NEMESIS
THE WARLOCK

Death To All Aliens

Pat Mills, Kevin O'Neill & Jesus Redondo

TITAN BOOKS
in association with *2000 AD*

NEMESIS THE WARLOCK: DEATH TO ALL ALIENS

ISBN 1 84023 794 5

Nemesis the Warlock created by Pat Mills and Kevin O'Neill

Published by Titan Books, a division of Titan Publishing Group Ltd.
144 Southwark St
London SE1 0UP
In association with Rebellion

A CIP catalogue record for this title is available from the British Library.

Originally published in hardback: March 2003
First paperback edition: March 2004
1 3 5 7 9 10 8 6 4 2

Cover Illustrations by Kevin O'Neill

Printed in Italy.

Other 2000 AD titles now available from Titan Books:
A.B.C. Warriors: The Black Hole (ISBN: 1 84023 529 2)
A.B.C. Warriors: The Mek-Nificent Seven (ISBN: 1 84023 347 8)
Judge Anderson: Death's Dark Dimension (ISBN: 1 84023 476 8)
Judge Anderson: Hour of the Wolf (ISBN: 1 84023 589 6)
Judge Anderson: Triad (ISBN: 1 84023 639 6)
Missionary Man (ISBN: 1 84023 465 2)
Nemesis the Warlock: Death to All Aliens (ISBN: 1 84023 475 X)
Rogue Trooper: Future War (ISBN: 1 84023 481 4)
Skizz (ISBN: 1 84023 450 4)
Sláine: The King (ISBN: 1 84023 416 4)
Sláine: The Horned God — Part One (ISBN: 1 84023 477 6)
Sláine: The Horned God — Part Two (ISBN: 1 84023 474 1)
Sláine: Time Killer (ISBN: 1 84023 645 0)
Sláine: The King (paperback) (ISBN: 1 84023 762 7)
Strontium Dog: Portrait of a Mutant (ISBN: 1 84023 479 2)
The Complete Ballad of Halo Jones (ISBN: 1 84023 772 4)
The Complete Ballad of Halo Jones (paperback) (ISBN: 1 84023 342 7)
The Complete D.R. & Quinch (paperback) (ISBN: 1 84023 345 1)
The Complete D.R. & Quinch (ISBN 1 84023 775 9)

A wide selection of Judge Dredd titles is also available. Check out our website at www.titanbooks.com for details.

To order from the UK telephone 01536 764 646

What did you think of this book? We love to hear from our readers. Please email us at: readerfeedback@titanemail.com, or write to us at the above address.
You can also visit us at www.titanbooks.com

***Nemesis the Warlock* is perhaps Pat Mills' most significant story contribution to the Galaxy's Greatest Comic — and it began with the Jam-inspired "Comic Rock" story 'Terror Tube', in *2000 AD* Prog #167. *2000 AD*'s most savage satirical strip of its early years begins with the mixture of humour and explosive violence which would shortly become its trademark — and provides the story's most chilling catchphrase at the same time, Torquemada's "Be pure... be vigilant... behave!"**

Progs #178–9 feature 'Killer Watt', the sequel to 'Terror Tube'. This second story occupies a rather strange part of *Nemesis* as a series, in that it sees the notional death of the future ultimate villain of the story — the terrifying fan-favourite, zealot-to-end-all-zealots, Tomas de Torquemada — in only his second appearance in the comic!

The last "preparatory" instalment is something of an oddity; Mills' "Olric" story, in 1981's *2000AD Sci-Fi Special*, appears at first glance to be a straight parody of the sword and sorcery genre, with the human protagonist's name a send-up of Michael Moorcock's enormously popular *Elric*. But the sardonic twist at the story's end — the victory of the Warlock and death of Olric — is the real set-up for *Nemesis* proper; as the alien narrator tells us:

"Nemesis went on to do many great deeds and killed many humans..."

Finally, we come to *Nemesis: Book One* (Progs #222–233, #238–240 and #243–244), wherein we see the motivating force behind the series: Mills' bilious hatred of authority, coupled with the detail-heavy, vicious caricaturing of Kevin O'Neill. The world of Termight is presented as a joyless totalitarian nightmare, controlled by a military-theocratic elite, and a single figurehead — "Inquisitor General" Tomas de Torquemada, a Ku Klux Klan-hooded killer who rules first as a terrifying, all-knowing spectre — Big Brother with a self-penned Bible — and later as a literal spectre, moving from body to body to bedevil Nemesis time and time again.

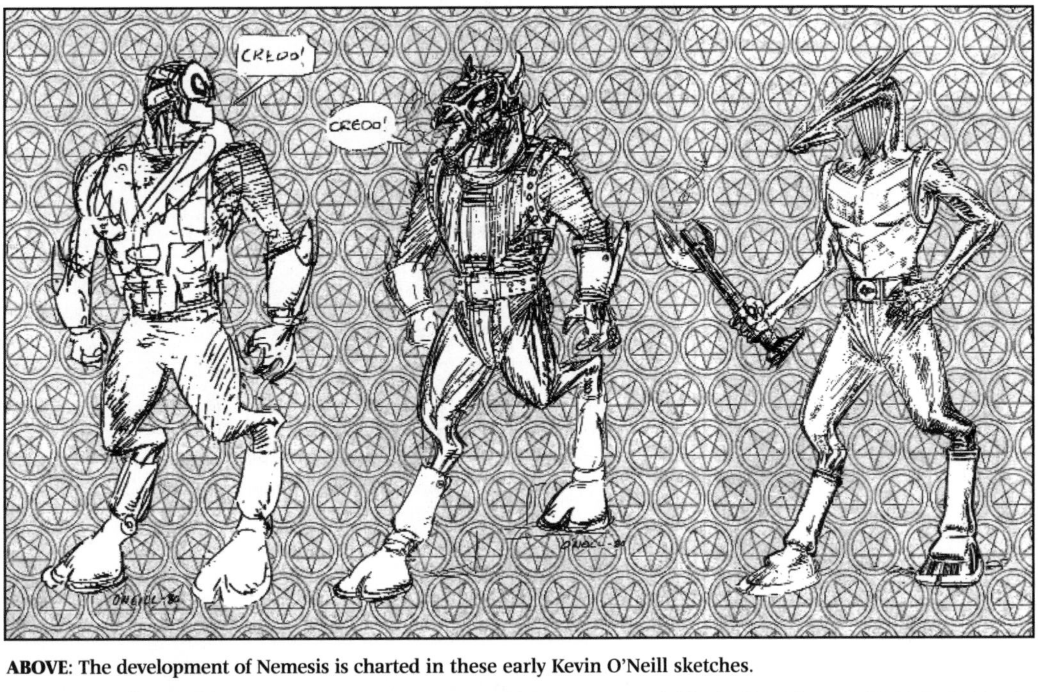
CREDO!
CREDO!

ABOVE: The development of Nemesis is charted in these early Kevin O'Neill sketches.

Book Two (Progs #246–257), drawn by Jesus Redondo, is something of a tangent from the first volume. Nemesis is portrayed as wanting to reconcile with the humans he slaughtered in Book One; but, of course, Torquemada intervenes. The near aside on Arachnos, the planet of the spiders, may seem incongruous at first, but — as with the Torquemada/Nemesis parallel — the actions of the Terminators show the contrast between human zealotry and the firm-but-fair attitude of their jailers. Torquemada is his usual sizzlingly evil self, but the real gem of this story is Mills' ability to make spiders — traditionally a figure of fear to humans — sympathetic characters. Nemesis is less of a cipher here, too; sparing Torquemada to save Purity, for example — and this sets up the quantum leap in character development to come in *Nemesis: Book Three...*

Also featured in this collection is the Nemesis story, 'The Secret Life of the Blitzspear', which originally appeared in 1983's *2000 AD Annual*. Though not "Book" specific, the David Attenborough-style slice of alien natural history expands upon the relationship between Nemesis and his symbiotic alien spacecraft, Seth.

TOP TO BOTTOM: The evolution of a *Nemesis* page; roughs, pencils, and inks.

THE TERROR TUBE. P. Mills and K. O'Neill

TERMIGHT - city planet and centre of a vast galactic empire. Above ground it is a desolate cold world - but below it teems with life . . . the entire planet has been hollowed out - it's like a gigantic malteser.

We meet some OVERLANDERS - country bumpkins - who have never been below ground before. They are going to see their daughter, Mabeline, who lives in NECROPOLIS deep inside the planet.

A t.v. commentator introduces them and us to the travel tube system - telling us how safe it is as yet another multiple pile-up takes place.

We cut to the TERMINATORS - the sinister police of TERMIGHT. We have now made them look more like <u>baddies</u> . . . they have Klu Klux Klan style metal hoods and flowing - Deadlock style - gowns. This will also give a more s.f. feeling to the strip. They carry strange weapons - long decorated lances . . . glowing orbs with spikes radiating from them . . . symbols of power! They may be chanting as we first see them into frame.

The chief terminator issues instructions . . . they've had a tip off . . . leader of the rebels - NEMESIS - is going to attack today. All units are warned to be on the look-out!

In a dark corner of the tube system - evil lights glow . . . a sinister car roars forward. It's . . . NEMESIS!

A slave wagon - a huge zeppelin-like vehicle - roars along one of the tubes and Nemesis zooms forward . . . cutting the vehicle in half. "CREDO!"

Prisoners pour out and make good their escape into the labyrinth of tunnels . . . "Credo be praised," they shout. CREDO . . . the name of the rebel organisation. It means "Trust"!
~~(appropriately appropriately appropriately appropriately appropriately appropriately appropriately)~~

There is a full scale alert . . .Terminators roar to intercept . . . At all costs they must stop Nemesis before he reaches the Black-Hole Bypass . . . they must stop before he gets out of town.

The Terminators smash other vehicles aside in their eagerness to catch Nemesis - he roars onwards expertly handling his sinister car, making it loop the loop, taking bends at fantastic speed, jumping lanes with wrists of steel. "CREDO!" Devastating action involving the tunnel floor itself opening. The Terminators crash into one another . . .the outriders smeared across the walls of tunnels . . . With their sinister hoods, and possibly glowing eyes they should provide a frightening image in the depths of the travel tube system.

Nemesis roars on towards "the Black Hole" Bypass. The chief terminator snarls to six wall-wagons who roar out of side tunnels to intercept . . . on the very lip of the bypass.

The feeling of the tube is one of murky labyrinth darkness . . . but now we are reaching its most sinister feature . . . a huge vertical drop . . . a gaping black maw . . . From here all vehicles leave the city, heading into open country . . . If he gets through the bypass they'll never find him.

Confident of success the wall wagons adjust their guns . . . Nemesis must slow down for the bypass, and . . .

We see the wall wagons roar forward . . . but Nemesis accelerates plunging past them. The wall wagons smash into one another - in a hideous pile-up . . . what's left of them falls into the bypass.

"CREDO!"

(The finer details of the last pile-up may need some further discussion, Kev . . . A) To enhance the heroism of Nemesis B) To enhance devastation)

Nemesis plunges into the bypass . . . it is like a black drain . . . It spins at incredible speed . . . hurtling the cars down it at collosal speed . . . a sheer horrifying drop . . . he guns his engines . . . faster . . . faster . . . faster . . .

. . . And emerges amidst the stars! We see now it is a Man-Made Black Hole . . . From it, Termight has controlled a thousand planets . . .

Nemesis makes good his escape - but he will back to strike another blow against the Termight Tyranny.

"CREDO!"

....

*Haven't got a name for his car yet, Steve - but something will occur in due course. As you can see Nemesis is an unseen version of Deadlock, without having the restraints of the latter . . . e.g. Volgans, Mars etc. In future adventures he can strike again at Termight or any other planet.

Handwritten margin notes:
They sins a hymn to the victims or road accidents that day.

- INCLUDING BUMPKINS -

Man's short cut to

gateways ... to the stars

TERMIGHT! CAPITAL PLANET OF A CRUEL GALACTIC EMPIRE... ABOVE GROUND IT IS A STRANGE, DESOLATE WORLD... DEVASTATED BY NUCLEAR WARS— WHERE ONLY A FEW POOR OVERLANDERS GRUB A LIVING. BUT BENEATH THE SURFACE...

Comic Rock ♪♫

HOLD ON! WE'RE GOING UNDERGROUND!

Story suggested by THE JAM'S GOING UNDERGROUND

O'NEILL

TERROR TUBE

TERMIGHT TEEMS WITH LIFE! THE PLANET HAS BEEN HOLLOWED OUT INTO AN AMAZING NET-WORK OF TRAVEL TUBES AND UNDERGROUND CITIES!

HEY, YOU OVERLANDERS! SHIFT THAT CRATE! THIS IS THE "SUPER-JUGGERNAUT" LANE!

WEEKEND TRIPPERS! YA MEANT TO DRIVE ON THE CEILING!

SORREEE!

WELCOME TO THE TRAVEL TUBE, FRIENDS! THE MOST ADVANCED ROAD SYSTEM IN THE GALAXY!

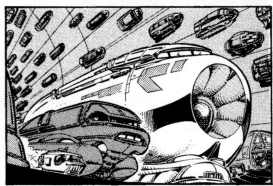

CAN'T WE GO BACK, MABELINE? I-I'M JUST A SIMPLE, OLD-FASHIONED OVERLANDER! I DON'T UNDERSTAND THIS NEW-FANGLED TRAVEL TUBE!

DON'T SHOW YER IGNORANCE, ELMER! WE'RE GOING TO VISIT OUR DAUGHTER DOWN IN NECROPOLIS! TAKE HER SOME OF MA HOME-MADE SYNTHI-COOKIES!

AND NOW, FRIENDS, IF YOU CAN HEAR ME ABOVE THE GENTLE THUNDER OF THE JUGGERNAUTS, IT'S TRAFFIC NEWS TIME!

ELMER! GET THE MAP OUT! HURRY!

Y-YES, MABELINE!

MICHELIN TUBE GUIDE VISIT THE BLACK HOLE TERMIGHT TUNNELS DINSDALE DRAINS

ROUTE 66

COME ON DOWN

GULP!

THERE'S BEEN ANOTHER MAJOR ROAD ACCIDENT NEAR THE JUNCTION OF "INQUEST ALLEY" WITH "RIGOR MORTIS ROUNDABOUT"...!

...DRIVERS HEADING FOR NECROPOLIS SHOULD TAKE AN ALTERNATIVE ROUTE DOWN "AUTOPSY UNDERPASS"— REFERENCE TR666/75T/F18/M16B!

I-I THINK SO, MABELINE!

ELMER! ELMER! CAN YOU FIND IT ON THE MAP?

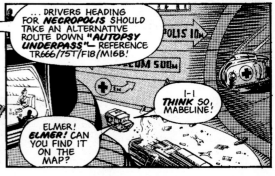

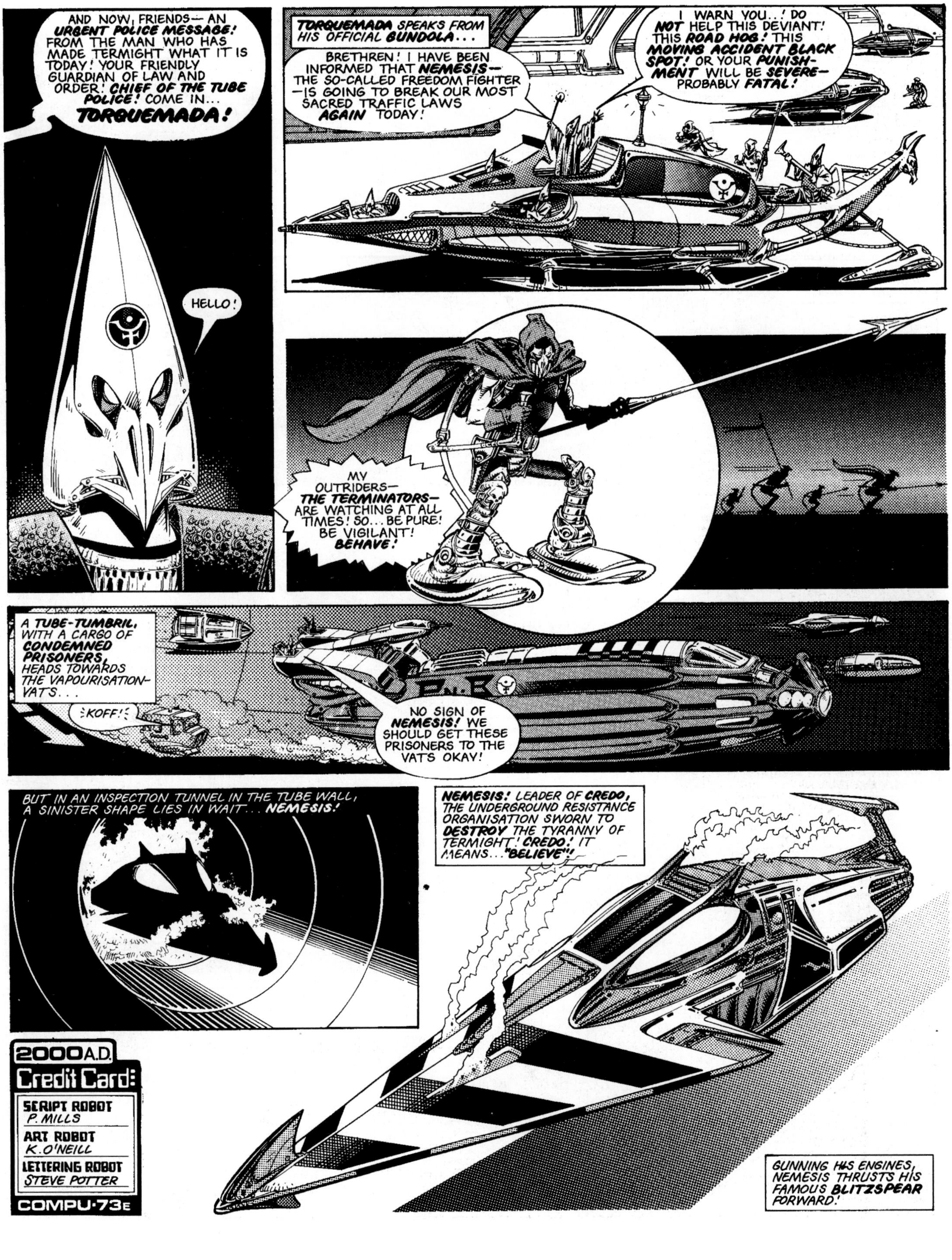

AND NOW, FRIENDS— AN URGENT POLICE MESSAGE! FROM THE MAN WHO HAS MADE TERMIGHT WHAT IT IS TODAY! YOUR FRIENDLY GUARDIAN OF LAW AND ORDER: CHIEF OF THE TUBE POLICE! COME IN... TORQUEMADA!
HELLO!
TORQUEMADA SPEAKS FROM HIS OFFICIAL GUNDOLA...
BRETHREN! I HAVE BEEN INFORMED THAT NEMESIS— THE SO-CALLED FREEDOM FIGHTER —IS GOING TO BREAK OUR MOST SACRED TRAFFIC LAWS AGAIN TODAY!
I WARN YOU..! DO NOT HELP THIS DEVIANT! THIS ROAD HOG! THIS MOVING ACCIDENT BLACK SPOT! OR YOUR PUNISHMENT WILL BE SEVERE— PROBABLY FATAL!
MY OUTRIDERS— THE TERMINATORS— ARE WATCHING AT ALL TIMES! SO... BE PURE! BE VIGILANT! BEHAVE!
A TUBE-TUMBRIL, WITH A CARGO OF CONDEMNED PRISONERS, HEADS TOWARDS THE VAPOURISATION-VATS...
KOFF!
NO SIGN OF NEMESIS! WE SHOULD GET THESE PRISONERS TO THE VATS OKAY!
BUT IN AN INSPECTION TUNNEL IN THE TUBE WALL, A SINISTER SHAPE LIES IN WAIT... NEMESIS!
NEMESIS! LEADER OF CREDO, THE UNDERGROUND RESISTANCE ORGANISATION SWORN TO DESTROY THE TYRANNY OF TERMIGHT! CREDO! IT MEANS... "BELIEVE"!
GUNNING HIS ENGINES, NEMESIS THRUSTS HIS FAMOUS BLITZSPEAR FORWARD!
2000 A.D. Credit Card:
SCRIPT ROBOT P. MILLS
ART ROBOT K. O'NEILL
LETTERING ROBOT STEVE POTTER
COMPU-73E

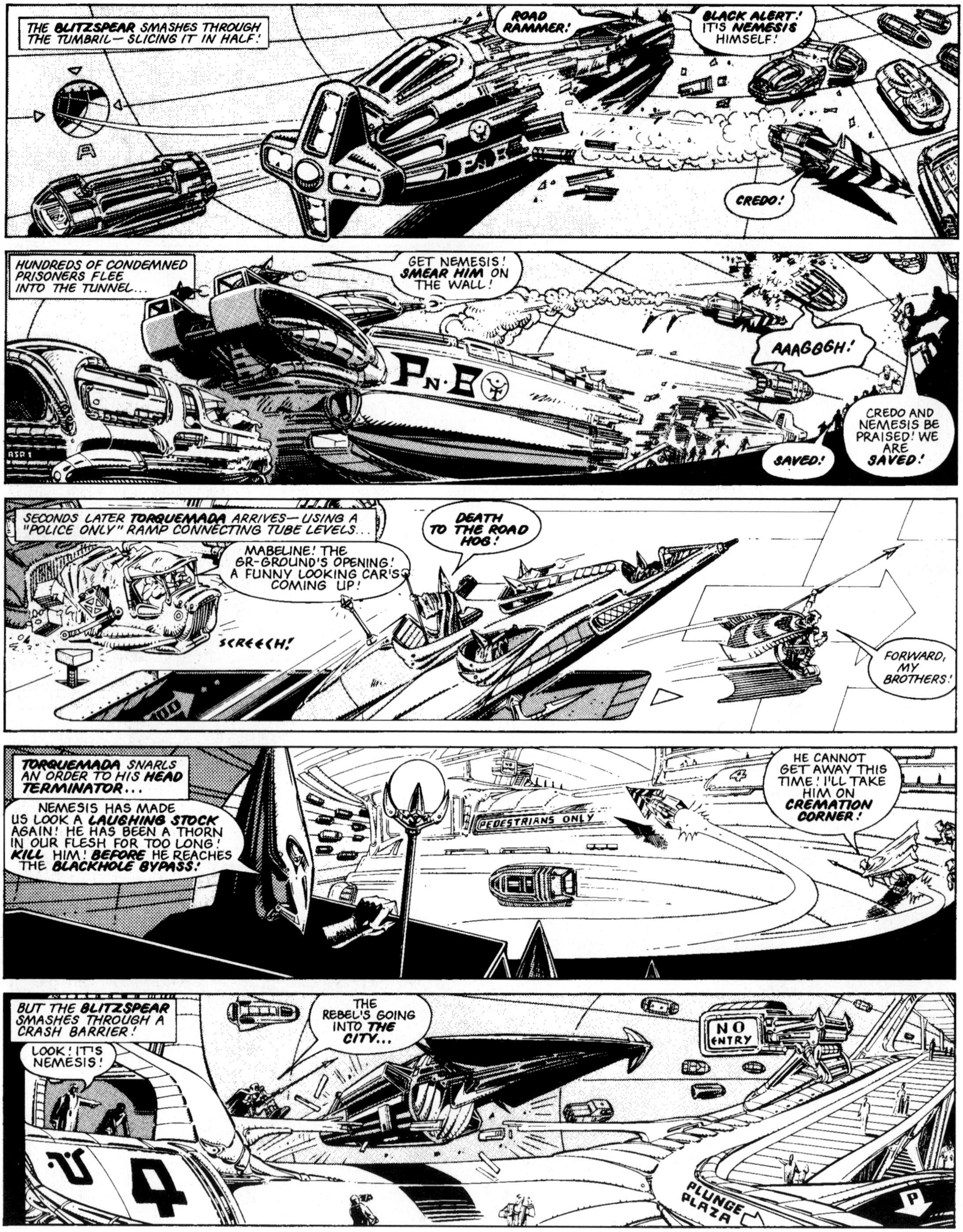
THE BLITZSPEAR SMASHES THROUGH THE TUMBRIL— SLICING IT IN HALF!
ROAD RAMMER!
BLACK ALERT! IT'S NEMESIS HIMSELF!
CREDO!
HUNDREDS OF CONDEMNED PRISONERS FLEE INTO THE TUNNEL...
GET NEMESIS! SMEAR HIM ON THE WALL!
AAAGGGH!
CREDO AND NEMESIS BE PRAISED! WE ARE SAVED!
SAVED!
SECONDS LATER TORQUEMADA ARRIVES— USING A "POLICE ONLY" RAMP CONNECTING TUBE LEVELS...
MABELINE! THE GR-GROUND'S OPENING! A FUNNY LOOKING CAR'S COMING UP!
DEATH TO THE ROAD HOG!
SCREEECH!
FORWARD, MY BROTHERS!
TORQUEMADA SNARLS AN ORDER TO HIS HEAD TERMINATOR...
NEMESIS HAS MADE US LOOK A LAUGHING STOCK AGAIN! HE HAS BEEN A THORN IN OUR FLESH FOR TOO LONG! KILL HIM! BEFORE HE REACHES THE BLACKHOLE BYPASS!
PEDESTRIANS ONLY
HE CANNOT GET AWAY THIS TIME! I'LL TAKE HIM ON CREMATION CORNER!
BUT THE BLITZSPEAR SMASHES THROUGH A CRASH BARRIER!
LOOK! IT'S NEMESIS!
THE REBEL'S GOING INTO THE CITY...
NO ENTRY
PLUNGE PLAZA

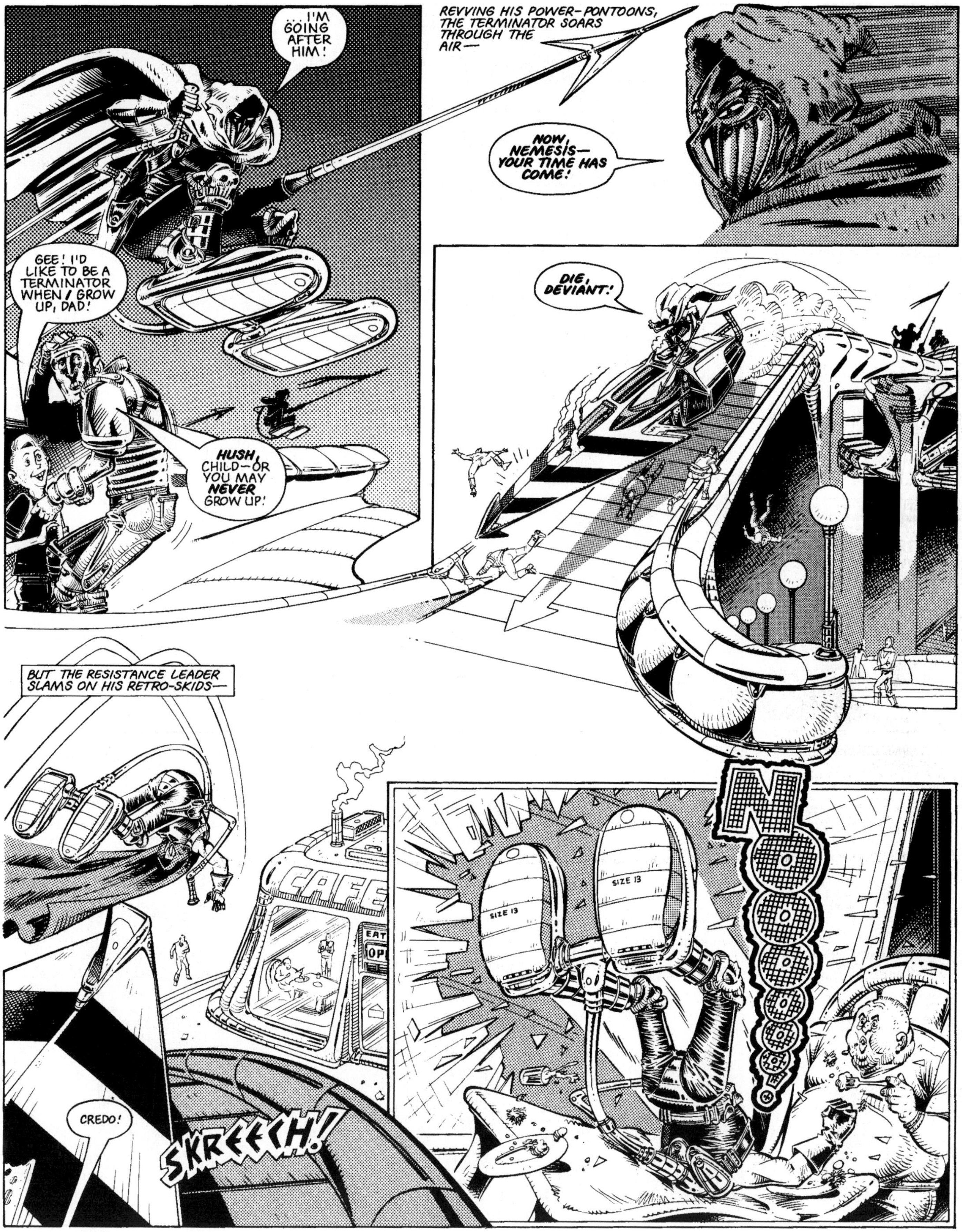

...I'M GOING AFTER HIM!
GEE! I'D LIKE TO BE A TERMINATOR WHEN I GROW UP, DAD!
HUSH, CHILD—OR YOU MAY NEVER GROW UP!
REVVING HIS POWER-PONTOONS, THE TERMINATOR SOARS THROUGH THE AIR—
NOW, NEMESIS—YOUR TIME HAS COME!
DIE, DEVIANT!
BUT THE RESISTANCE LEADER SLAMS ON HIS RETRO-SKIDS—
CAFE
SIZE 13
SIZE 13
NOOOOOOO!
CREDO!
SKREECH!

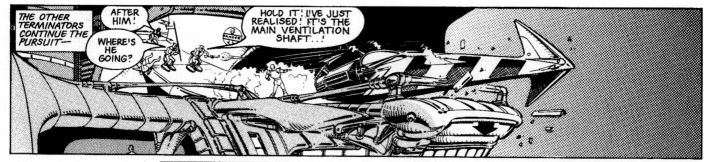

THE OTHER TERMINATORS CONTINUE THE PURSUIT—

AFTER HIM!

WHERE'S HE GOING?

HOLD IT! I'VE JUST REALISED! IT'S THE MAIN VENTILATION SHAFT..!

AAAAAAA!

..."DEATH DRAIN"!

Credo!

AS THE BLITZSPEAR DROPS DOWN TOWARDS THE **BLACKHOLE BY-PASS**, IT IS SPOTTED BY ONE OF THE **WATCH-TOWERS** OVERLOOKING THE BYPASS...

KEEP LEFT

HAVE A GOOD DROP

NEMESIS!

AAAAAAA!

PLUNGE PLATEAU

THE BLACKHOLE BYPASS!

ATTENTION ALL WATCHTOWERS! NEMESIS IS ESCAPING! ACTIVATE **RACK BEAMS**...!

INSIDE THE TOWERS, TUBE POLICE CONTROL THE BYPASS — RAISING AND LOWERING ROADS — TIPPING TRAFFIC INTO THE BLACKHOLE, WHICH SPINS WITH INCREDIBLE CENTRIFUGAL SPEED, HURLING CARS DOWN IT!

... NOW!

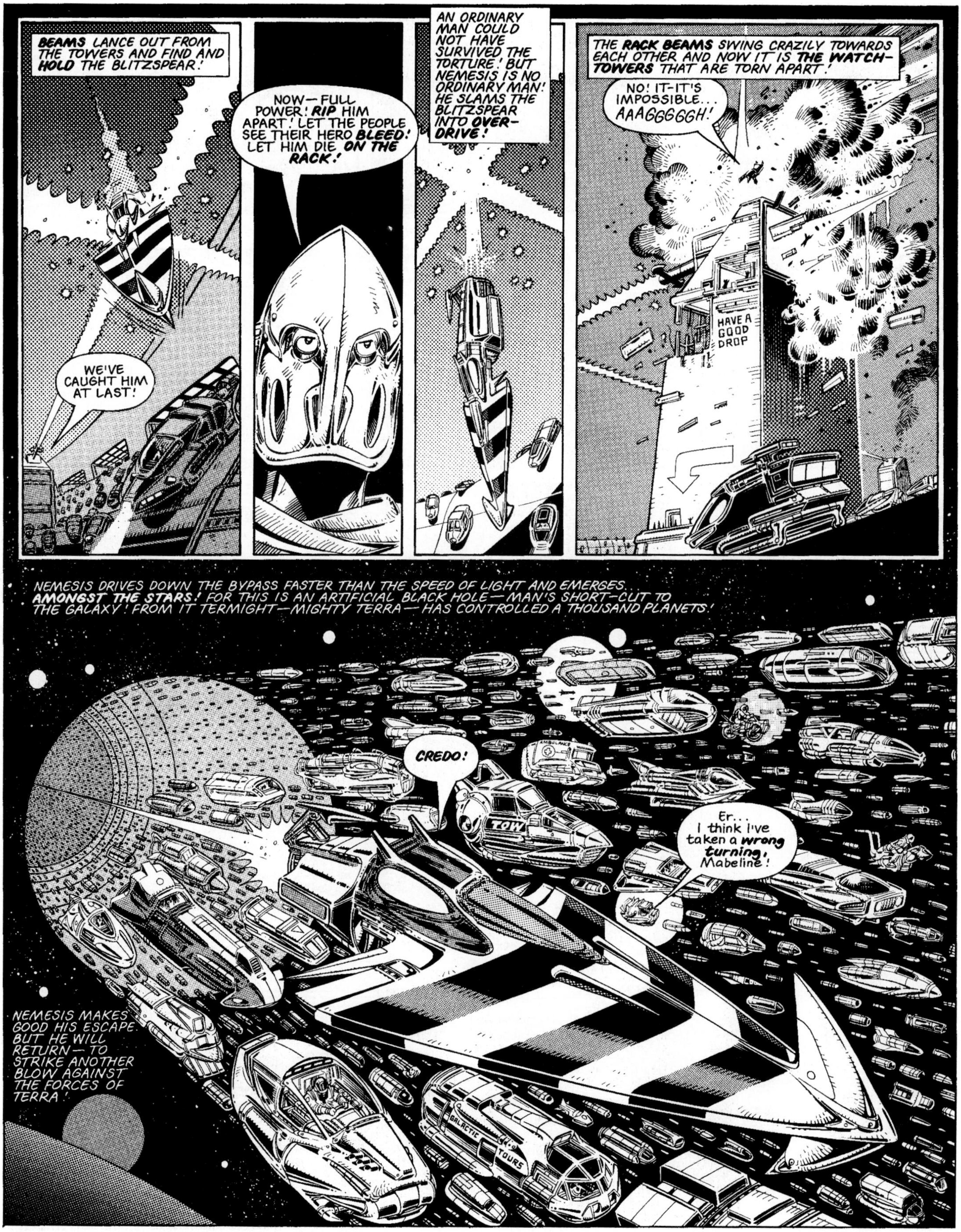

BEAMS LANCE OUT FROM THE TOWERS AND FIND AND HOLD THE BLITZSPEAR!
WE'VE CAUGHT HIM AT LAST!
NOW—FULL POWER! RIP HIM APART! LET THE PEOPLE SEE THEIR HERO BLEED! LET HIM DIE ON THE RACK!
AN ORDINARY MAN COULD NOT HAVE SURVIVED THE TORTURE! BUT NEMESIS IS NO ORDINARY MAN! HE SLAMS THE BLITZSPEAR INTO OVER-DRIVE!
THE RACK BEAMS SWING CRAZILY TOWARDS EACH OTHER AND NOW IT IS THE WATCH-TOWERS THAT ARE TORN APART!
NO! IT-IT'S IMPOSSIBLE... AAAGGGGGH!
HAVE A GOOD DROP
NEMESIS DRIVES DOWN THE BYPASS FASTER THAN THE SPEED OF LIGHT AND EMERGES... AMONGST THE STARS! FOR THIS IS AN ARTIFICIAL BLACK HOLE—MAN'S SHORT-CUT TO THE GALAXY! FROM IT TERMIGHT—MIGHTY TERRA—HAS CONTROLLED A THOUSAND PLANETS!
CREDO!
AMBULANCE
TOW
Er... I think I've taken a wrong turning, Mabeline!
NEMESIS MAKES GOOD HIS ESCAPE. BUT HE WILL RETURN—TO STRIKE ANOTHER BLOW AGAINST THE FORCES OF TERRA!
GALACTIC TOURS

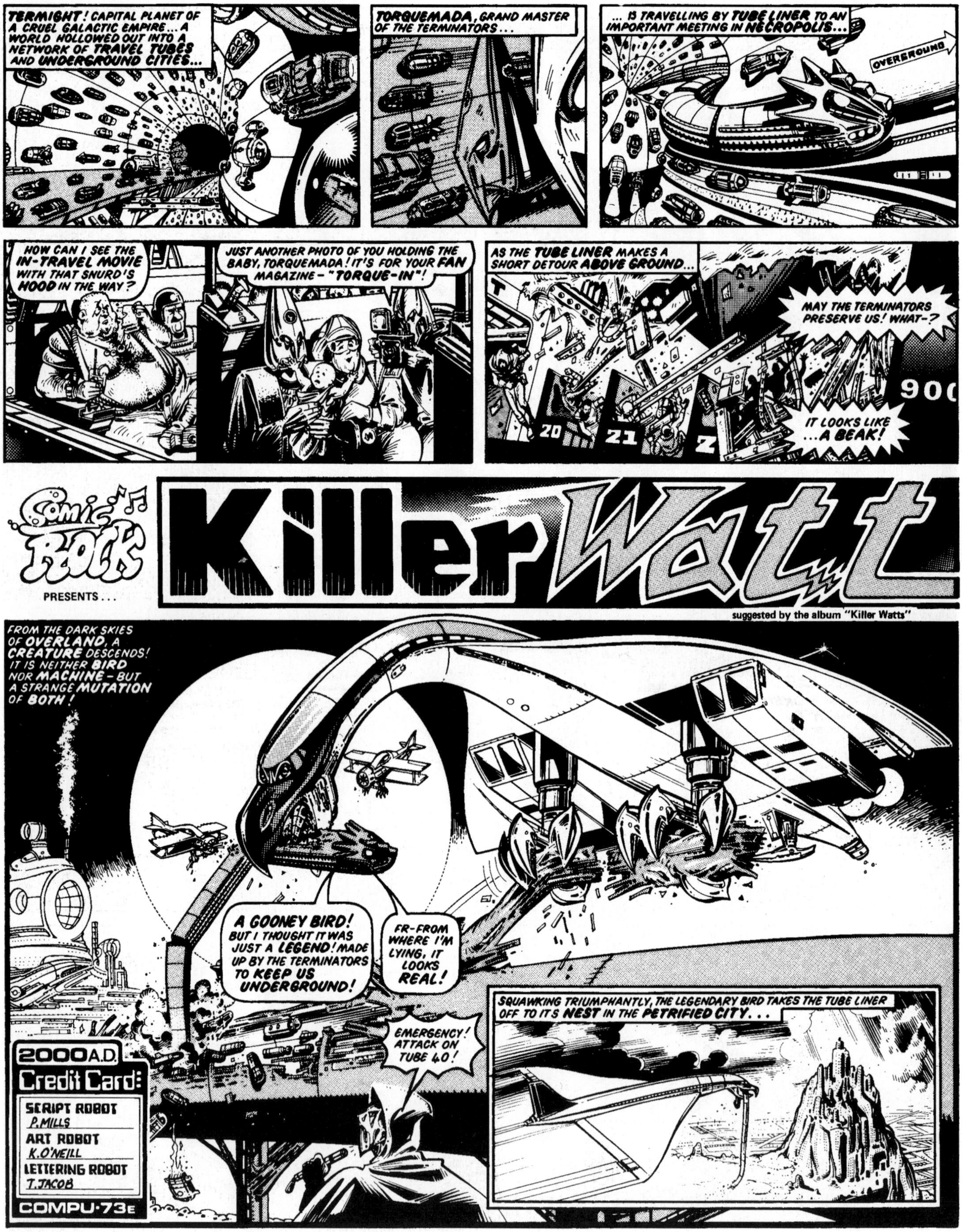
TERMIGHT! CAPITAL PLANET OF A CRUEL GALACTIC EMPIRE... A WORLD HOLLOWED OUT INTO A NETWORK OF TRAVEL TUBES AND UNDERGROUND CITIES...
TORQUEMADA, GRAND MASTER OF THE TERMINATORS...
... IS TRAVELLING BY TUBE LINER TO AN IMPORTANT MEETING IN NECROPOLIS...
OVERGROUND
HOW CAN I SEE THE IN-TRAVEL MOVIE WITH THAT SNURD'S HOOD IN THE WAY?
JUST ANOTHER PHOTO OF YOU HOLDING THE BABY, TORQUEMADA! IT'S FOR YOUR FAN MAGAZINE – "TORQUE-IN"!
AS THE TUBE LINER MAKES A SHORT DETOUR ABOVE GROUND...
MAY THE TERMINATORS PRESERVE US! WHAT-?
900
IT LOOKS LIKE ...A BEAK!
20
21
Comic ROCK PRESENTS...
Killer Watt
suggested by the album "Killer Watts"
FROM THE DARK SKIES OF OVERLAND, A CREATURE DESCENDS! IT IS NEITHER BIRD NOR MACHINE – BUT A STRANGE MUTATION OF BOTH!
A GOONEY BIRD! BUT I THOUGHT IT WAS JUST A LEGEND! MADE UP BY THE TERMINATORS TO KEEP US UNDERGROUND!
FR-FROM WHERE I'M LYING, IT LOOKS REAL!
EMERGENCY! ATTACK ON TUBE 40!
2000 A.D. Credit Card:
SCRIPT ROBOT P. MILLS
ART ROBOT K. O'NEILL
LETTERING ROBOT T. JACOB
COMPU-73E
SQUAWKING TRIUMPHANTLY, THE LEGENDARY BIRD TAKES THE TUBE LINER OFF TO ITS NEST IN THE PETRIFIED CITY...

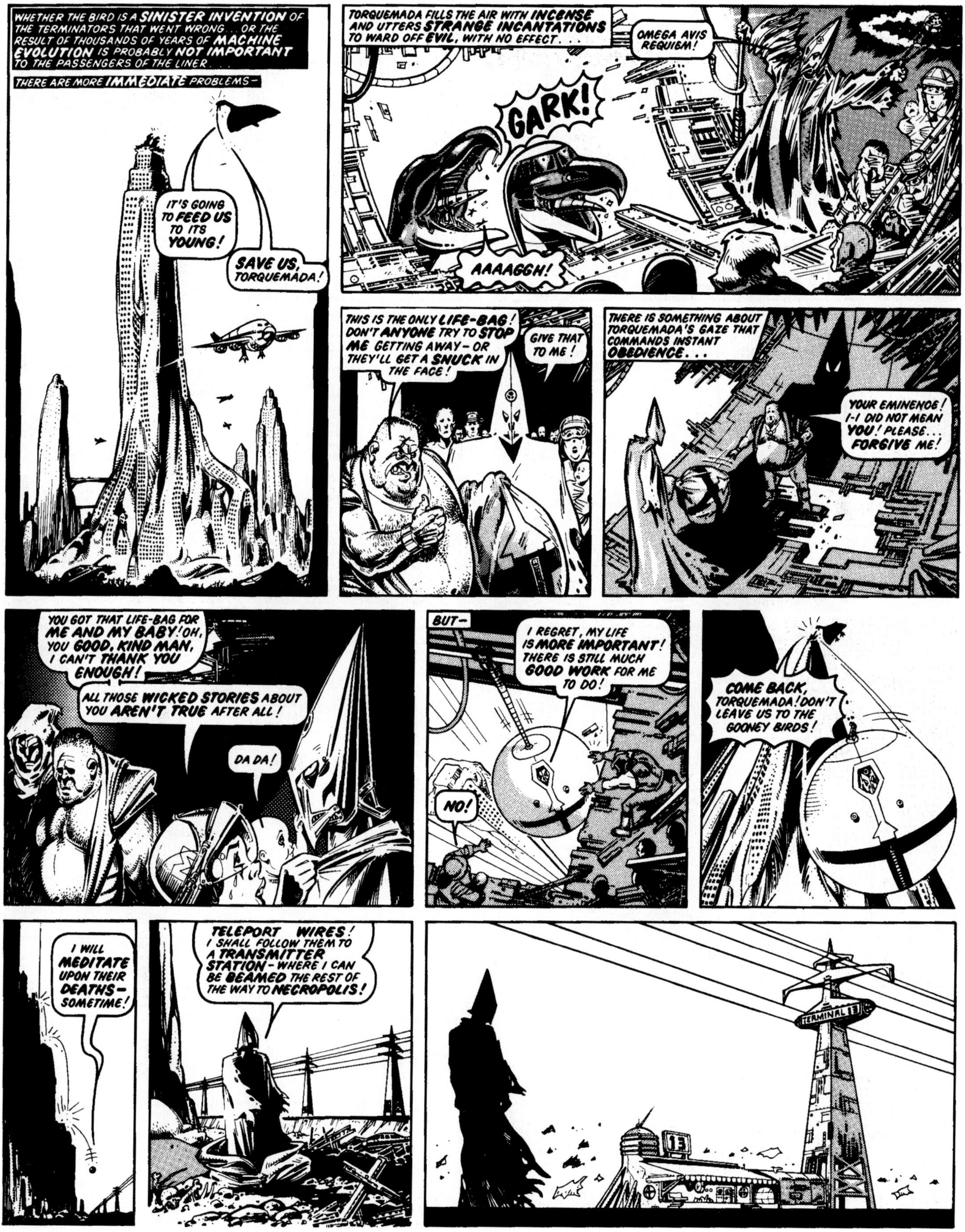
WHETHER THE BIRD IS A SINISTER INVENTION OF THE TERMINATORS THAT WENT WRONG... OR THE RESULT OF THOUSANDS OF YEARS OF MACHINE EVOLUTION IS PROBABLY NOT IMPORTANT TO THE PASSENGERS OF THE LINER.
THERE ARE MORE IMMEDIATE PROBLEMS—
IT'S GOING TO FEED US TO ITS YOUNG!
SAVE US, TORQUEMADA!
TORQUEMADA FILLS THE AIR WITH INCENSE AND UTTERS STRANGE INCANTATIONS TO WARD OFF EVIL, WITH NO EFFECT...
OMEGA AVIS REQUIEM!
GARK!
AAAAGGH!
THIS IS THE ONLY LIFE-BAG! DON'T ANYONE TRY TO STOP ME GETTING AWAY - OR THEY'LL GET A SNUCK IN THE FACE!
GIVE THAT TO ME!
THERE IS SOMETHING ABOUT TORQUEMADA'S GAZE THAT COMMANDS INSTANT OBEDIENCE...
YOUR EMINENCE! I-I DID NOT MEAN YOU! PLEASE... FORGIVE ME!
YOU GOT THAT LIFE-BAG FOR ME AND MY BABY! OH, YOU GOOD, KIND MAN, I CAN'T THANK YOU ENOUGH!
ALL THOSE WICKED STORIES ABOUT YOU AREN'T TRUE AFTER ALL!
DA DA!
BUT—
I REGRET, MY LIFE IS MORE IMPORTANT! THERE IS STILL MUCH GOOD WORK FOR ME TO DO!
NO!
COME BACK, TORQUEMADA! DON'T LEAVE US TO THE GOONEY BIRDS!
I WILL MEDITATE UPON THEIR DEATHS— SOMETIME!
TELEPORT WIRES! I SHALL FOLLOW THEM TO A TRANSMITTER STATION - WHERE I CAN BE BEAMED THE REST OF THE WAY TO NECROPOLIS!
TERMINAL 13
13

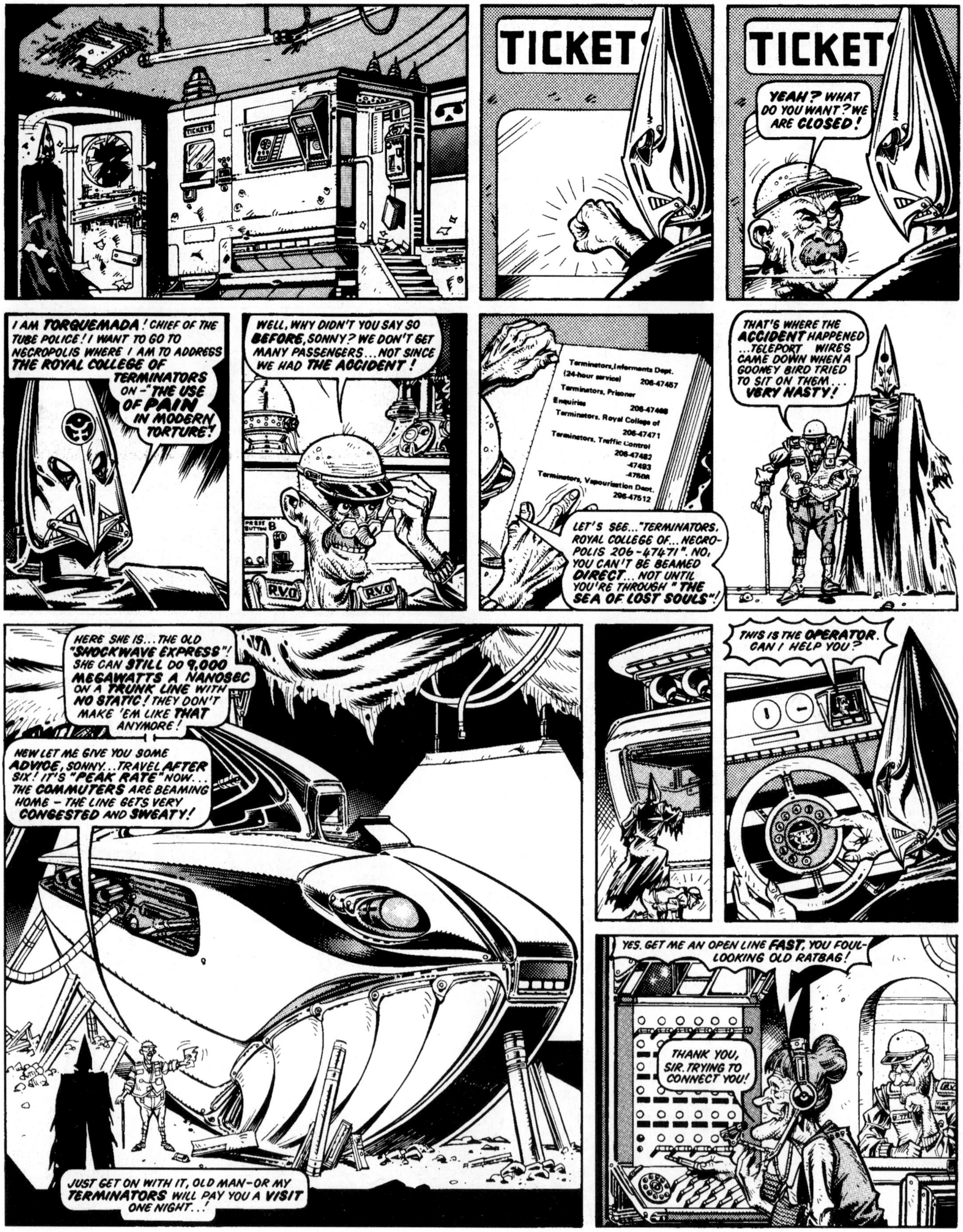
TICKETS
TICKETS
YEAH? WHAT DO YOU WANT? WE ARE CLOSED!
I AM TORQUEMADA! CHIEF OF THE TUBE POLICE! I WANT TO GO TO NECROPOLIS WHERE I AM TO ADDRESS THE ROYAL COLLEGE OF TERMINATORS ON-"THE USE OF PAIN IN MODERN TORTURE"!
WELL, WHY DIDN'T YOU SAY SO BEFORE, SONNY? WE DON'T GET MANY PASSENGERS... NOT SINCE WE HAD THE ACCIDENT!
PRESS BUTTON B
R.V.O
Terminators,Informants Dept.
(24-hour service) 206-47457
Terminators, Prisoner
Enquiries
Terminators, Royal College of
206-47471
Terminators, Traffic Control
206-47482
-47493
Terminators, Vapourisation Dept.
206-47512
LET'S SEE..."TERMINATORS, ROYAL COLLEGE OF... NECROPOLIS 206-47471". NO, YOU CAN'T BE BEAMED DIRECT... NOT UNTIL YOU'RE THROUGH "THE SEA OF LOST SOULS"!
THAT'S WHERE THE ACCIDENT HAPPENED ...TELEPORT WIRES CAME DOWN WHEN A GOONEY BIRD TRIED TO SIT ON THEM... VERY NASTY!
HERE SHE IS... THE OLD "SHOCKWAVE EXPRESS"! SHE CAN STILL DO 9,000 MEGAWATTS A NANOSEC ON A TRUNK LINE WITH NO STATIC! THEY DON'T MAKE 'EM LIKE THAT ANYMORE!
NEW LET ME GIVE YOU SOME ADVICE, SONNY... TRAVEL AFTER SIX! IT'S "PEAK RATE" NOW... THE COMMUTERS ARE BEAMING HOME - THE LINE GETS VERY CONGESTED AND SWEATY!
JUST GET ON WITH IT, OLD MAN-OR MY TERMINATORS WILL PAY YOU A VISIT ONE NIGHT...!
THIS IS THE OPERATOR. CAN I HELP YOU?
YES, GET ME AN OPEN LINE FAST, YOU FOUL-LOOKING OLD RATBAG!
THANK YOU, SIR. TRYING TO CONNECT YOU!

BRRR... BRRR...
BRRR
PIP PIP PIP
VRRROOOM
YOU'RE THROUGH!

BUT THERE IS MORE TO THE OLD TELE-PORTER THAN MEETS THE EYE...!

BRRR. BRRR. BRRR. CLICK!

NEMESIS...? AGENT RAFFERTY HERE! YOU'RE NOT GOING TO BELIEVE THIS...! TORQUEMADA HIMSELF JUST LEFT MY TRANSMITTER STATION — ALONE!

HE'S HEADING TOWARDS THE "SEA OF LOST SOULS"!

NEMESIS, MYSTERIOUS LEADER OF THE SECRET RESISTANCE ORGANISATION — CREDO! THIS IS THE CHANCE HE HAS BEEN WAITING FOR — TO DESTROY THE EVIL TORQUEMADA!

CREDO!

HE GUNS HIS BLITZSPEAR DOWN THE TELEPORT WIRE!

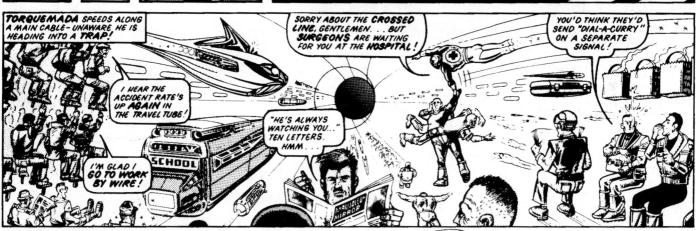
TORQUEMADA SPEEDS ALONG A MAIN CABLE — UNAWARE, HE IS HEADING INTO A TRAP!

I HEAR THE ACCIDENT RATE'S UP AGAIN IN THE TRAVEL TUBE!

I'M GLAD I GO TO WORK BY WIRE!

SCHOOL

SORRY ABOUT THE CROSSED LINE, GENTLEMEN... BUT SURGEONS ARE WAITING FOR YOU AT THE HOSPITAL!

"HE'S ALWAYS WATCHING YOU..." TEN LETTERS. HMM...

YOU'D THINK THEY'D SEND "DIAL-A-CURRY" ON A SEPARATE SIGNAL!

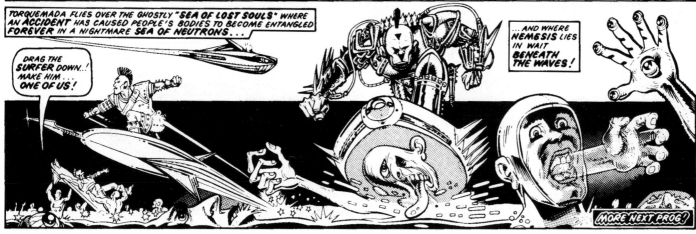
TORQUEMADA FLIES OVER THE GHOSTLY "SEA OF LOST SOULS" WHERE AN ACCIDENT HAS CAUSED PEOPLE'S BODIES TO BECOME ENTANGLED FOREVER IN A NIGHTMARE SEA OF NEUTRONS...

DRAG THE SURFER DOWN...! MAKE HIM... ONE OF US!

...AND WHERE NEMESIS LIES IN WAIT BENEATH THE WAVES!

MORE NEXT PROG!

Comic Rock
PRESENTS
PART 2 of...
Killer Watt
suggested by the album "Killer Watts"
INSIDE THE TELEPORT SYSTEM, TORQUEMADA FLIES OVER THE "SEA OF LOST SOULS" - WHERE PEOPLE ARE ENTANGLED FOREVER IN A NIGHTMARE SEA OF NEUTRONS!
GIVE ME YOUR BODY! I WANT YOUR BODY!
BUT TORQUEMADA HAS FALLEN INTO A TRAP! HIS SWORN ENEMY, NEMESIS - MYSTERIOUS LEADER OF CREDO - RISES FROM THE DEPTHS!
THE BLITZSPEAR BREAKS THE SURFACE OF THE GHOST OCEAN AND BLASTS THE SHOCKWAVE EXPRESS.! DESPERATELY, TORQUEMADA CALLS HIS TERMINATORS...
I AM UNDER ATTACK BY THE DEVIANT, NEMESIS, IN THE "SEA OF LOST SOULS"! I WANT A KILL-TRACKER TEAM HERE... FAST!
WITHIN MINUTES, A TEAM OF KILL-TRACKERS ARE ON THE SCENE... THEY "TAP" THE FALLEN TELEPORT CABLES THAT HAVE CAUSED THE "SEA OF LOST SOULS"...
YOUR EMINENCE! WE HAVE LOCATED YOU AND THE DEVIANT INSIDE THE CABLE! BUT IF WE ELECTROCUTE NEMESIS NOW - WE WILL ALSO KILL THOUSANDS OF INNOCENT TRAVELLERS!
A MERE TECHNICALITY! BUT WAIT...! NEMESIS IS TOO CLOSE - MY OWN LIFE WOULD BE IN DANGER! TELL ALL KILL-TRACKERS TO REMAIN ON STAND-BY!
KILL-TRACKERS ON STAND-BY!
TORQUEMADA ACCELERATES - BUT THE BLITZSPEAR WRAPS ITSELF ROUND THE SHOCKWAVE EXPRESS AS THEY HURTLE FORWARD - THE TWO VEHICLES WARPING AT INCREDIBLE SPEEDS!
I'VE GOT TO LOSE HIM! THE OLD TELEPORTER SAID THE EXPRESS COULD DO 9,000 MEGAWATTS A NANOSEC - WELL, WE'LL SEE....!
THIS IS KILL-TRACKER 5! SIGNALMAN REPORTING! TORQUEMADA IS GETTING AWAY FROM TARGET! LOCATION 95 RZ!
2000 A.D. Credit Card:
SCRIPT ROBOT PAT MILLS
ART ROBOT KEVIN O'NEILL
LETTERING ROBOT TONY JACOB
COMPU-73E

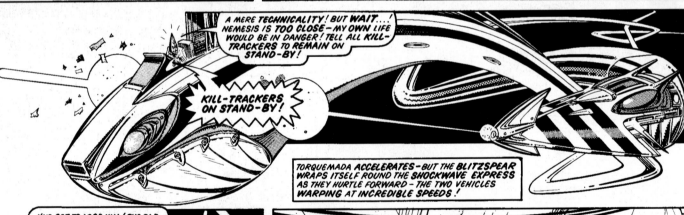

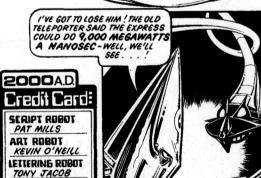

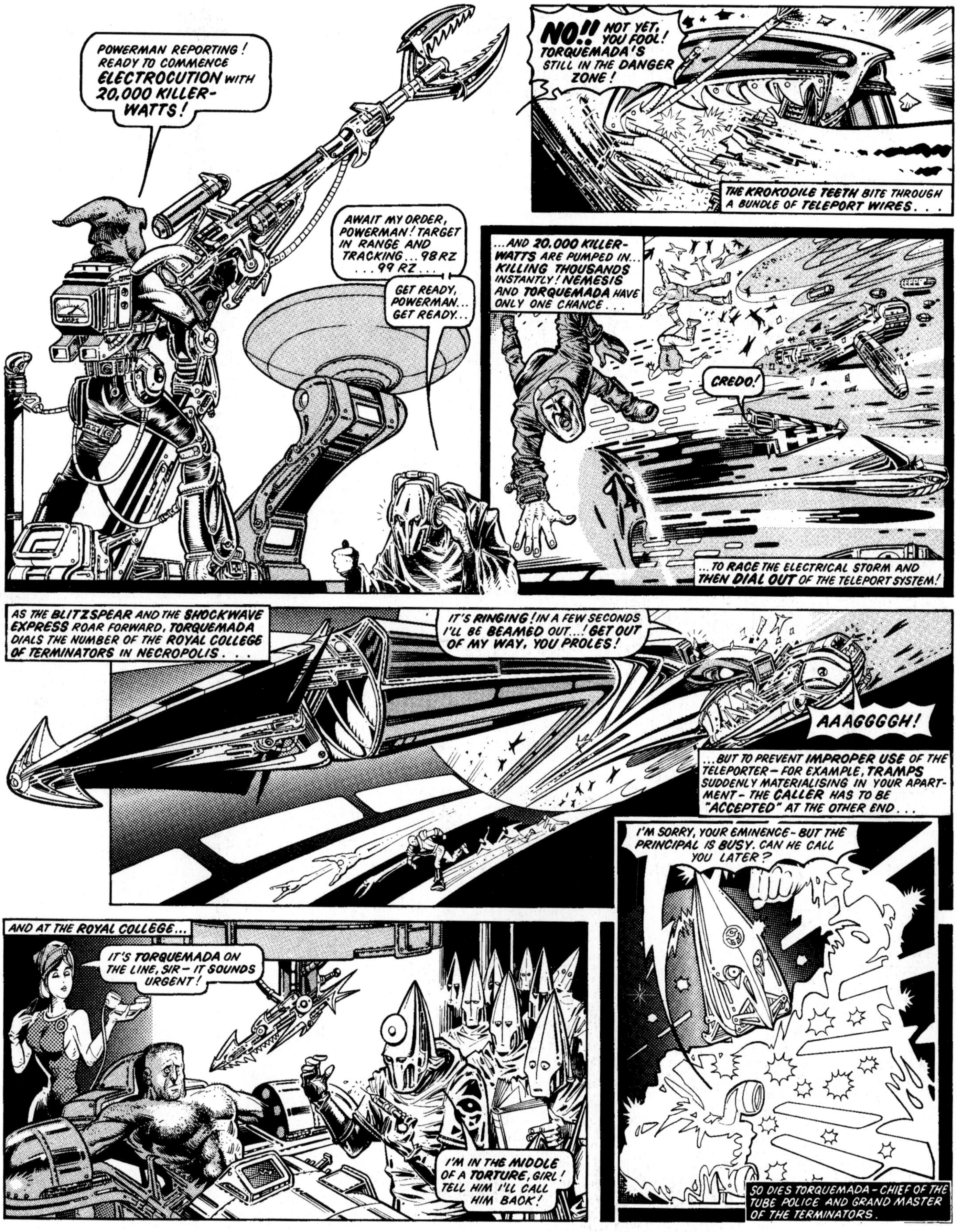
POWERMAN REPORTING! READY TO COMMENCE ELECTROCUTION WITH 20,000 KILLER-WATTS!
AWAIT MY ORDER, POWERMAN! TARGET IN RANGE AND TRACKING... 98 RZ ... 99 RZ ...
GET READY, POWERMAN... GET READY...
NO!! NOT YET, YOU FOOL! TORQUEMADA'S STILL IN THE DANGER ZONE!
THE KROKODILE TEETH BITE THROUGH A BUNDLE OF TELEPORT WIRES...
...AND 20,000 KILLER-WATTS ARE PUMPED IN... KILLING THOUSANDS INSTANTLY! NEMESIS AND TORQUEMADA HAVE ONLY ONE CHANCE...
CREDO!
...TO RACE THE ELECTRICAL STORM AND THEN DIAL OUT OF THE TELEPORT SYSTEM!
AS THE BLITZSPEAR AND THE SHOCKWAVE EXPRESS ROAR FORWARD, TORQUEMADA DIALS THE NUMBER OF THE ROYAL COLLEGE OF TERMINATORS IN NECROPOLIS...
IT'S RINGING! IN A FEW SECONDS I'LL BE BEAMED OUT...! GET OUT OF MY WAY, YOU PROLES!
AAAGGGGH!
...BUT TO PREVENT IMPROPER USE OF THE TELEPORTER - FOR EXAMPLE, TRAMPS SUDDENLY MATERIALISING IN YOUR APARTMENT - THE CALLER HAS TO BE "ACCEPTED" AT THE OTHER END...
AND AT THE ROYAL COLLEGE...
IT'S TORQUEMADA ON THE LINE, SIR - IT SOUNDS URGENT!
I'M IN THE MIDDLE OF A TORTURE, GIRL! TELL HIM I'LL CALL HIM BACK!
I'M SORRY, YOUR EMINENCE - BUT THE PRINCIPAL IS BUSY. CAN HE CALL YOU LATER?
SO DIES TORQUEMADA - CHIEF OF THE TUBE POLICE AND GRAND MASTER OF THE TERMINATORS.

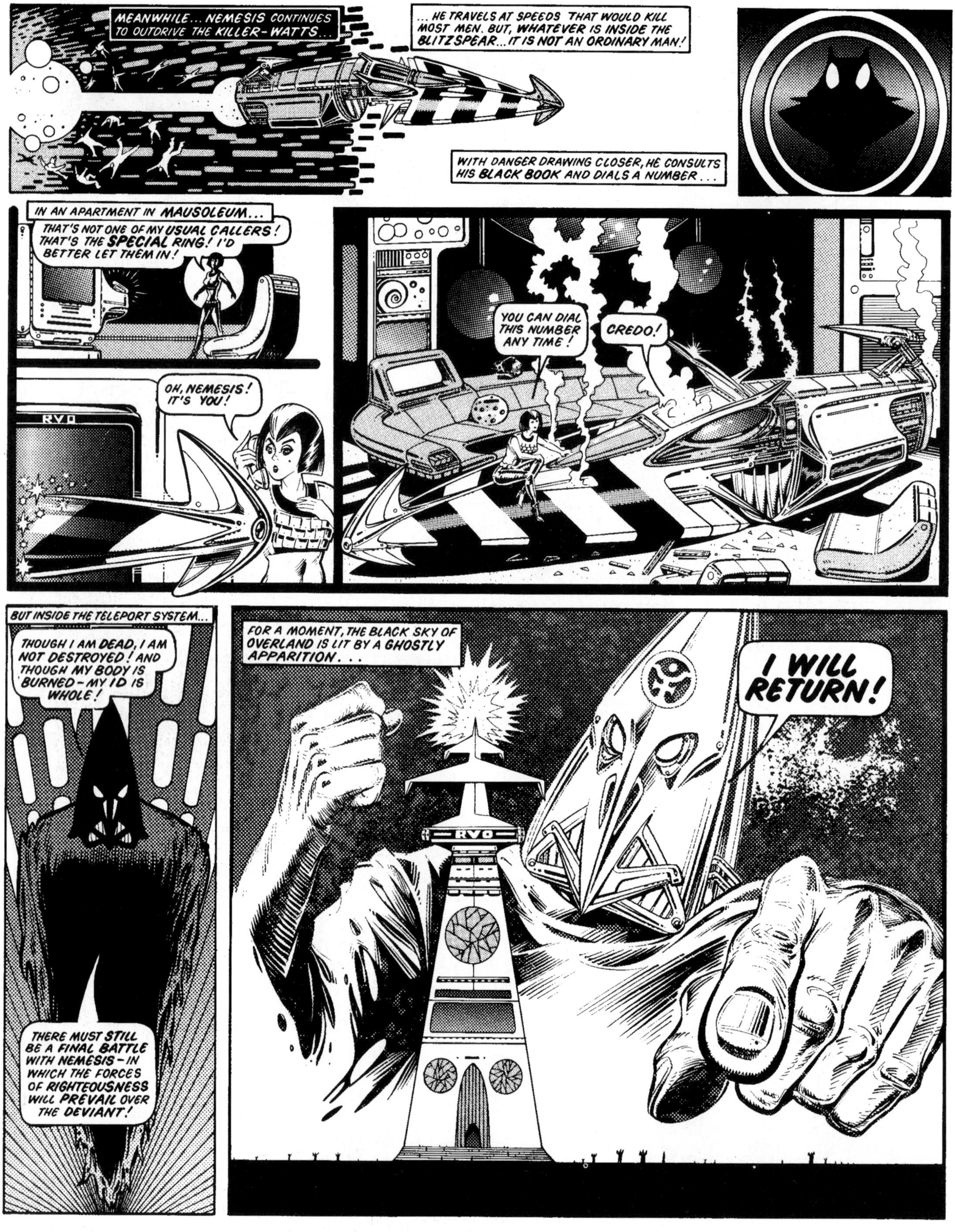
MEANWHILE... NEMESIS CONTINUES TO OUTDRIVE THE KILLER-WATTS...
... HE TRAVELS AT SPEEDS THAT WOULD KILL MOST MEN. BUT, WHATEVER IS INSIDE THE BLITZSPEAR... IT IS NOT AN ORDINARY MAN!
WITH DANGER DRAWING CLOSER, HE CONSULTS HIS BLACK BOOK AND DIALS A NUMBER...
IN AN APARTMENT IN MAUSOLEUM...
THAT'S NOT ONE OF MY USUAL CALLERS! THAT'S THE SPECIAL RING! I'D BETTER LET THEM IN!
OH, NEMESIS! IT'S YOU!
RVO
YOU CAN DIAL THIS NUMBER ANY TIME!
CREDO!
BUT INSIDE THE TELEPORT SYSTEM...
THOUGH I AM DEAD, I AM NOT DESTROYED! AND THOUGH MY BODY IS 'BURNED'- MY ID IS WHOLE!
THERE MUST STILL BE A FINAL BATTLE WITH NEMESIS - IN WHICH THE FORCES OF RIGHTEOUSNESS WILL PREVAIL OVER THE DEVIANT!
FOR A MOMENT, THE BLACK SKY OF OVERLAND IS LIT BY A GHOSTLY APPARITION...
RVO
I WILL RETURN!

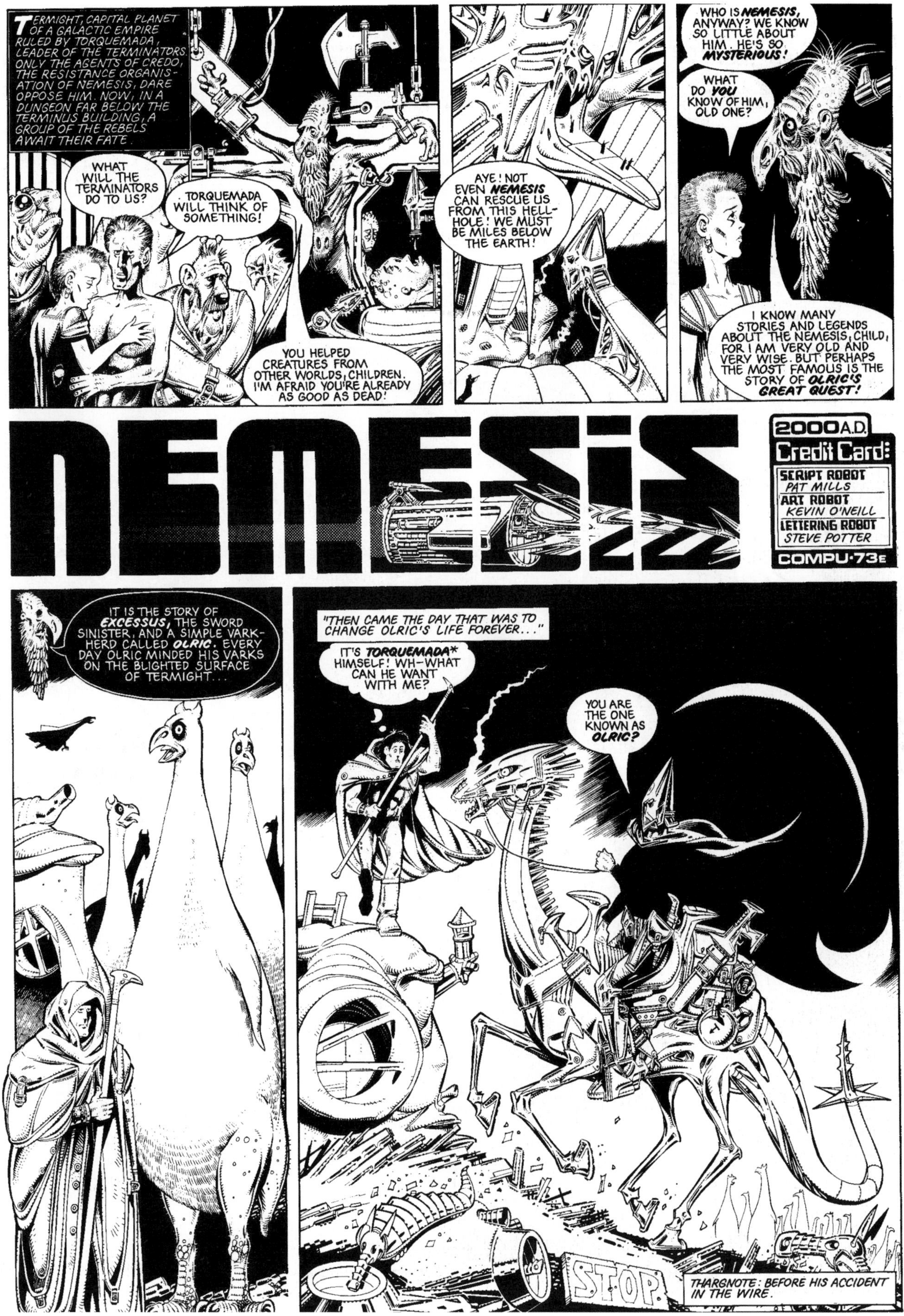
TERMIGHT, CAPITAL PLANET OF A GALACTIC EMPIRE RULED BY TORQUEMADA, LEADER OF THE TERMINATORS. ONLY THE AGENTS OF CREDO, THE RESISTANCE ORGANISATION OF NEMESIS, DARE OPPOSE HIM. NOW, IN A DUNGEON FAR BELOW THE TERMINUS BUILDING, A GROUP OF THE REBELS AWAIT THEIR FATE.
WHAT WILL THE TERMINATORS DO TO US?
TORQUEMADA WILL THINK OF SOMETHING!
YOU HELPED CREATURES FROM OTHER WORLDS, CHILDREN. I'M AFRAID YOU'RE ALREADY AS GOOD AS DEAD!
AYE! NOT EVEN NEMESIS CAN RESCUE US FROM THIS HELL-HOLE! WE MUST BE MILES BELOW THE EARTH!
WHO IS NEMESIS, ANYWAY? WE KNOW SO LITTLE ABOUT HIM. HE'S SO MYSTERIOUS!
WHAT DO YOU KNOW OF HIM, OLD ONE?
I KNOW MANY STORIES AND LEGENDS ABOUT THE NEMESIS, CHILD, FOR I AM VERY OLD AND VERY WISE. BUT PERHAPS THE MOST FAMOUS IS THE STORY OF OLRIC'S GREAT QUEST!
NEMESIS
2000 A.D.
Credit Card:
SCRIPT ROBOT
PAT MILLS
ART ROBOT
KEVIN O'NEILL
LETTERING ROBOT
STEVE POTTER
COMPU-73E
IT IS THE STORY OF EXCESSUS, THE SWORD SINISTER, AND A SIMPLE VARK-HERD CALLED OLRIC. EVERY DAY OLRIC MINDED HIS VARKS ON THE BLIGHTED SURFACE OF TERMIGHT...
"THEN CAME THE DAY THAT WAS TO CHANGE OLRIC'S LIFE FOREVER..."
IT'S TORQUEMADA* HIMSELF! WH-WHAT CAN HE WANT WITH ME?
YOU ARE THE ONE KNOWN AS OLRIC?
STOP
THARGNOTE: BEFORE HIS ACCIDENT IN THE WIRE.

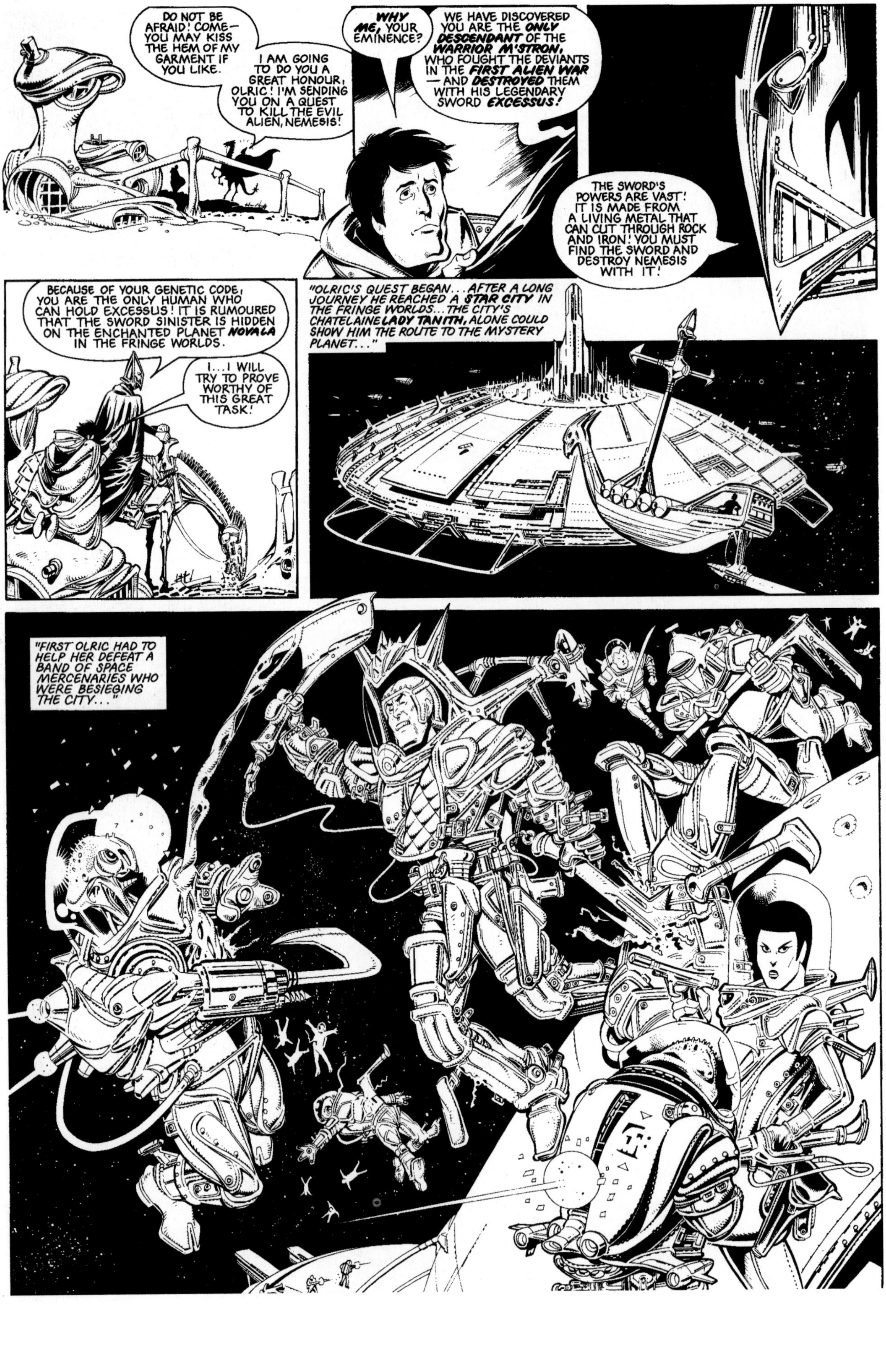

DO NOT BE AFRAID! COME— YOU MAY KISS THE HEM OF MY GARMENT IF YOU LIKE.
I AM GOING TO DO YOU A GREAT HONOUR, OLRIC! I'M SENDING YOU ON A QUEST TO KILL THE EVIL ALIEN, NEMESIS!
WHY ME, YOUR EMINENCE?
WE HAVE DISCOVERED YOU ARE THE ONLY DESCENDANT OF THE WARRIOR M'STRON, WHO FOUGHT THE DEVIANTS IN THE FIRST ALIEN WAR —AND DESTROYED THEM WITH HIS LEGENDARY SWORD EXCESSUS!
THE SWORD'S POWERS ARE VAST! IT IS MADE FROM A LIVING METAL THAT CAN CUT THROUGH ROCK AND IRON! YOU MUST FIND THE SWORD AND DESTROY NEMESIS WITH IT!
BECAUSE OF YOUR GENETIC CODE, YOU ARE THE ONLY HUMAN WHO CAN HOLD EXCESSUS! IT IS RUMOURED THAT THE SWORD SINISTER IS HIDDEN ON THE ENCHANTED PLANET NOVALA IN THE FRINGE WORLDS.
I...I WILL TRY TO PROVE WORTHY OF THIS GREAT TASK!
"OLRIC'S QUEST BEGAN...AFTER A LONG JOURNEY HE REACHED A STAR CITY IN THE FRINGE WORLDS...THE CITY'S CHATELAINE LADY TANITH, ALONE COULD SHOW HIM THE ROUTE TO THE MYSTERY PLANET..."
"FIRST OLRIC HAD TO HELP HER DEFEAT A BAND OF SPACE MERCENARIES WHO WERE BESIEGING THE CITY..."

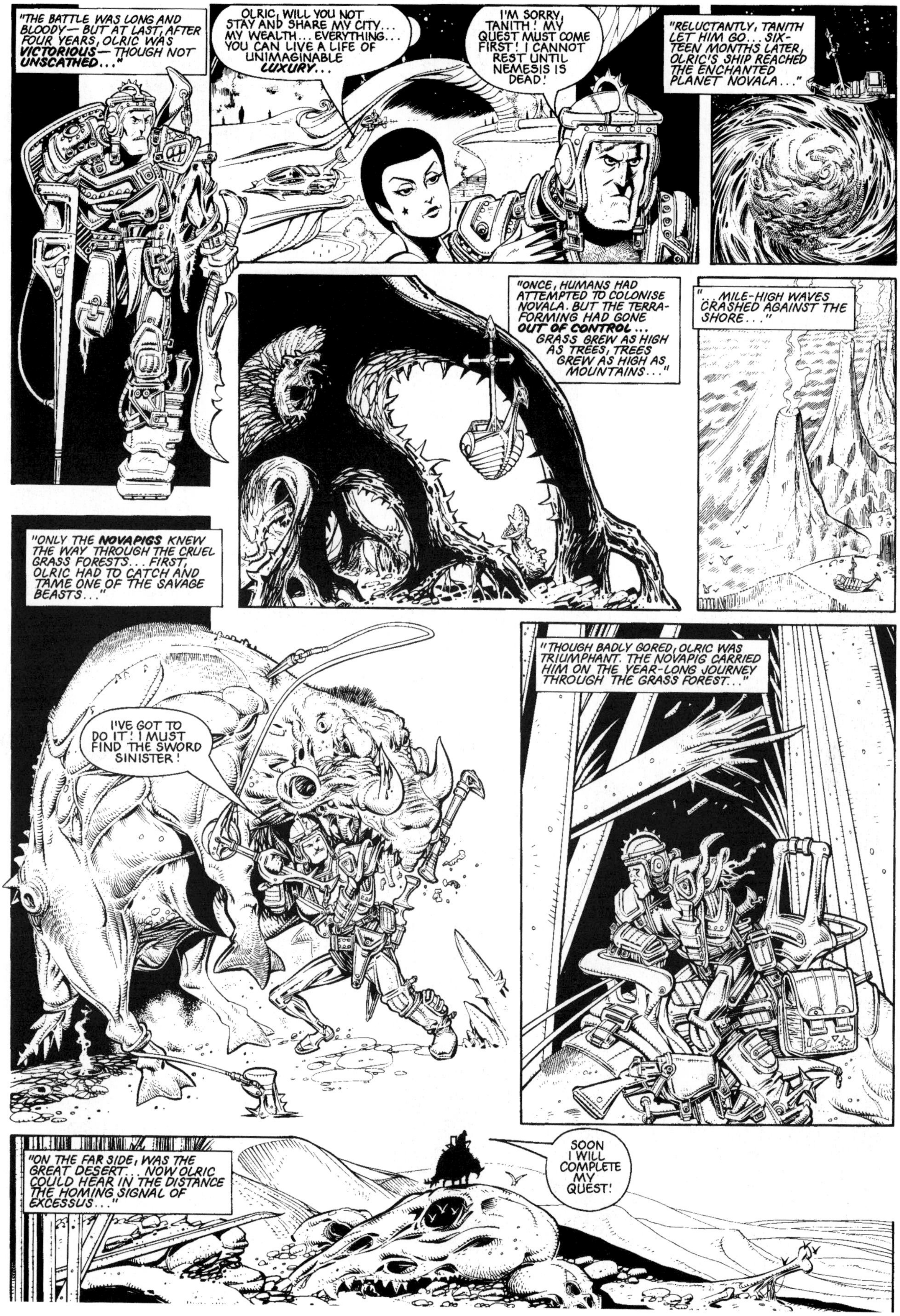
"THE BATTLE WAS LONG AND BLOODY — BUT AT LAST, AFTER FOUR YEARS, OLRIC WAS VICTORIOUS — THOUGH NOT UNSCATHED..."
OLRIC, WILL YOU NOT STAY AND SHARE MY CITY... MY WEALTH... EVERYTHING... YOU CAN LIVE A LIFE OF UNIMAGINABLE LUXURY...
I'M SORRY, TANITH! MY QUEST MUST COME FIRST! I CANNOT REST UNTIL NEMESIS IS DEAD!
"RELUCTANTLY, TANITH LET HIM GO... SIXTEEN MONTHS LATER, OLRIC'S SHIP REACHED THE ENCHANTED PLANET NOVALA..."
"ONCE, HUMANS HAD ATTEMPTED TO COLONISE NOVALA. BUT THE TERRAFORMING HAD GONE OUT OF CONTROL... GRASS GREW AS HIGH AS TREES, TREES GREW AS HIGH AS MOUNTAINS..."
"... MILE-HIGH WAVES CRASHED AGAINST THE SHORE..."
"ONLY THE NOVAPIGS KNEW THE WAY THROUGH THE CRUEL GRASS FORESTS... FIRST, OLRIC HAD TO CATCH AND TAME ONE OF THE SAVAGE BEASTS..."
I'VE GOT TO DO IT! I MUST FIND THE SWORD SINISTER!
"THOUGH BADLY GORED, OLRIC WAS TRIUMPHANT. THE NOVAPIG CARRIED HIM ON THE YEAR-LONG JOURNEY THROUGH THE GRASS FOREST..."
"ON THE FAR SIDE, WAS THE GREAT DESERT... NOW OLRIC COULD HEAR IN THE DISTANCE THE HOMING SIGNAL OF EXCESSUS..."
SOON I WILL COMPLETE MY QUEST!

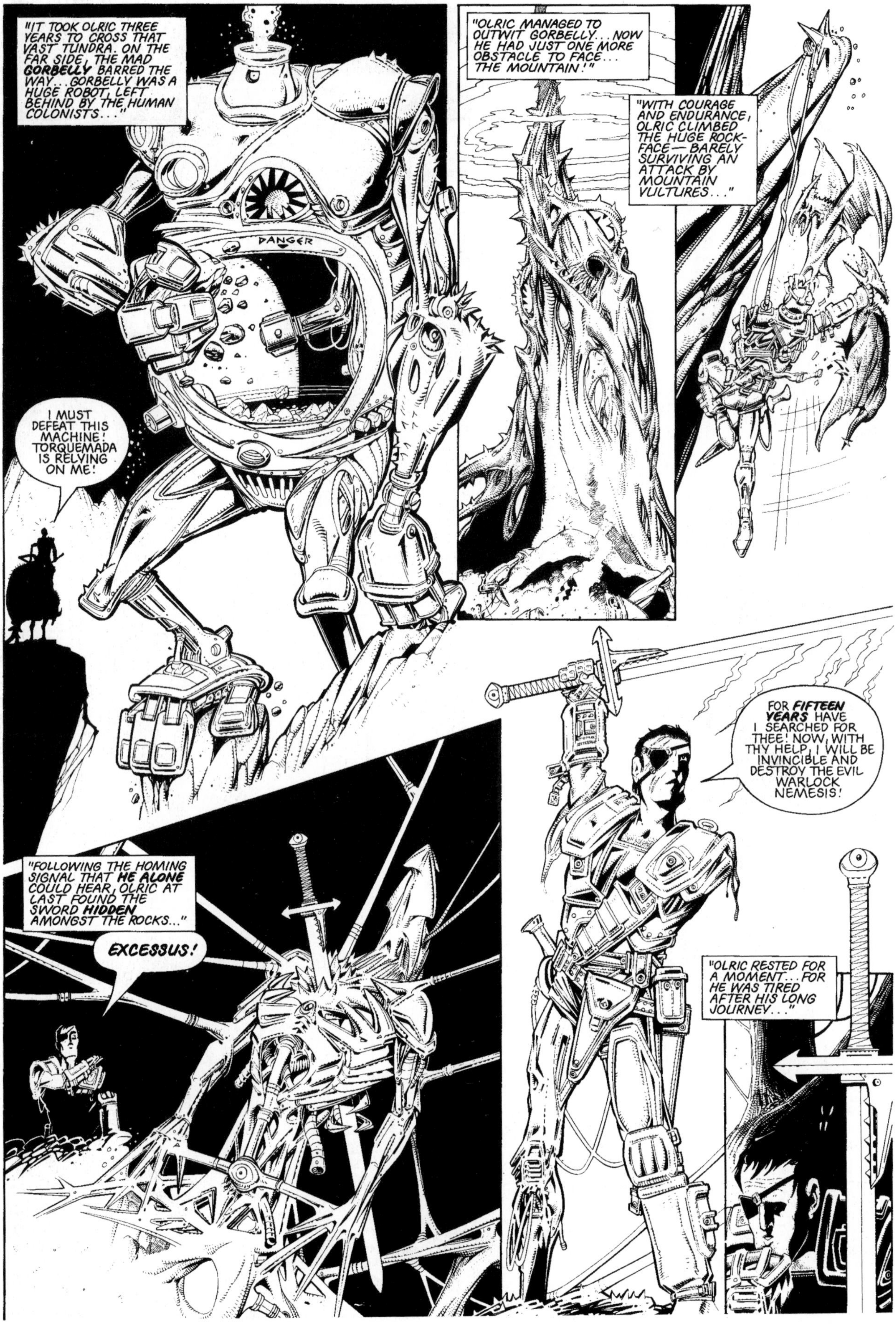
"IT TOOK OLRIC THREE YEARS TO CROSS THAT VAST TUNDRA. ON THE FAR SIDE, THE MAD GORBELLY BARRED THE WAY... GORBELLY WAS A HUGE ROBOT, LEFT BEHIND BY THE HUMAN COLONISTS..."
DANGER
I MUST DEFEAT THIS MACHINE! TORQUEMADA IS RELYING ON ME!
"OLRIC MANAGED TO OUTWIT GORBELLY... NOW HE HAD JUST ONE MORE OBSTACLE TO FACE... THE MOUNTAIN!"
"WITH COURAGE AND ENDURANCE, OLRIC CLIMBED THE HUGE ROCK-FACE — BARELY SURVIVING AN ATTACK BY MOUNTAIN VULTURES..."
"FOLLOWING THE HOMING SIGNAL THAT HE ALONE COULD HEAR, OLRIC AT LAST FOUND THE SWORD HIDDEN AMONGST THE ROCKS..."
EXCESSUS!
FOR FIFTEEN YEARS HAVE I SEARCHED FOR THEE! NOW, WITH THY HELP, I WILL BE INVINCIBLE AND DESTROY THE EVIL WARLOCK NEMESIS!
"OLRIC RESTED FOR A MOMENT... FOR HE WAS TIRED AFTER HIS LONG JOURNEY..."

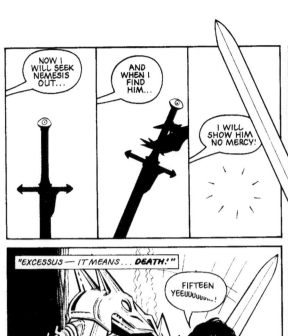

NOW I WILL SEEK NEMESIS OUT...

AND WHEN I FIND HIM...

I WILL SHOW HIM NO MERCY!

"EXCESSUS — IT MEANS... DEATH!"

FIFTEEN YEEUUUUUUU...!

NEMESIS!!

"OLRIC'S GREAT QUEST WAS OVER. HE HAD FAILED."

"BUT NEMESIS WENT ON TO DO MANY GREAT DEEDS AND KILLED MANY HUMANS WITH THE SWORD!"

I LIKE A STORY WITH A HAPPY ENDING!

AND THAT IS HOW OUR GREAT LEADER RE-GAINED HIS SWORD. FOR THE HUMAN, M'STRON, HAD STOLEN IT FROM THE WAR-LOCK MANY YEARS BEFORE—AND FASHIONED IT TO HIS GRASP. BUT THAT'S ANOTHER STORY FOR ANOTHER DAY, CHILDREN.

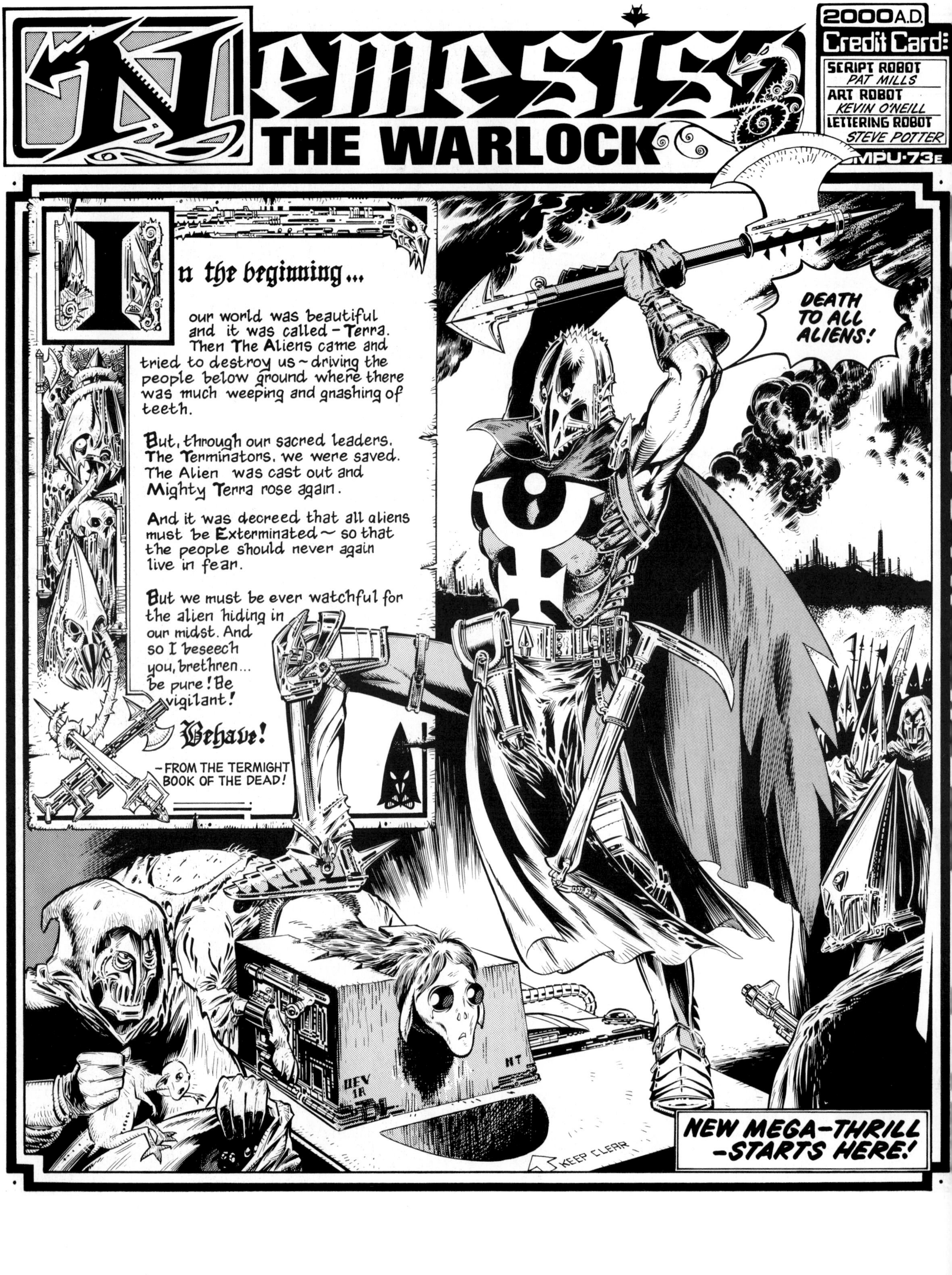

Nemesis THE WARLOCK
2000 A.D. Credit Card:
SCRIPT ROBOT PAT MILLS
ART ROBOT KEVIN O'NEILL
LETTERING ROBOT STEVE POTTER
MPU·73E
In the beginning...
our world was beautiful and it was called - Terra. Then The Aliens came and tried to destroy us ~ driving the people below ground where there was much weeping and gnashing of teeth.
But, through our sacred leaders, The Terminators, we were saved. The Alien was cast out and Mighty Terra rose again.
And it was decreed that all aliens must be Exterminated ~ so that the people should never again live in fear.
But we must be ever watchful for the alien hiding in our midst. And so I beseech you, brethren... be pure! Be vigilant!
Behave!
- FROM THE TERMIGHT BOOK OF THE DEAD!
DEATH TO ALL ALIENS!
KEEP CLEAR
NEW MEGA-THRILL -STARTS HERE!

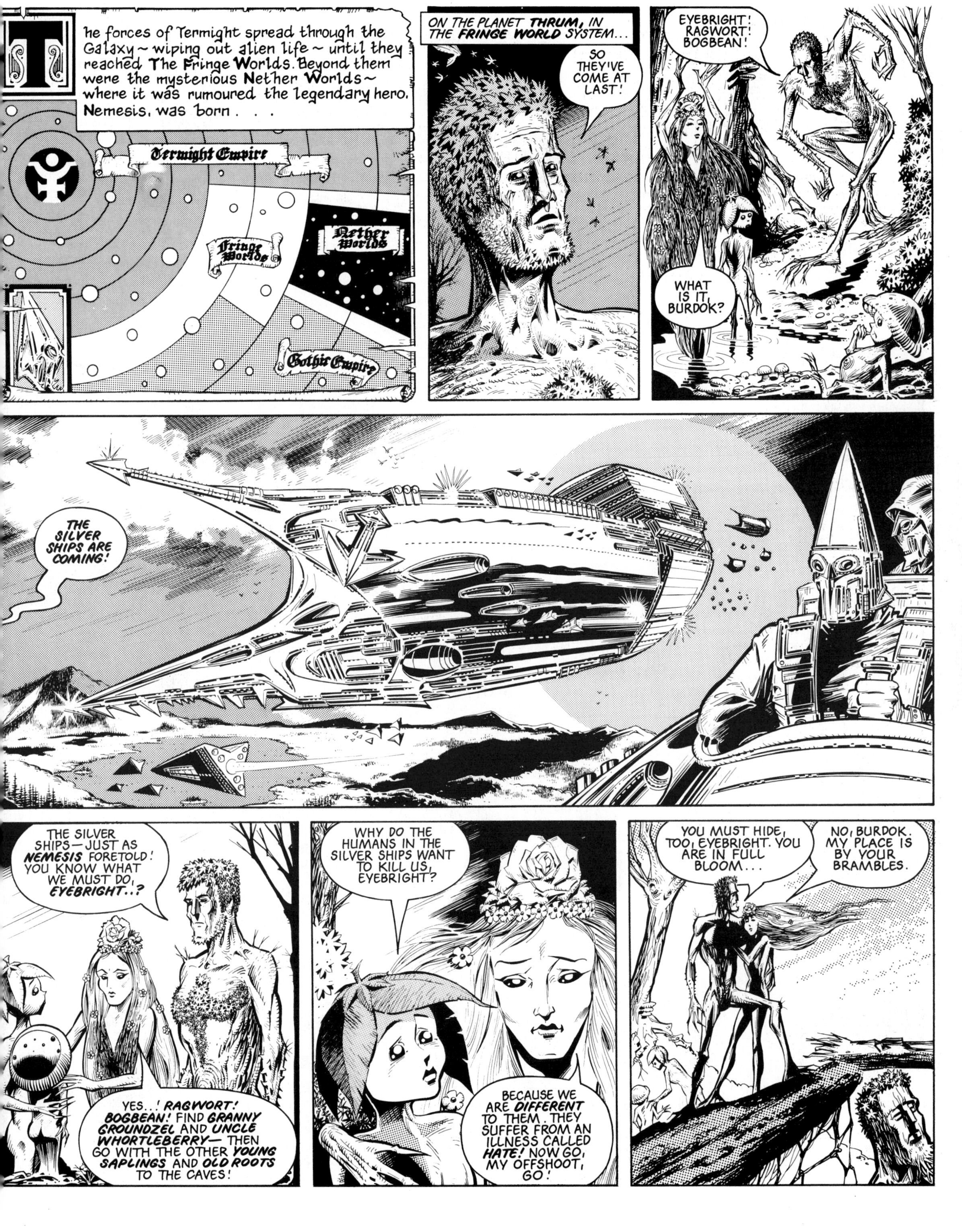
The forces of Termight spread through the Galaxy ~ wiping out alien life ~ until they reached The Fringe Worlds. Beyond them were the mysterious Nether Worlds ~ where it was rumoured the legendary hero, Nemesis, was born . . .
Termight Empire
Fringe Worlds
Nether Worlds
Gothic Empire
ON THE PLANET THRUM, IN THE FRINGE WORLD SYSTEM...
SO THEY'VE COME AT LAST!
EYEBRIGHT! RAGWORT! BOGBEAN!
WHAT IS IT, BURDOK?
THE SILVER SHIPS ARE COMING!
THE SILVER SHIPS—JUST AS NEMESIS FORETOLD! YOU KNOW WHAT WE MUST DO, EYEBRIGHT..?
YES..! RAGWORT! BOGBEAN! FIND GRANNY GROUNDZEL AND UNCLE WHORTLEBERRY— THEN GO WITH THE OTHER YOUNG SAPLINGS AND OLD ROOTS TO THE CAVES!
WHY DO THE HUMANS IN THE SILVER SHIPS WANT TO KILL US, EYEBRIGHT?
BECAUSE WE ARE DIFFERENT TO THEM. THEY SUFFER FROM AN ILLNESS CALLED HATE! NOW GO, MY OFFSHOOT, GO!
YOU MUST HIDE, TOO, EYEBRIGHT. YOU ARE IN FULL BLOOM...
NO, BURDOK. MY PLACE IS BY YOUR BRAMBLES.

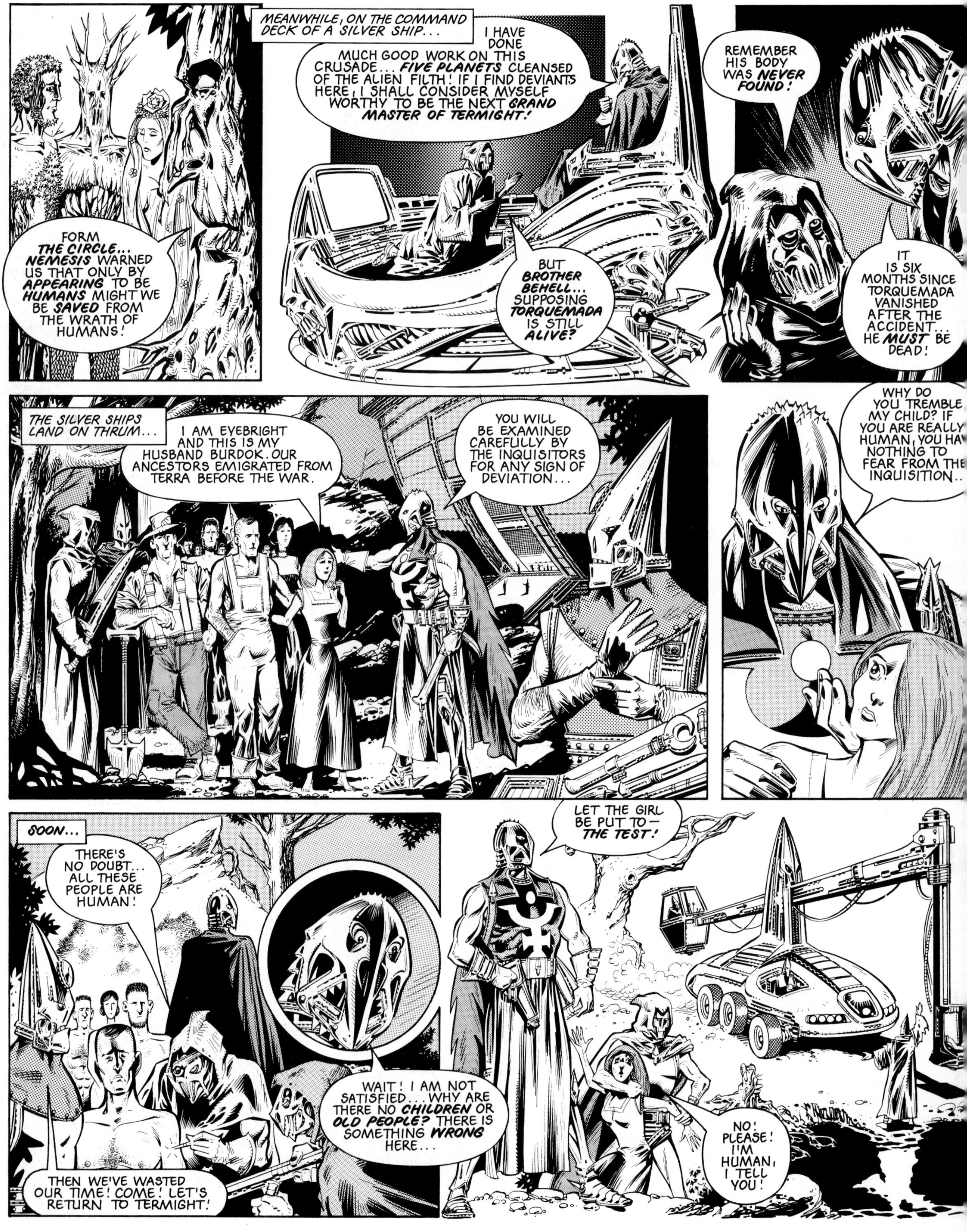
FORM THE CIRCLE... NEMESIS WARNED US THAT ONLY BY APPEARING TO BE HUMANS MIGHT WE BE SAVED FROM THE WRATH OF HUMANS!
MEANWHILE, ON THE COMMAND DECK OF A SILVER SHIP...
I HAVE DONE MUCH GOOD WORK ON THIS CRUSADE... FIVE PLANETS CLEANSED OF THE ALIEN FILTH! IF I FIND DEVIANTS HERE, I SHALL CONSIDER MYSELF WORTHY TO BE THE NEXT GRAND MASTER OF TERMIGHT!
BUT BROTHER BEHELL... SUPPOSING TORQUEMADA IS STILL ALIVE?
REMEMBER HIS BODY WAS NEVER FOUND!
IT IS SIX MONTHS SINCE TORQUEMADA VANISHED AFTER THE ACCIDENT... HE MUST BE DEAD!
THE SILVER SHIPS LAND ON THRUM...
I AM EYEBRIGHT AND THIS IS MY HUSBAND BURDOK. OUR ANCESTORS EMIGRATED FROM TERRA BEFORE THE WAR.
YOU WILL BE EXAMINED CAREFULLY BY THE INQUISITORS FOR ANY SIGN OF DEVIATION...
WHY DO YOU TREMBLE MY CHILD? IF YOU ARE REALLY HUMAN, YOU HA NOTHING TO FEAR FROM THE INQUISITION...
SOON...
THERE'S NO DOUBT... ALL THESE PEOPLE ARE HUMAN!
THEN WE'VE WASTED OUR TIME! COME! LET'S RETURN TO TERMIGHT!
WAIT! I AM NOT SATISFIED... WHY ARE THERE NO CHILDREN OR OLD PEOPLE? THERE IS SOMETHING WRONG HERE...
LET THE GIRL BE PUT TO— THE TEST!
NO! PLEASE! I'M HUMAN, I TELL YOU!

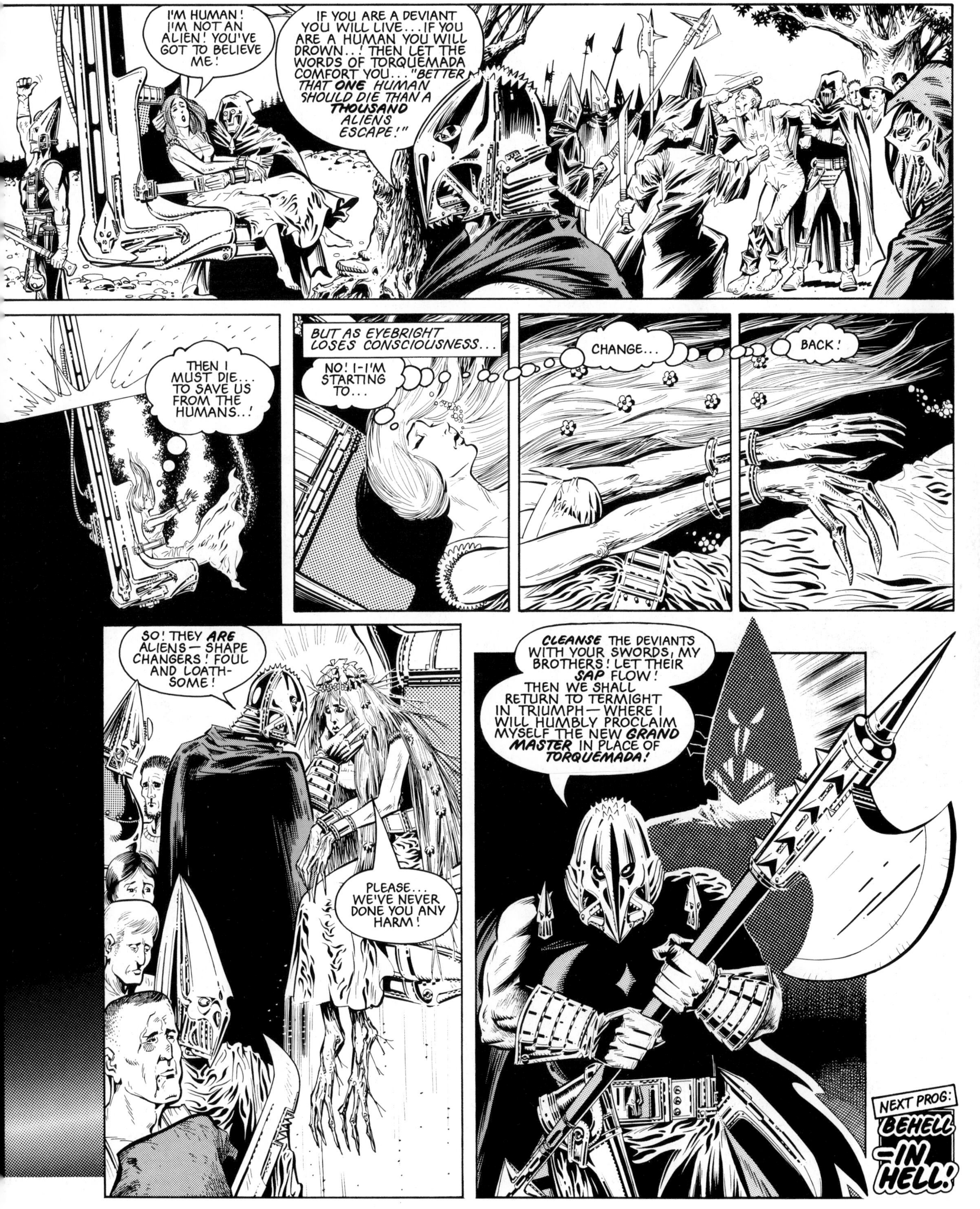

I'M HUMAN! I'M NOT AN ALIEN! YOU'VE GOT TO BELIEVE ME!
IF YOU ARE A DEVIANT YOU WILL LIVE... IF YOU ARE A HUMAN YOU WILL DROWN..! THEN LET THE WORDS OF TORQUEMADA COMFORT YOU... "BETTER THAT ONE HUMAN SHOULD DIE THAN A THOUSAND ALIENS ESCAPE!"
THEN I MUST DIE... TO SAVE US FROM THE HUMANS..!
BUT AS EYEBRIGHT LOSES CONSCIOUSNESS...
NO! I-I'M STARTING TO...
CHANGE...
BACK!
SO! THEY ARE ALIENS— SHAPE CHANGERS! FOUL AND LOATH-SOME!
PLEASE... WE'VE NEVER DONE YOU ANY HARM!
CLEANSE THE DEVIANTS WITH YOUR SWORDS, MY BROTHERS! LET THEIR SAP FLOW! THEN WE SHALL RETURN TO TERMIGHT IN TRIUMPH— WHERE I WILL HUMBLY PROCLAIM MYSELF THE NEW GRAND MASTER IN PLACE OF TORQUEMADA!
NEXT PROG:
BEHELL —IN HELL!

Nemesis THE WARLOCK

2000 A.D. Credit Card
SCRIPT ROBOT PAT MILLS
ART ROBOT KEVIN O'NEILL
LETTERING ROBOT STEVE POTTER
COMPU-73E

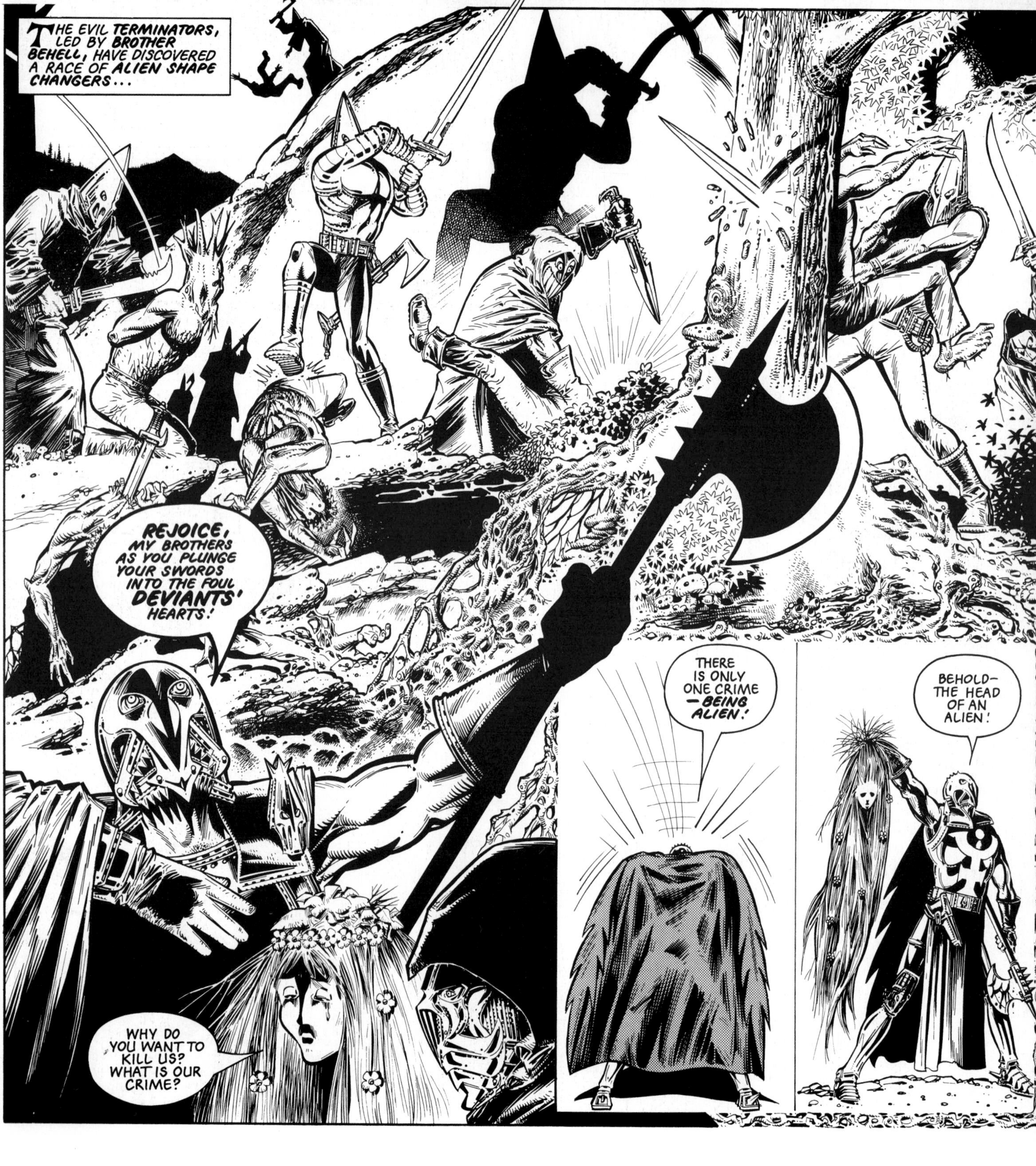

THE EVIL TERMINATORS, LED BY BROTHER BEHELL, HAVE DISCOVERED A RACE OF ALIEN SHAPE CHANGERS...
REJOICE, MY BROTHERS AS YOU PLUNGE YOUR SWORDS INTO THE FOUL DEVIANTS' HEARTS!
WHY DO YOU WANT TO KILL US? WHAT IS OUR CRIME?
THERE IS ONLY ONE CRIME —BEING ALIEN!
BEHOLD— THE HEAD OF AN ALIEN!

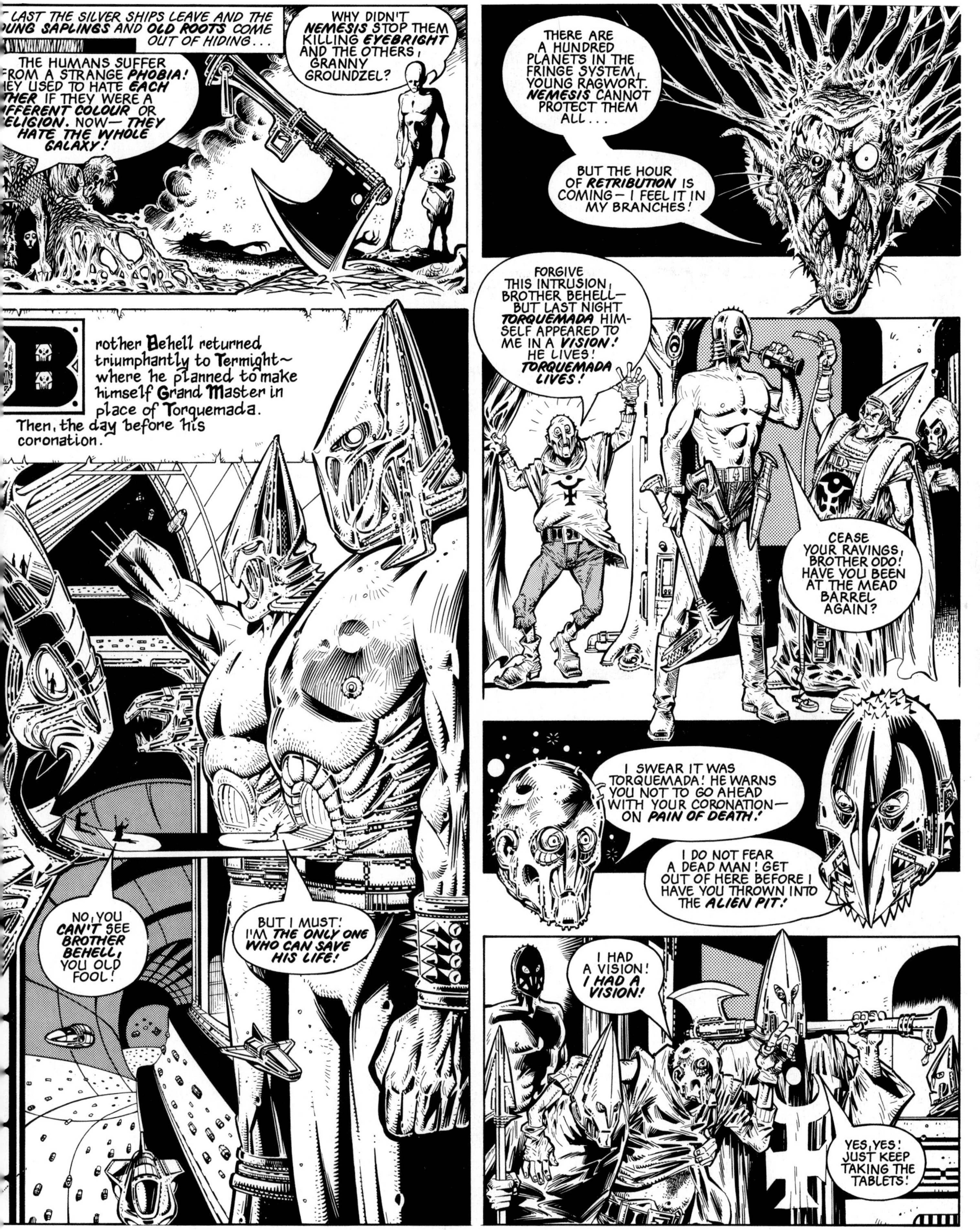
T LAST THE SILVER SHIPS LEAVE AND THE UNG SAPLINGS AND OLD ROOTS COME OUT OF HIDING . . .
WHY DIDN'T NEMESIS STOP THEM KILLING EYEBRIGHT AND THE OTHERS, GRANNY GROUNDZEL?
THE HUMANS SUFFER FROM A STRANGE PHOBIA! HEY USED TO HATE EACH THER IF THEY WERE A IFFERENT COLOUR OR ELIGION. NOW— THEY HATE THE WHOLE GALAXY!
THERE ARE A HUNDRED PLANETS IN THE FRINGE SYSTEM, YOUNG RAGWORT. NEMESIS CANNOT PROTECT THEM ALL . . .
BUT THE HOUR OF RETRIBUTION IS COMING— I FEEL IT IN MY BRANCHES!
Brother Behell returned triumphantly to Termight~ where he planned to make himself Grand Master in place of Torquemada. Then, the day before his coronation.
NO, YOU CAN'T SEE BROTHER BEHELL, YOU OLD FOOL!
BUT I MUST! I'M THE ONLY ONE WHO CAN SAVE HIS LIFE!
FORGIVE THIS INTRUSION, BROTHER BEHELL— BUT LAST NIGHT TORQUEMADA HIMSELF APPEARED TO ME IN A VISION! HE LIVES! TORQUEMADA LIVES!
CEASE YOUR RAVINGS, BROTHER ODO! HAVE YOU BEEN AT THE MEAD BARREL AGAIN?
I SWEAR IT WAS TORQUEMADA! HE WARNS YOU NOT TO GO AHEAD WITH YOUR CORONATION— ON PAIN OF DEATH!
I DO NOT FEAR A DEAD MAN! GET OUT OF HERE BEFORE I HAVE YOU THROWN INTO THE ALIEN PIT!
I HAD A VISION! I HAD A VISION!
YES, YES! JUST KEEP TAKING THE TABLETS!

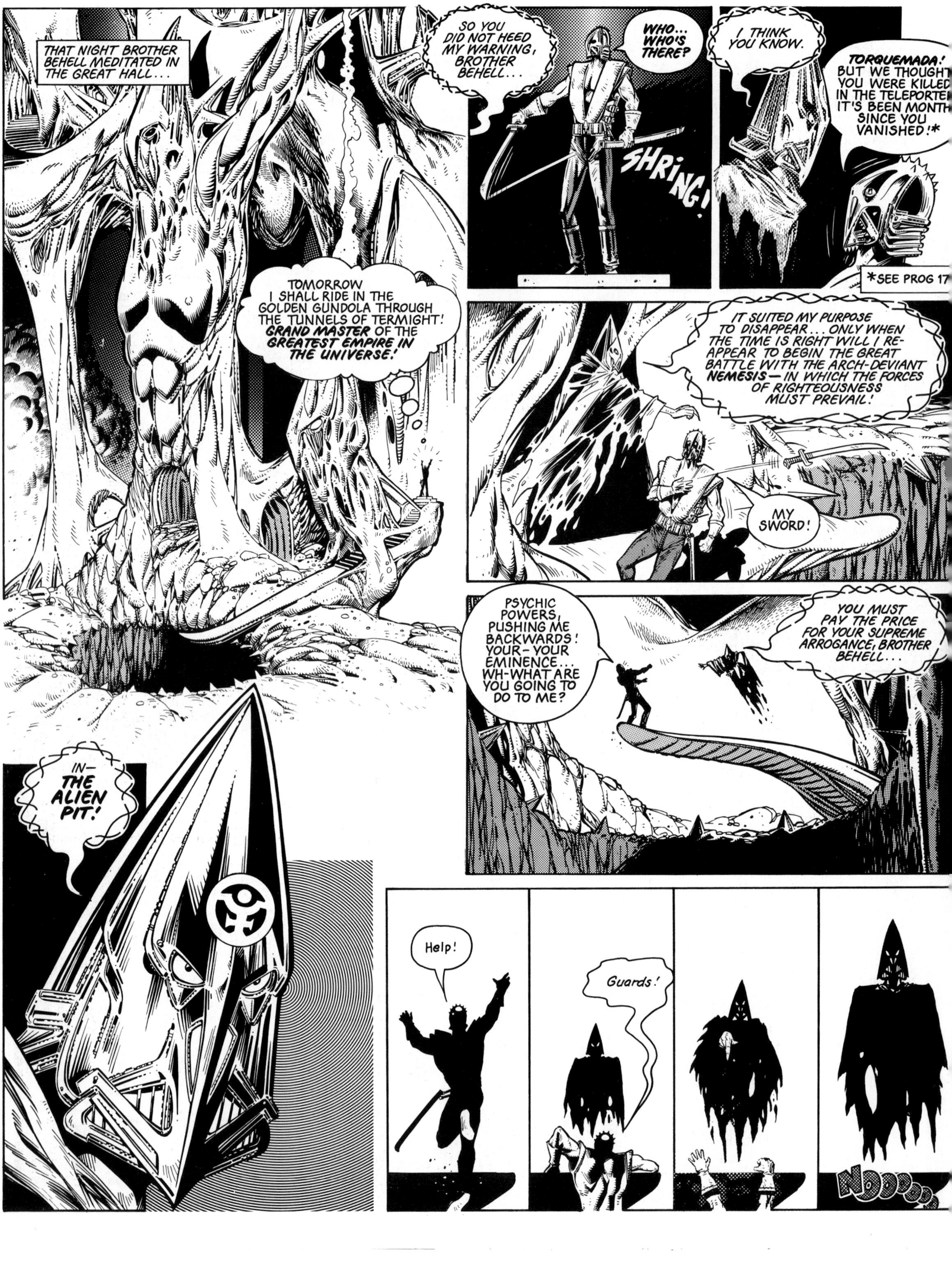

THAT NIGHT BROTHER BEHELL MEDITATED IN THE GREAT HALL...
TOMORROW I SHALL RIDE IN THE GOLDEN GUNDOLA THROUGH THE TUNNELS OF TERMIGHT! GRAND MASTER OF THE GREATEST EMPIRE IN THE UNIVERSE!
SO YOU DID NOT HEED MY WARNING, BROTHER BEHELL...
WHO... WHO'S THERE?
SHRING!
I THINK YOU KNOW.
TORQUEMADA! BUT WE THOUGHT YOU WERE KILLED IN THE TELEPORTER IT'S BEEN MONTHS SINCE YOU VANISHED!*
*SEE PROG 17
IT SUITED MY PURPOSE TO DISAPPEAR... ONLY WHEN THE TIME IS RIGHT WILL I RE-APPEAR TO BEGIN THE GREAT BATTLE WITH THE ARCH-DEVIANT NEMESIS — IN WHICH THE FORCES OF RIGHTEOUSNESS MUST PREVAIL!
MY SWORD!
PSYCHIC POWERS, PUSHING ME BACKWARDS! YOUR- YOUR EMINENCE... WH-WHAT ARE YOU GOING TO DO TO ME?
YOU MUST PAY THE PRICE FOR YOUR SUPREME ARROGANCE, BROTHER BEHELL...
IN— THE ALIEN PIT!
Help!
Guards!
NOOOOOO

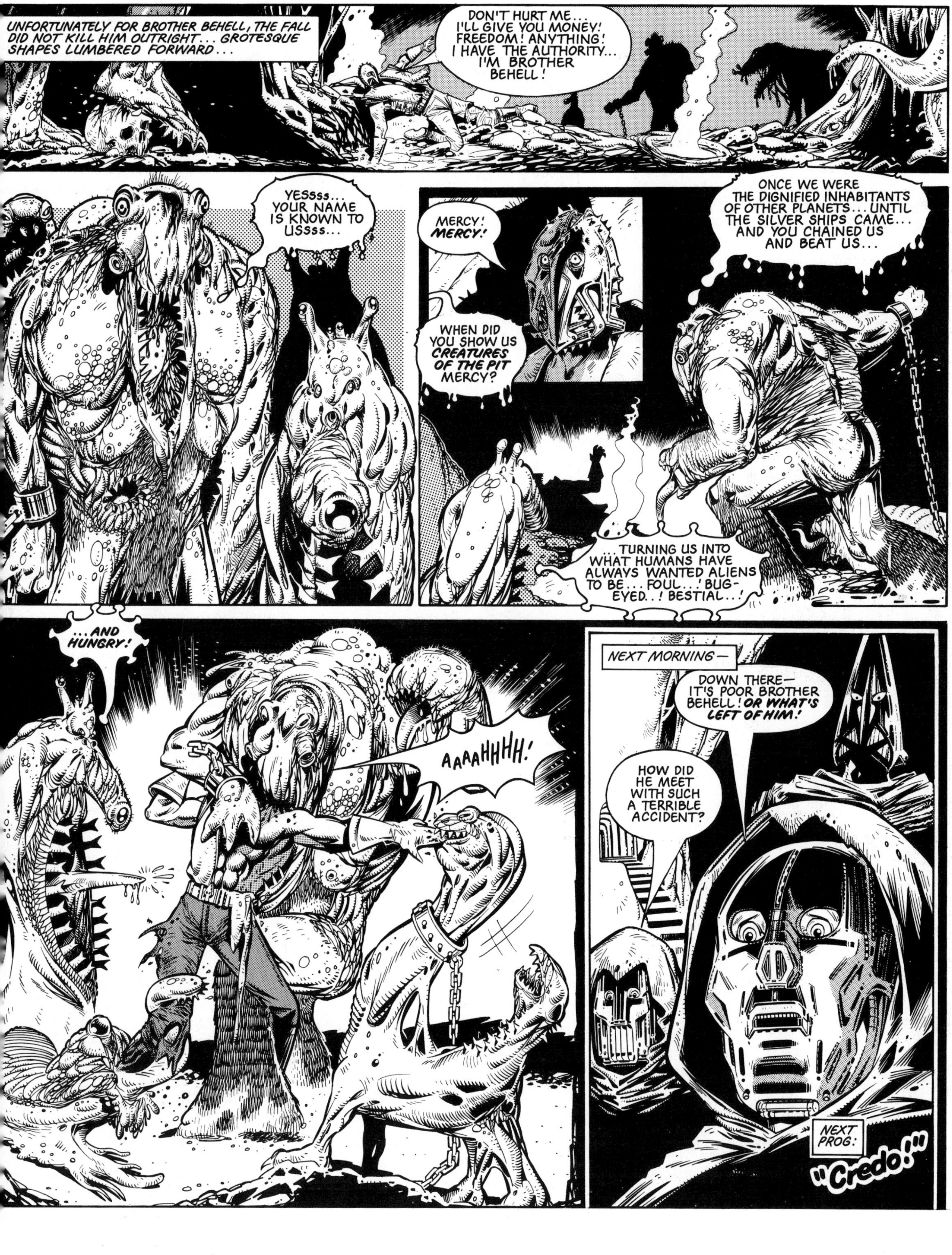

UNFORTUNATELY FOR BROTHER BEHELL, THE FALL DID NOT KILL HIM OUTRIGHT... GROTESQUE SHAPES LUMBERED FORWARD...
DON'T HURT ME... I'LL GIVE YOU MONEY! FREEDOM! ANYTHING! I HAVE THE AUTHORITY... I'M BROTHER BEHELL!
YESSSS... YOUR NAME IS KNOWN TO USSSS...
MERCY! MERCY!
WHEN DID YOU SHOW US CREATURES OF THE PIT MERCY?
ONCE WE WERE THE DIGNIFIED INHABITANTS OF OTHER PLANETS... UNTIL THE SILVER SHIPS CAME... AND YOU CHAINED US AND BEAT US...
...TURNING US INTO WHAT HUMANS HAVE ALWAYS WANTED ALIENS TO BE... FOUL...! BUG-EYED...! BESTIAL...!
...AND HUNGRY!
AAAAHHHH!
NEXT MORNING—
DOWN THERE— IT'S POOR BROTHER BEHELL! OR WHAT'S LEFT OF HIM!
HOW DID HE MEET WITH SUCH A TERRIBLE ACCIDENT?
NEXT PROG:
"Credo!"

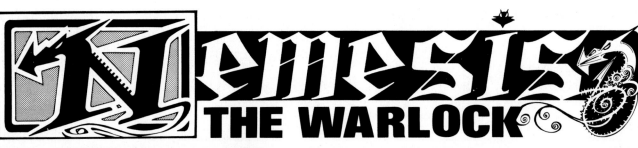

Nemesis THE WARLOCK

2000 A.D.
Credit Car
SCRIPT ROBOT PAT MILLS
ART ROBOT KEVIN O'NEILL
LETTERING ROBOT STEVE POTTER
COMPU·73

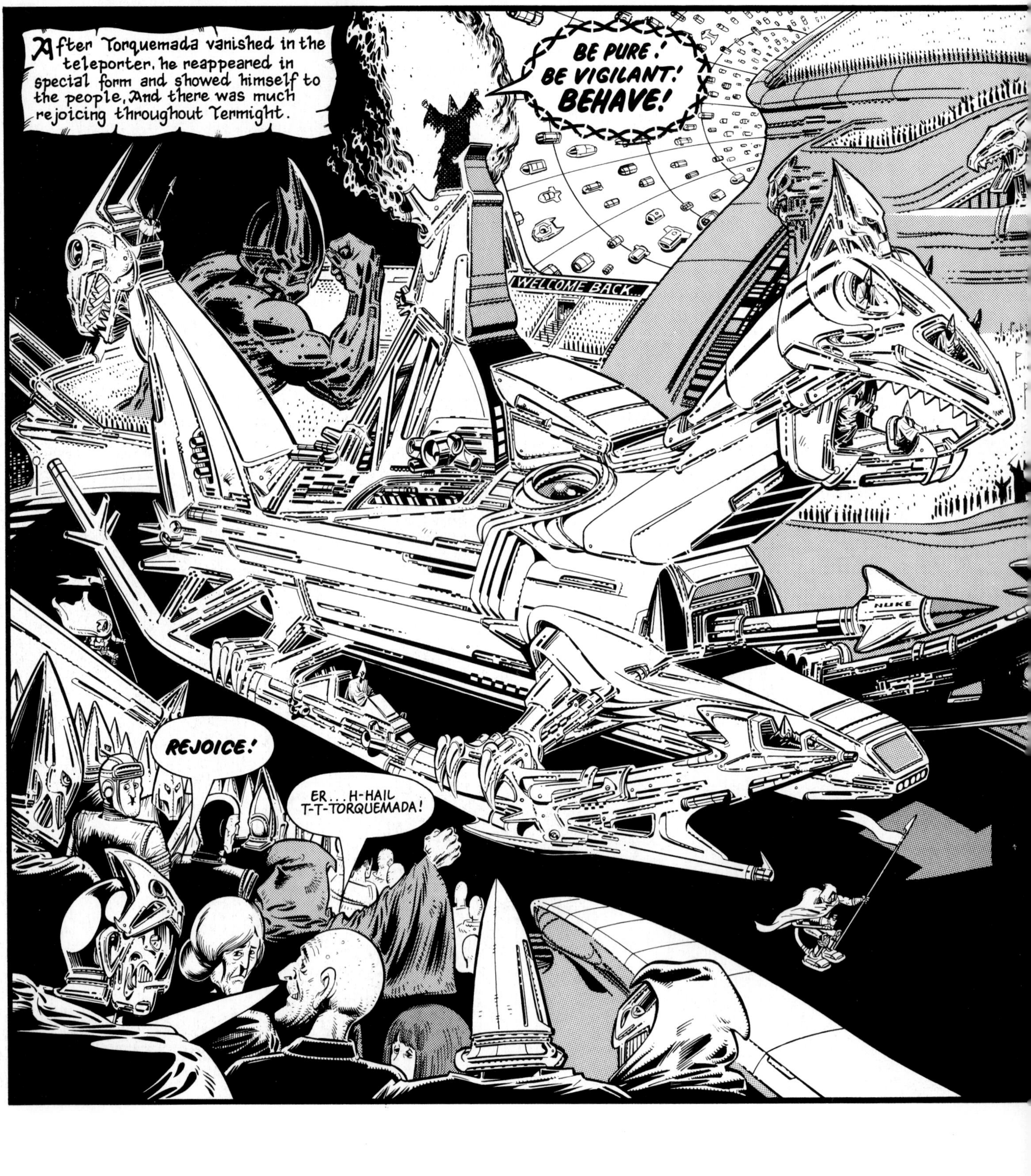

After Torquemada vanished in the teleporter, he reappeared in special form and showed himself to the people, And there was much rejoicing throughout Termight.
BE PURE! BE VIGILANT! BEHAVE!
WELCOME BACK...
NUKE
REJOICE!
ER... H-HAIL T-T-TORQUEMADA!

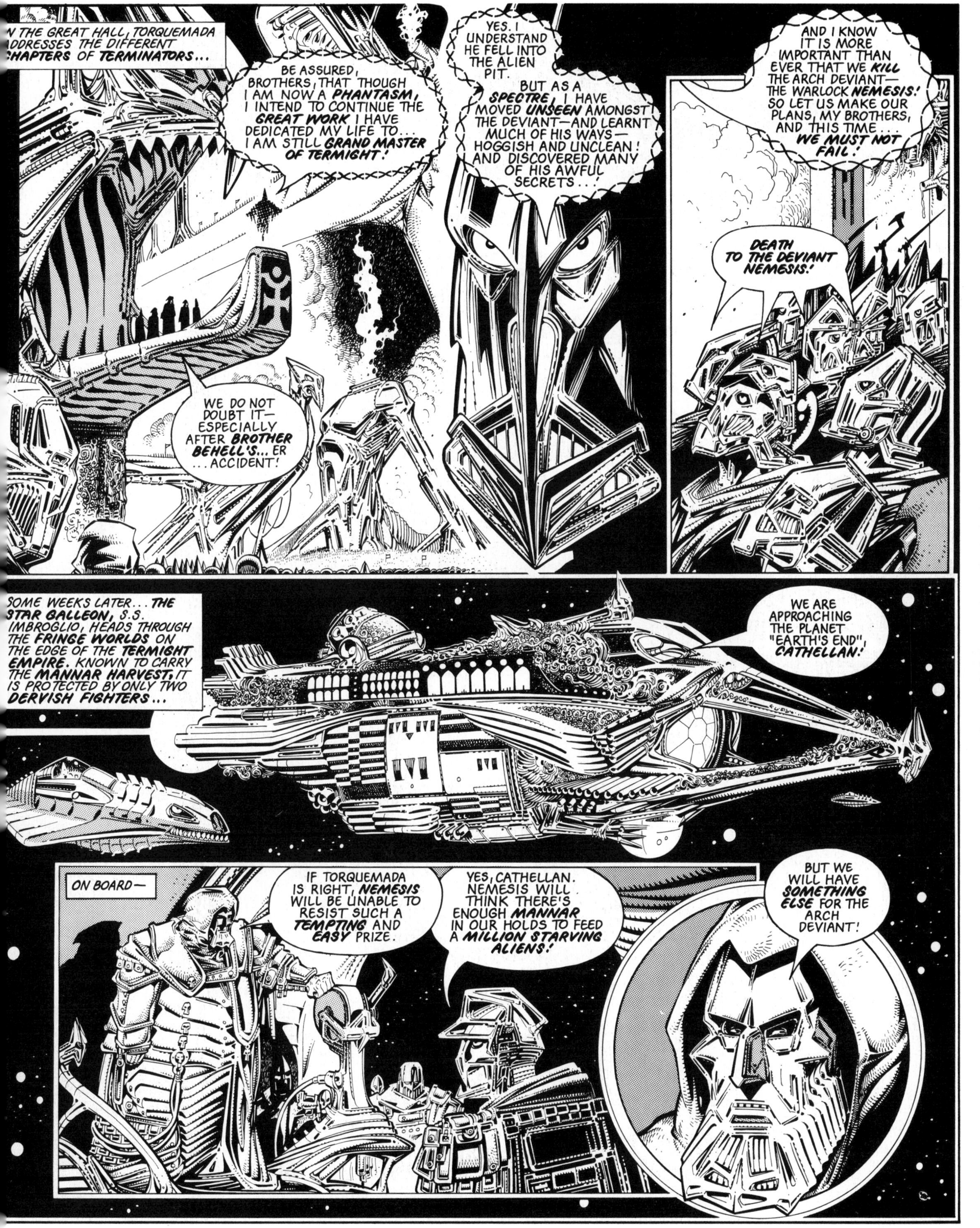
IN THE GREAT HALL, TORQUEMADA ADDRESSES THE DIFFERENT CHAPTERS OF TERMINATORS...
BE ASSURED, BROTHERS, THAT THOUGH I AM NOW A PHANTASM, I INTEND TO CONTINUE THE GREAT WORK I HAVE DEDICATED MY LIFE TO... I AM STILL GRAND MASTER OF TERMIGHT!
WE DO NOT DOUBT IT— ESPECIALLY AFTER BROTHER BEHELL'S... ER ...ACCIDENT!
YES. I UNDERSTAND HE FELL INTO THE ALIEN PIT.
BUT AS A SPECTRE, I HAVE MOVED UNSEEN AMONGST THE DEVIANT—AND LEARNT MUCH OF HIS WAYS— HOGGISH AND UNCLEAN! AND DISCOVERED MANY OF HIS AWFUL SECRETS...!
AND I KNOW IT IS MORE IMPORTANT THAN EVER THAT WE KILL THE ARCH DEVIANT— THE WARLOCK NEMESIS! SO LET US MAKE OUR PLANS, MY BROTHERS, AND THIS TIME... WE MUST NOT FAIL!
DEATH TO THE DEVIANT NEMESIS!
SOME WEEKS LATER... THE STAR GALLEON, S.S. IMBROGLIO, HEADS THROUGH THE FRINGE WORLDS ON THE EDGE OF THE TERMIGHT EMPIRE. KNOWN TO CARRY THE MANNAR HARVEST, IT IS PROTECTED BY ONLY TWO DERVISH FIGHTERS...
WE ARE APPROACHING THE PLANET "EARTH'S END", CATHELLAN!
ON BOARD—
IF TORQUEMADA IS RIGHT, NEMESIS WILL BE UNABLE TO RESIST SUCH A TEMPTING AND EASY PRIZE.
YES, CATHELLAN. NEMESIS WILL THINK THERE'S ENOUGH MANNAR IN OUR HOLDS TO FEED A MILLION STARVING ALIENS!
BUT WE WILL HAVE SOMETHING ELSE FOR THE ARCH DEVIANT!

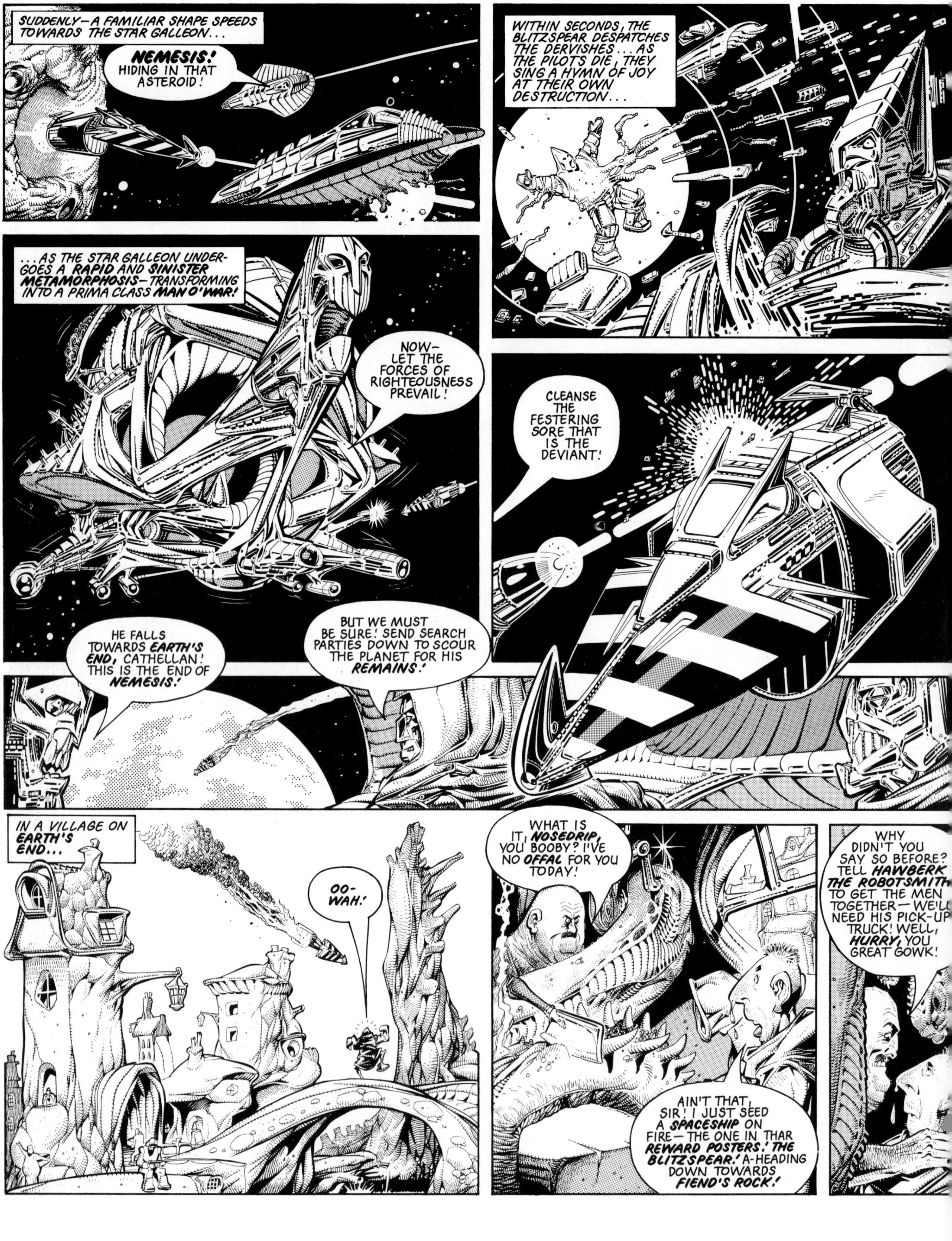
SUDDENLY—A FAMILIAR SHAPE SPEEDS TOWARDS THE STAR GALLEON...
NEMESIS! HIDING IN THAT ASTEROID!
WITHIN SECONDS, THE BLITZSPEAR DESPATCHES THE DERVISHES... AS THE PILOTS DIE, THEY SING A HYMN OF JOY AT THEIR OWN DESTRUCTION...
...AS THE STAR GALLEON UNDERGOES A RAPID AND SINISTER METAMORPHOSIS—TRANSFORMING INTO A PRIMA CLASS MAN O'WAR!
NOW—LET THE FORCES OF RIGHTEOUSNESS PREVAIL!
CLEANSE THE FESTERING SORE THAT IS THE DEVIANT!
HE FALLS TOWARDS EARTH'S END, CATHELLAN! THIS IS THE END OF NEMESIS!
BUT WE MUST BE SURE! SEND SEARCH PARTIES DOWN TO SCOUR THE PLANET FOR HIS REMAINS!
IN A VILLAGE ON EARTH'S END...
OO-WAH!
WHAT IS IT, NOSEDRIP, YOU BOOBY? I'VE NO OFFAL FOR YOU TODAY!
AIN'T THAT, SIR! I JUST SEED A SPACESHIP ON FIRE—THE ONE IN THAR REWARD POSTERS! THE BLITZSPEAR! A-HEADING DOWN TOWARDS FIEND'S ROCK!
WHY DIDN'T YOU SAY SO BEFORE? TELL HAWBERK THE ROBOTSMITH TO GET THE MEN TOGETHER—WE'LL NEED HIS PICK-UP TRUCK! WELL, HURRY, YOU GREAT GOWK!

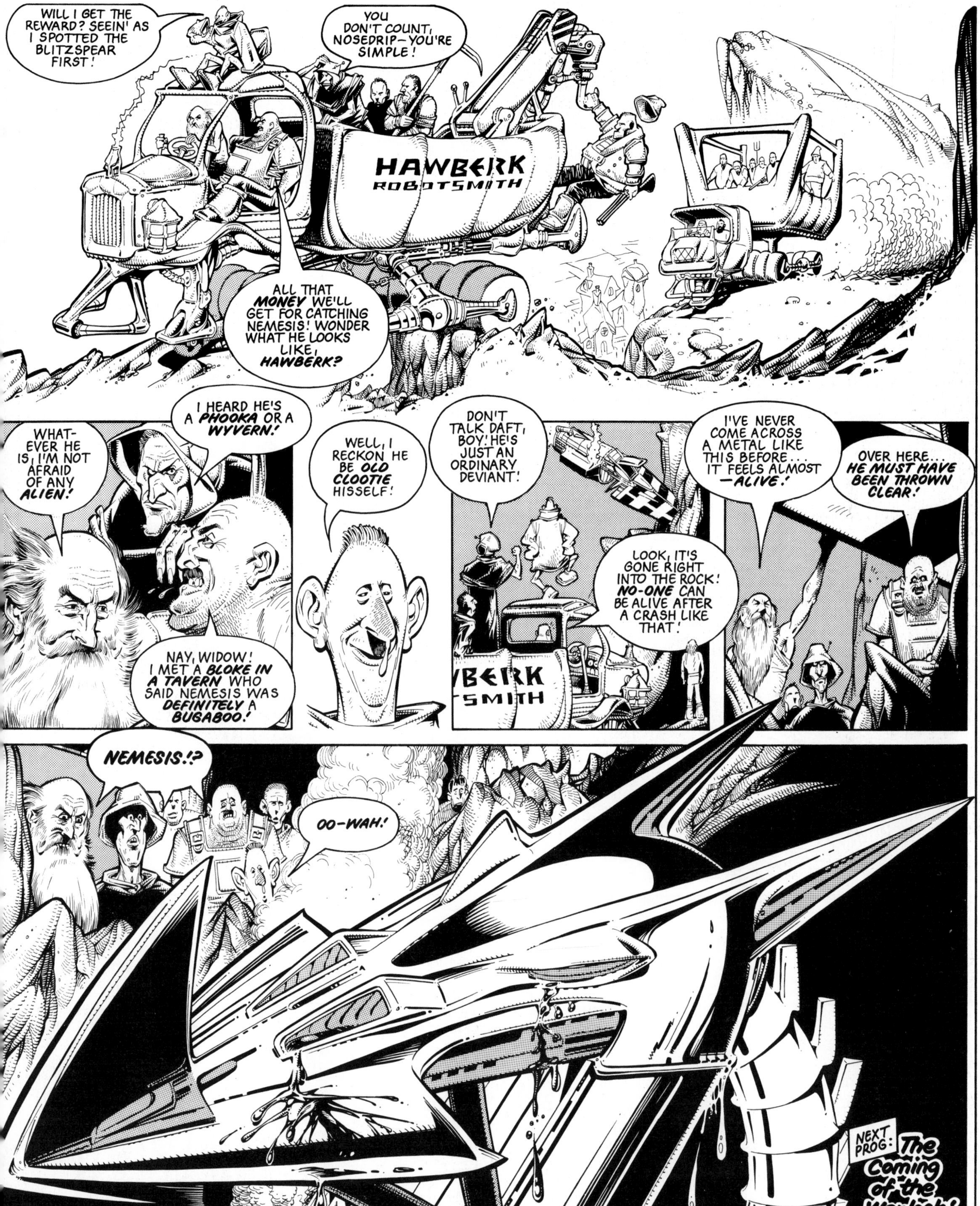
WILL I GET THE REWARD? SEEIN' AS I SPOTTED THE BLITZSPEAR FIRST!
YOU DON'T COUNT, NOSEDRIP—YOU'RE SIMPLE!
HAWBERK ROBOTSMITH
ALL THAT MONEY WE'LL GET FOR CATCHING NEMESIS! WONDER WHAT HE LOOKS LIKE, HAWBERK?
WHAT-EVER HE IS, I'M NOT AFRAID OF ANY ALIEN!
I HEARD HE'S A PHOOKA OR A WYVERN!
NAY, WIDOW! I MET A BLOKE IN A TAVERN WHO SAID NEMESIS WAS DEFINITELY A BUGABOO!
WELL, I RECKON HE BE OLD CLOOTIE HISSELF!
DON'T TALK DAFT, BOY! HE'S JUST AN ORDINARY DEVIANT!
LOOK, IT'S GONE RIGHT INTO THE ROCK! NO-ONE CAN BE ALIVE AFTER A CRASH LIKE THAT!
I'VE NEVER COME ACROSS A METAL LIKE THIS BEFORE... IT FEELS ALMOST —ALIVE!
OVER HERE... HE MUST HAVE BEEN THROWN CLEAR!
NEMESIS!?
OO-WAH!
NEXT PROG: The Coming of the Warlock!

Nemesis THE WARLOCK

2000 A.D.
Credit Car

SCRIPT ROBOT
PAT MILLS
ART ROBOT
KEVIN O'NEILL
LETTERING ROBOT
STEVE POTTER
COMPU·73

THE BLITZSPEAR HAS CRASHED ON "EARTH'S END" WHERE A GROUP OF SETTLERS FIND THE VEHICLE AND ITS MYSTERIOUS OCCUPANT... *NEMESIS!*

IT— IT BE A *FIEND* FROM HELL!

SOMEONE PUT A TARPAULIN OVER IT! I DON'T LIKE TO LOOK AT IT!

THE CREATURE'S *DEAD,* ALL RIGHT, HAWBERK! AND WE STAND TO GET THE *REWARD!*

WHAT ABOUT ME? I SAW IT CRASH!

YOU DON'T COUNT, NOSEDRIP! NOW GIVE ME A HAND WITH THESE CHAINS. I'M GOING TO PULL THE BLITZ-SPEAR FREE.

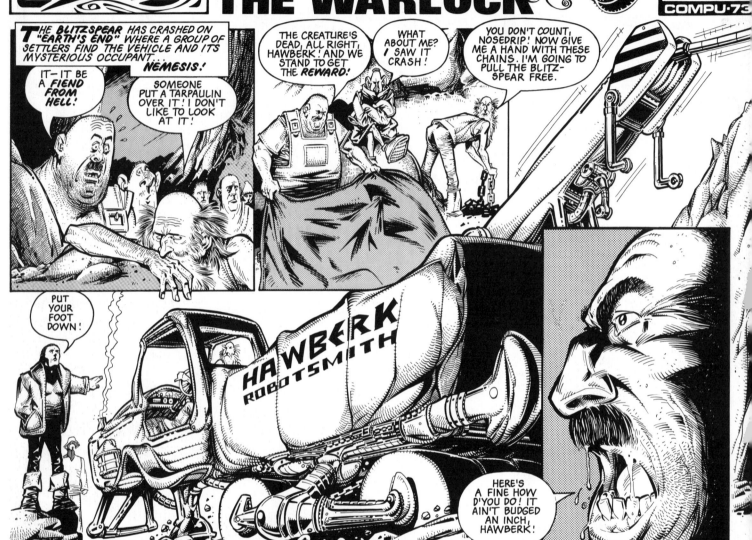

PUT YOUR FOOT DOWN!

HAWBERK ROBOTSMITH

HERE'S A FINE HOW D'YOU DO! IT AIN'T BUDGED AN INCH, HAWBERK!

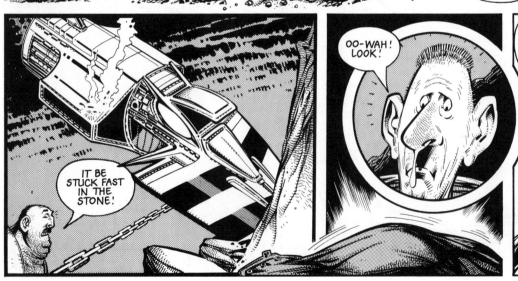

IT BE STUCK FAST IN THE STONE!

OO-WAH! LOOK!

QUICK! *GET THE GUNS!* THAT *THING* UNDER THE TARPAULIN... IT'S STARTING TO *MOVE!*

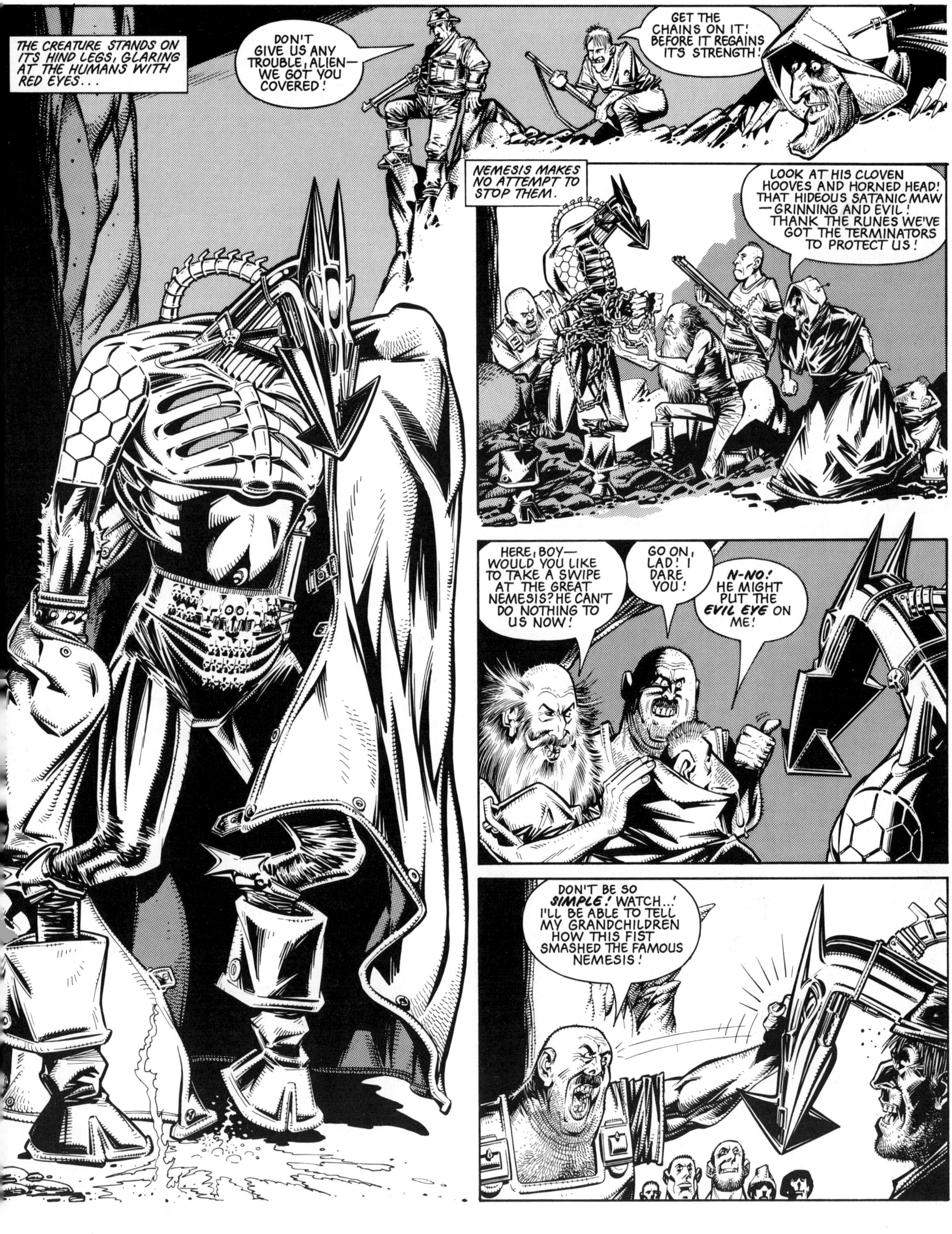
THE CREATURE STANDS ON IT'S HIND LEGS, GLARING AT THE HUMANS WITH RED EYES...
DON'T GIVE US ANY TROUBLE, ALIEN— WE GOT YOU COVERED!
GET THE CHAINS ON IT! BEFORE IT REGAINS IT'S STRENGTH!
NEMESIS MAKES NO ATTEMPT TO STOP THEM.
LOOK AT HIS CLOVEN HOOVES AND HORNED HEAD! THAT HIDEOUS SATANIC MAW —GRINNING AND EVIL! THANK THE RUNES WE'VE GOT THE TERMINATORS TO PROTECT US!
HERE, BOY— WOULD YOU LIKE TO TAKE A SWIPE AT THE GREAT NEMESIS? HE CAN'T DO NOTHING TO US NOW!
GO ON, LAD! I DARE YOU!
N-NO! HE MIGHT PUT THE EVIL EYE ON ME!
DON'T BE SO SIMPLE! WATCH...' I'LL BE ABLE TO TELL MY GRANDCHILDREN HOW THIS FIST SMASHED THE FAMOUS NEMESIS!

AFTER THAT, SOME OF THE OTHER SETTLERS FOLLOWED SUIT, UNTIL...

THAT'S ENOUGH— LET'S GET HIM BACK TO THE VILLAGE. I DON'T WANT NO ALIEN IN MY TRUCK, I'LL *DRAG* HIM BEHIND.

WHAT WE GOING TO DO WITH HIM?

WE CAN'T WAIT UNTIL A TERMINATOR PATROL ARRIVES! WE'LL HAVE TO KILL HIM *OURSELVES!*

HOW WE GONNA DO IT... *BEHEAD* HIM?

IT'S A BIT RISKY, WIDOW... SOME OF THESE ALIENS HAVE *ACIDIC* BLOOD.

THE TERMINATORS *BURN* A LOT OF 'EM AT THE STAKE!

I DUNNO... I RECKON *HE* MIGHT *ENJOY* THAT!

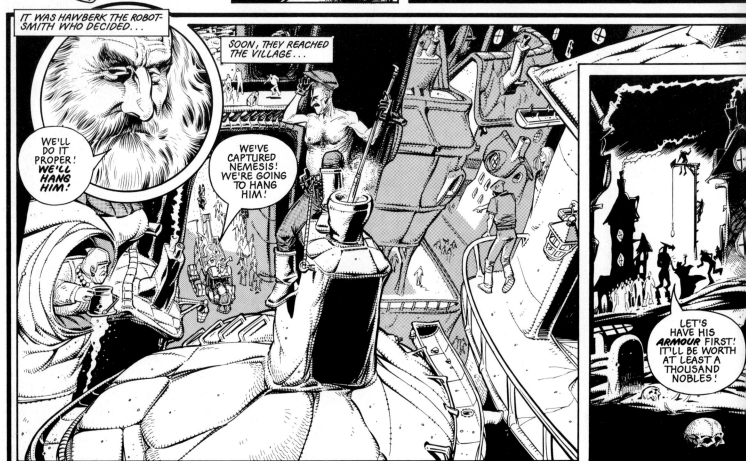

IT WAS HAWBERK THE ROBOT-SMITH WHO DECIDED...

WE'LL DO IT PROPER! *WE'LL HANG HIM!*

SOON, THEY REACHED THE VILLAGE...

WE'VE CAPTURED NEMESIS! WE'RE GOING TO HANG HIM!

LET'S HAVE HIS *ARMOUR* FIRST! IT'LL BE WORTH AT LEAST A THOUSAND NOBLES!

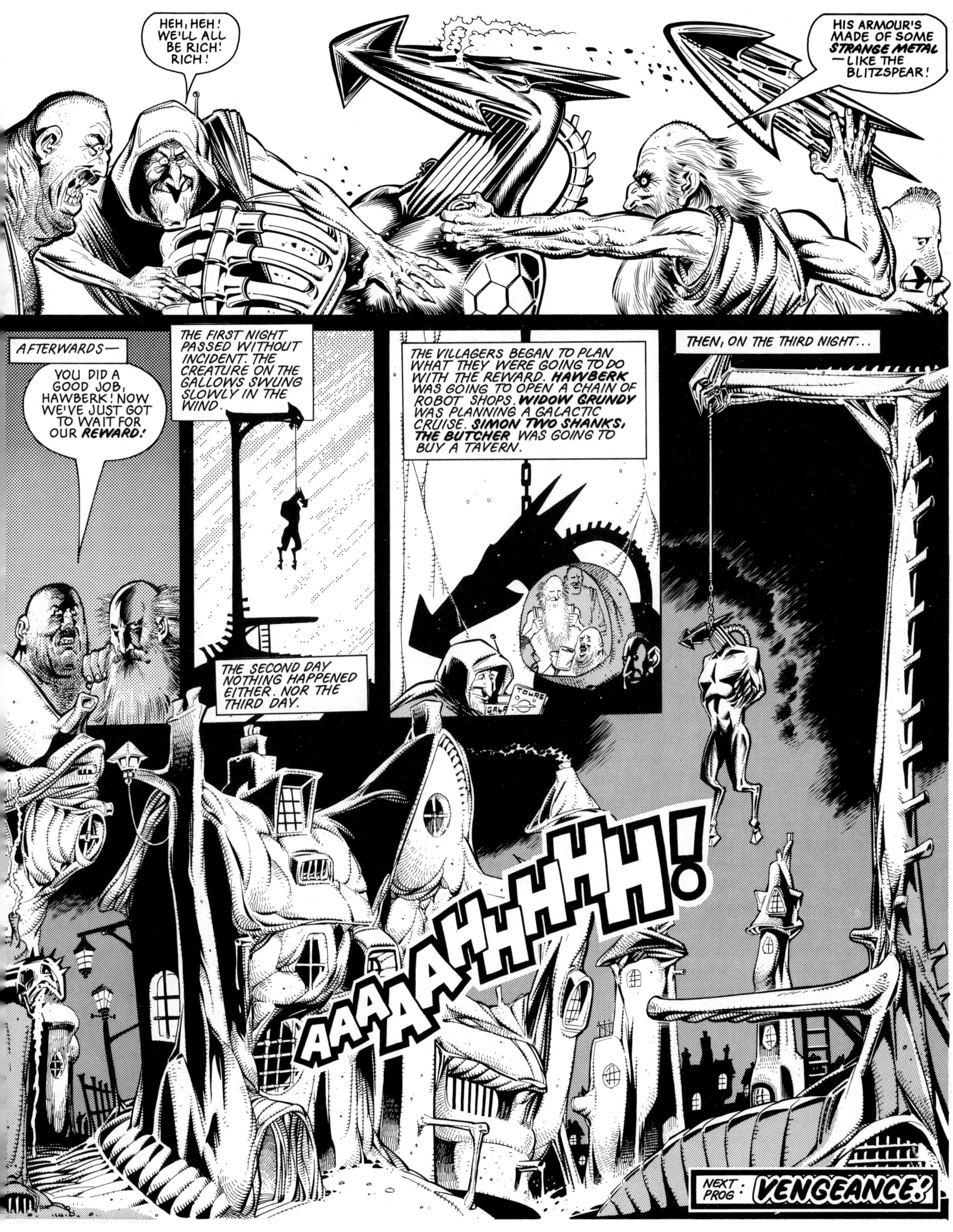
HEH, HEH! WE'LL ALL BE RICH! RICH!
HIS ARMOUR'S MADE OF SOME **STRANGE METAL** —LIKE THE BLITZSPEAR!
AFTERWARDS—
YOU DID A GOOD JOB, HAWBERK! NOW WE'VE JUST GOT TO WAIT FOR OUR **REWARD!**
THE FIRST NIGHT PASSED WITHOUT INCIDENT. THE CREATURE ON THE GALLOWS SWUNG SLOWLY IN THE WIND.
THE SECOND DAY NOTHING HAPPENED EITHER. NOR THE THIRD DAY.
THE VILLAGERS BEGAN TO PLAN WHAT THEY WERE GOING TO DO WITH THE REWARD. **HAWBERK** WAS GOING TO OPEN A CHAIN OF ROBOT SHOPS. **WIDOW GRUNDY** WAS PLANNING A GALACTIC CRUISE. **SIMON TWO SHANKS, THE BUTCHER** WAS GOING TO BUY A TAVERN.
THEN, ON THE THIRD NIGHT...
AAAAAHHHHHH!
NEXT PROG: VENGEANCE!

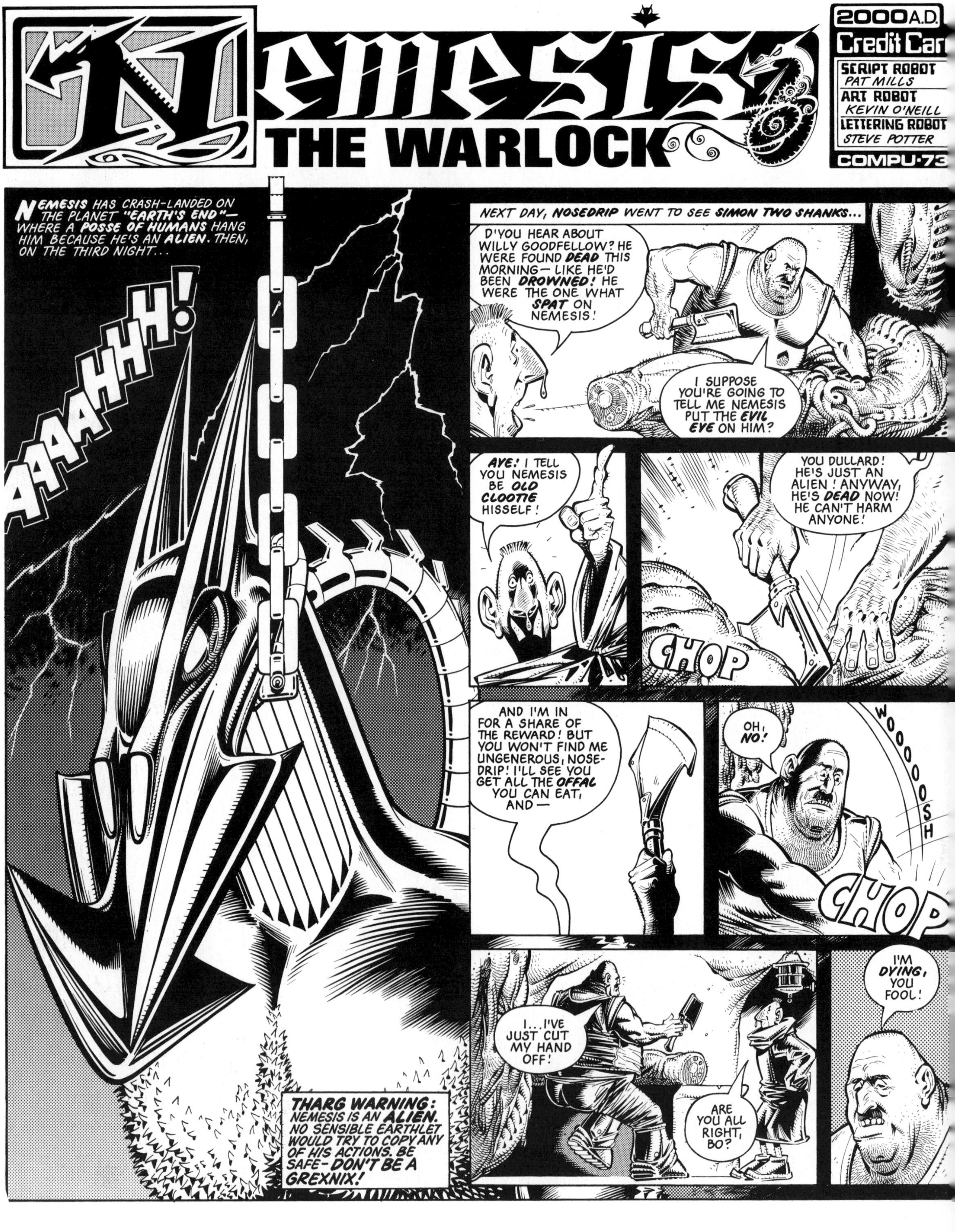

NEMESIS THE WARLOCK
2000 A.D. Credit Car
SCRIPT ROBOT PAT MILLS
ART ROBOT KEVIN O'NEILL
LETTERING ROBOT STEVE POTTER
COMPU-73
NEMESIS HAS CRASH-LANDED ON THE PLANET "EARTH'S END"— WHERE A POSSE OF HUMANS HANG HIM BECAUSE HE'S AN ALIEN. THEN, ON THE THIRD NIGHT...
AAAAHHH!
THARG WARNING: NEMESIS IS AN ALIEN. NO SENSIBLE EARTHLET WOULD TRY TO COPY ANY OF HIS ACTIONS. BE SAFE—DON'T BE A GREXNIX!
NEXT DAY, NOSEDRIP WENT TO SEE SIMON TWO SHANKS...
D'YOU HEAR ABOUT WILLY GOODFELLOW? HE WERE FOUND DEAD THIS MORNING— LIKE HE'D BEEN DROWNED! HE WERE THE ONE WHAT SPAT ON NEMESIS!
I SUPPOSE YOU'RE GOING TO TELL ME NEMESIS PUT THE EVIL EYE ON HIM?
AYE! I TELL YOU NEMESIS BE OLD CLOOTIE HISSELF!
YOU DULLARD! HE'S JUST AN ALIEN! ANYWAY, HE'S DEAD NOW! HE CAN'T HARM ANYONE!
CHOP
AND I'M IN FOR A SHARE OF THE REWARD! BUT YOU WON'T FIND ME UNGENEROUS, NOSE-DRIP! I'LL SEE YOU GET ALL THE OFFAL YOU CAN EAT, AND—
OH, NO!
WOOOOOOSH
CHOP
I...I'VE JUST CUT MY HAND OFF!
ARE YOU ALL RIGHT, BO?
I'M DYING, YOU FOOL!

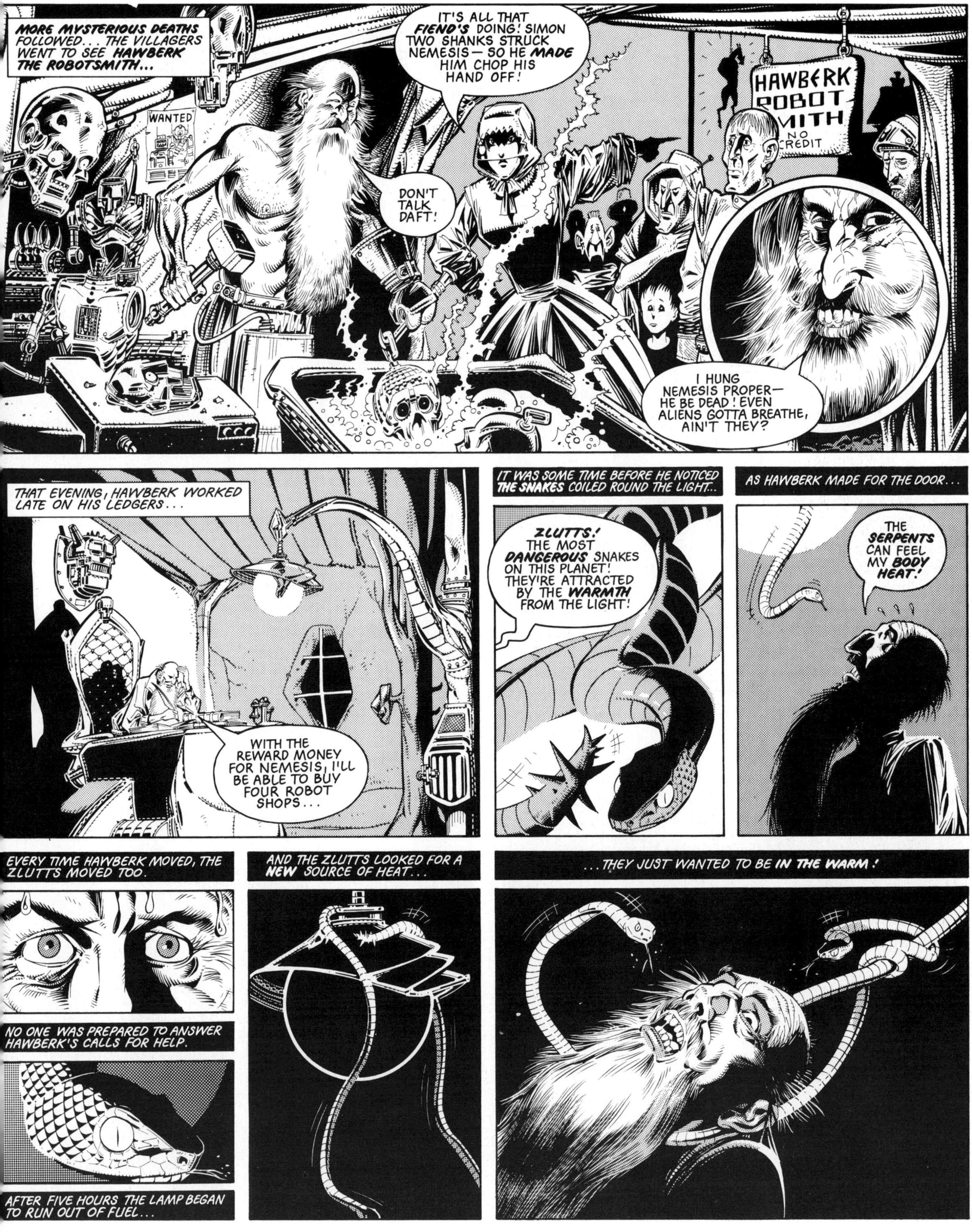
MORE MYSTERIOUS DEATHS FOLLOWED... THE VILLAGERS WENT TO SEE HAWBERK THE ROBOTSMITH...
IT'S ALL THAT FIEND'S DOING! SIMON TWO SHANKS STRUCK NEMESIS — SO HE MADE HIM CHOP HIS HAND OFF!
WANTED
HAWBERK ROBOT SMITH NO CREDIT
DON'T TALK DAFT!
I HUNG NEMESIS PROPER— HE BE DEAD! EVEN ALIENS GOTTA BREATHE, AIN'T THEY?
THAT EVENING, HAWBERK WORKED LATE ON HIS LEDGERS...
WITH THE REWARD MONEY FOR NEMESIS, I'LL BE ABLE TO BUY FOUR ROBOT SHOPS...
IT WAS SOME TIME BEFORE HE NOTICED THE SNAKES COILED ROUND THE LIGHT...
ZLUTTS! THE MOST DANGEROUS SNAKES ON THIS PLANET! THEY'RE ATTRACTED BY THE WARMTH FROM THE LIGHT!
AS HAWBERK MADE FOR THE DOOR...
THE SERPENTS CAN FEEL MY BODY HEAT!
EVERY TIME HAWBERK MOVED, THE ZLUTTS MOVED TOO.
NO ONE WAS PREPARED TO ANSWER HAWBERK'S CALLS FOR HELP.
AFTER FIVE HOURS THE LAMP BEGAN TO RUN OUT OF FUEL...
AND THE ZLUTTS LOOKED FOR A NEW SOURCE OF HEAT...
...THEY JUST WANTED TO BE IN THE WARM!

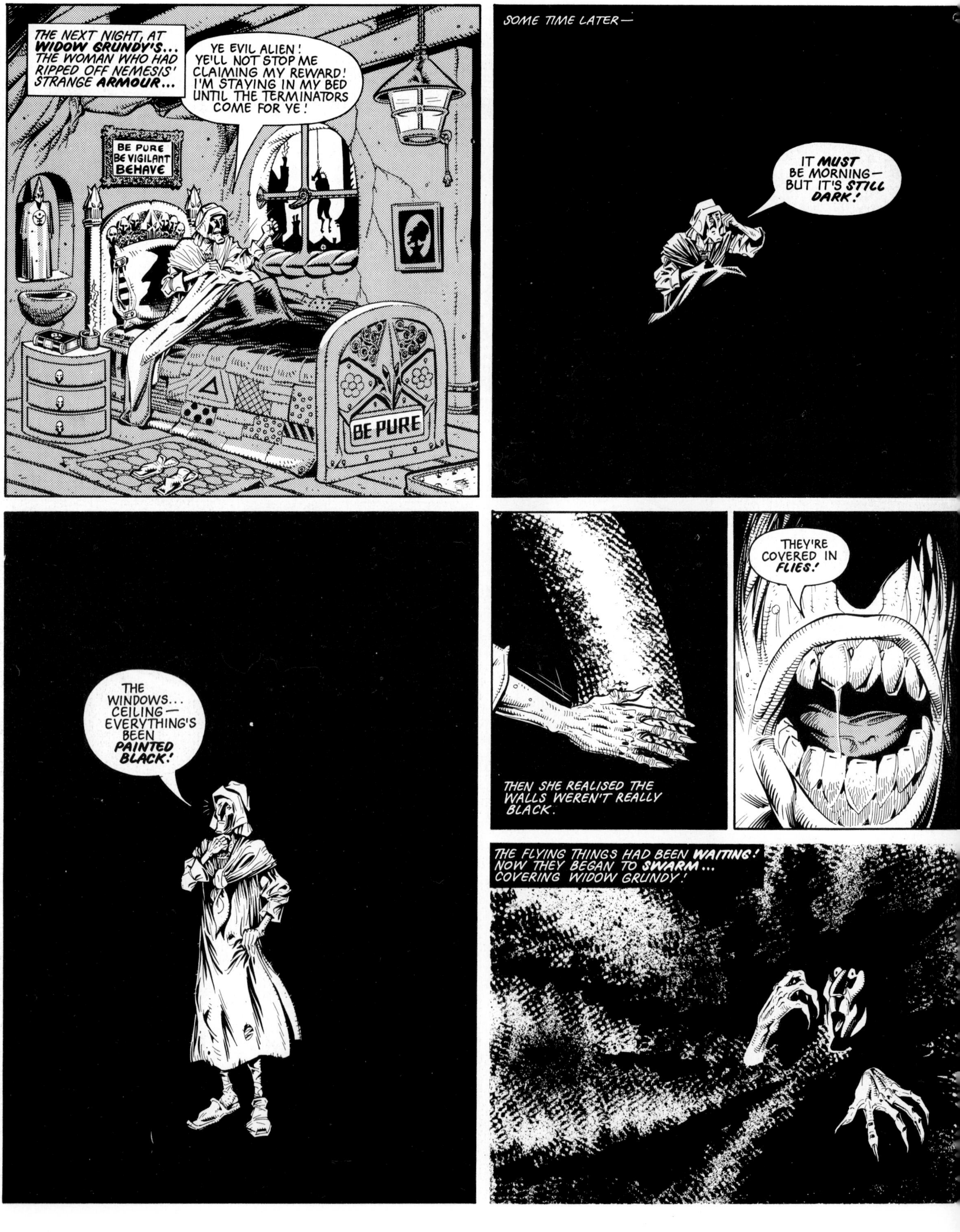
THE NEXT NIGHT, AT WIDOW GRUNDY'S... THE WOMAN WHO HAD RIPPED OFF NEMESIS' STRANGE ARMOUR...
YE EVIL ALIEN! YE'LL NOT STOP ME CLAIMING MY REWARD! I'M STAYING IN MY BED UNTIL THE TERMINATORS COME FOR YE!
BE PURE BE VIGILANT BEHAVE
BE PURE
SOME TIME LATER—
IT MUST BE MORNING— BUT IT'S STILL DARK!
THE WINDOWS... CEILING— EVERYTHING'S BEEN PAINTED BLACK!
THEN SHE REALISED THE WALLS WEREN'T REALLY BLACK.
THEY'RE COVERED IN FLIES!
THE FLYING THINGS HAD BEEN WAITING! NOW THEY BEGAN TO SWARM... COVERING WIDOW GRUNDY!

THE VILLAGERS WENT TO SEE NEMESIS.

PLEASE... LEAVE US ALONE! WE WON'T HARM YOU AGAIN!

LOOK... HERE'S YOUR ARMOUR BACK!

USING SOME STRANGE POWER OF LEVITATION OR ANTI-GRAVITY, THE ALIEN WALKED DOWN THROUGH THE AIR.

MAY TORQUEMADA AND HIS TERMINATORS PROTECT US!

AS NEMESIS DONNED HIS ARMOUR, THE BLITZSPEAR APPEARED — AS IF ANSWERING A SECRET SUMMONS...

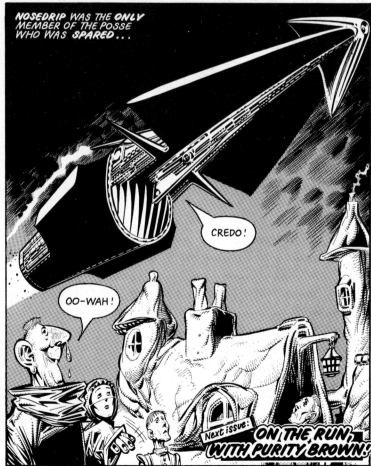

NOSEDRIP WAS THE ONLY MEMBER OF THE POSSE WHO WAS SPARED...

CREDO!

OO-WAH!

Next issue: ON THE RUN, WITH PURITY BROWN!

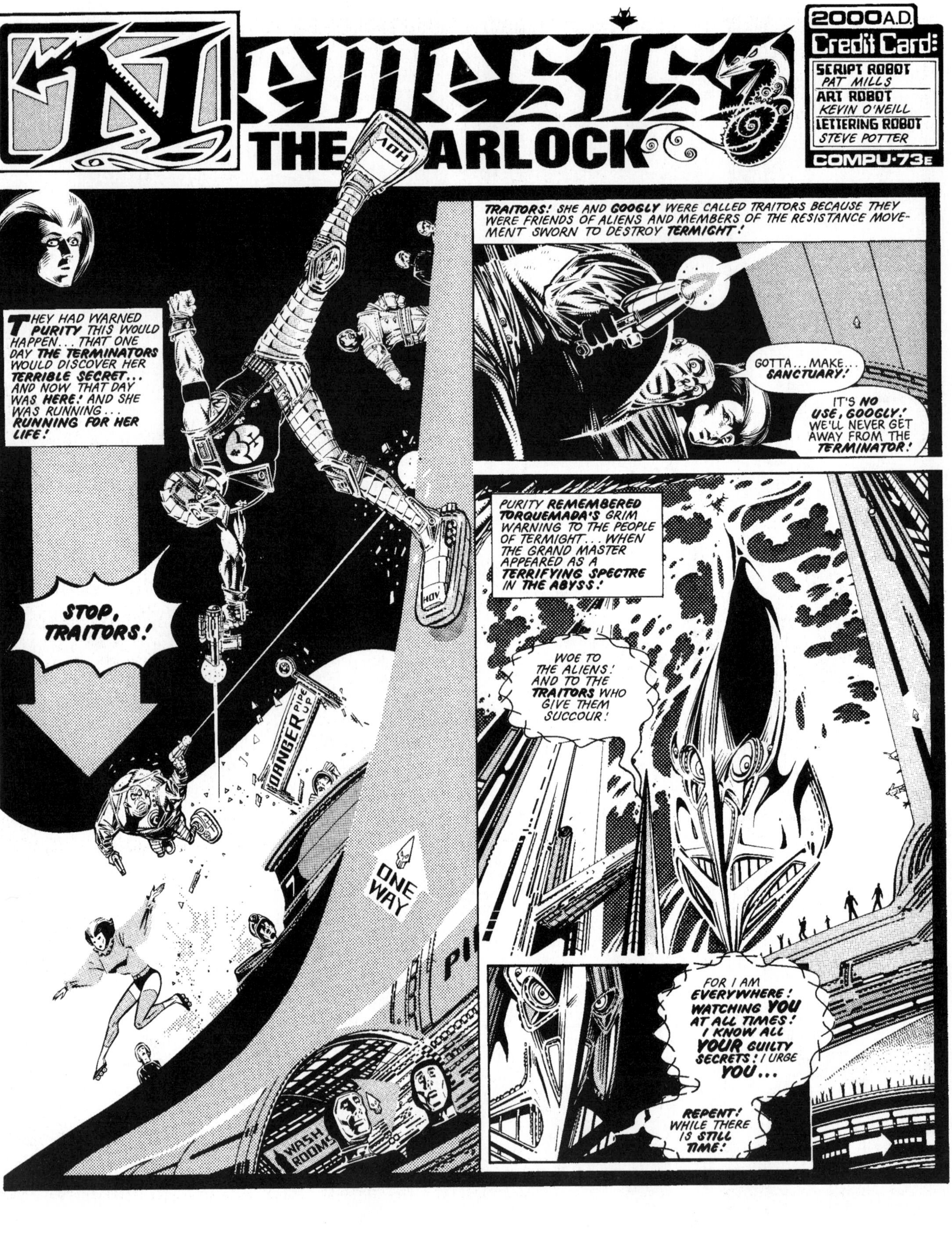
NEMESIS THE WARLOCK
2000 A.D. Credit Card:
SCRIPT ROBOT PAT MILLS
ART ROBOT KEVIN O'NEILL
LETTERING ROBOT STEVE POTTER
COMPU-73E
THEY HAD WARNED PURITY THIS WOULD HAPPEN... THAT ONE DAY THE TERMINATORS WOULD DISCOVER HER TERRIBLE SECRET... AND NOW THAT DAY WAS HERE! AND SHE WAS RUNNING... RUNNING FOR HER LIFE!
STOP, TRAITORS!
DANGER PIPE UP
ONE WAY
WASH ROOMS
TRAITORS! SHE AND GOOGLY WERE CALLED TRAITORS BECAUSE THEY WERE FRIENDS OF ALIENS AND MEMBERS OF THE RESISTANCE MOVEMENT SWORN TO DESTROY TERMIGHT!
GOTTA... MAKE... SANCTUARY!
IT'S NO USE, GOOGLY! WE'LL NEVER GET AWAY FROM THE TERMINATOR!
PURITY REMEMBERED TORQUEMADA'S GRIM WARNING TO THE PEOPLE OF TERMIGHT... WHEN THE GRAND MASTER APPEARED AS A TERRIFYING SPECTRE IN THE ABYSS!
WOE TO THE ALIENS! AND TO THE TRAITORS WHO GIVE THEM SUCCOUR!
FOR I AM EVERYWHERE! WATCHING YOU AT ALL TIMES! I KNOW ALL YOUR GUILTY SECRETS! I URGE YOU...
REPENT! WHILE THERE IS STILL TIME!

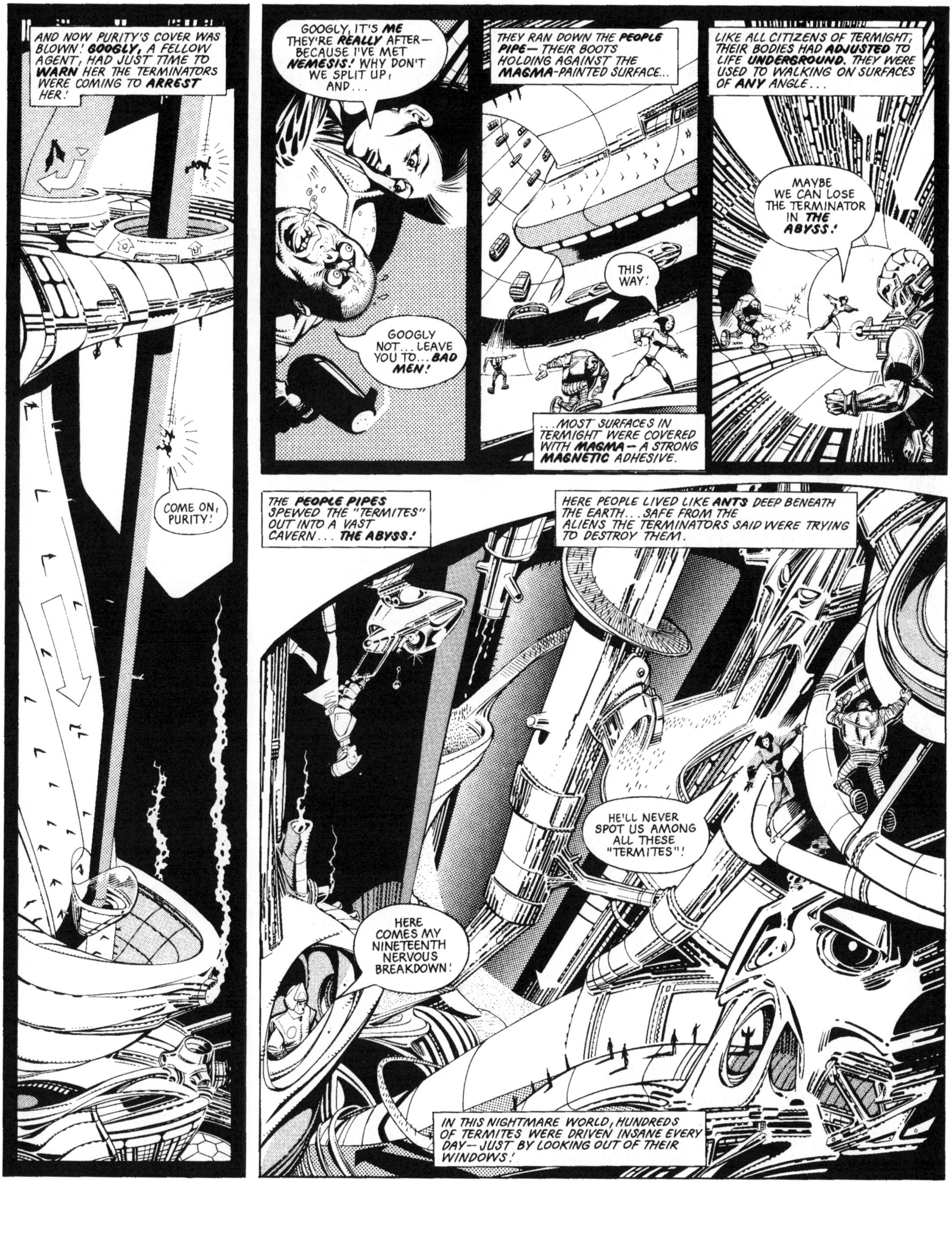
AND NOW PURITY'S COVER WAS BLOWN! GOOGLY, A FELLOW AGENT, HAD JUST TIME TO WARN HER THE TERMINATORS WERE COMING TO ARREST HER!
COME ON, PURITY!
GOOGLY, IT'S ME THEY'RE REALLY AFTER— BECAUSE I'VE MET NEMESIS! WHY DON'T WE SPLIT UP, AND...
GOOGLY NOT... LEAVE YOU TO... BAD MEN!
THEY RAN DOWN THE PEOPLE PIPE— THEIR BOOTS HOLDING AGAINST THE MAGMA-PAINTED SURFACE...
THIS WAY!
...MOST SURFACES IN TERMIGHT WERE COVERED WITH MAGMA— A STRONG MAGNETIC ADHESIVE.
LIKE ALL CITIZENS OF TERMIGHT, THEIR BODIES HAD ADJUSTED TO LIFE UNDERGROUND. THEY WERE USED TO WALKING ON SURFACES OF ANY ANGLE...
MAYBE WE CAN LOSE THE TERMINATOR IN THE ABYSS!
THE PEOPLE PIPES SPEWED THE "TERMITES" OUT INTO A VAST CAVERN... THE ABYSS!
HERE PEOPLE LIVED LIKE ANTS DEEP BENEATH THE EARTH... SAFE FROM THE ALIENS THE TERMINATORS SAID WERE TRYING TO DESTROY THEM.
HE'LL NEVER SPOT US AMONG ALL THESE "TERMITES"!
HERE COMES MY NINETEENTH NERVOUS BREAKDOWN!
IN THIS NIGHTMARE WORLD, HUNDREDS OF TERMITES WERE DRIVEN INSANE EVERY DAY— JUST BY LOOKING OUT OF THEIR WINDOWS!

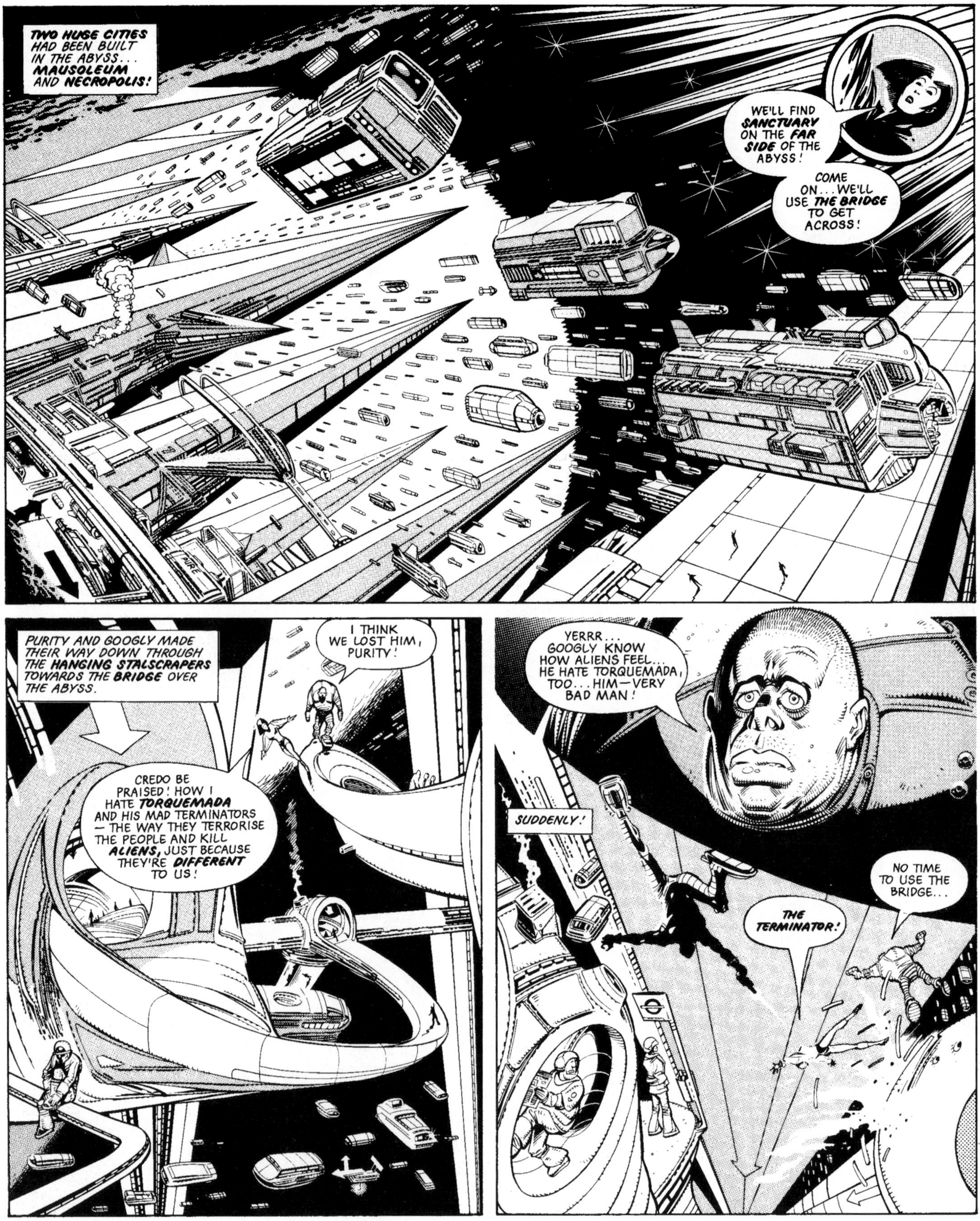
TWO HUGE CITIES HAD BEEN BUILT IN THE ABYSS... MAUSOLEUM AND NECROPOLIS!
WE'LL FIND SANCTUARY ON THE FAR SIDE OF THE ABYSS!
COME ON... WE'LL USE THE BRIDGE TO GET ACROSS!
PURITY AND GOOGLY MADE THEIR WAY DOWN THROUGH THE HANGING STALSCRAPERS TOWARDS THE BRIDGE OVER THE ABYSS.
I THINK WE LOST HIM, PURITY!
CREDO BE PRAISED! HOW I HATE TORQUEMADA AND HIS MAD TERMINATORS — THE WAY THEY TERRORISE THE PEOPLE AND KILL ALIENS, JUST BECAUSE THEY'RE DIFFERENT TO US!
YERRR... GOOGLY KNOW HOW ALIENS FEEL... HE HATE TORQUEMADA, TOO... HIM—VERY BAD MAN!
SUDDENLY!
NO TIME TO USE THE BRIDGE...
THE TERMINATOR!

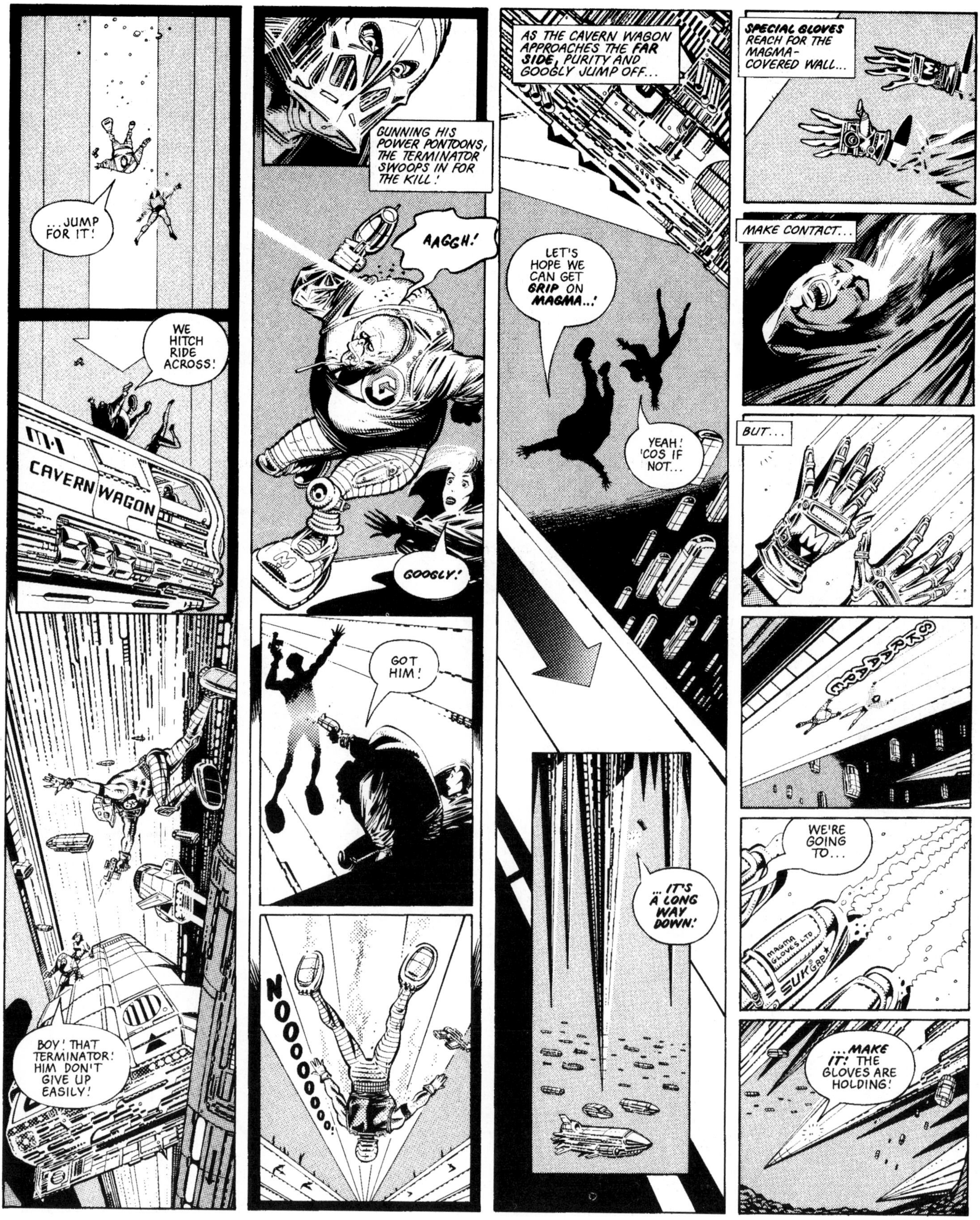
...JUMP FOR IT!
WE HITCH RIDE ACROSS!
CAVERN WAGON
BOY! THAT TERMINATOR! HIM DON'T GIVE UP EASILY!
GUNNING HIS POWER PONTOONS, THE TERMINATOR SWOOPS IN FOR THE KILL!
AAGGH!
GOOGLY!
GOT HIM!
NOOOOOOOOOOO!
AS THE CAVERN WAGON APPROACHES THE FAR SIDE, PURITY AND GOOGLY JUMP OFF...
LET'S HOPE WE CAN GET GRIP ON MAGMA...!
YEAH! 'COS IF NOT...
...IT'S A LONG WAY DOWN!
SPECIAL GLOVES REACH FOR THE MAGMA-COVERED WALL...
MAKE CONTACT...
BUT...
WE'RE GOING TO...
MAGMA GLOVES LTD
...MAKE IT! THE GLOVES ARE HOLDING!

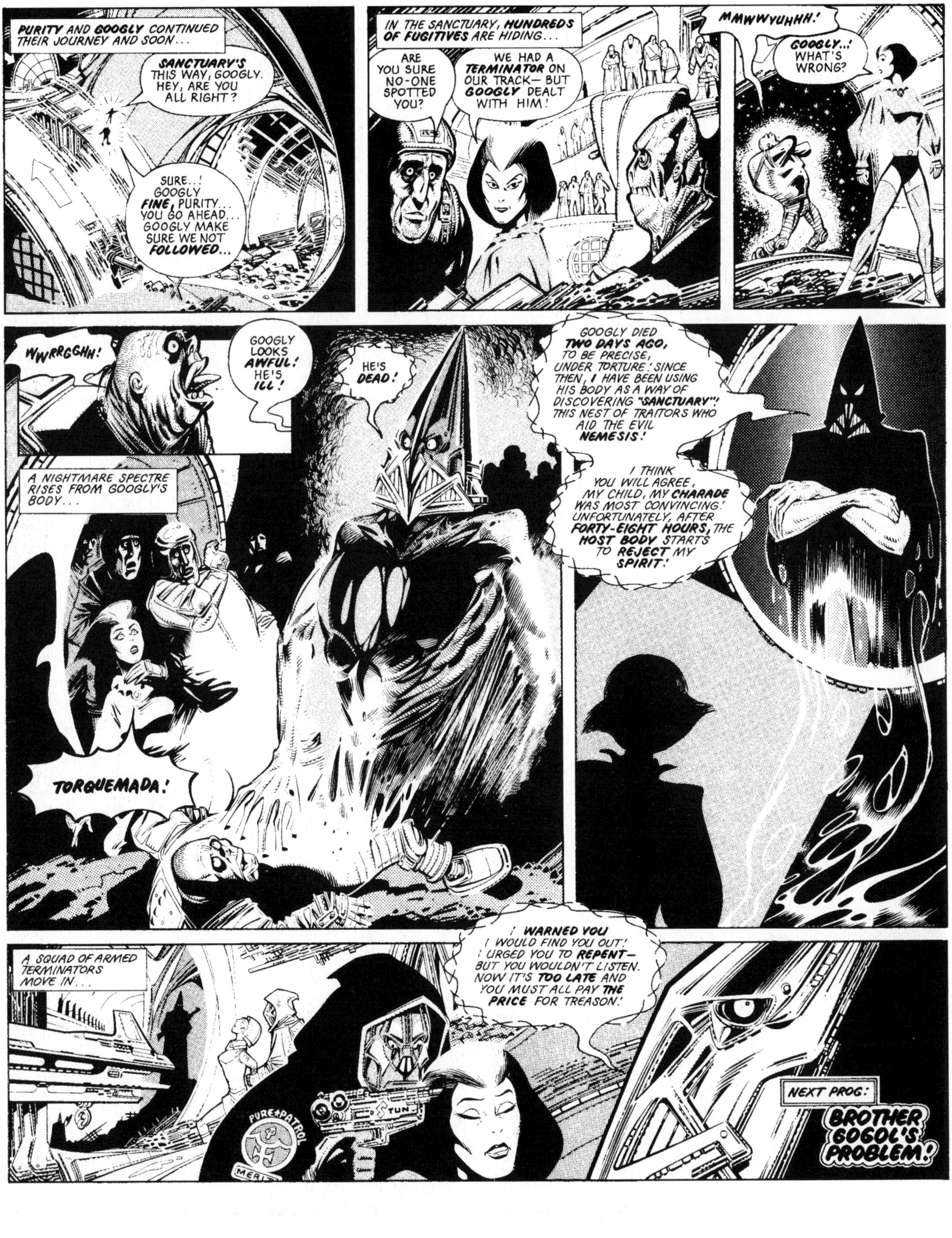

PURITY AND GOOGLY CONTINUED THEIR JOURNEY AND SOON...
SANCTUARY'S THIS WAY, GOOGLY. HEY, ARE YOU ALL RIGHT?
SURE..! GOOGLY FINE, PURITY... YOU GO AHEAD... GOOGLY MAKE SURE WE NOT FOLLOWED...
IN THE SANCTUARY, HUNDREDS OF FUGITIVES ARE HIDING...
ARE YOU SURE NO-ONE SPOTTED YOU?
WE HAD A TERMINATOR ON OUR TRACK— BUT GOOGLY DEALT WITH HIM!
MMWWYUHHH!
GOOGLY..! WHAT'S WRONG?
WWRRGGHH!
GOOGLY LOOKS AWFUL! HE'S ILL!
HE'S DEAD!
GOOGLY DIED TWO DAYS AGO, TO BE PRECISE, UNDER TORTURE! SINCE THEN, I HAVE BEEN USING HIS BODY AS A WAY OF DISCOVERING "SANCTUARY"! THIS NEST OF TRAITORS WHO AID THE EVIL NEMESIS!
A NIGHTMARE SPECTRE RISES FROM GOOGLY'S BODY...
I THINK YOU WILL AGREE, MY CHILD, MY CHARADE WAS MOST CONVINCING! UNFORTUNATELY, AFTER FORTY-EIGHT HOURS, THE HOST BODY STARTS TO REJECT MY SPIRIT!
TORQUEMADA!
A SQUAD OF ARMED TERMINATORS MOVE IN...
I WARNED YOU I WOULD FIND YOU OUT! I URGED YOU TO REPENT— BUT YOU WOULDN'T LISTEN. NOW IT'S TOO LATE AND YOU MUST ALL PAY THE PRICE FOR TREASON!
STUN
PURE PATROL
NEXT PROG:
BROTHER GOGOL'S PROBLEM!

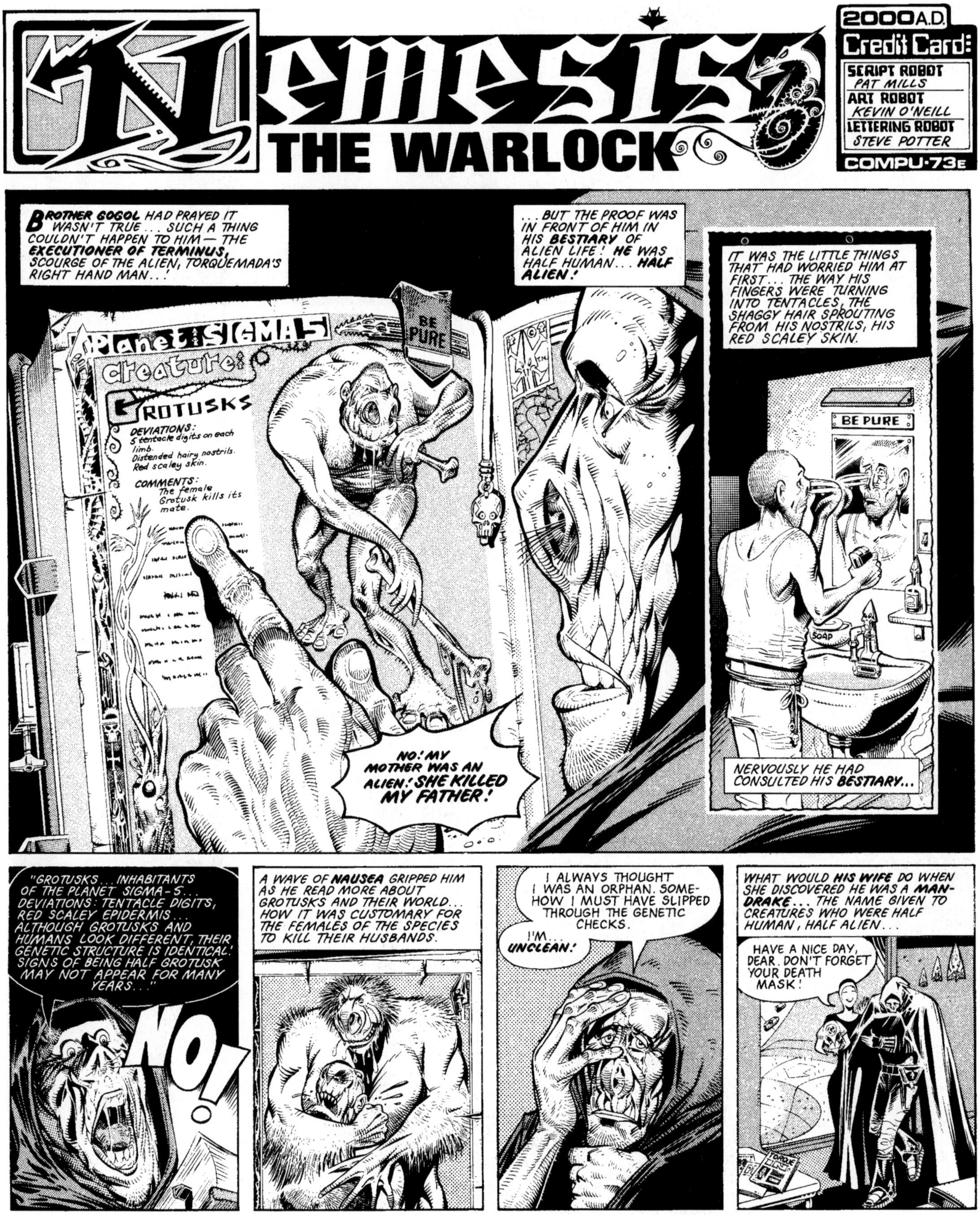

NEMESIS THE WARLOCK
2000 A.D. Credit Card:
SCRIPT ROBOT PAT MILLS
ART ROBOT KEVIN O'NEILL
LETTERING ROBOT STEVE POTTER
COMPU-73E
BROTHER GOGOL HAD PRAYED IT WASN'T TRUE... SUCH A THING COULDN'T HAPPEN TO HIM — THE EXECUTIONER OF TERMINUS, SCOURGE OF THE ALIEN, TORQUEMADA'S RIGHT HAND MAN...!
...BUT THE PROOF WAS IN FRONT OF HIM IN HIS BESTIARY OF ALIEN LIFE! HE WAS HALF HUMAN... HALF ALIEN!
Planet SIGMA 5
creature:
GROTUSKS
DEVIATIONS: 5 tentacle digits on each limb. Distended hairy nostrils. Red scaley skin.
COMMENTS: The female Grotusk kills its mate.
BE PURE
NO! MY MOTHER WAS AN ALIEN! SHE KILLED MY FATHER!
IT WAS THE LITTLE THINGS THAT HAD WORRIED HIM AT FIRST... THE WAY HIS FINGERS WERE TURNING INTO TENTACLES, THE SHAGGY HAIR SPROUTING FROM HIS NOSTRILS, HIS RED SCALEY SKIN.
BE PURE
SOAP
NERVOUSLY HE HAD CONSULTED HIS BESTIARY...
"GROTUSKS... INHABITANTS OF THE PLANET SIGMA-5... DEVIATIONS: TENTACLE DIGITS, RED SCALEY EPIDERMIS... ALTHOUGH GROTUSKS AND HUMANS LOOK DIFFERENT, THEIR GENETIC STRUCTURE IS IDENTICAL! SIGNS OF BEING HALF GROTUSK MAY NOT APPEAR FOR MANY YEARS..."
NO!
A WAVE OF NAUSEA GRIPPED HIM AS HE READ MORE ABOUT GROTUSKS AND THEIR WORLD... HOW IT WAS CUSTOMARY FOR THE FEMALES OF THE SPECIES TO KILL THEIR HUSBANDS.
I ALWAYS THOUGHT I WAS AN ORPHAN. SOMEHOW I MUST HAVE SLIPPED THROUGH THE GENETIC CHECKS.
I'M... UNCLEAN!
WHAT WOULD HIS WIFE DO WHEN SHE DISCOVERED HE WAS A MAN-DRAKE... THE NAME GIVEN TO CREATURES WHO WERE HALF HUMAN, HALF ALIEN...
HAVE A NICE DAY, DEAR. DON'T FORGET YOUR DEATH MASK!

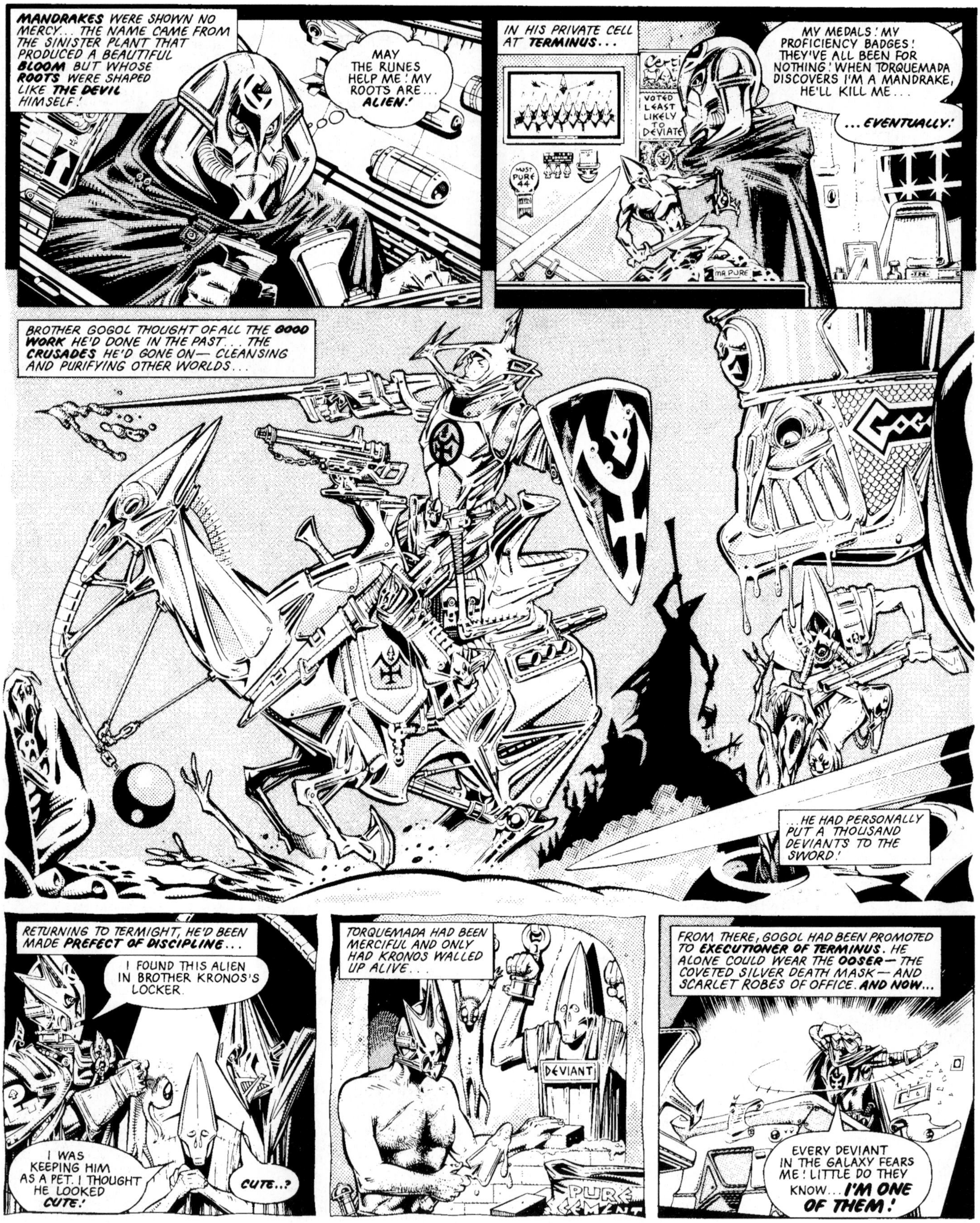
MANDRAKES WERE SHOWN NO MERCY... THE NAME CAME FROM THE SINISTER PLANT THAT PRODUCED A BEAUTIFUL BLOOM BUT WHOSE ROOTS WERE SHAPED LIKE THE DEVIL HIMSELF!
MAY THE RUNES HELP ME! MY ROOTS ARE... ALIEN!
IN HIS PRIVATE CELL AT TERMINUS...
VOTED LEAST LIKELY TO DEVIATE
MOST PURE 44
MR PURE
MY MEDALS! MY PROFICIENCY BADGES! THEY'VE ALL BEEN FOR NOTHING! WHEN TORQUEMADA DISCOVERS I'M A MANDRAKE, HE'LL KILL ME...
...EVENTUALLY!
BROTHER GOGOL THOUGHT OF ALL THE GOOD WORK HE'D DONE IN THE PAST... THE CRUSADES HE'D GONE ON— CLEANSING AND PURIFYING OTHER WORLDS...
...HE HAD PERSONALLY PUT A THOUSAND DEVIANTS TO THE SWORD!
RETURNING TO TERMIGHT, HE'D BEEN MADE PREFECT OF DISCIPLINE...
I FOUND THIS ALIEN IN BROTHER KRONOS'S LOCKER.
I WAS KEEPING HIM AS A PET. I THOUGHT HE LOOKED CUTE!
CUTE..?
TORQUEMADA HAD BEEN MERCIFUL AND ONLY HAD KRONOS WALLED UP ALIVE...
DEVIANT
PURE CEMENT
FROM THERE, GOGOL HAD BEEN PROMOTED TO EXECUTIONER OF TERMINUS. HE ALONE COULD WEAR THE OOSER— THE COVETED SILVER DEATH MASK— AND SCARLET ROBES OF OFFICE. AND NOW...
EVERY DEVIANT IN THE GALAXY FEARS ME! LITTLE DO THEY KNOW... I'M ONE OF THEM!

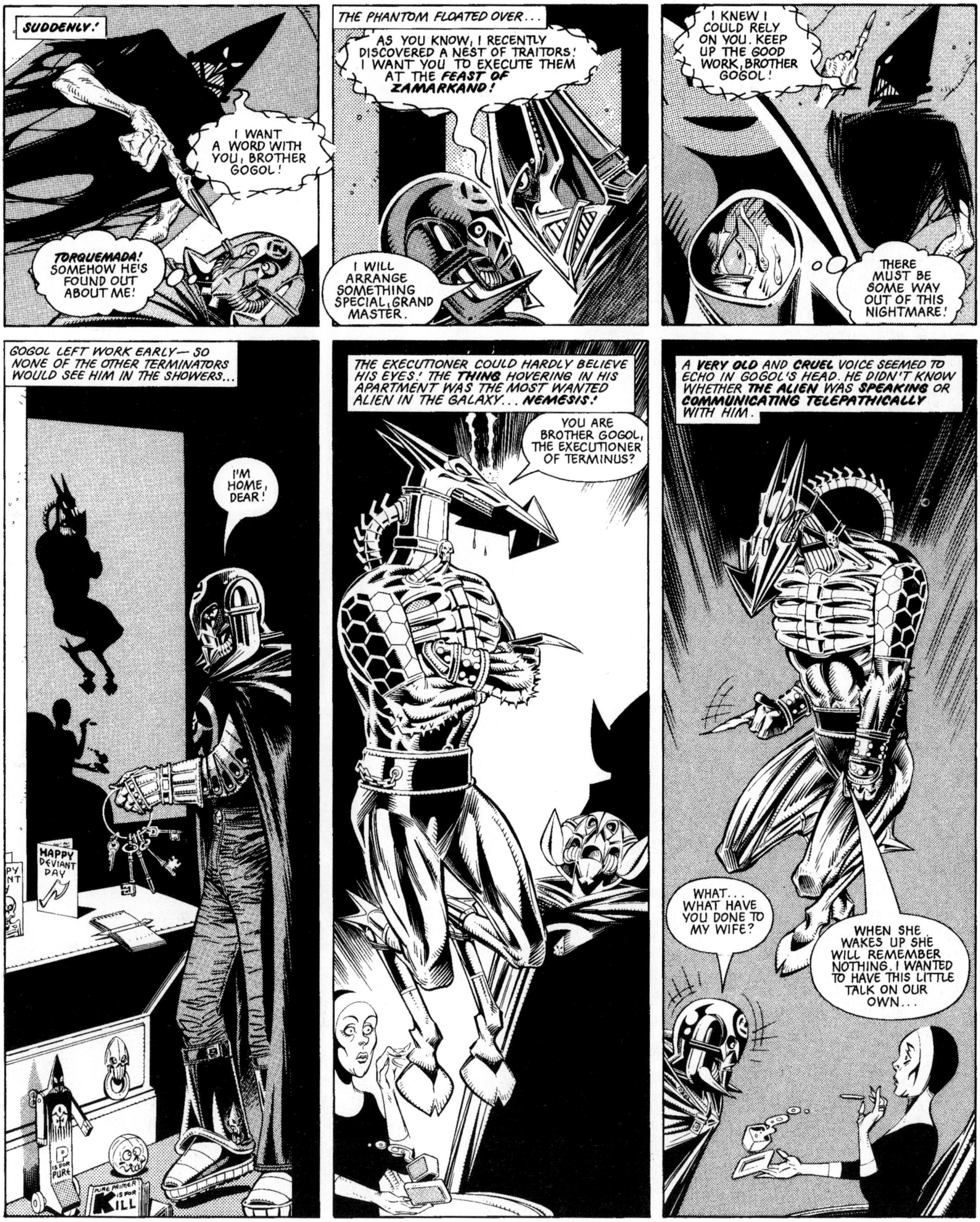
SUDDENLY!
I WANT A WORD WITH YOU, BROTHER GOGOL!
TORQUEMADA! SOMEHOW HE'S FOUND OUT ABOUT ME!
THE PHANTOM FLOATED OVER...
AS YOU KNOW, I RECENTLY DISCOVERED A NEST OF TRAITORS! I WANT YOU TO EXECUTE THEM AT THE FEAST OF ZAMARKAND!
I WILL ARRANGE SOMETHING SPECIAL, GRAND MASTER.
I KNEW I COULD RELY ON YOU. KEEP UP THE GOOD WORK, BROTHER GOGOL!
THERE MUST BE SOME WAY OUT OF THIS NIGHTMARE!
GOGOL LEFT WORK EARLY— SO NONE OF THE OTHER TERMINATORS WOULD SEE HIM IN THE SHOWERS...
I'M HOME, DEAR!
HAPPY DEVIANT DAY
P IS FOR PURE
PURE PRIMER K IS FOR KILL
THE EXECUTIONER COULD HARDLY BELIEVE HIS EYES! THE THING HOVERING IN HIS APARTMENT WAS THE MOST WANTED ALIEN IN THE GALAXY... NEMESIS!
YOU ARE BROTHER GOGOL, THE EXECUTIONER OF TERMINUS?
A VERY OLD AND CRUEL VOICE SEEMED TO ECHO IN GOGOL'S HEAD. HE DIDN'T KNOW WHETHER THE ALIEN WAS SPEAKING OR COMMUNICATING TELEPATHICALLY WITH HIM.
WHAT... WHAT HAVE YOU DONE TO MY WIFE?
WHEN SHE WAKES UP SHE WILL REMEMBER NOTHING. I WANTED TO HAVE THIS LITTLE TALK ON OUR OWN...

THE CREATURE DIDN'T LOOK LIKE THE PICTURES OF IT IN THE BESTIARY... IT LOOKED WORSE... MUCH WORSE!

IN SEVEN DAYS, MANY OF MY AGENTS ARE GOING TO BE EXECUTED AT THE FEAST OF ZAMARKAND. YOU, BROTHER GOGOL, ARE PART OF MY PLAN FOR THEIR ESCAPE!

WHY SHOULD I HELP THE ALIEN WHO I HATE ABOVE ALL ALIENS?

THE WARLOCK LEERED AT HIM—

BECAUSE YOU'RE TURNING INTO A MANDRAKE!

THAT'S A LIE! A FILTHY LIE! I'M PURE!

ANYWAY, EVEN IF IT WAS TRUE, ESCAPE IS IMPOSSIBLE...NO PRISONER'S GOT OUT OF TERMINUS ALIVE!

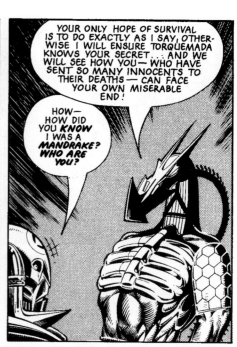

YOUR ONLY HOPE OF SURVIVAL IS TO DO EXACTLY AS I SAY, OTHERWISE I WILL ENSURE TORQUEMADA KNOWS YOUR SECRET... AND WE WILL SEE HOW YOU—WHO HAVE SENT SO MANY INNOCENTS TO THEIR DEATHS—CAN FACE YOUR OWN MISERABLE END!

HOW— HOW DID YOU KNOW I WAS A MANDRAKE? WHO ARE YOU?

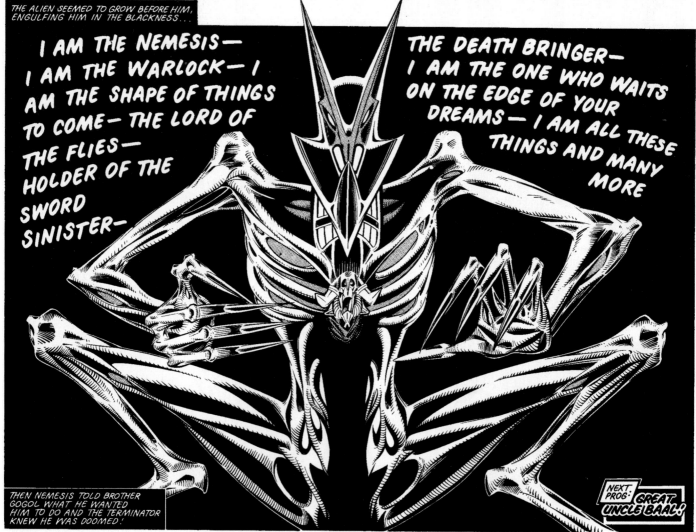

THE ALIEN SEEMED TO GROW BEFORE HIM, ENGULFING HIM IN THE BLACKNESS...

I AM THE NEMESIS— I AM THE WARLOCK— I AM THE SHAPE OF THINGS TO COME— THE LORD OF THE FLIES— HOLDER OF THE SWORD SINISTER—

THE DEATH BRINGER— I AM THE ONE WHO WAITS ON THE EDGE OF YOUR DREAMS— I AM ALL THESE THINGS AND MANY MORE

THEN NEMESIS TOLD BROTHER GOGOL WHAT HE WANTED HIM TO DO AND THE TERMINATOR KNEW HE WAS DOOMED!

NEXT PROG: GREAT UNCLE BAAL!

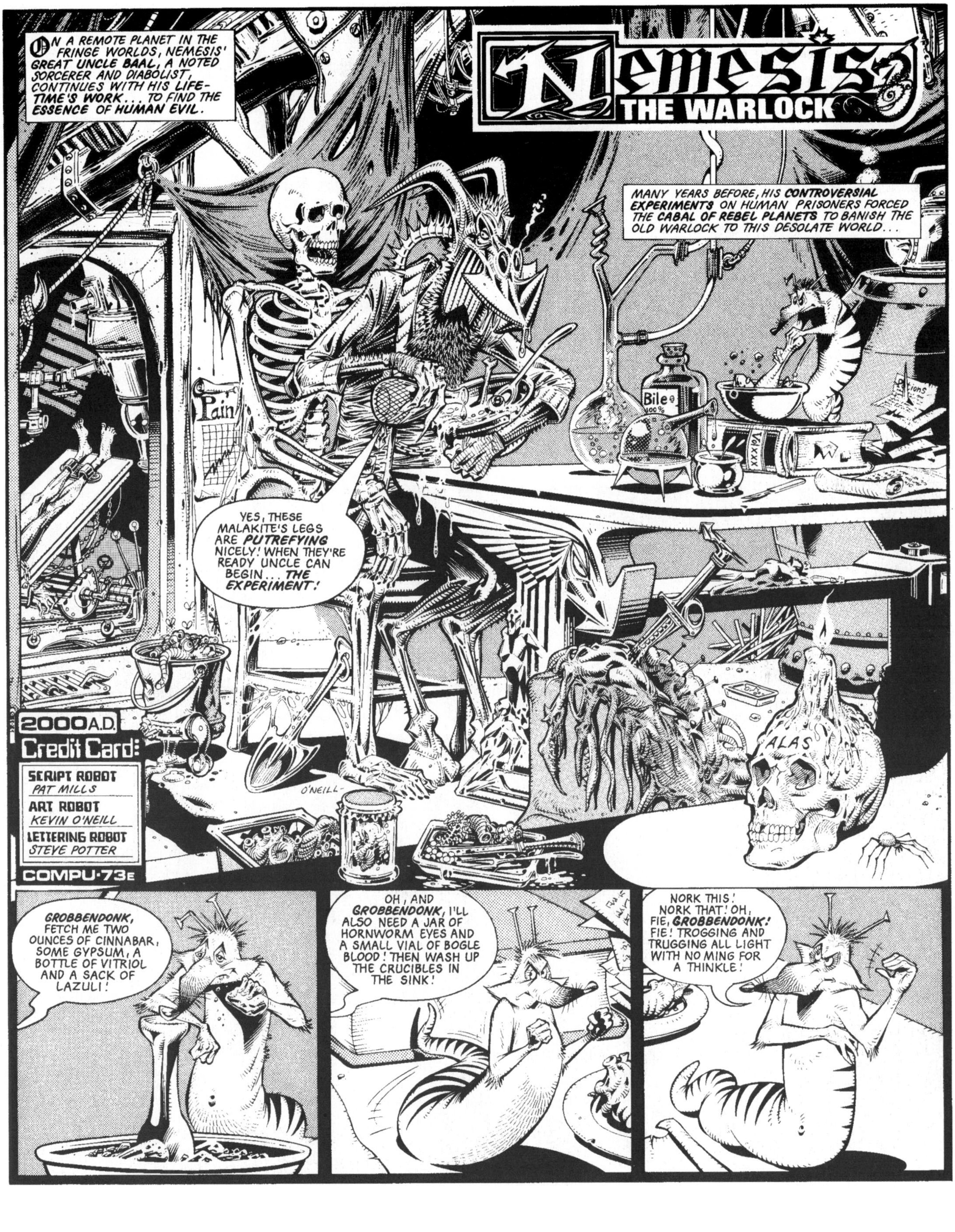

ON A REMOTE PLANET IN THE FRINGE WORLDS, NEMESIS' GREAT UNCLE BAAL, A NOTED SORCERER AND DIABOLIST, CONTINUES WITH HIS LIFE-TIME'S WORK... TO FIND THE ESSENCE OF HUMAN EVIL.
Nemesis THE WARLOCK
MANY YEARS BEFORE, HIS CONTROVERSIAL EXPERIMENTS ON HUMAN PRISONERS FORCED THE CABAL OF REBEL PLANETS TO BANISH THE OLD WARLOCK TO THIS DESOLATE WORLD...
Pain
Bile 100%
YES, THESE MALAKITE'S LEGS ARE PUTREFYING NICELY! WHEN THEY'RE READY UNCLE CAN BEGIN... THE EXPERIMENT!
ALAS
O'NEILL
2000 A.D. Credit Card:
SCRIPT ROBOT PAT MILLS
ART ROBOT KEVIN O'NEILL
LETTERING ROBOT STEVE POTTER
COMPU-73E
GROBBENDONK, FETCH ME TWO OUNCES OF CINNABAR, SOME GYPSUM, A BOTTLE OF VITRIOL AND A SACK OF LAZULI!
OH, AND GROBBENDONK, I'LL ALSO NEED A JAR OF HORNWORM EYES AND A SMALL VIAL OF BOGLE BLOOD! THEN WASH UP THE CRUCIBLES IN THE SINK!
NORK THIS! NORK THAT! OH, FIE, GROBBENDONK! FIE! TROGGING AND TRUGGING ALL LIGHT WITH NO MING FOR A THINKLE!

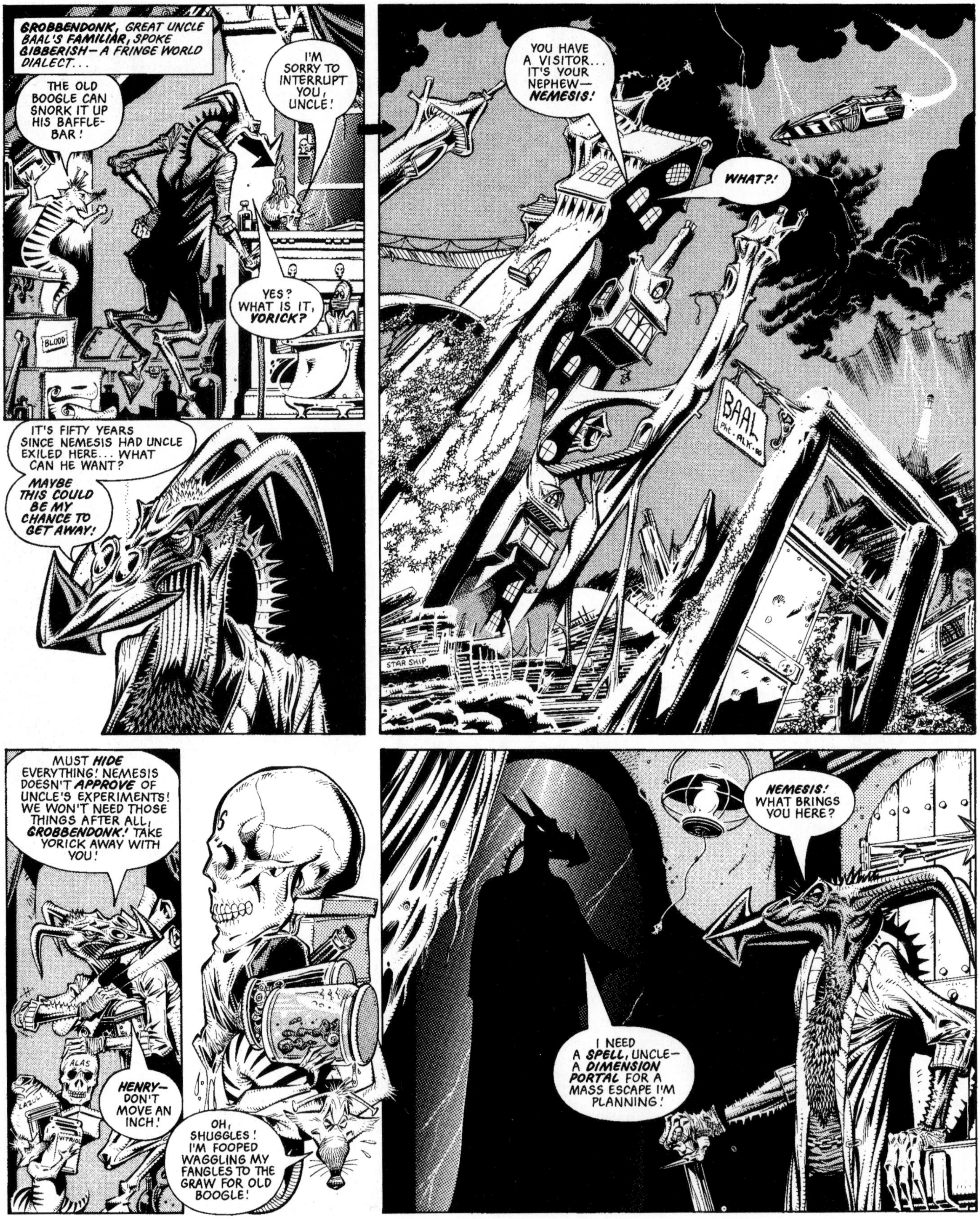

GROBBENDONK, GREAT UNCLE BAAL'S FAMILIAR, SPOKE GIBBERISH— A FRINGE WORLD DIALECT...
THE OLD BOOGLE CAN SNORK IT UP HIS BAFFLE-BAR!
I'M SORRY TO INTERRUPT YOU, UNCLE!
YES? WHAT IS IT, YORICK?
BLOOD
YOU HAVE A VISITOR... IT'S YOUR NEPHEW— NEMESIS!
WHAT?!
BAAL
STAR SHIP
IT'S FIFTY YEARS SINCE NEMESIS HAD UNCLE EXILED HERE... WHAT CAN HE WANT?
MAYBE THIS COULD BE MY CHANCE TO GET AWAY!
MUST HIDE EVERYTHING! NEMESIS DOESN'T APPROVE OF UNCLE'S EXPERIMENTS! WE WON'T NEED THOSE THINGS AFTER ALL, GROBBENDONK! TAKE YORICK AWAY WITH YOU!
HENRY— DON'T MOVE AN INCH!
OH, SHUGGLES! I'M FOOPED WAGGLING MY FANGLES TO THE GRAW FOR OLD BOOGLE!
ALAS
LAZULI
VITRIOL
NEMESIS! WHAT BRINGS YOU HERE?
I NEED A SPELL, UNCLE— A DIMENSION PORTAL FOR A MASS ESCAPE I'M PLANNING!

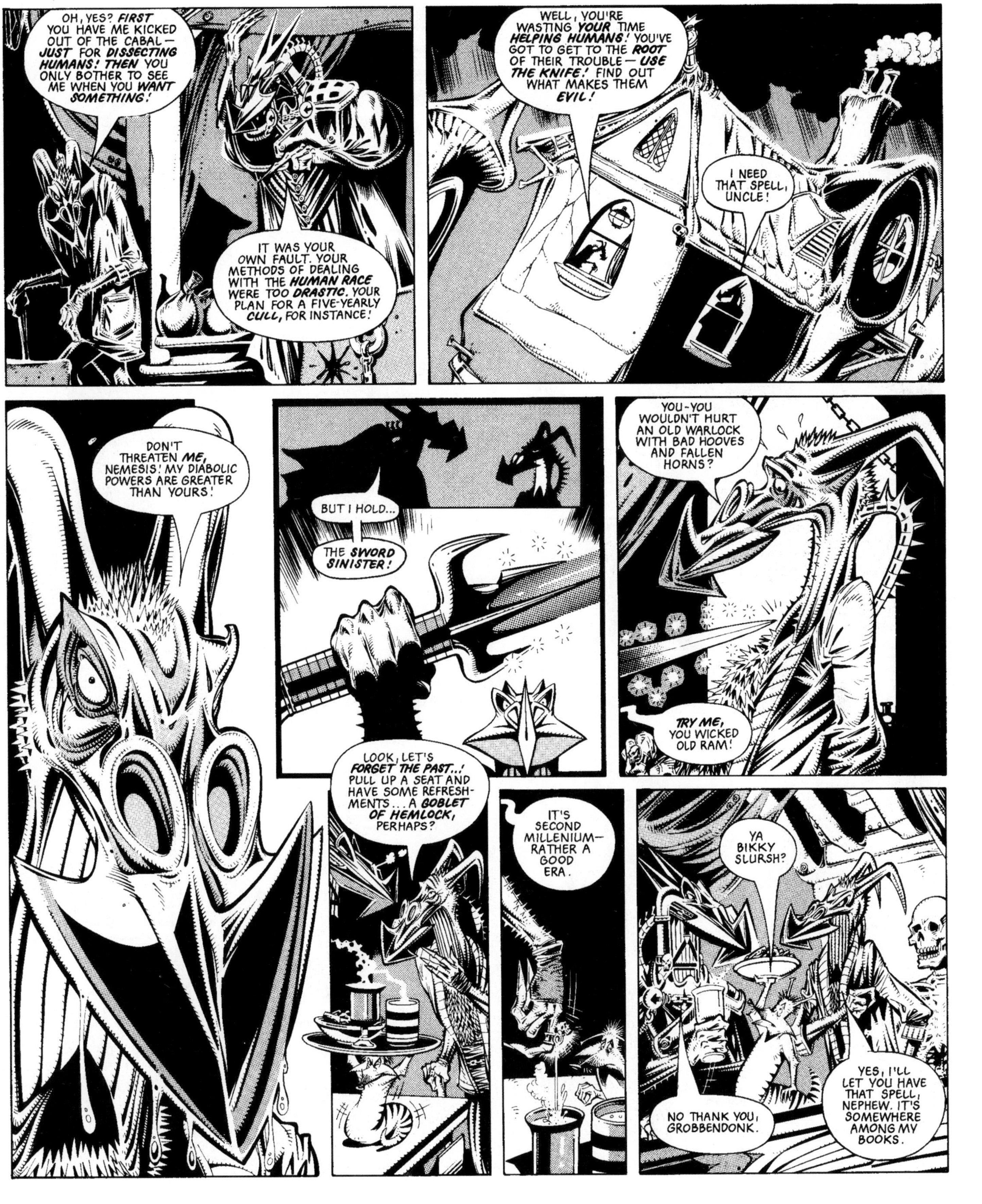

OH, YES? FIRST YOU HAVE ME KICKED OUT OF THE CABAL— JUST FOR DISSECTING HUMANS! THEN YOU ONLY BOTHER TO SEE ME WHEN YOU WANT SOMETHING!
IT WAS YOUR OWN FAULT. YOUR METHODS OF DEALING WITH THE HUMAN RACE WERE TOO DRASTIC. YOUR PLAN FOR A FIVE-YEARLY CULL, FOR INSTANCE!
WELL, YOU'RE WASTING YOUR TIME HELPING HUMANS! YOU'VE GOT TO GET TO THE ROOT OF THEIR TROUBLE— USE THE KNIFE! FIND OUT WHAT MAKES THEM EVIL!
I NEED THAT SPELL, UNCLE!
DON'T THREATEN ME, NEMESIS! MY DIABOLIC POWERS ARE GREATER THAN YOURS!
BUT I HOLD...
THE SWORD SINISTER!
YOU-YOU WOULDN'T HURT AN OLD WARLOCK WITH BAD HOOVES AND FALLEN HORNS?
TRY ME, YOU WICKED OLD RAM!
LOOK, LET'S FORGET THE PAST...! PULL UP A SEAT AND HAVE SOME REFRESH-MENTS... A GOBLET OF HEMLOCK, PERHAPS?
IT'S SECOND MILLENIUM— RATHER A GOOD ERA.
YA BIKKY SLURSH?
NO THANK YOU, GROBBENDONK.
YES, I'LL LET YOU HAVE THAT SPELL, NEPHEW. IT'S SOMEWHERE AMONG MY BOOKS.

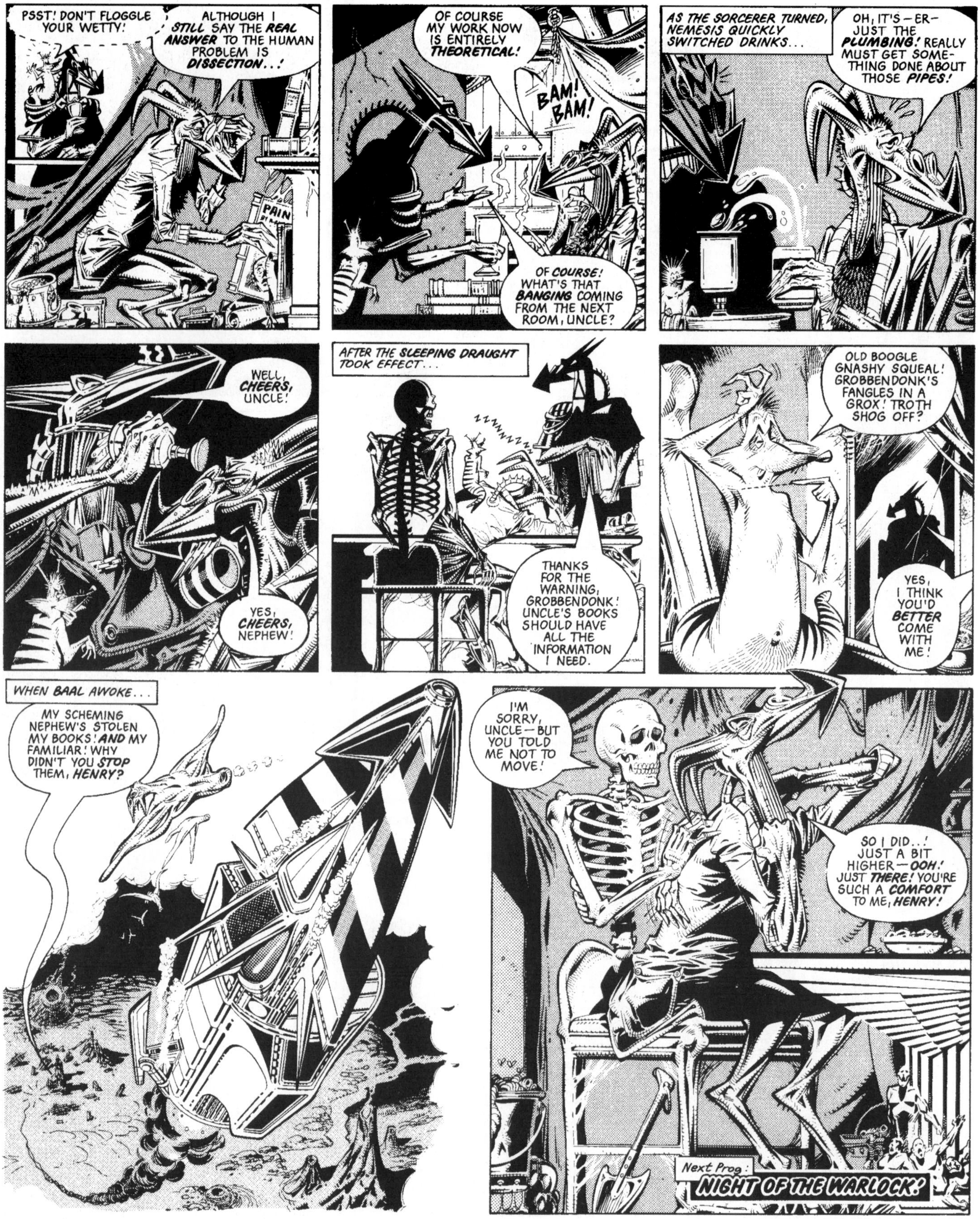
PSST! DON'T FLOGGLE YOUR WETTY!
ALTHOUGH I STILL SAY THE REAL ANSWER TO THE HUMAN PROBLEM IS DISSECTION..!
PAIN
OF COURSE MY WORK NOW IS ENTIRELY THEORETICAL!
BAM! BAM!
OF COURSE! WHAT'S THAT BANGING COMING FROM THE NEXT ROOM, UNCLE?
AS THE SORCERER TURNED, NEMESIS QUICKLY SWITCHED DRINKS...
OH, IT'S—ER—JUST THE PLUMBING! REALLY MUST GET SOMETHING DONE ABOUT THOSE PIPES!
WELL, CHEERS, UNCLE!
YES, CHEERS, NEPHEW!
AFTER THE SLEEPING DRAUGHT TOOK EFFECT...
ZZZZZZZZ
THANKS FOR THE WARNING, GROBBENDONK! UNCLE'S BOOKS SHOULD HAVE ALL THE INFORMATION I NEED.
OLD BOOGLE GNASHY SQUEAL! GROBBENDONK'S FANGLES IN A GROX! TROTH SHOG OFF?
YES, I THINK YOU'D BETTER COME WITH ME!
WHEN BAAL AWOKE...
MY SCHEMING NEPHEW'S STOLEN MY BOOKS! AND MY FAMILIAR! WHY DIDN'T YOU STOP THEM, HENRY?
I'M SORRY, UNCLE—BUT YOU TOLD ME NOT TO MOVE!
SO I DID..! JUST A BIT HIGHER—OOH! JUST THERE! YOU'RE SUCH A COMFORT TO ME, HENRY!
Next Prog: NIGHT OF THE WARLOCK!

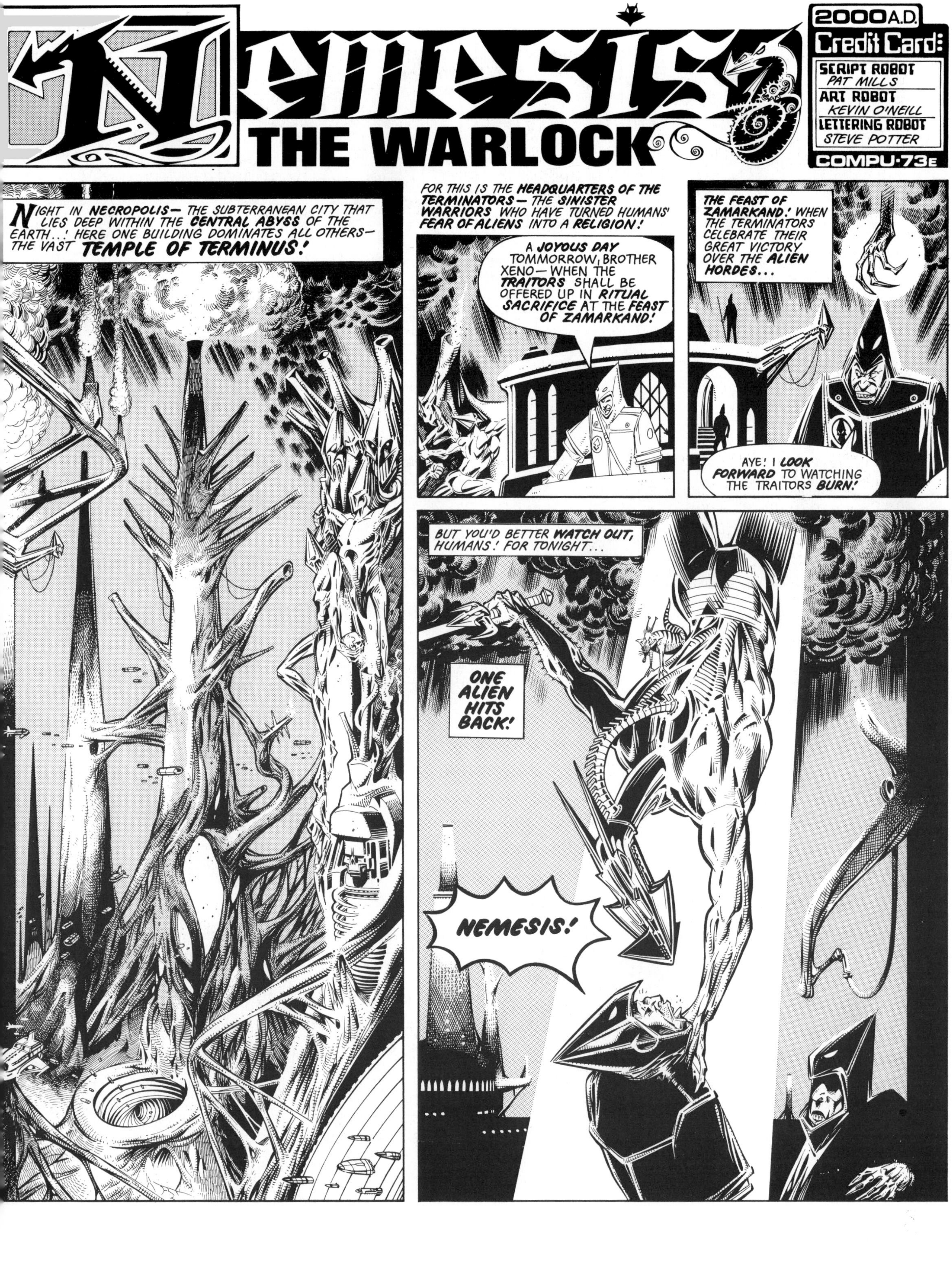
NEMESIS THE WARLOCK
2000 A.D. Credit Card:
SCRIPT ROBOT PAT MILLS
ART ROBOT KEVIN O'NEILL
LETTERING ROBOT STEVE POTTER
COMPU-73E
NIGHT IN NECROPOLIS— THE SUBTERRANEAN CITY THAT LIES DEEP WITHIN THE CENTRAL ABYSS OF THE EARTH..! HERE ONE BUILDING DOMINATES ALL OTHERS— THE VAST TEMPLE OF TERMINUS!
FOR THIS IS THE HEADQUARTERS OF THE TERMINATORS— THE SINISTER WARRIORS WHO HAVE TURNED HUMANS' FEAR OF ALIENS INTO A RELIGION!
A JOYOUS DAY TOMMORROW, BROTHER XENO— WHEN THE TRAITORS SHALL BE OFFERED UP IN RITUAL SACRIFICE AT THE FEAST OF ZAMARKAND!
THE FEAST OF ZAMARKAND! WHEN THE TERMINATORS CELEBRATE THEIR GREAT VICTORY OVER THE ALIEN HORDES...
AYE! I LOOK FORWARD TO WATCHING THE TRAITORS BURN!
BUT YOU'D BETTER WATCH OUT, HUMANS! FOR TONIGHT...
ONE ALIEN HITS BACK!
NEMESIS!

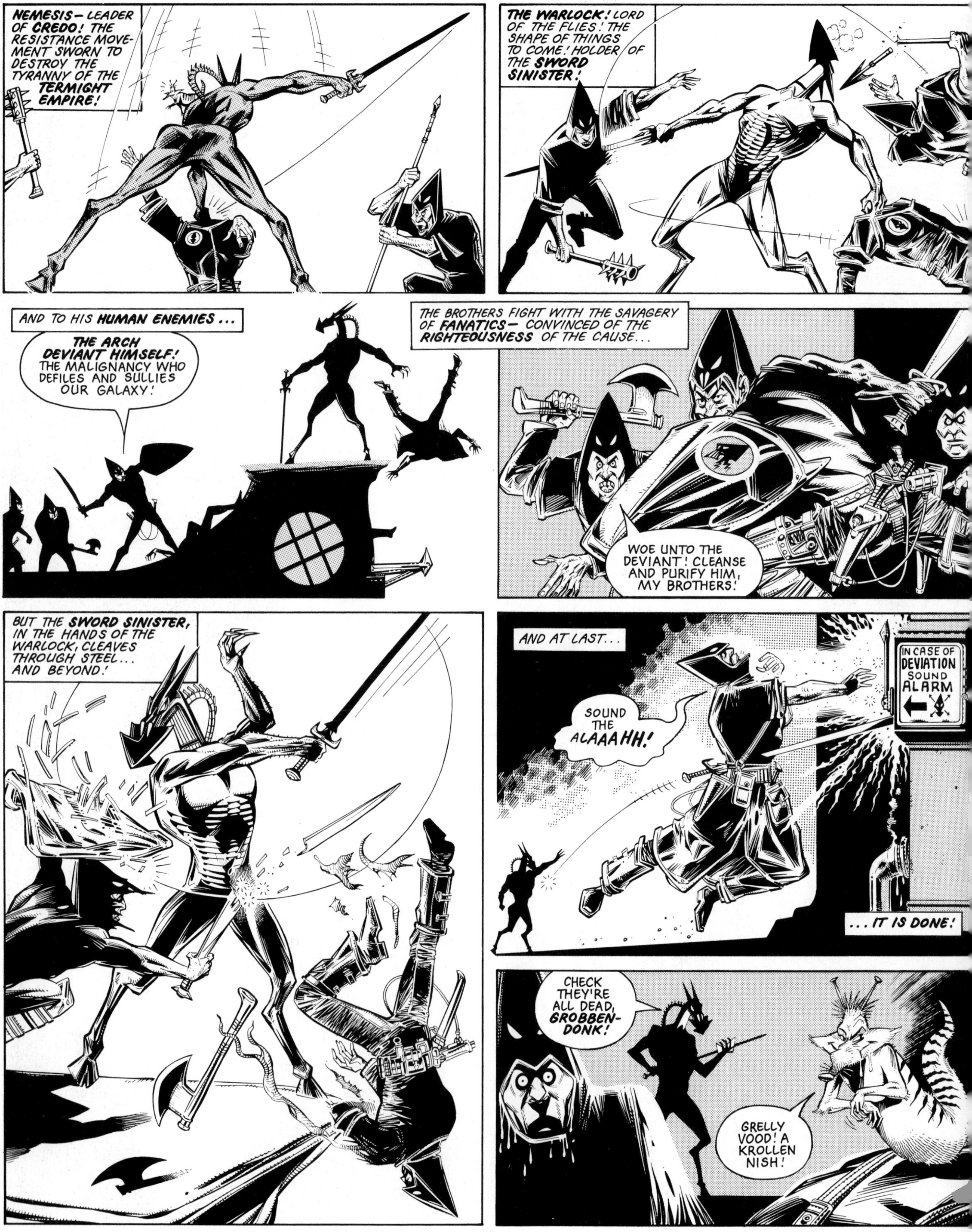
NEMESIS— LEADER OF CREDO! THE RESISTANCE MOVEMENT SWORN TO DESTROY THE TYRANNY OF THE TERMIGHT EMPIRE!
THE WARLOCK! LORD OF THE FLIES! THE SHAPE OF THINGS TO COME! HOLDER OF THE SWORD SINISTER!
AND TO HIS HUMAN ENEMIES ...
THE ARCH DEVIANT HIMSELF! THE MALIGNANCY WHO DEFILES AND SULLIES OUR GALAXY!
THE BROTHERS FIGHT WITH THE SAVAGERY OF FANATICS— CONVINCED OF THE RIGHTEOUSNESS OF THE CAUSE...
WOE UNTO THE DEVIANT! CLEANSE AND PURIFY HIM, MY BROTHERS!
BUT THE SWORD SINISTER, IN THE HANDS OF THE WARLOCK, CLEAVES THROUGH STEEL... AND BEYOND!
AND AT LAST...
SOUND THE ALAAAHH!
IN CASE OF DEVIATION SOUND ALARM
... IT IS DONE!
CHECK THEY'RE ALL DEAD, GROBBENDONK!
GRELLY VOOD! A KROLLEN NISH!

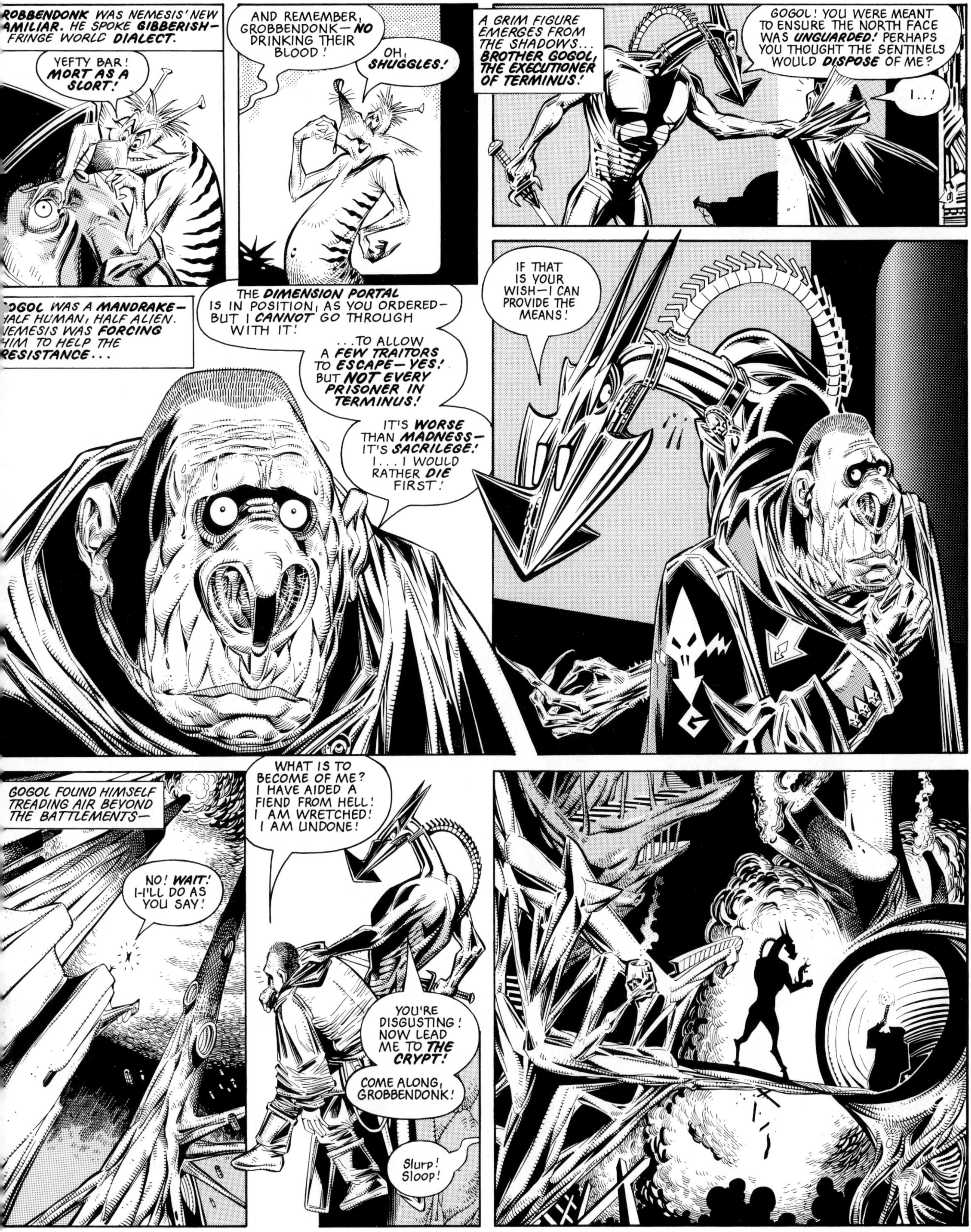

ROBBENDONK WAS NEMESIS' NEW AMILIAR. HE SPOKE GIBBERISH-FRINGE WORLD DIALECT.
YEFTY BAR! MORT AS A SLORT!
AND REMEMBER, GROBBENDONK—NO DRINKING THEIR BLOOD!
OH, SHUGGLES!
A GRIM FIGURE EMERGES FROM THE SHADOWS... BROTHER GOGOL, THE EXECUTIONER OF TERMINUS!
GOGOL! YOU WERE MEANT TO ENSURE THE NORTH FACE WAS UNGUARDED! PERHAPS YOU THOUGHT THE SENTINELS WOULD DISPOSE OF ME?
I...!
OGOL WAS A MANDRAKE—HALF HUMAN, HALF ALIEN. NEMESIS WAS FORCING HIM TO HELP THE RESISTANCE...
THE DIMENSION PORTAL IS IN POSITION, AS YOU ORDERED—BUT I CANNOT GO THROUGH WITH IT!
...TO ALLOW A FEW TRAITORS TO ESCAPE—YES! BUT NOT EVERY PRISONER IN TERMINUS!
IT'S WORSE THAN MADNESS—IT'S SACRILEGE! I...I WOULD RATHER DIE FIRST!
IF THAT IS YOUR WISH—I CAN PROVIDE THE MEANS!
GOGOL FOUND HIMSELF TREADING AIR BEYOND THE BATTLEMENTS—
NO! WAIT! I-I'LL DO AS YOU SAY!
WHAT IS TO BECOME OF ME? I HAVE AIDED A FIEND FROM HELL! I AM WRETCHED! I AM UNDONE!
YOU'RE DISGUSTING! NOW LEAD ME TO THE CRYPT!
COME ALONG, GROBBENDONK!
Slurp! Sloop!

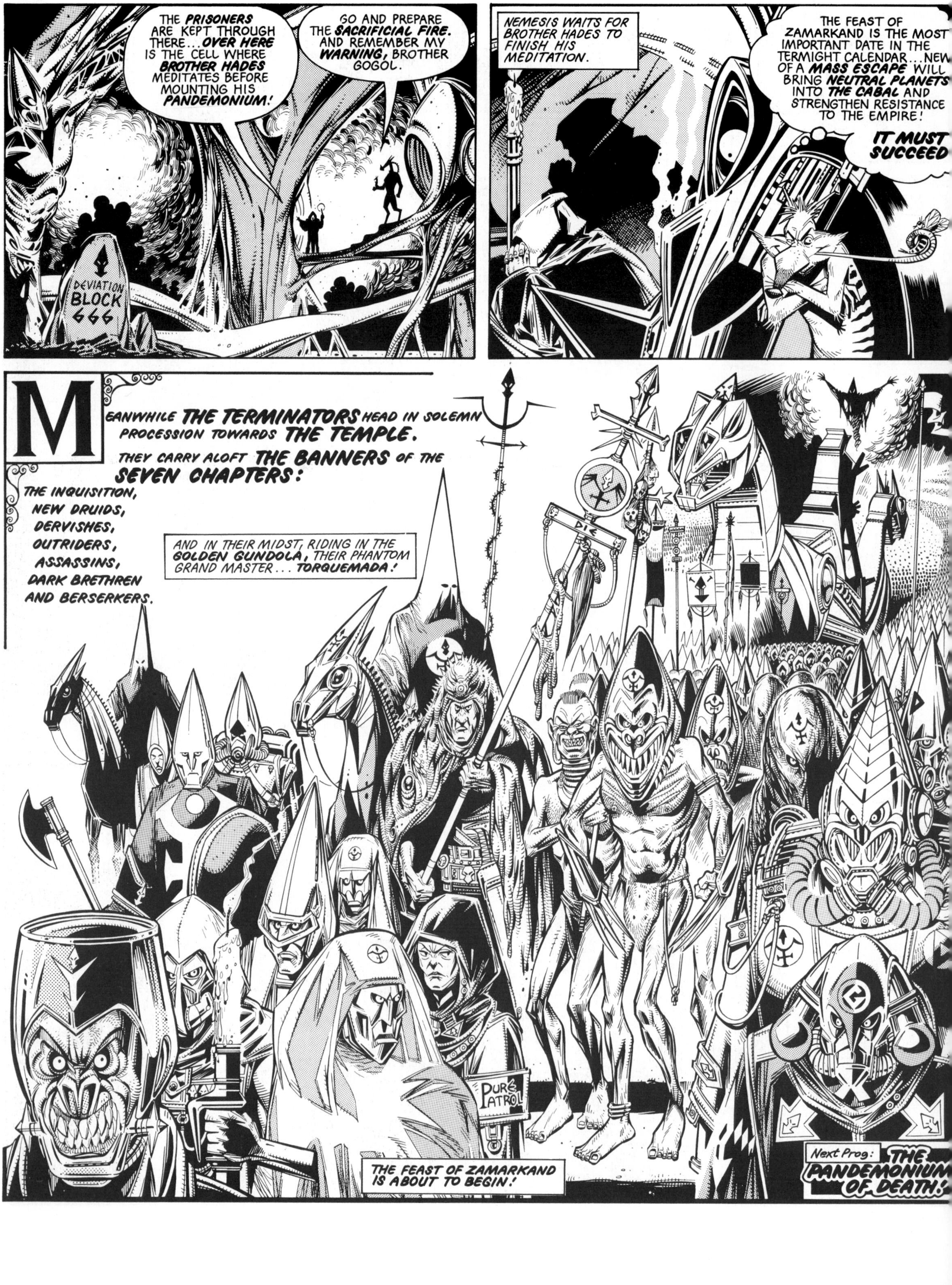
THE PRISONERS ARE KEPT THROUGH THERE... OVER HERE IS THE CELL WHERE BROTHER HADES MEDITATES BEFORE MOUNTING HIS PANDEMONIUM!
GO AND PREPARE THE SACRIFICIAL FIRE. AND REMEMBER MY WARNING, BROTHER GOGOL.
DEVIATION BLOCK 666
NEMESIS WAITS FOR BROTHER HADES TO FINISH HIS MEDITATION.
THE FEAST OF ZAMARKAND IS THE MOST IMPORTANT DATE IN THE TERMIGHT CALENDAR... NEW OF A MASS ESCAPE WILL BRING NEUTRAL PLANETS INTO THE CABAL AND STRENGTHEN RESISTANCE TO THE EMPIRE!
IT MUST SUCCEED
MEANWHILE THE TERMINATORS HEAD IN SOLEMN PROCESSION TOWARDS THE TEMPLE.
THEY CARRY ALOFT THE BANNERS OF THE SEVEN CHAPTERS:
THE INQUISITION, NEW DRUIDS, DERVISHES, OUTRIDERS, ASSASSINS, DARK BRETHREN AND BERSERKERS.
AND IN THEIR MIDST, RIDING IN THE GOLDEN GUNDOLA, THEIR PHANTOM GRAND MASTER... TORQUEMADA!
DIE
PURE PATROL
THE FEAST OF ZAMARKAND IS ABOUT TO BEGIN!
Next Prog: THE PANDEMONIUM OF DEATH!

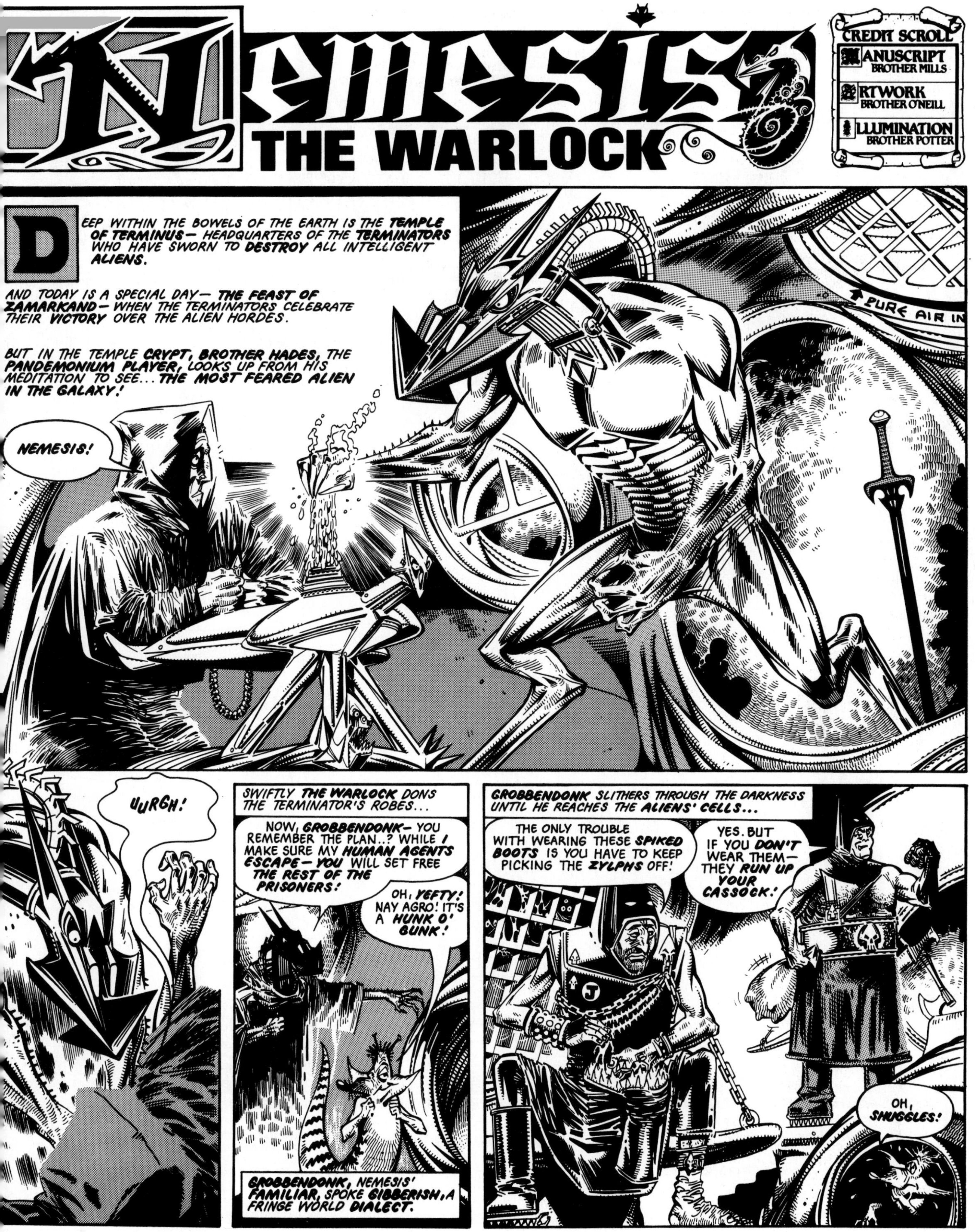

NEMESIS THE WARLOCK
CREDIT SCROLL
MANUSCRIPT BROTHER MILLS
ARTWORK BROTHER O'NEILL
ILLUMINATION BROTHER POTTER
DEEP WITHIN THE BOWELS OF THE EARTH IS THE TEMPLE OF TERMINUS— HEADQUARTERS OF THE TERMINATORS WHO HAVE SWORN TO DESTROY ALL INTELLIGENT ALIENS.
AND TODAY IS A SPECIAL DAY— THE FEAST OF ZAMARKAND— WHEN THE TERMINATORS CELEBRATE THEIR VICTORY OVER THE ALIEN HORDES.
BUT IN THE TEMPLE CRYPT, BROTHER HADES, THE PANDEMONIUM PLAYER, LOOKS UP FROM HIS MEDITATION TO SEE... THE MOST FEARED ALIEN IN THE GALAXY!
NEMESIS!
PURE AIR IN
UURGH!
SWIFTLY THE WARLOCK DONS THE TERMINATOR'S ROBES...
NOW, GROBBENDONK— YOU REMEMBER THE PLAN..? WHILE I MAKE SURE MY HUMAN AGENTS ESCAPE— YOU WILL SET FREE THE REST OF THE PRISONERS!
OH, YEFTY! NAY AGRO! IT'S A HUNK O' BUNK!
GROBBENDONK, NEMESIS' FAMILIAR, SPOKE GIBBERISH, A FRINGE WORLD DIALECT.
GROBBENDONK SLITHERS THROUGH THE DARKNESS UNTIL HE REACHES THE ALIENS' CELLS...
THE ONLY TROUBLE WITH WEARING THESE SPIKED BOOTS IS YOU HAVE TO KEEP PICKING THE ZYLPHS OFF!
YES. BUT IF YOU DON'T WEAR THEM— THEY RUN UP YOUR CASSOCK!
OH, SHUGGLES!

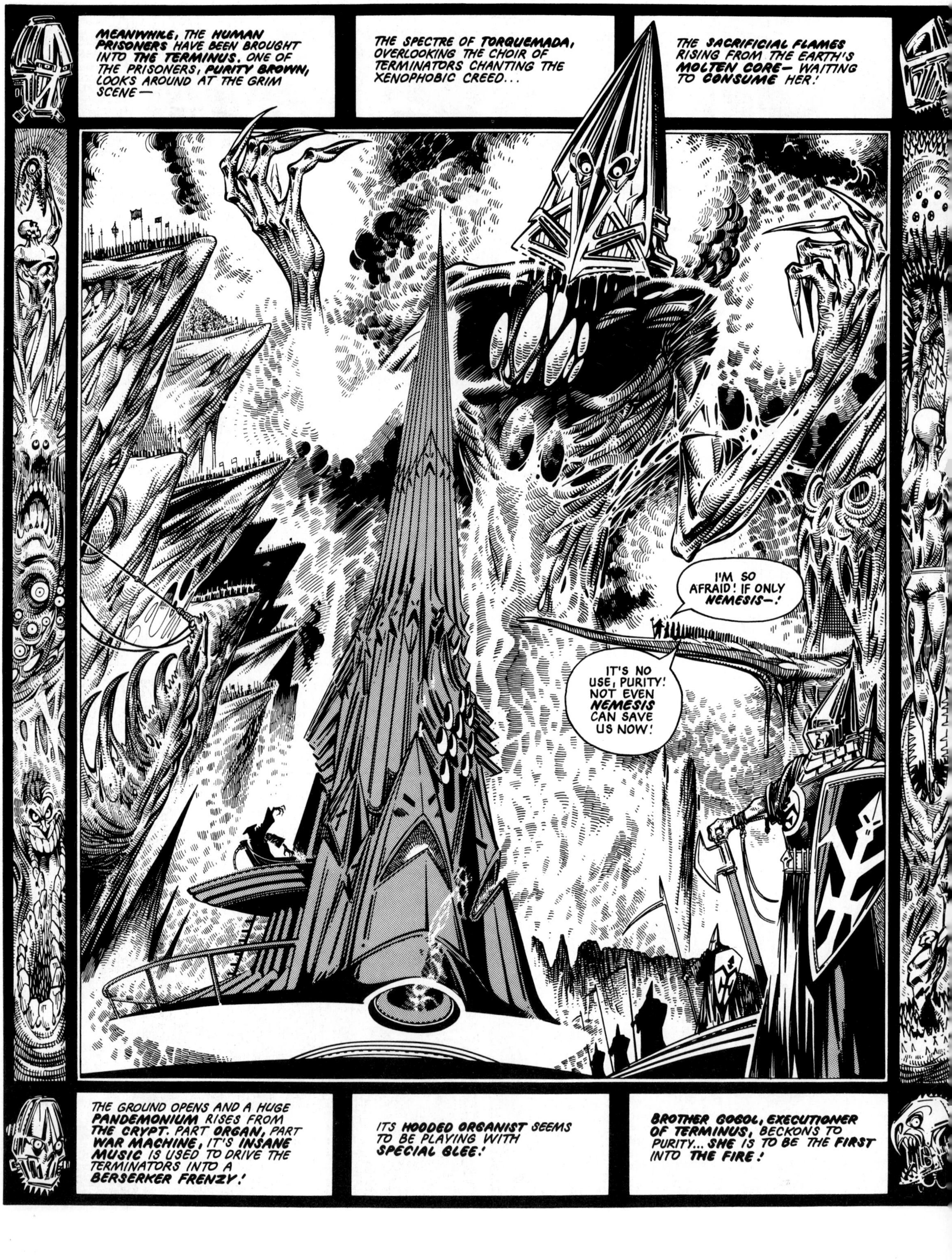
MEANWHILE, THE HUMAN PRISONERS HAVE BEEN BROUGHT INTO THE TERMINUS. ONE OF THE PRISONERS, PURITY BROWN, LOOKS AROUND AT THE GRIM SCENE—
THE SPECTRE OF TORQUEMADA, OVERLOOKING THE CHOIR OF TERMINATORS CHANTING THE XENOPHOBIC CREED...
THE SACRIFICIAL FLAMES RISING FROM THE EARTH'S MOLTEN CORE— WAITING TO CONSUME HER!
I'M SO AFRAID! IF ONLY NEMESIS—!
IT'S NO USE, PURITY! NOT EVEN NEMESIS CAN SAVE US NOW!
THE GROUND OPENS AND A HUGE PANDEMONIUM RISES FROM THE CRYPT. PART ORGAN, PART WAR MACHINE, IT'S INSANE MUSIC IS USED TO DRIVE THE TERMINATORS INTO A BERSERKER FRENZY!
ITS HOODED ORGANIST SEEMS TO BE PLAYING WITH SPECIAL GLEE!
BROTHER GOGOL, EXECUTIONER OF TERMINUS, BECKONS TO PURITY... SHE IS TO BE THE FIRST INTO THE FIRE!

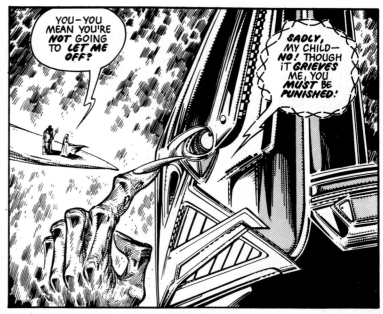

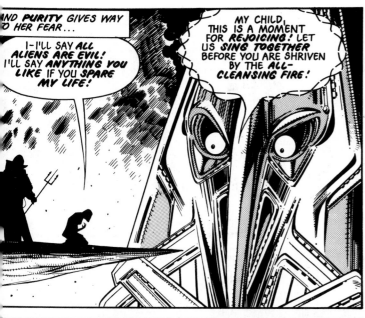

AND PURITY GIVES WAY TO HER FEAR...

I-I'LL SAY *ALL* ALIENS ARE *EVIL!* I'LL SAY *ANYTHING* YOU LIKE IF YOU *SPARE MY LIFE!*

MY CHILD, THIS IS A MOMENT FOR *REJOICING!* LET US *SING TOGETHER* BEFORE YOU ARE SHRIVEN BY THE *ALL-CLEANSING FIRE!*

YOU—YOU MEAN YOU'RE *NOT* GOING TO *LET ME OFF?*

SADLY, MY CHILD— *NO!* THOUGH IT *GRIEVES* ME, YOU *MUST BE PUNISHED!*

WHY ARE YOU ALL SO... *EVIL?* DON'T YOU THINK IT'S *WRONG* TO *HATE ALIENS— JUST* BECAUSE THEY'RE *DIFFERENT* TO US?

NO.

WHAT ARE YOU ALL *HIDING* BEHIND YOUR *MASKS?*

IN HER RAGE, SHE DOESN'T NOTICE BROTHER GOGOL TREMBLE AT HER LAST WORDS.

YOU'VE LED THE HUMAN RACE INTO A NEW *DARK AGE!* BUT *NEMESIS* WILL *AVENGE* OUR *DEATHS!*

AS THE MUSIC OF THE PANDEMONIUM HOWLS AN INSANE SYMPHONY, THE TERMINATORS GET TO THEIR FEET...

BURN HER! *BURN* THE *WITCH!*

THEN SHE HEARS A VOICE *INSIDE* HER HEAD—

NEMESIS!

DO NOT BE AFRAID

YOU MUST ENTER THE PIT

THE FLAMES ARE YOUR GATEWAY...

...TO *FREEDOM!*

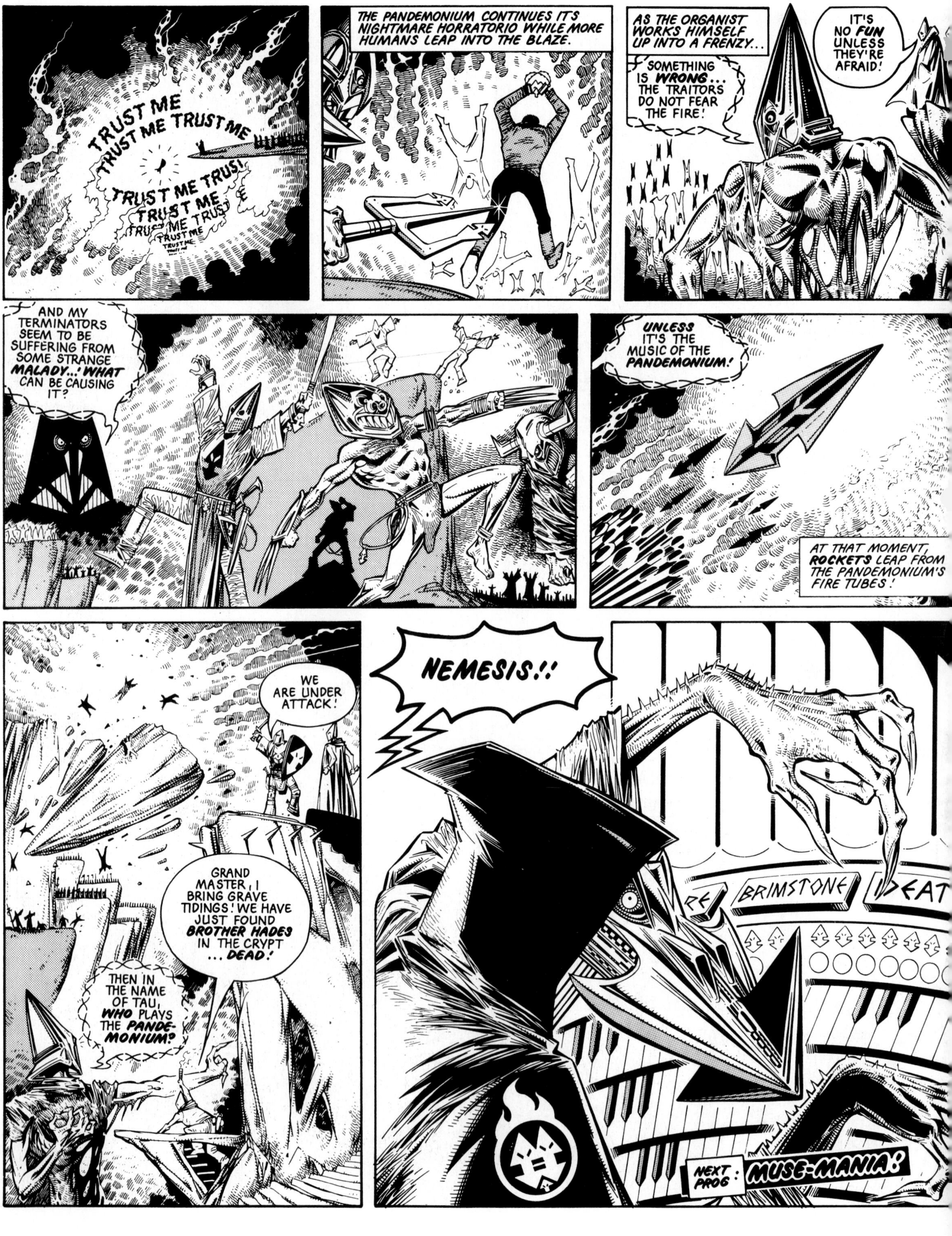

TRUST ME TRUST ME TRUST ME
TRUST ME TRUST TRUST ME TRUST ME TRUST ME
THE PANDEMONIUM CONTINUES ITS NIGHTMARE HORRATORIO WHILE MORE HUMANS LEAP INTO THE BLAZE.
AS THE ORGANIST WORKS HIMSELF UP INTO A FRENZY...
SOMETHING IS WRONG... THE TRAITORS DO NOT FEAR THE FIRE!
IT'S NO FUN UNLESS THEY'RE AFRAID!
AND MY TERMINATORS SEEM TO BE SUFFERING FROM SOME STRANGE MALADY...! WHAT CAN BE CAUSING IT?
UNLESS IT'S THE MUSIC OF THE PANDEMONIUM!
AT THAT MOMENT, ROCKETS LEAP FROM THE PANDEMONIUM'S FIRE TUBES!
WE ARE UNDER ATTACK!
GRAND MASTER, I BRING GRAVE TIDINGS! WE HAVE JUST FOUND BROTHER HADES IN THE CRYPT ... DEAD!
THEN IN THE NAME OF TAU, WHO PLAYS THE PANDEMONIUM?
NEMESIS!!
BRIMSTONE
NEXT PROG: MUSE-MANIA!

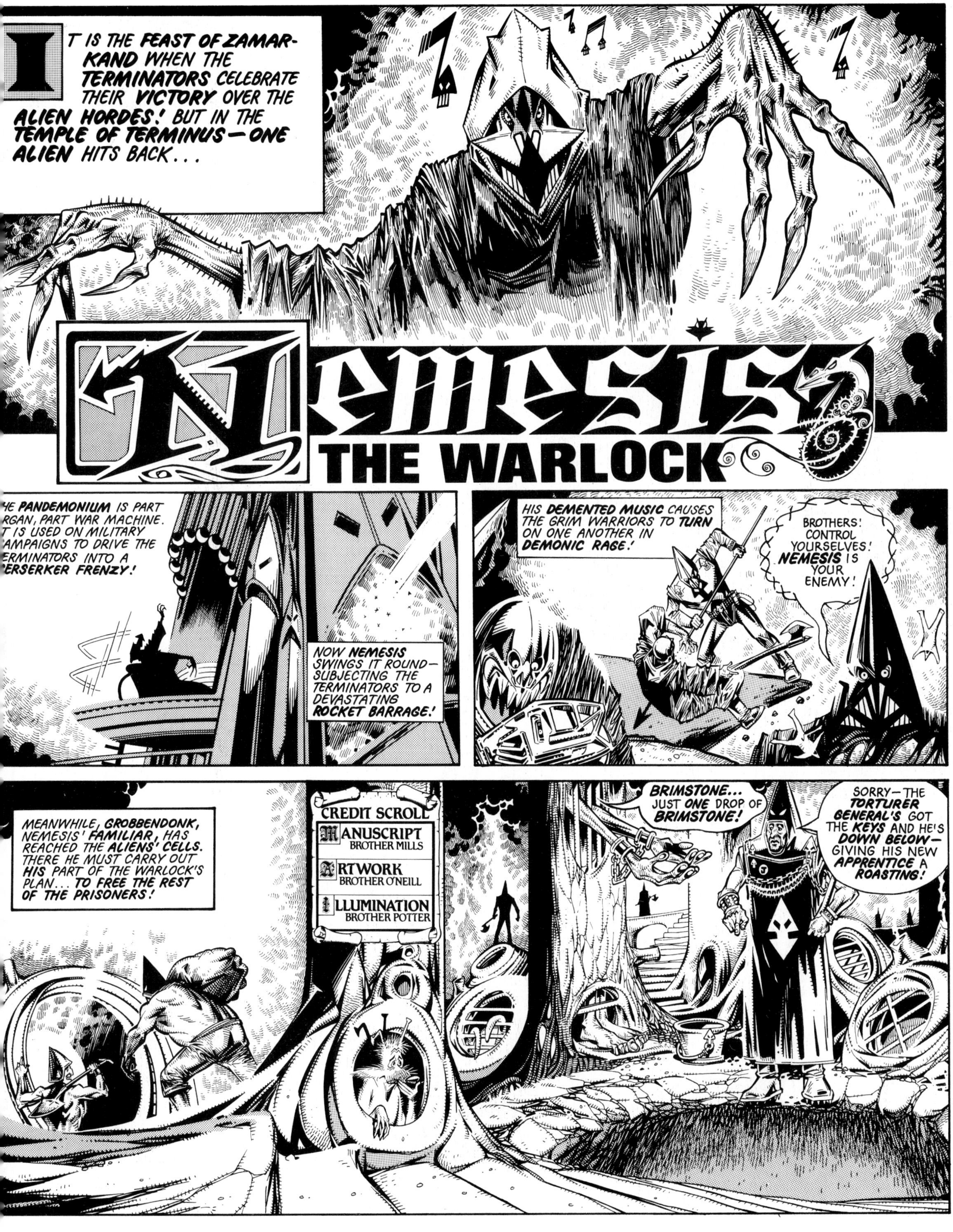

IT IS THE FEAST OF ZAMARKAND WHEN THE TERMINATORS CELEBRATE THEIR VICTORY OVER THE ALIEN HORDES! BUT IN THE TEMPLE OF TERMINUS—ONE ALIEN HITS BACK...
NEMESIS THE WARLOCK
HE PANDEMONIUM IS PART RGAN, PART WAR MACHINE. T IS USED ON MILITARY AMPAIGNS TO DRIVE THE ERMINATORS INTO A ERSERKER FRENZY!
NOW NEMESIS SWINGS IT ROUND—SUBJECTING THE TERMINATORS TO A DEVASTATING ROCKET BARRAGE!
HIS DEMENTED MUSIC CAUSES THE GRIM WARRIORS TO TURN ON ONE ANOTHER IN DEMONIC RAGE!
BROTHERS! CONTROL YOURSELVES! NEMESIS IS YOUR ENEMY!
MEANWHILE, GROBBENDONK, NEMESIS' FAMILIAR, HAS REACHED THE ALIENS' CELLS. THERE HE MUST CARRY OUT HIS PART OF THE WARLOCK'S PLAN... TO FREE THE REST OF THE PRISONERS!
CREDIT SCROLL
MANUSCRIPT BROTHER MILLS
ARTWORK BROTHER O'NEILL
ILLUMINATION BROTHER POTTER
BRIMSTONE... JUST ONE DROP OF BRIMSTONE!
SORRY—THE TORTURER GENERAL'S GOT THE KEYS AND HE'S DOWN BELOW—GIVING HIS NEW APPRENTICE A ROASTING!

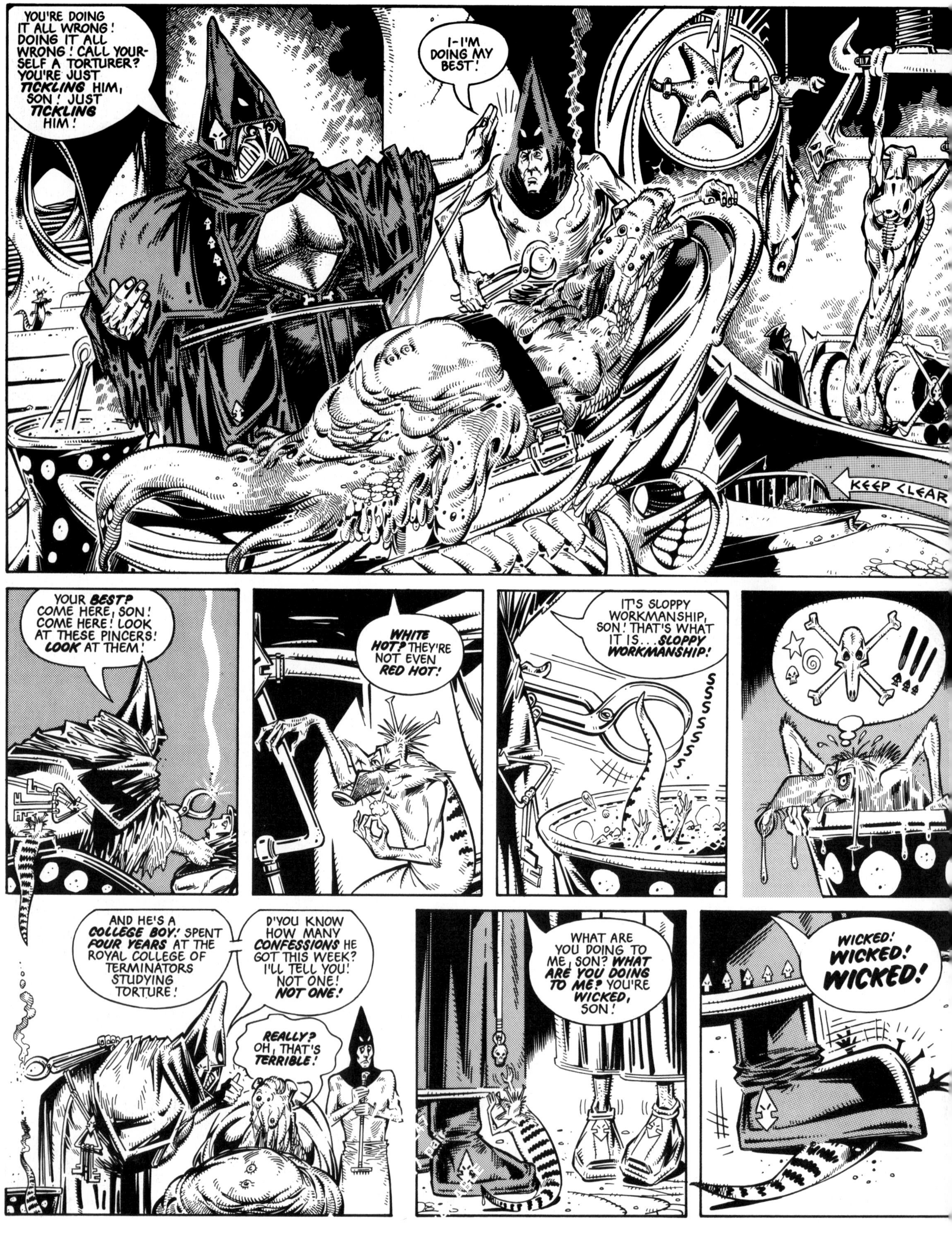

YOU'RE DOING IT ALL WRONG! DOING IT ALL WRONG! CALL YOURSELF A TORTURER? YOU'RE JUST TICKLING HIM, SON! JUST TICKLING HIM!
I-I'M DOING MY BEST!
KEEP CLEAR
YOUR BEST? COME HERE, SON! COME HERE! LOOK AT THESE PINCERS! LOOK AT THEM!
WHITE HOT? THEY'RE NOT EVEN RED HOT!
IT'S SLOPPY WORKMANSHIP, SON! THAT'S WHAT IT IS... SLOPPY WORKMANSHIP!
SSSSSSSS
AND HE'S A COLLEGE BOY! SPENT FOUR YEARS AT THE ROYAL COLLEGE OF TERMINATORS STUDYING TORTURE!
D'YOU KNOW HOW MANY CONFESSIONS HE GOT THIS WEEK? I'LL TELL YOU! NOT ONE! NOT ONE!
REALLY? OH, THAT'S TERRIBLE!
WHAT ARE YOU DOING TO ME, SON? WHAT ARE YOU DOING TO ME? YOU'RE WICKED, SON!
WICKED! WICKED! WICKED!

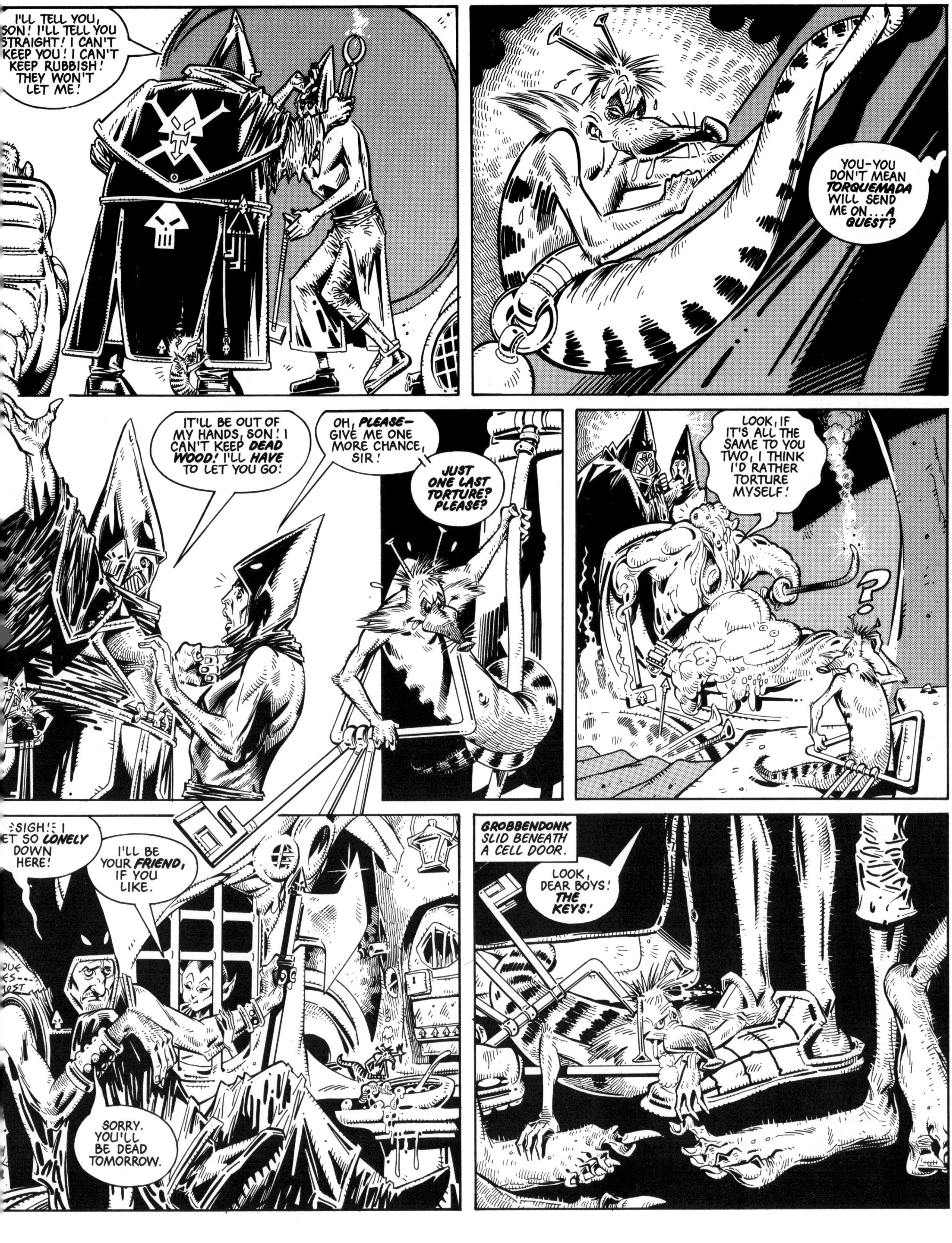
I'LL TELL YOU, SON! I'LL TELL YOU STRAIGHT! I CAN'T KEEP YOU! I CAN'T KEEP RUBBISH! THEY WON'T LET ME!
YOU-YOU DON'T MEAN TORQUEMADA WILL SEND ME ON... A QUEST?
IT'LL BE OUT OF MY HANDS, SON! I CAN'T KEEP DEAD WOOD! I'LL HAVE TO LET YOU GO!
OH, PLEASE- GIVE ME ONE MORE CHANCE, SIR!
JUST ONE LAST TORTURE? PLEASE?
LOOK, IF IT'S ALL THE SAME TO YOU TWO, I THINK I'D RATHER TORTURE MYSELF!
SIGH! I
ET SO LONELY DOWN HERE!
I'LL BE YOUR FRIEND, IF YOU LIKE.
SORRY. YOU'LL BE DEAD TOMORROW.
GROBBENDONK SLID BENEATH A CELL DOOR.
LOOK, DEAR BOYS! THE KEYS!

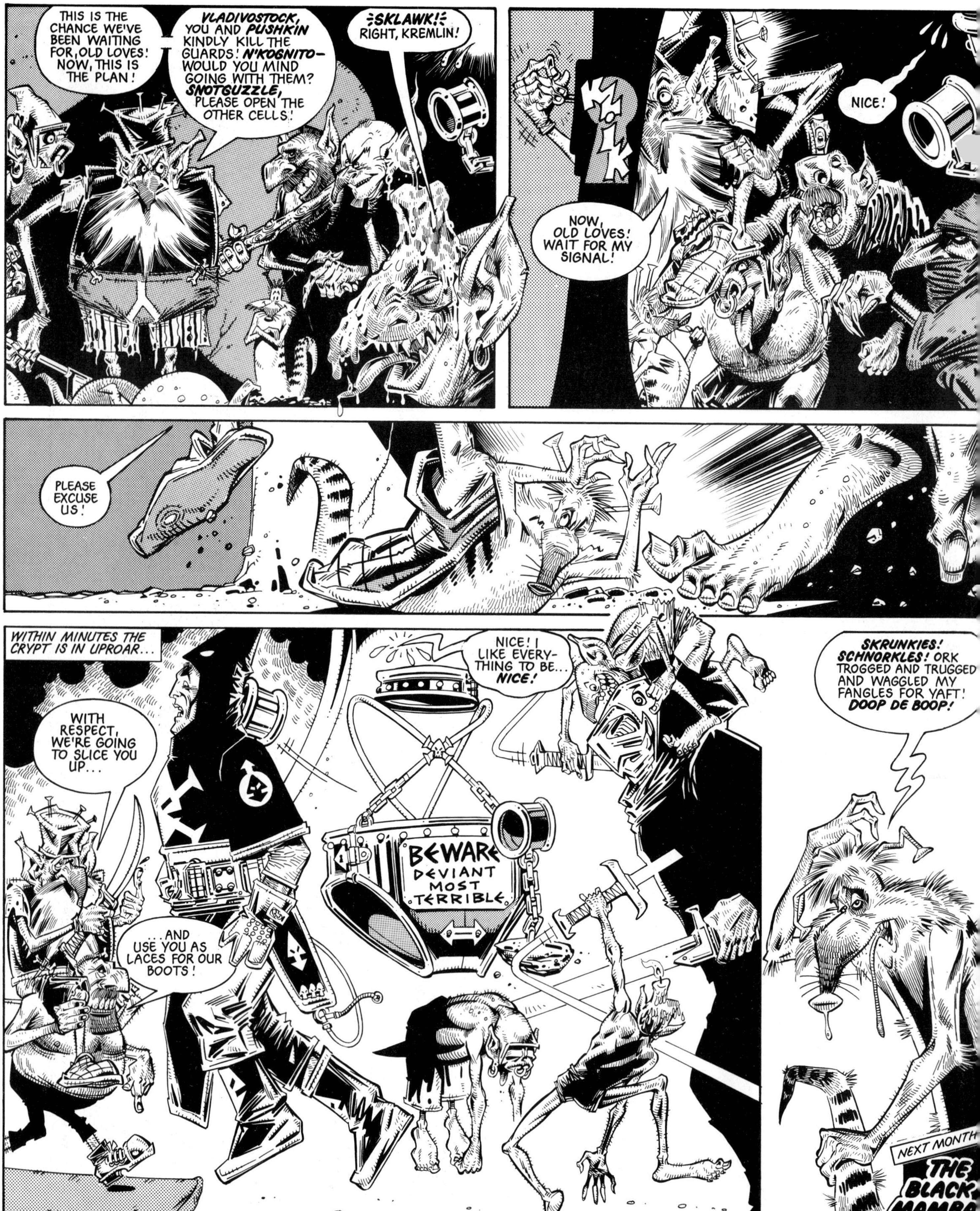
THIS IS THE CHANCE WE'VE BEEN WAITING FOR, OLD LOVES! NOW, THIS IS THE PLAN!
VLADIVOSTOCK, YOU AND PUSHKIN KINDLY KILL THE GUARDS! N'KOGNITO - WOULD YOU MIND GOING WITH THEM? SNOTGUZZLE, PLEASE OPEN THE OTHER CELLS!
SKLAWK! RIGHT, KREMLIN!
KRIK
NICE!
NOW, OLD LOVES! WAIT FOR MY SIGNAL!
PLEASE EXCUSE US!
WITHIN MINUTES THE CRYPT IS IN UPROAR...
WITH RESPECT, WE'RE GOING TO SLICE YOU UP...
...AND USE YOU AS LACES FOR OUR BOOTS!
NICE! I LIKE EVERYTHING TO BE... NICE!
BEWARE DEVIANT MOST TERRIBLE
SKRUNKIES! SCHNORKLES! ORK TROGGED AND TRUGGED AND WAGGLED MY FANGLES FOR YAFT! DOOP DE BOOP!
NEXT MONTH
THE BLACK MAMBA

Nemesis THE WARLOCK

CREDIT SCROLL
MANUSCRIPT
BROTHER MILLS
ARTWORK
BROTHER O'NEILL
ILLUMINATION
BROTHER POTTER

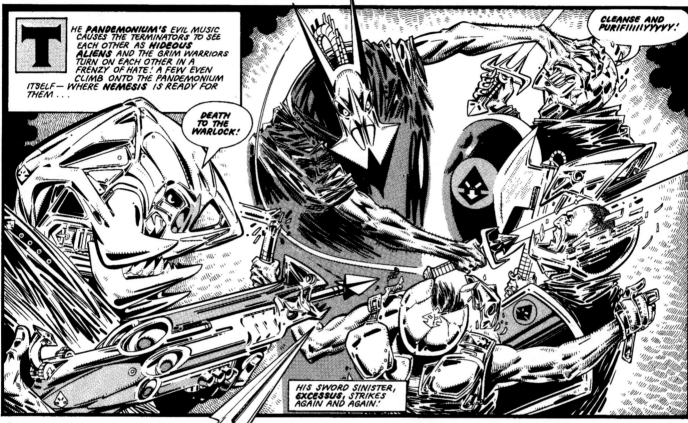

THE PANDEMONIUM'S EVIL MUSIC CAUSES THE TERMINATORS TO SEE EACH OTHER AS HIDEOUS ALIENS AND THE GRIM WARRIORS TURN ON EACH OTHER IN A FRENZY OF HATE! A FEW EVEN CLIMB ONTO THE PANDEMONIUM ITSELF— WHERE NEMESIS IS READY FOR THEM . . .

DEATH TO THE WARLOCK!

CLEANSE AND PURIFIIIIIYYYYY!

HIS SWORD SINISTER, EXCESSUS, STRIKES AGAIN AND AGAIN!

IN THE CRYPT BELOW THE TERMINUS, GROBBENDONK — NEMESIS' FAMILIAR — HAS RELEASED THE HORDES OF ALIEN PRISONERS HELD THERE. AMONG THEM ARE THE SINISTER YOLOGS, LED BY THEIR CHIEF, KREMLIN.

FORWARD! AND REMEMBER, OLD LOVES— BE POLITE! GOOD MANNERS COST NOTHING!

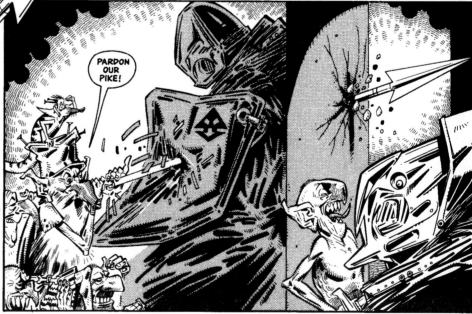

PARDON OUR PIKE!

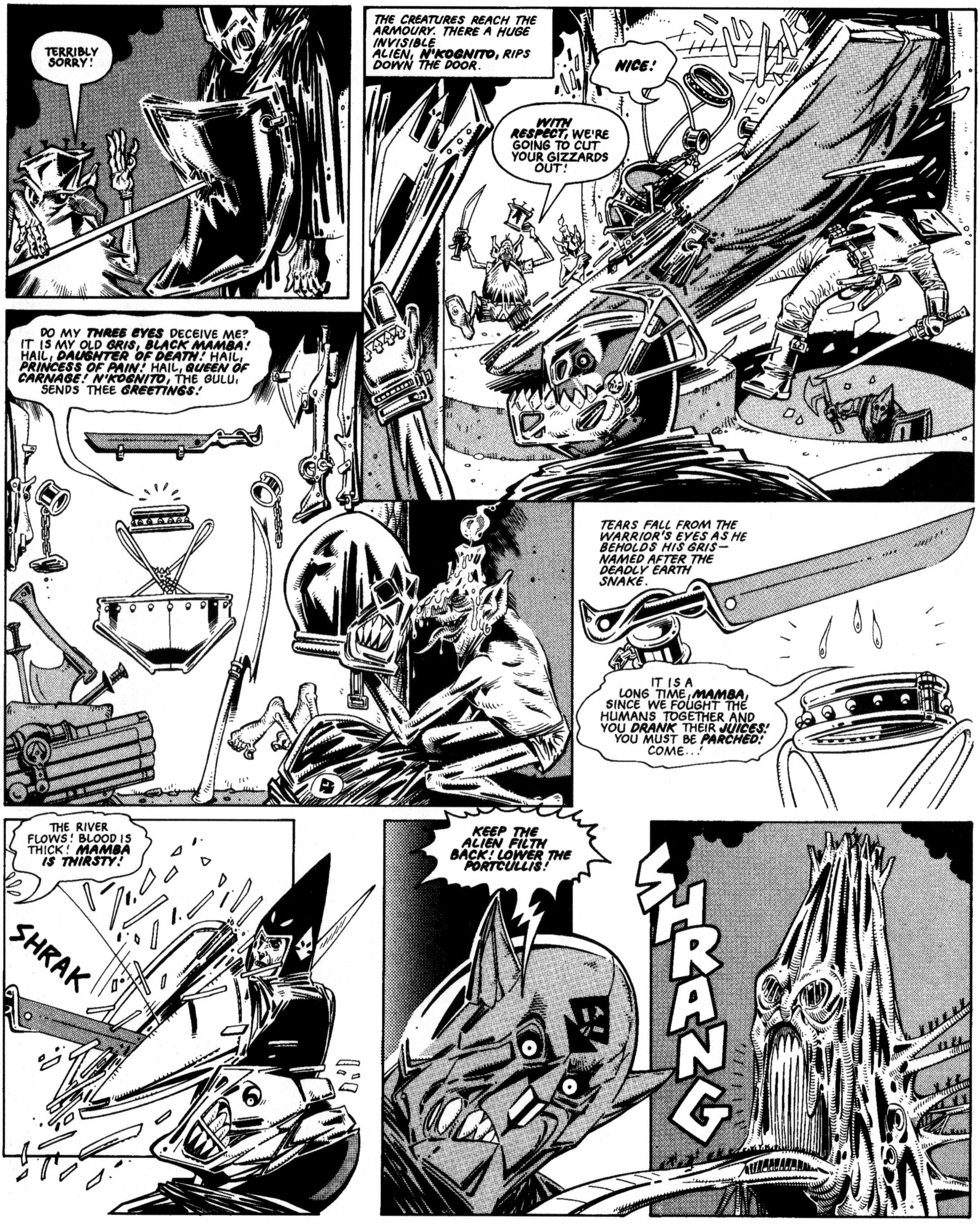
TERRIBLY SORRY!
THE CREATURES REACH THE ARMOURY. THERE A HUGE INVISIBLE ALIEN, N'KOGNITO, RIPS DOWN THE DOOR.
NICE!
WITH RESPECT, WE'RE GOING TO CUT YOUR GIZZARDS OUT!
DO MY THREE EYES DECEIVE ME? IT IS MY OLD GRIS, BLACK MAMBA! HAIL, DAUGHTER OF DEATH! HAIL, PRINCESS OF PAIN! HAIL, QUEEN OF CARNAGE! N'KOGNITO, THE GULU, SENDS THEE GREETINGS!
TEARS FALL FROM THE WARRIOR'S EYES AS HE BEHOLDS HIS GRIS— NAMED AFTER THE DEADLY EARTH SNAKE.
IT IS A LONG TIME, MAMBA, SINCE WE FOUGHT THE HUMANS TOGETHER AND YOU DRANK THEIR JUICES! YOU MUST BE PARCHED! COME..!
THE RIVER FLOWS! BLOOD IS THICK! MAMBA IS THIRSTY!
SHRAK
KEEP THE ALIEN FILTH BACK! LOWER THE PORTCULLIS!
SHRANG

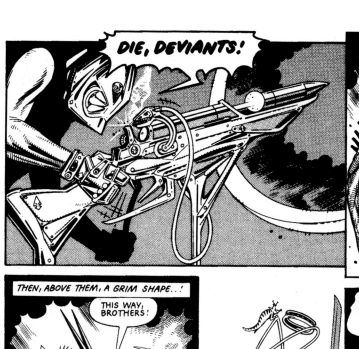

DIE, DEVIANTS!

BACK! WE'LL HAVE TO FIND ANOTHER WAY OUT!

PLEASE EXCUSE US!

THEN, ABOVE THEM, A GRIM SHAPE..!

THIS WAY, BROTHERS!

IT IS OUR MASTER—THE WARLOCK!

GREETINGS, LORD! CAN I BE WORTHY TO SERVE YOU AGAIN? I N'KOGNITO, THE BULU, WHO HAS FALLEN IN BATTLE!

OFF YOUR KNEES, N'KOGNITO! I STILL HAVE NEED OF YOUR SKILLS!

GOOD DAY TO YOU, NEMESIS OLD LOVE!

KREMLIN! STRANGE THAT YOU AND I SHOULD FIGHT ON THE SAME SIDE!

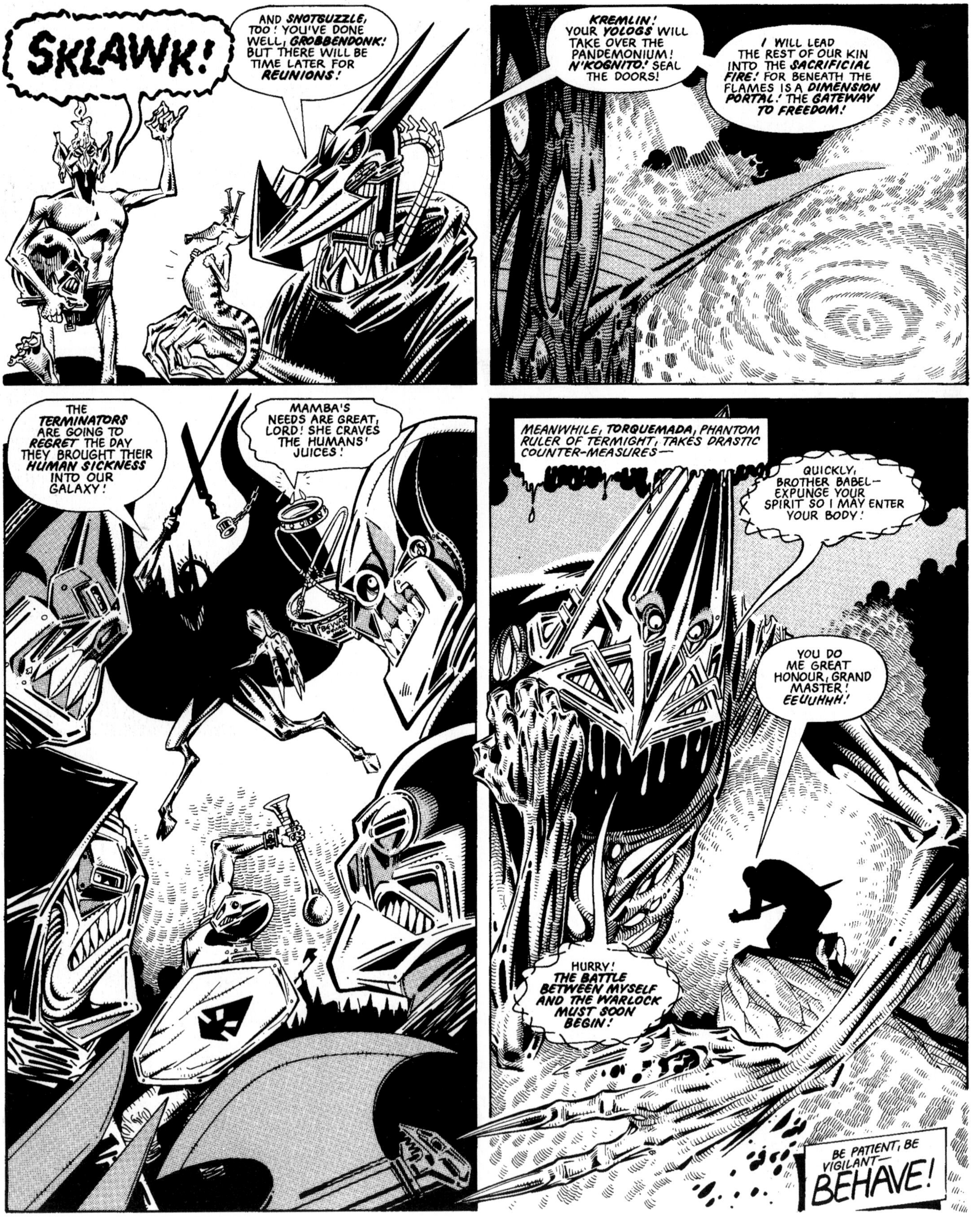
SKLAWK!
AND SNOTSUZZLE, TOO! YOU'VE DONE WELL, GROBBENDONK! BUT THERE WILL BE TIME LATER FOR REUNIONS!
KREMLIN! YOUR YOLOGS WILL TAKE OVER THE PANDEMONIUM! N'KOGNITO! SEAL THE DOORS!
I WILL LEAD THE REST OF OUR KIN INTO THE SACRIFICIAL FIRE! FOR BENEATH THE FLAMES IS A DIMENSION PORTAL! THE GATEWAY TO FREEDOM!
THE TERMINATORS ARE GOING TO REGRET THE DAY THEY BROUGHT THEIR HUMAN SICKNESS INTO OUR GALAXY!
MAMBA'S NEEDS ARE GREAT, LORD! SHE CRAVES THE HUMANS' JUICES!
MEANWHILE, TORQUEMADA, PHANTOM RULER OF TERMIGHT, TAKES DRASTIC COUNTER-MEASURES—
QUICKLY, BROTHER BABEL—EXPUNGE YOUR SPIRIT SO I MAY ENTER YOUR BODY!
YOU DO ME GREAT HONOUR, GRAND MASTER! EEUUHHH!
HURRY! THE BATTLE BETWEEN MYSELF AND THE WARLOCK MUST SOON BEGIN!
BE PATIENT, BE VIGILANT— BEHAVE!

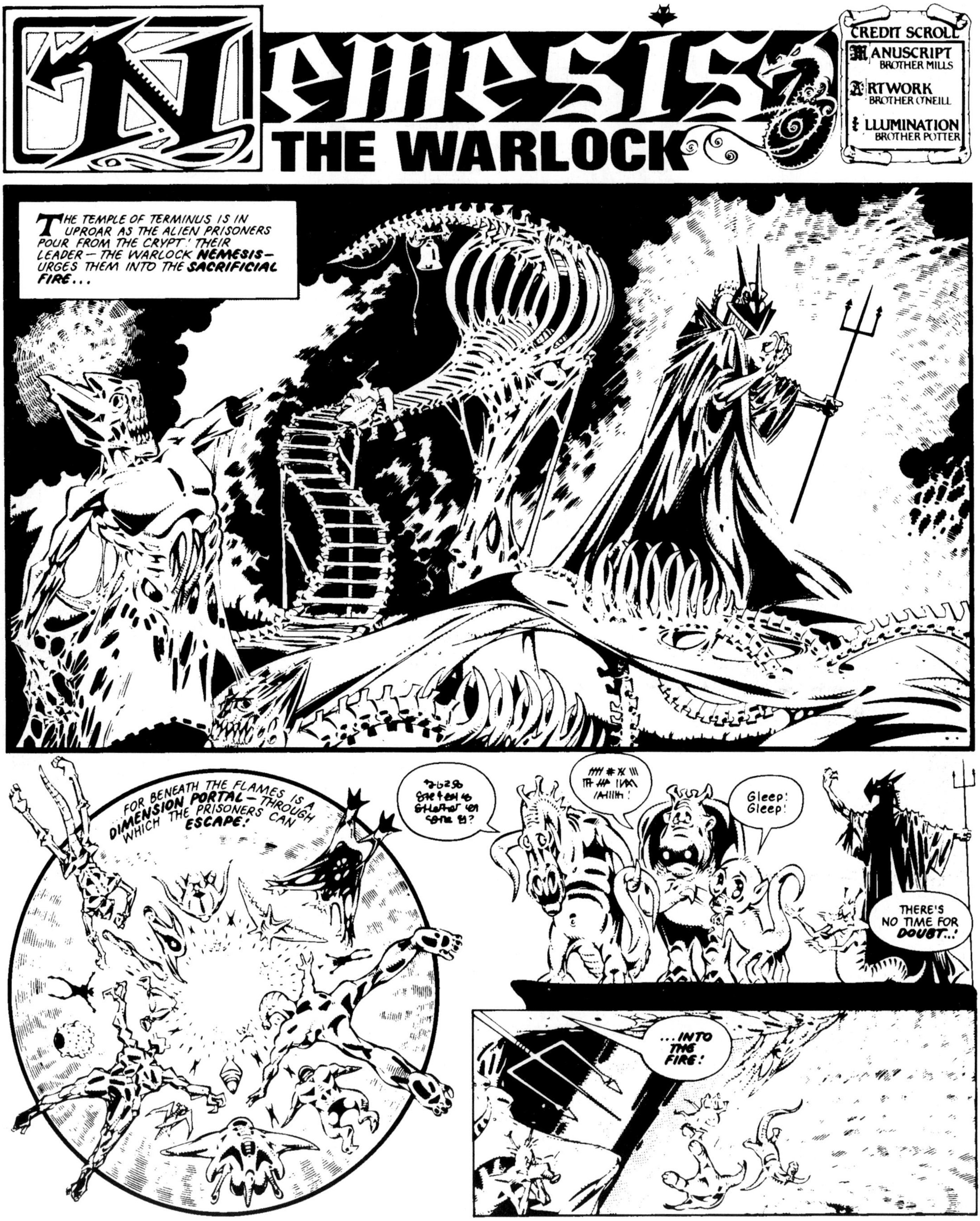
Nemesis
THE WARLOCK
CREDIT SCROLL
MANUSCRIPT BROTHER MILLS
ARTWORK BROTHER O'NEILL
ILLUMINATION BROTHER POTTER
THE TEMPLE OF TERMINUS IS IN UPROAR AS THE ALIEN PRISONERS POUR FROM THE CRYPT! THEIR LEADER — THE WARLOCK NEMESIS — URGES THEM INTO THE SACRIFICIAL FIRE...
FOR BENEATH THE FLAMES IS A DIMENSION PORTAL — THROUGH WHICH THE PRISONERS CAN ESCAPE!
Gleep! Gleep!
THERE'S NO TIME FOR DOUBT..!
...INTO THE FIRE!

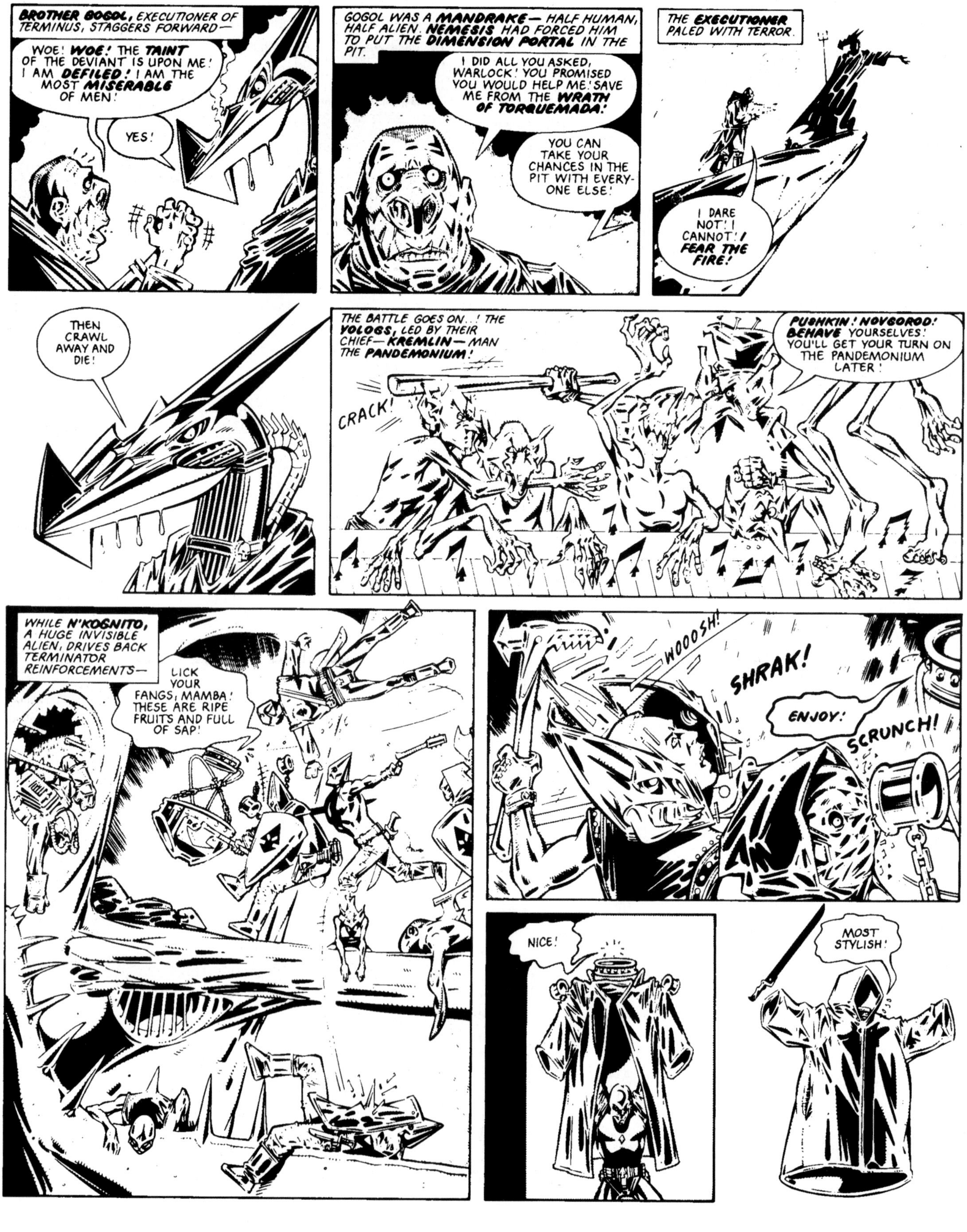

BROTHER GOGOL, EXECUTIONER OF TERMINUS, STAGGERS FORWARD—
WOE! WOE! THE TAINT OF THE DEVIANT IS UPON ME! I AM DEFILED! I AM THE MOST MISERABLE OF MEN!
YES!
GOGOL WAS A MANDRAKE— HALF HUMAN, HALF ALIEN. NEMESIS HAD FORCED HIM TO PUT THE DIMENSION PORTAL IN THE PIT.
I DID ALL YOU ASKED, WARLOCK! YOU PROMISED YOU WOULD HELP ME! SAVE ME FROM THE WRATH OF TORQUEMADA!
YOU CAN TAKE YOUR CHANCES IN THE PIT WITH EVERY-ONE ELSE!
THE EXECUTIONER PALED WITH TERROR.
I DARE NOT! I CANNOT! I FEAR THE FIRE!
THEN CRAWL AWAY AND DIE!
THE BATTLE GOES ON..! THE VOLOGS, LED BY THEIR CHIEF— KREMLIN— MAN THE PANDEMONIUM!
CRACK!
PUSHKIN! NOVGOROD! BEHAVE YOURSELVES! YOU'LL GET YOUR TURN ON THE PANDEMONIUM LATER!
WHILE N'KOGNITO, A HUGE INVISIBLE ALIEN, DRIVES BACK TERMINATOR REINFORCEMENTS—
LICK YOUR FANGS, MAMBA! THESE ARE RIPE FRUITS AND FULL OF SAP!
WOOOSH!
SHRAK!
ENJOY!
SCRUNCH!
NICE!
MOST STYLISH!

MEANWHILE, *TORQUEMADA*, GRAND MASTER OF TERMIGHT, PLANS TO JOIN THE FRAY...

HURRY UP AND DIE, BROTHER BABEL!

I-I'M DOING MY BEST, GRAND MASTER!

UUUUGHH

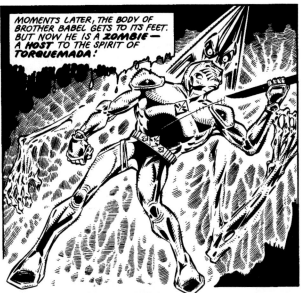

MOMENTS LATER, THE BODY OF BROTHER BABEL GETS TO ITS FEET. BUT NOW HE IS A *ZOMBIE*— A *HOST* TO THE SPIRIT OF *TORQUEMADA!*

THE WARLOCK HAS... *RUINED*... OUR GREAT FEAST OF ZAMARKAND! BUT HE WILL... *PAYYYYYY!*

AND... *DEARLY!*

HE COMES UPON THE WRETCHED FIGURE OF BROTHER GOGOL...

I SENSE YOU HAD A PART IN THIS BETRAYAL...

TORQUEMADA..?!

UGH! YOU BEAR THE FEATURES OF... A *MANDRAKE!* I SEE NOW WHY YOU GAVE AID TO THE DEVIANT!

I-I HAD NO CHOICE, GRAND MASTER!

PLEASE... DON'T *KILL* ME!

KILL YOU..? *SHAME* ON YOU, BROTHER GOGOL! SURELY YOU KNOW ME BETTER THAN THAT?

⟨CRUNCH!⟩

DEATH IS *TOO GOOD* FOR YOU!

I WILL DEAL WITH YOU... *LATER!*

TORQUEMADA HEADS TOWARDS THE SACRIFICIAL FIRE...

OUT OF MY WAY! THERE IS ONE DEVIANT WHO I MUST DESTROY *PERSONALLY!* THE ARCH DEVIANT— *NEMESIS!*

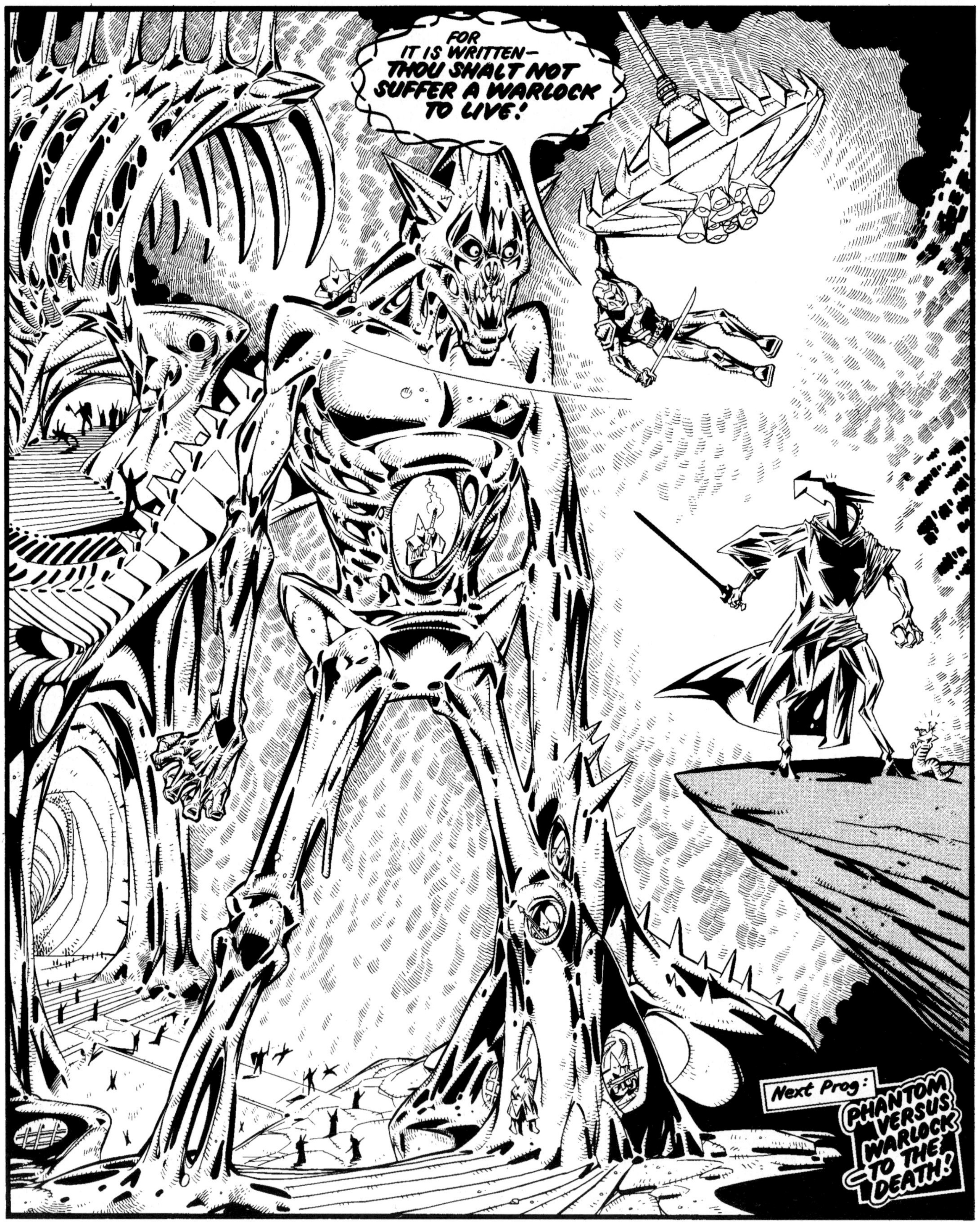
FOR IT IS WRITTEN— THOU SHALT NOT SUFFER A WARLOCK TO LIVE!
Next Prog:
PHANTOM VERSUS WARLOCK —TO THE DEATH!

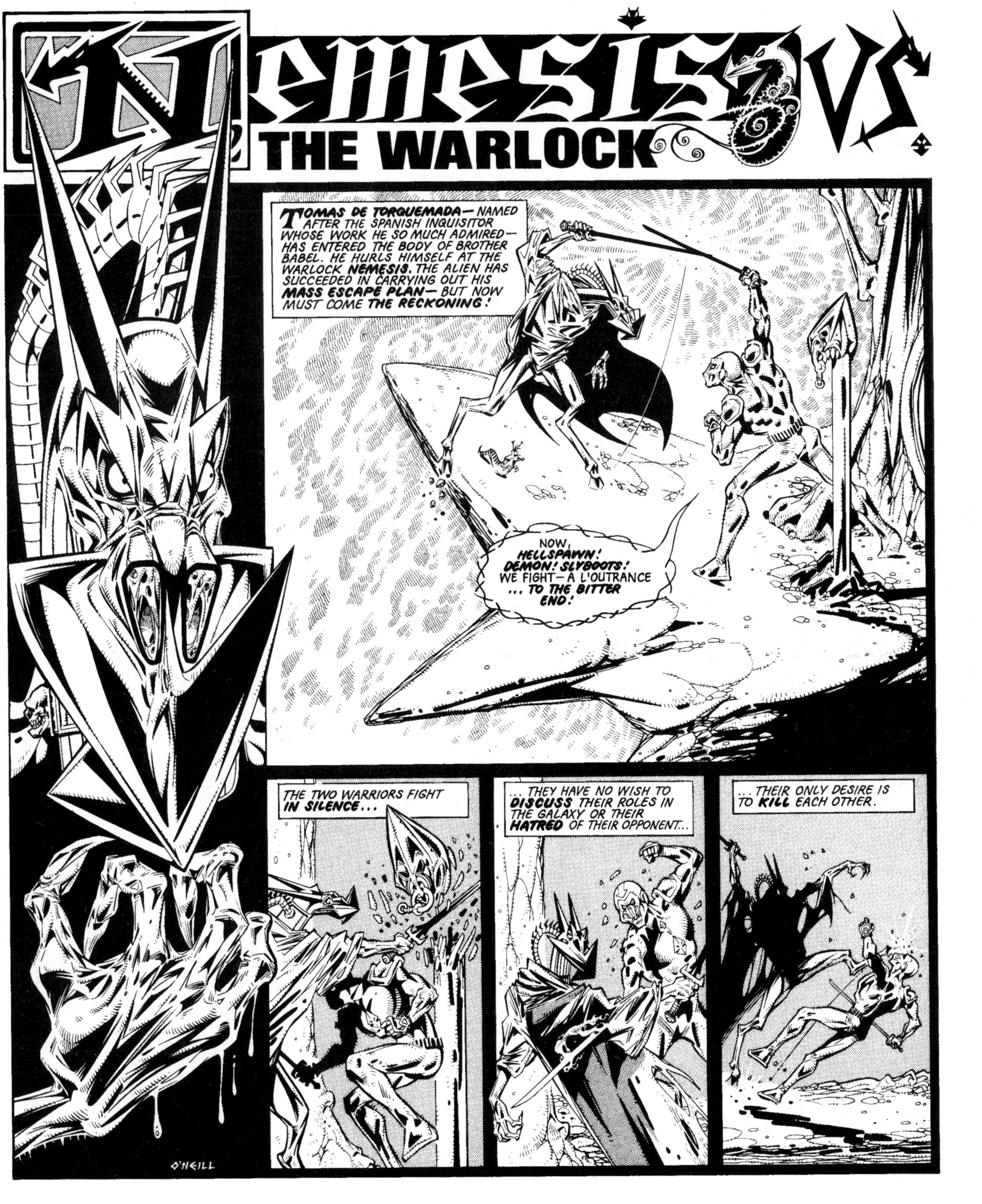
NEMESIS VS THE WARLOCK
TOMAS DE TORQUEMADA— NAMED AFTER THE SPANISH INQUISITOR WHOSE WORK HE SO MUCH ADMIRED— HAS ENTERED THE BODY OF BROTHER BABEL. HE HURLS HIMSELF AT THE WARLOCK NEMESIS. THE ALIEN HAS SUCCEEDED IN CARRYING OUT HIS MASS ESCAPE PLAN— BUT NOW MUST COME THE RECKONING!
NOW, HELLSPAWN! DEMON! SLYBOOTS! WE FIGHT— A L'OUTRANCE ... TO THE BITTER END!
THE TWO WARRIORS FIGHT IN SILENCE...
... THEY HAVE NO WISH TO DISCUSS THEIR ROLES IN THE GALAXY OR THEIR HATRED OF THEIR OPPONENT...
... THEIR ONLY DESIRE IS TO KILL EACH OTHER.
O'NEILL

TORQUEMADA
GRAND MASTER of TERMIGHT

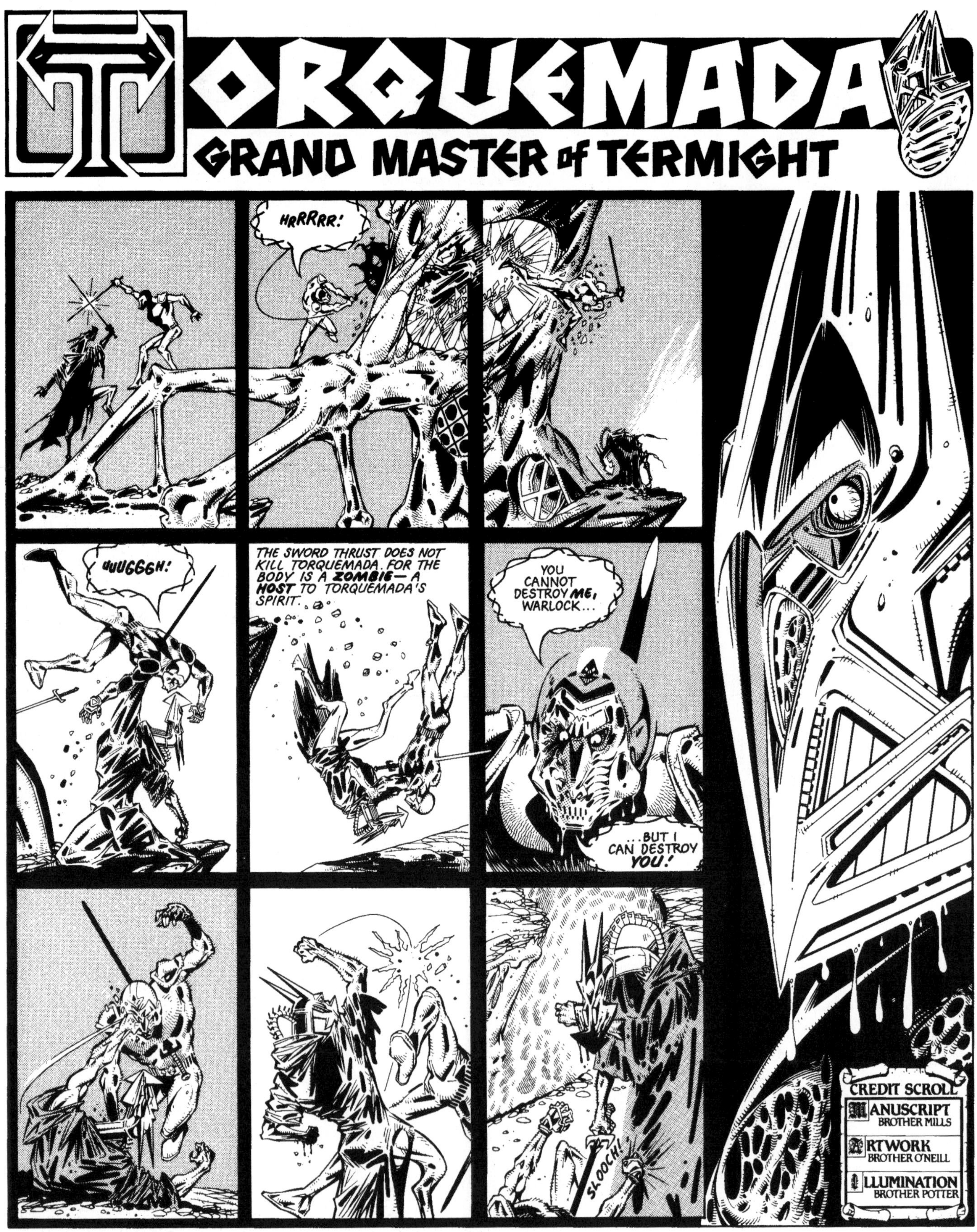

HRRRRR!
UUUGGGH!
THE SWORD THRUST DOES NOT KILL TORQUEMADA. FOR THE BODY IS A ZOMBIE— A HOST TO TORQUEMADA'S SPIRIT.
YOU CANNOT DESTROY ME, WARLOCK...
...BUT I CAN DESTROY YOU!
SLOOCH!
CREDIT SCROLL
MANUSCRIPT BROTHER MILLS
ARTWORK BROTHER O'NEILL
ILLUMINATION BROTHER POTTER

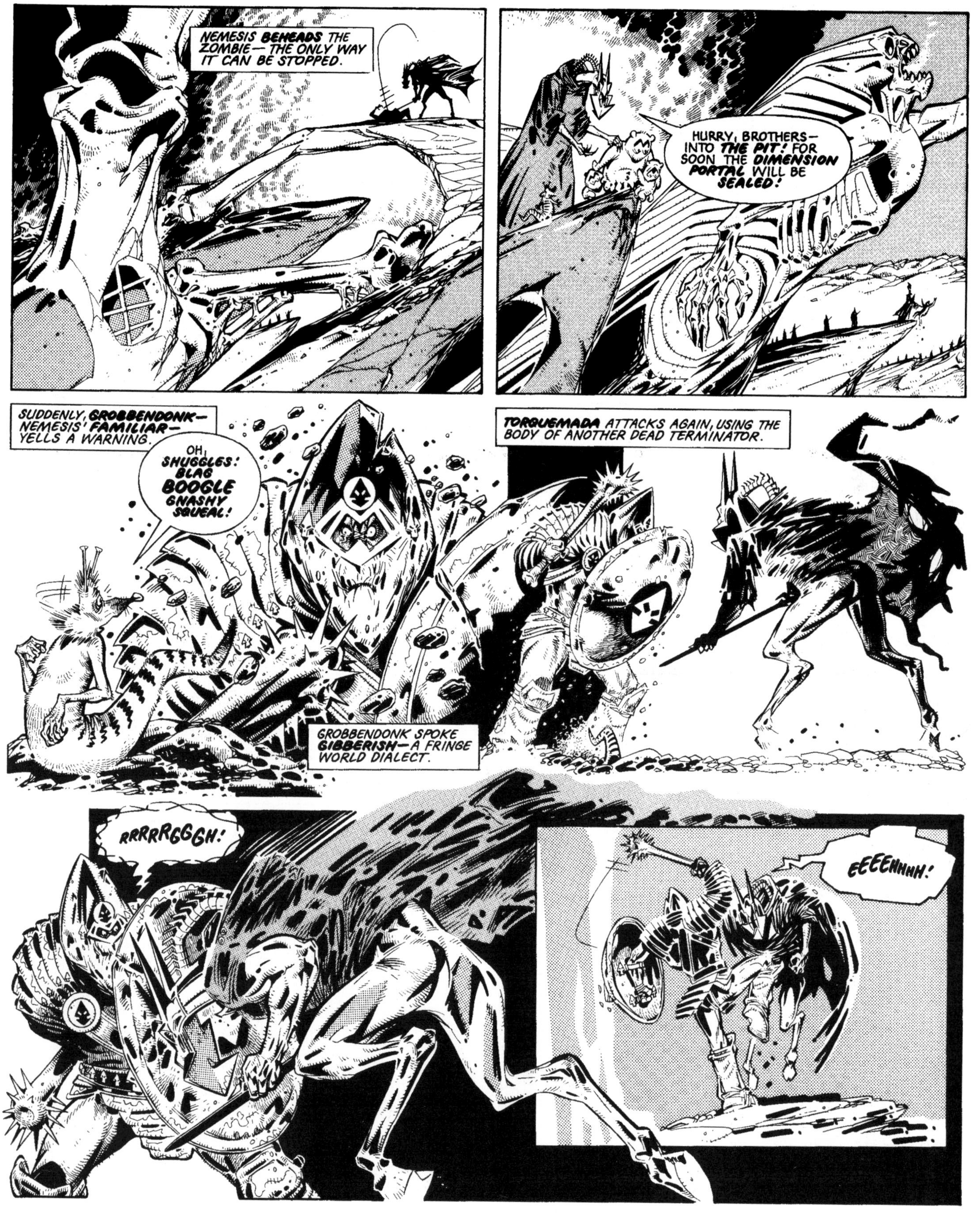

NEMESIS BEHEADS THE ZOMBIE— THE ONLY WAY IT CAN BE STOPPED.
HURRY, BROTHERS— INTO THE PIT! FOR SOON THE DIMENSION PORTAL WILL BE SEALED!
SUDDENLY, GROBBENDONK— NEMESIS' FAMILIAR— YELLS A WARNING.
OH, SHUGGLES! BLAG BOOGLE GNASHY SQUEAL!
GROBBENDONK SPOKE GIBBERISH— A FRINGE WORLD DIALECT.
TORQUEMADA ATTACKS AGAIN, USING THE BODY OF ANOTHER DEAD TERMINATOR.
RRRRRGGGH!
EEEEHHHH!

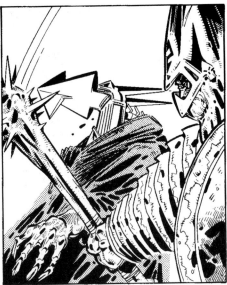

HURRRRR!

SPITTING FIRE AND VENOM, THE WARLOCK COUNTER-ATTACKS...

?

AAAGGGGGGHH!

BUT NOW ANOTHER DEAD TERMINATOR RISES TO ITS FEET.

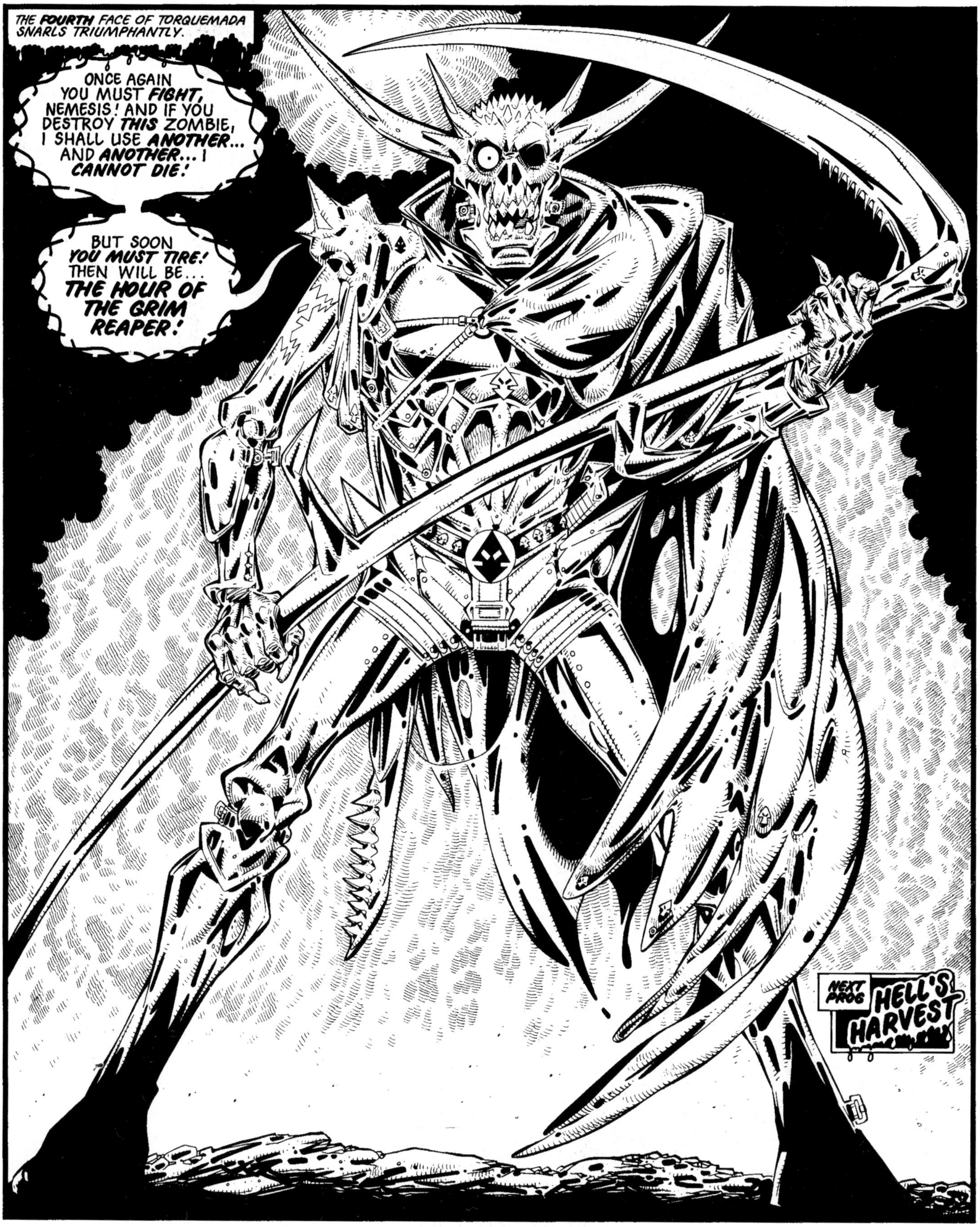
THE FOURTH FACE OF TORQUEMADA SNARLS TRIUMPHANTLY.
ONCE AGAIN YOU MUST FIGHT, NEMESIS! AND IF YOU DESTROY THIS ZOMBIE, I SHALL USE ANOTHER... AND ANOTHER... I CANNOT DIE!
BUT SOON YOU MUST TIRE! THEN WILL BE... THE HOUR OF THE GRIM REAPER!
NEXT PROG HELL'S HARVEST

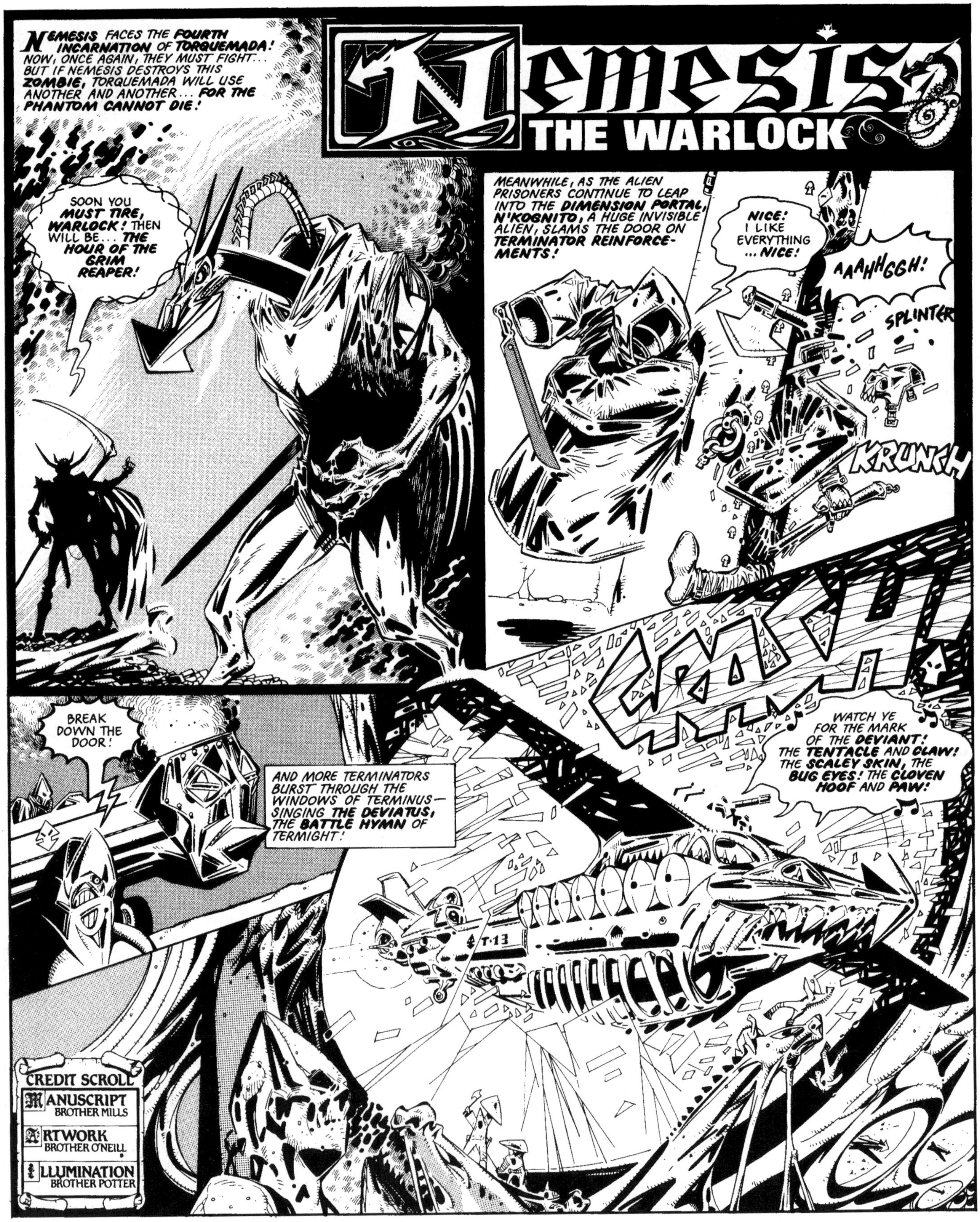

NEMESIS FACES THE FOURTH INCARNATION OF TORQUEMADA! NOW, ONCE AGAIN, THEY MUST FIGHT... BUT IF NEMESIS DESTROYS THIS ZOMBIE, TORQUEMADA WILL USE ANOTHER AND ANOTHER... FOR THE PHANTOM CANNOT DIE!
NEMESIS THE WARLOCK
SOON YOU MUST TIRE, WARLOCK! THEN WILL BE... THE HOUR OF THE GRIM REAPER!
MEANWHILE, AS THE ALIEN PRISONERS CONTINUE TO LEAP INTO THE DIMENSION PORTAL, N'KOGNITO, A HUGE INVISIBLE ALIEN, SLAMS THE DOOR ON TERMINATOR REINFORCEMENTS!
NICE! I LIKE EVERYTHING ...NICE!
AAAHHGGH!
SPLINTER
KRUNCH
CRASH!
BREAK DOWN THE DOOR!
AND MORE TERMINATORS BURST THROUGH THE WINDOWS OF TERMINUS— SINGING THE DEVIATUS, THE BATTLE HYMN OF TERMIGHT!
WATCH YE FOR THE MARK OF THE DEVIANT! THE TENTACLE AND CLAW! THE SCALEY SKIN, THE BUG EYES! THE CLOVEN HOOF AND PAW!
T·13
CREDIT SCROLL
MANUSCRIPT BROTHER MILLS
ARTWORK BROTHER O'NEILL
ILLUMINATION BROTHER POTTER

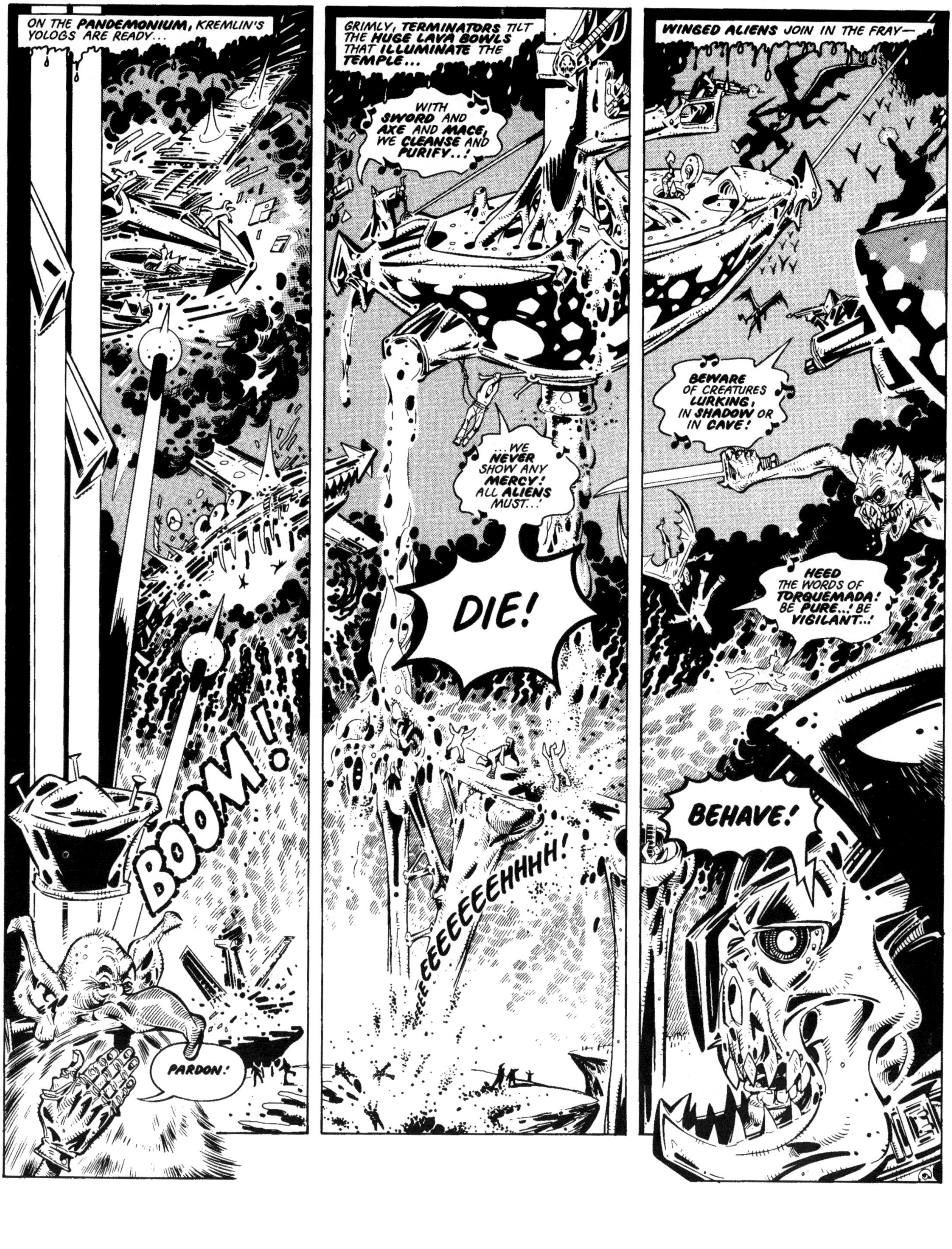
ON THE PANDEMONIUM, KREMLIN'S YOLOGS ARE READY...
BOOM!
PARDON!
GRIMLY, TERMINATORS TILT THE HUGE LAVA BOWLS THAT ILLUMINATE THE TEMPLE...
WITH SWORD AND AXE AND MACE, WE CLEANSE AND PURIFY...!
...WE NEVER SHOW ANY MERCY! ALL ALIENS MUST...!
DIE!
EEEEEEEEEEEEHHHH!
WINGED ALIENS JOIN IN THE FRAY—
BEWARE OF CREATURES LURKING, IN SHADOW OR IN CAVE!
HEED THE WORDS OF TORQUEMADA! BE PURE...! BE VIGILANT...!
BEHAVE!

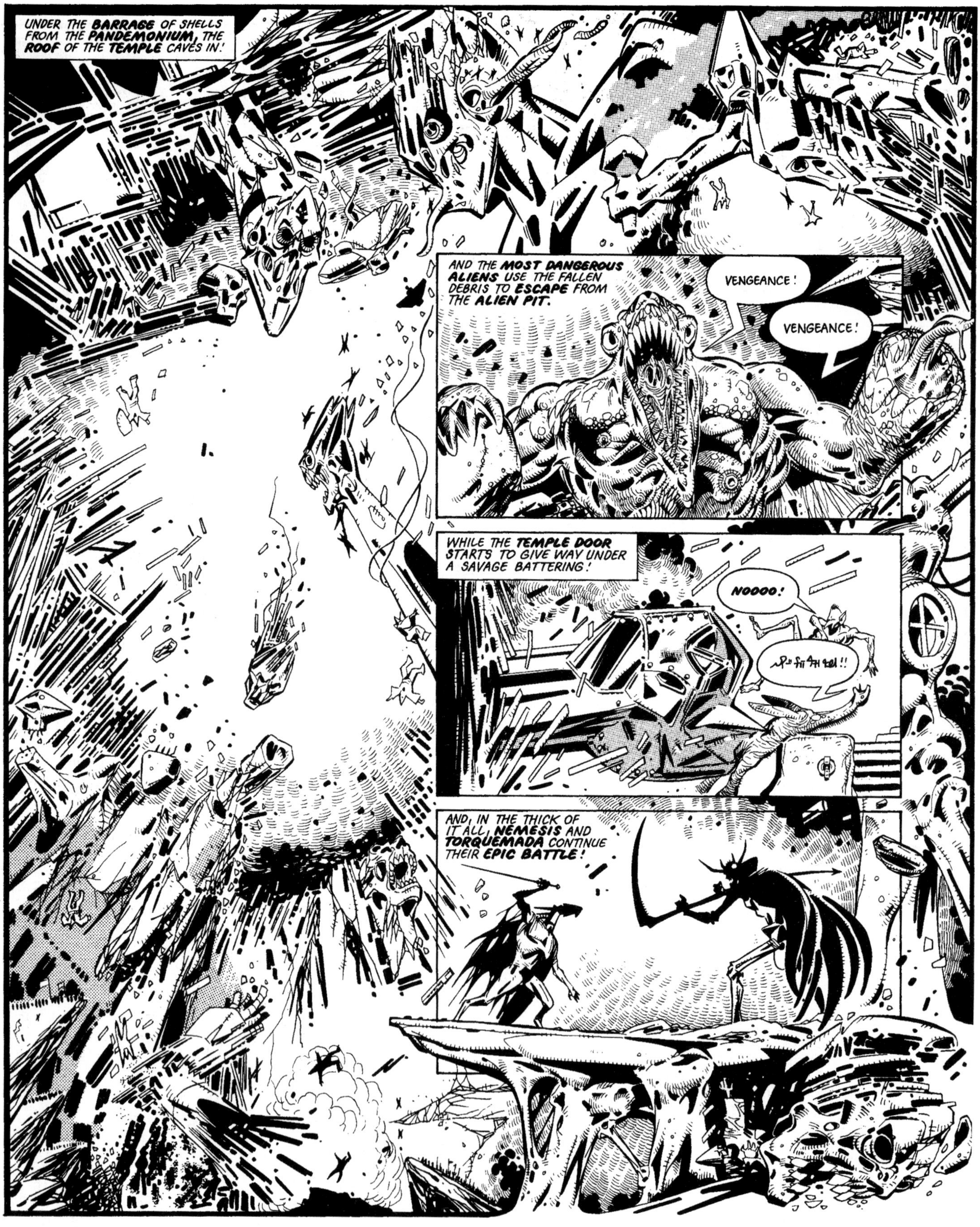
UNDER THE BARRAGE OF SHELLS FROM THE PANDEMONIUM, THE ROOF OF THE TEMPLE CAVES IN!
AND THE MOST DANGEROUS ALIENS USE THE FALLEN DEBRIS TO ESCAPE FROM THE ALIEN PIT.
VENGEANCE!
VENGEANCE!
WHILE THE TEMPLE DOOR STARTS TO GIVE WAY UNDER A SAVAGE BATTERING!
NOOOO!
AND, IN THE THICK OF IT ALL, NEMESIS AND TORQUEMADA CONTINUE THEIR EPIC BATTLE!

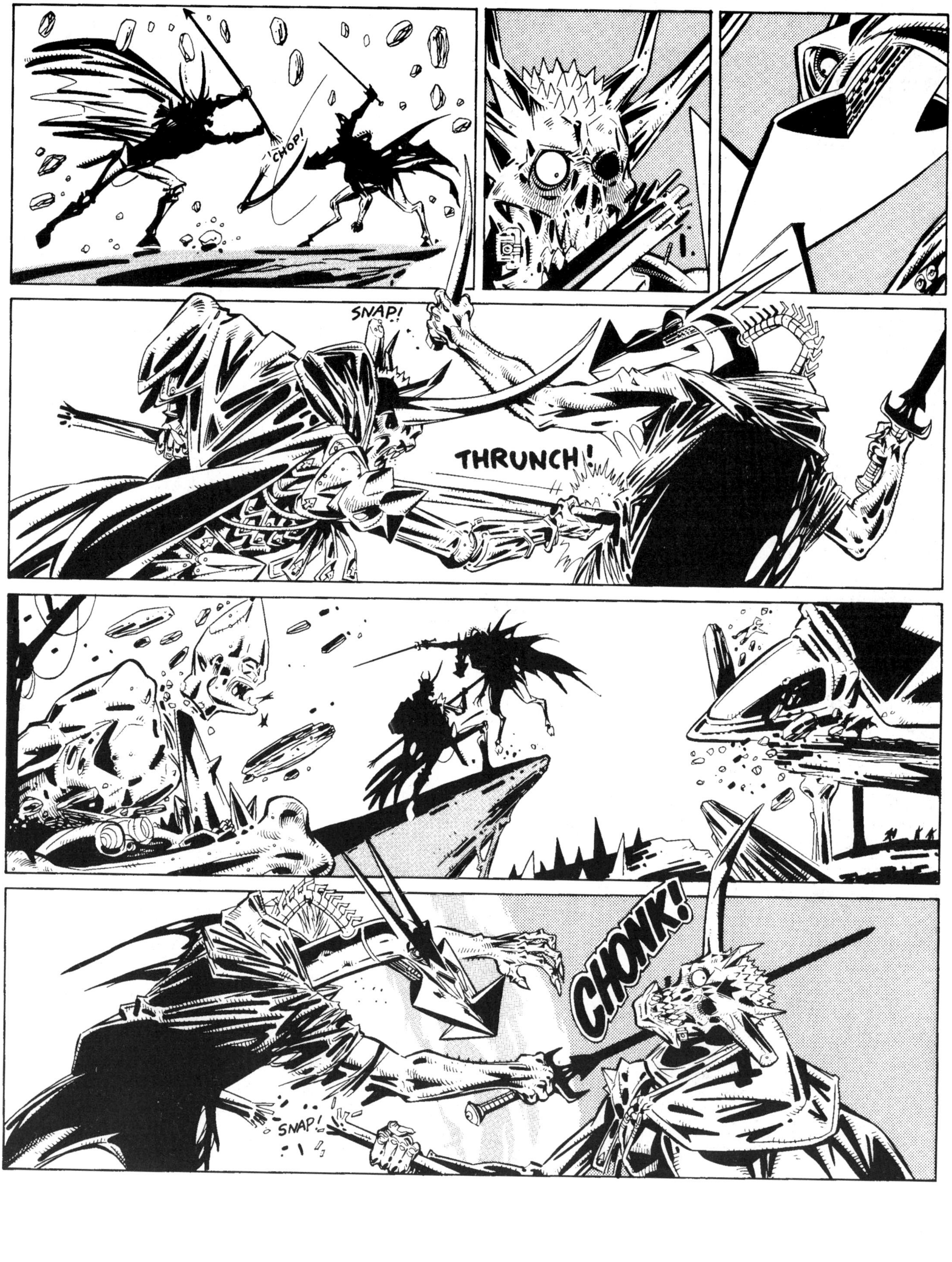
CHOP!
SNAP!
THRUNCH!
CHONK!
SNAP!

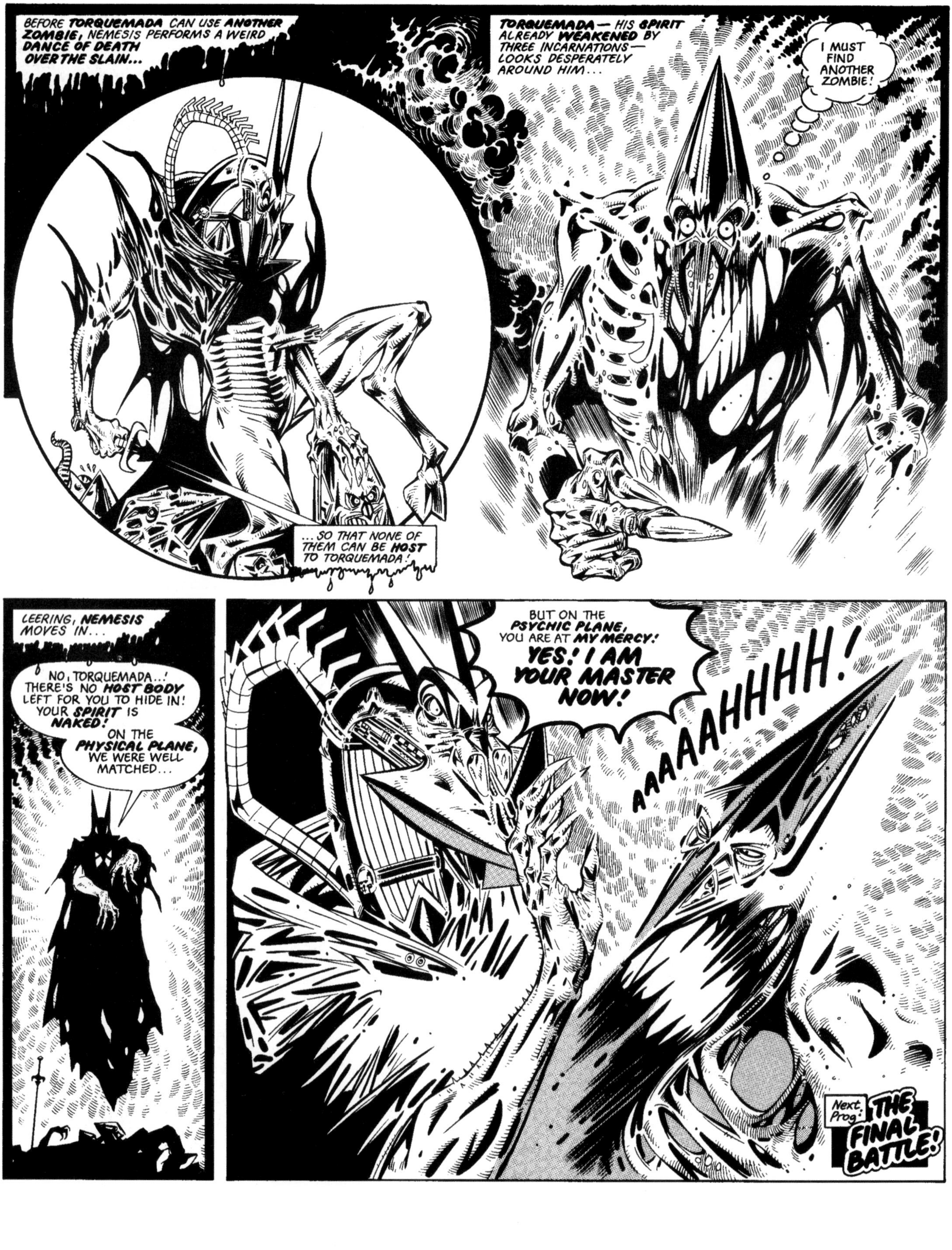
BEFORE TORQUEMADA CAN USE ANOTHER ZOMBIE, NEMESIS PERFORMS A WEIRD DANCE OF DEATH OVER THE SLAIN...
...SO THAT NONE OF THEM CAN BE HOST TO TORQUEMADA!
TORQUEMADA— HIS SPIRIT ALREADY WEAKENED BY THREE INCARNATIONS— LOOKS DESPERATELY AROUND HIM...
I MUST FIND ANOTHER ZOMBIE!
LEERING, NEMESIS MOVES IN...
NO, TORQUEMADA..! THERE'S NO HOST BODY LEFT FOR YOU TO HIDE IN! YOUR SPIRIT IS NAKED!
ON THE PHYSICAL PLANE, WE WERE WELL MATCHED...
BUT ON THE PSYCHIC PLANE, YOU ARE AT MY MERCY! YES! I AM YOUR MASTER NOW!
AAAAAHHHHH!
Next Prog: THE FINAL BATTLE!

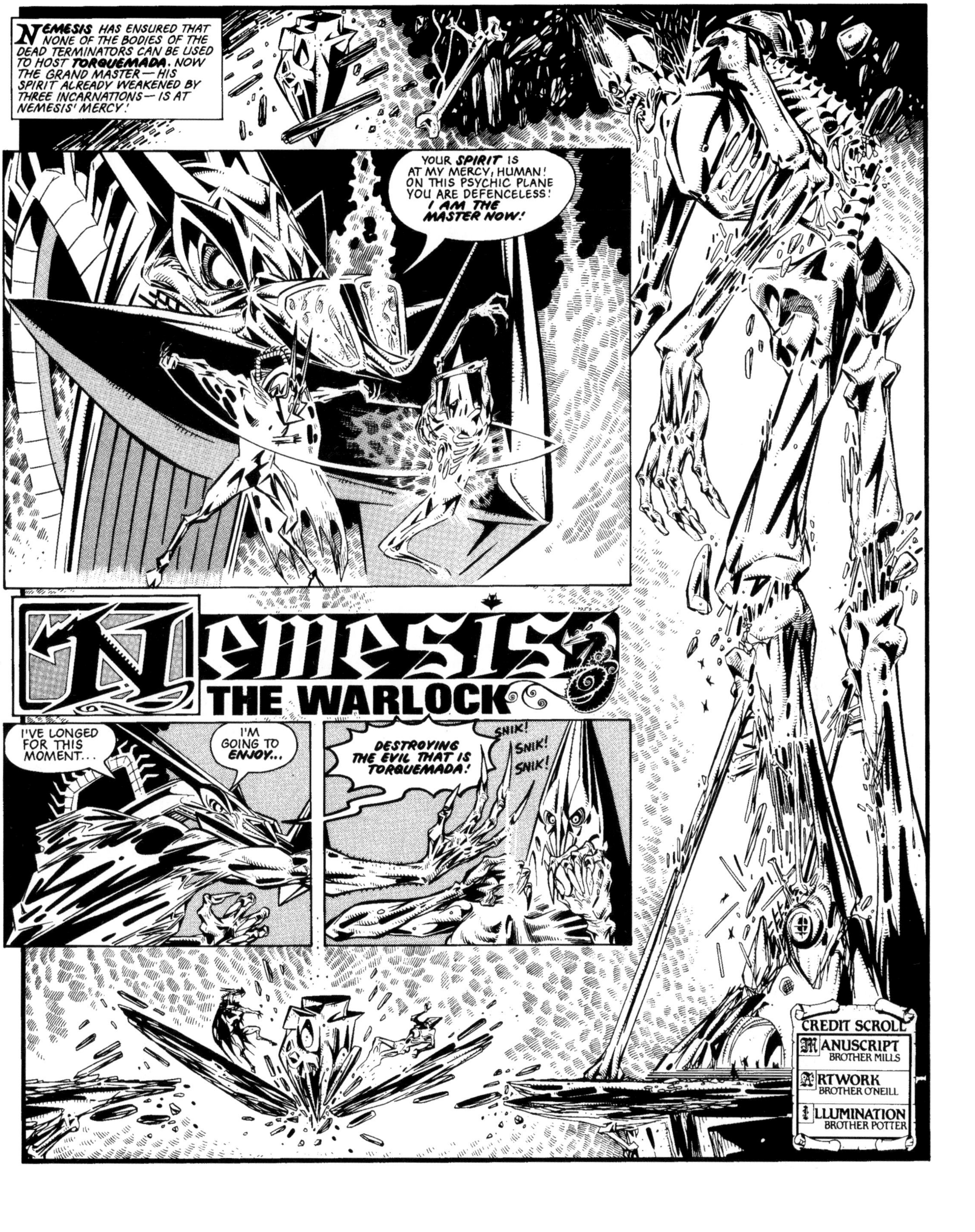
NEMESIS HAS ENSURED THAT NONE OF THE BODIES OF THE DEAD TERMINATORS CAN BE USED TO HOST TORQUEMADA. NOW THE GRAND MASTER — HIS SPIRIT ALREADY WEAKENED BY THREE INCARNATIONS — IS AT NEMESIS' MERCY!
YOUR SPIRIT IS AT MY MERCY, HUMAN! ON THIS PSYCHIC PLANE YOU ARE DEFENCELESS! I AM THE MASTER NOW!
NEMESIS THE WARLOCK
I'VE LONGED FOR THIS MOMENT...
I'M GOING TO ENJOY...
DESTROYING THE EVIL THAT IS TORQUEMADA!
SNIK! SNIK! SNIK!
CREDIT SCROLL
MANUSCRIPT BROTHER MILLS
ARTWORK BROTHER O'NEILL
ILLUMINATION BROTHER POTTER

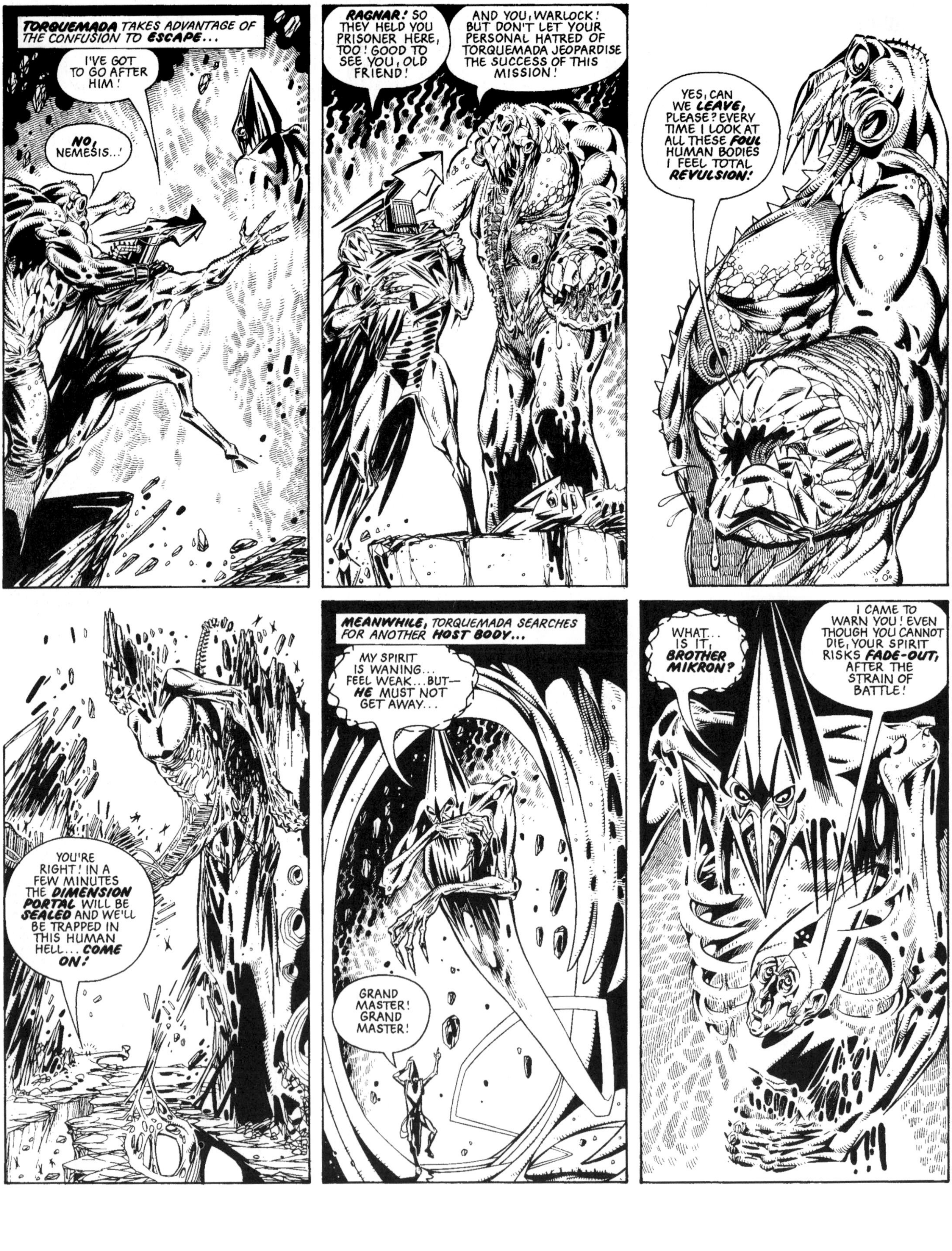

TORQUEMADA TAKES ADVANTAGE OF THE CONFUSION TO ESCAPE...
I'VE GOT TO GO AFTER HIM!
NO, NEMESIS..!
RAGNAR! SO THEY HELD YOU PRISONER HERE, TOO! GOOD TO SEE YOU, OLD FRIEND!
AND YOU, WARLOCK! BUT DON'T LET YOUR PERSONAL HATRED OF TORQUEMADA JEOPARDISE THE SUCCESS OF THIS MISSION!
YES, CAN WE LEAVE, PLEASE? EVERY TIME I LOOK AT ALL THESE FOUL HUMAN BODIES I FEEL TOTAL REVULSION!
YOU'RE RIGHT! IN A FEW MINUTES THE DIMENSION PORTAL WILL BE SEALED AND WE'LL BE TRAPPED IN THIS HUMAN HELL... COME ON!
MEANWHILE, TORQUEMADA SEARCHES FOR ANOTHER HOST BODY...
MY SPIRIT IS WANING... FEEL WEAK... BUT— HE MUST NOT GET AWAY...
GRAND MASTER! GRAND MASTER!
WHAT... IS IT, BROTHER MIKRON?
I CAME TO WARN YOU! EVEN THOUGH YOU CANNOT DIE, YOUR SPIRIT RISKS FADE-OUT, AFTER THE STRAIN OF BATTLE!

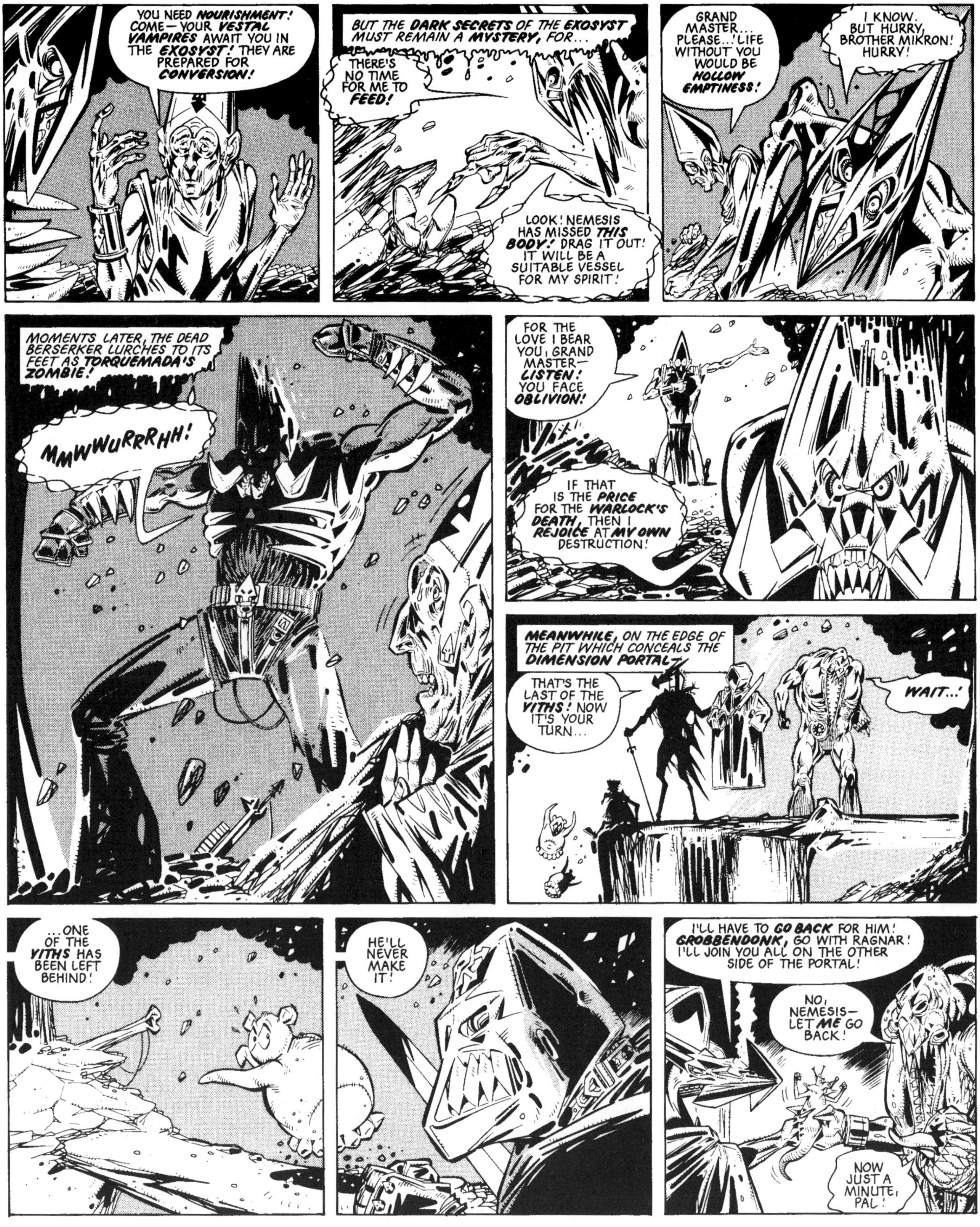

YOU NEED NOURISHMENT! COME—YOUR VESTAL VAMPIRES AWAIT YOU IN THE EXOSYST! THEY ARE PREPARED FOR CONVERSION!
BUT THE DARK SECRETS OF THE EXOSYST MUST REMAIN A MYSTERY, FOR...
THERE'S NO TIME FOR ME TO FEED!
LOOK! NEMESIS HAS MISSED THIS BODY! DRAG IT OUT! IT WILL BE A SUITABLE VESSEL FOR MY SPIRIT!
GRAND MASTER... PLEASE...! LIFE WITHOUT YOU WOULD BE HOLLOW EMPTINESS!
I KNOW. BUT HURRY, BROTHER MIKRON! HURRY!
MOMENTS LATER, THE DEAD BERSERKER LURCHES TO ITS FEET AS TORQUEMADA'S ZOMBIE!
MMWWURRRHH!
FOR THE LOVE I BEAR YOU, GRAND MASTER—LISTEN! YOU FACE OBLIVION!
IF THAT IS THE PRICE FOR THE WARLOCK'S DEATH, THEN I REJOICE AT MY OWN DESTRUCTION!
MEANWHILE, ON THE EDGE OF THE PIT WHICH CONCEALS THE DIMENSION PORTAL—
THAT'S THE LAST OF THE VITHS! NOW IT'S YOUR TURN...
WAIT...!
...ONE OF THE VITHS HAS BEEN LEFT BEHIND!
HE'LL NEVER MAKE IT!
I'LL HAVE TO GO BACK FOR HIM! GROBBENDONK, GO WITH RAGNAR! I'LL JOIN YOU ALL ON THE OTHER SIDE OF THE PORTAL!
NO, NEMESIS—LET ME GO BACK!
NOW JUST A MINUTE, PAL!

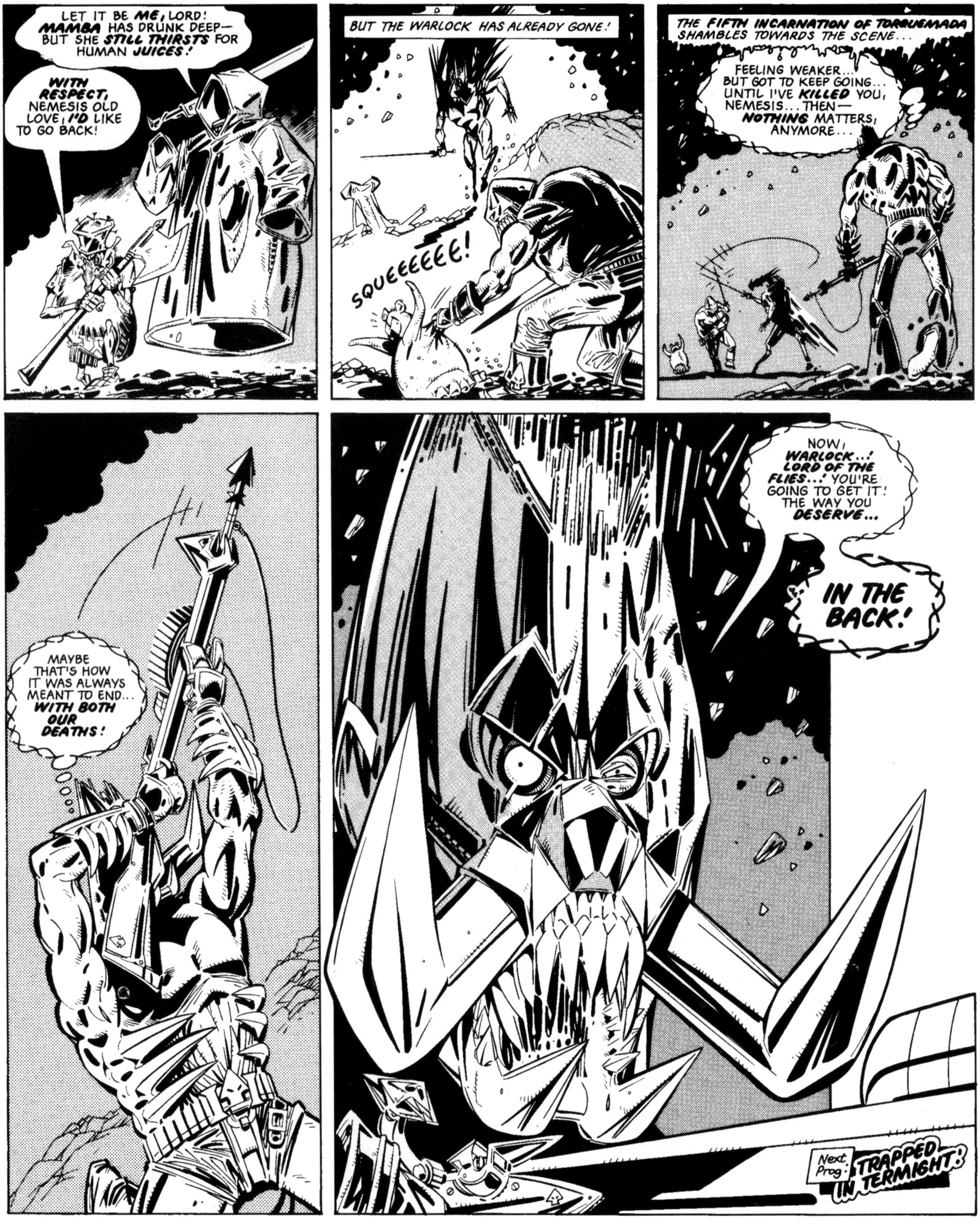
LET IT BE ME, LORD! MAMBA HAS DRUNK DEEP— BUT SHE STILL THIRSTS FOR HUMAN JUICES!
WITH RESPECT, NEMESIS OLD LOVE, I'D LIKE TO GO BACK!
BUT THE WARLOCK HAS ALREADY GONE!
SQUEEEEEEE!
THE FIFTH INCARNATION OF TORQUEMADA SHAMBLES TOWARDS THE SCENE...
FEELING WEAKER... BUT GOT TO KEEP GOING... UNTIL I'VE KILLED YOU, NEMESIS... THEN— NOTHING MATTERS, ANYMORE...
MAYBE THAT'S HOW IT WAS ALWAYS MEANT TO END... WITH BOTH OUR DEATHS!
NOW, WARLOCK..! LORD OF THE FLIES..! YOU'RE GOING TO GET IT! THE WAY YOU DESERVE...
IN THE BACK!
Next Prog: TRAPPED IN TERMIGHT!

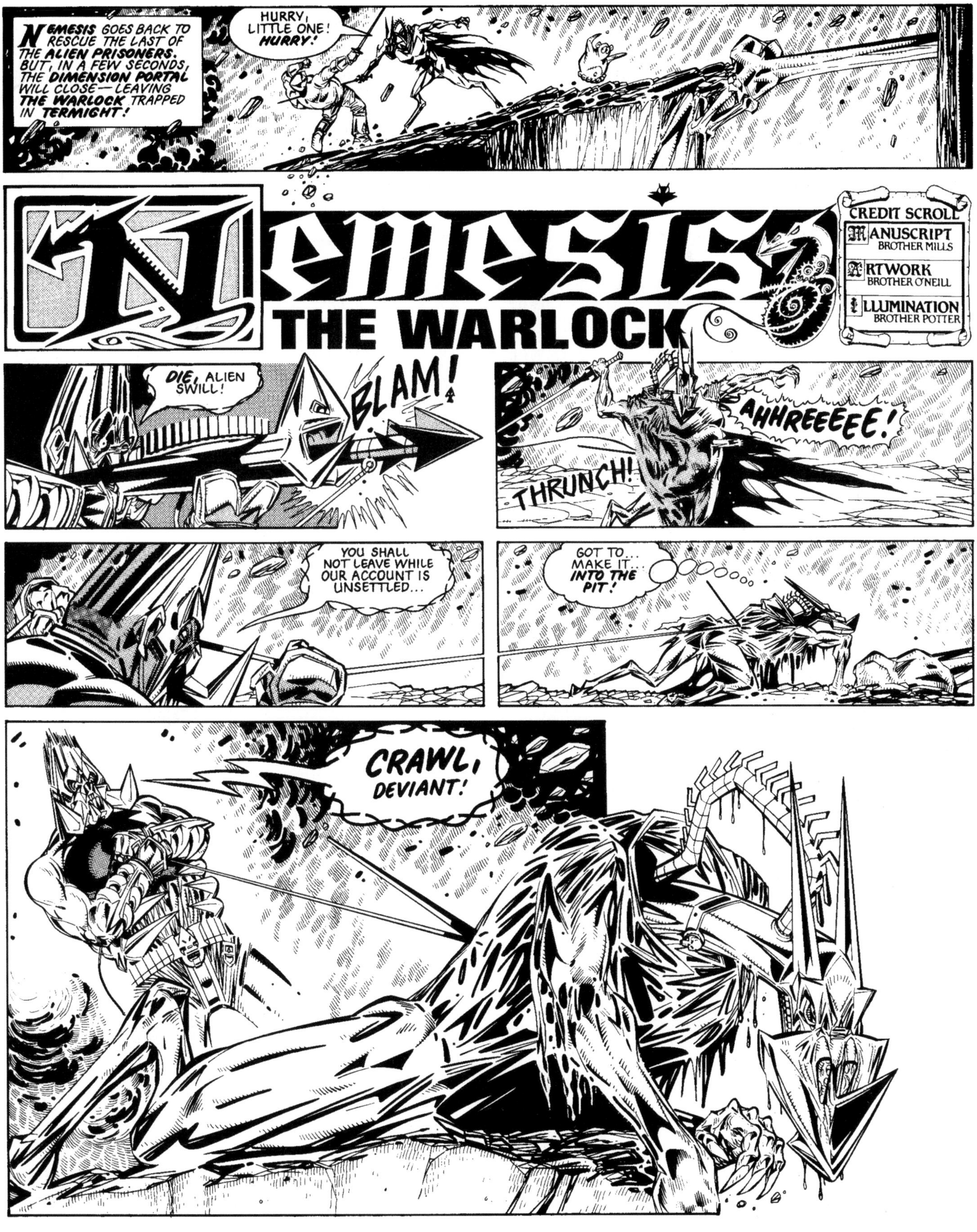

NEMESIS GOES BACK TO RESCUE THE LAST OF THE ALIEN PRISONERS. BUT, IN A FEW SECONDS, THE DIMENSION PORTAL WILL CLOSE—LEAVING THE WARLOCK TRAPPED IN TERMIGHT!
HURRY, LITTLE ONE! HURRY!
NEMESIS THE WARLOCK
CREDIT SCROLL
MANUSCRIPT BROTHER MILLS
ARTWORK BROTHER O'NEILL
ILLUMINATION BROTHER POTTER
DIE, ALIEN SWILL!
BLAM!
AHHREEEEE!
THRUNCH!
YOU SHALL NOT LEAVE WHILE OUR ACCOUNT IS UNSETTLED...
GOT TO... MAKE IT... INTO THE PIT!
CRAWL, DEVIANT!

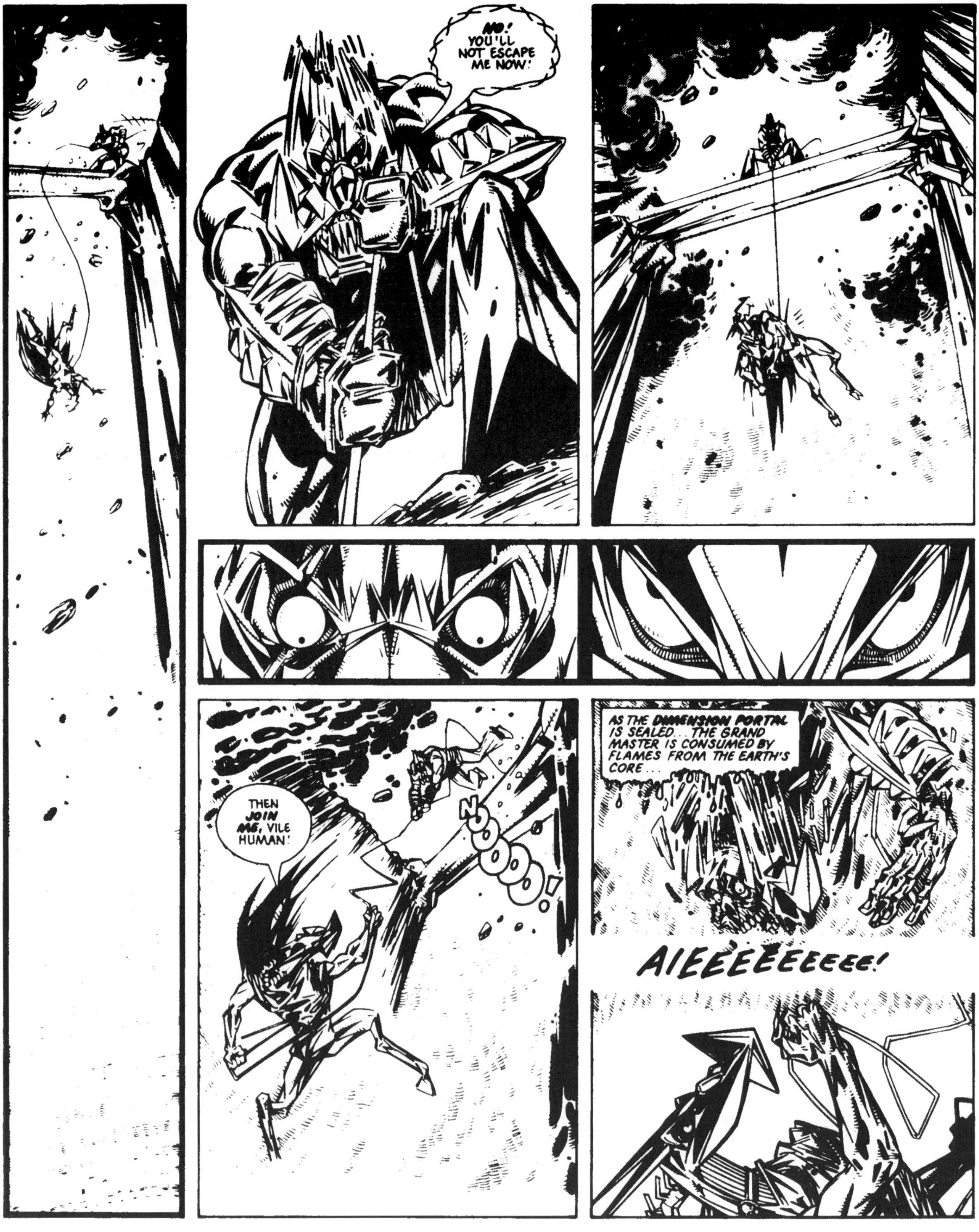

NO! YOU'LL NOT ESCAPE ME NOW!
THEN JOIN ME, VILE HUMAN!
NOOOOOO!
AS THE DIMENSION PORTAL IS SEALED... THE GRAND MASTER IS CONSUMED BY FLAMES FROM THE EARTH'S CORE...
AIEEEEEEeeee!

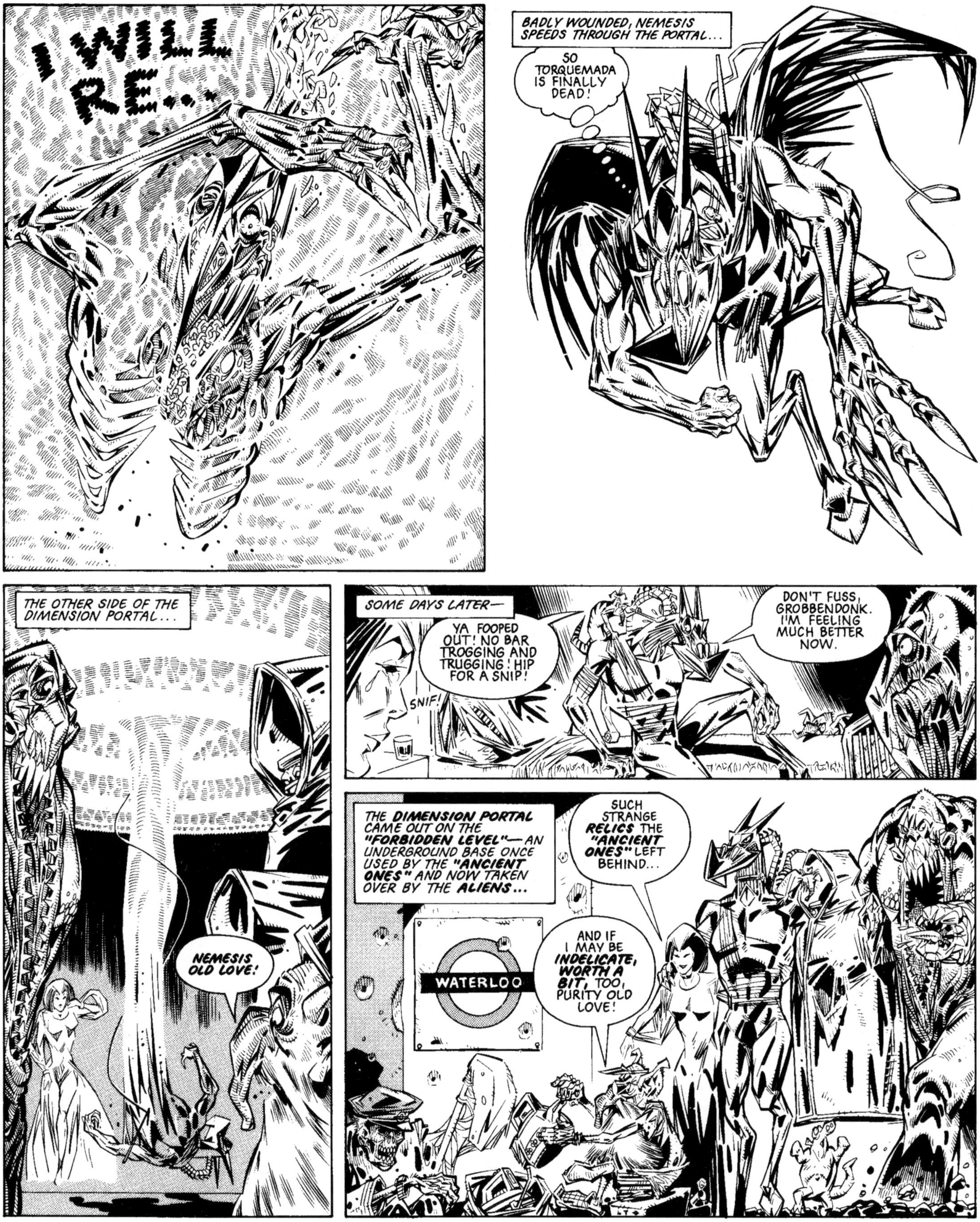
I WILL RE...
BADLY WOUNDED, NEMESIS SPEEDS THROUGH THE PORTAL...
SO TORQUEMADA IS FINALLY DEAD!
THE OTHER SIDE OF THE DIMENSION PORTAL...
NEMESIS OLD LOVE!
SOME DAYS LATER—
YA FOOPED OUT! NO BAR TROGGING AND TRUGGING! HIP FOR A SNIP!
SNIF!
DON'T FUSS, GROBBENDONK. I'M FEELING MUCH BETTER NOW.
THE DIMENSION PORTAL CAME OUT ON THE "FORBIDDEN LEVEL"—AN UNDERGROUND BASE ONCE USED BY THE "ANCIENT ONES" AND NOW TAKEN OVER BY THE ALIENS...
SUCH STRANGE RELICS THE "ANCIENT ONES" LEFT BEHIND...
WATERLOO
AND IF I MAY BE INDELICATE, WORTH A BIT, TOO, PURITY OLD LOVE!

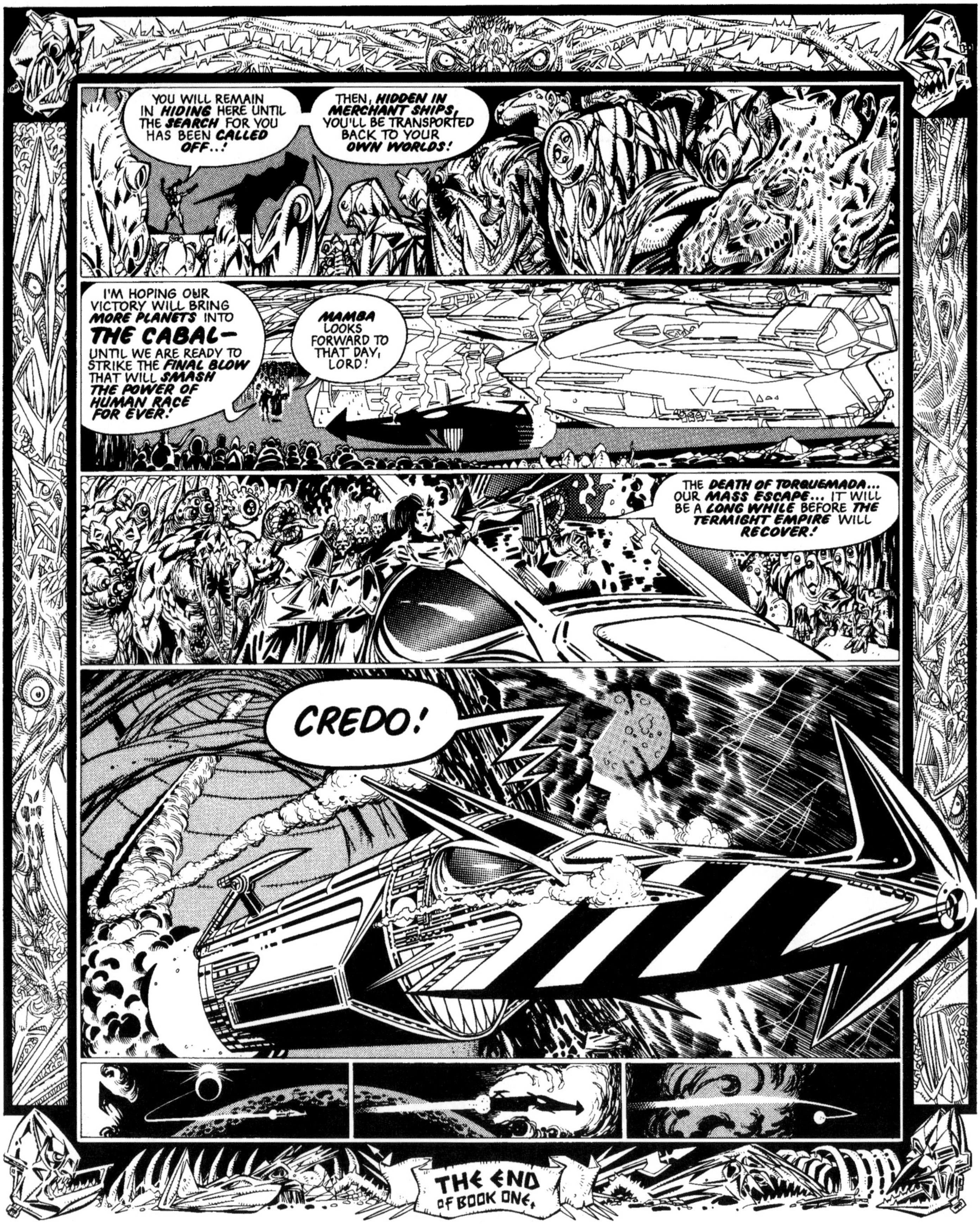
YOU WILL REMAIN IN HIDING HERE UNTIL THE SEARCH FOR YOU HAS BEEN CALLED OFF...!
THEN, HIDDEN IN MERCHANT SHIPS, YOU'LL BE TRANSPORTED BACK TO YOUR OWN WORLDS!
I'M HOPING OUR VICTORY WILL BRING MORE PLANETS INTO THE CABAL— UNTIL WE ARE READY TO STRIKE THE FINAL BLOW THAT WILL SMASH THE POWER OF HUMAN RACE FOR EVER!
MAMBA LOOKS FORWARD TO THAT DAY, LORD!
THE DEATH OF TORQUEMADA... OUR MASS ESCAPE... IT WILL BE A LONG WHILE BEFORE THE TERMIGHT EMPIRE WILL RECOVER!
CREDO!
THE END OF BOOK ONE.

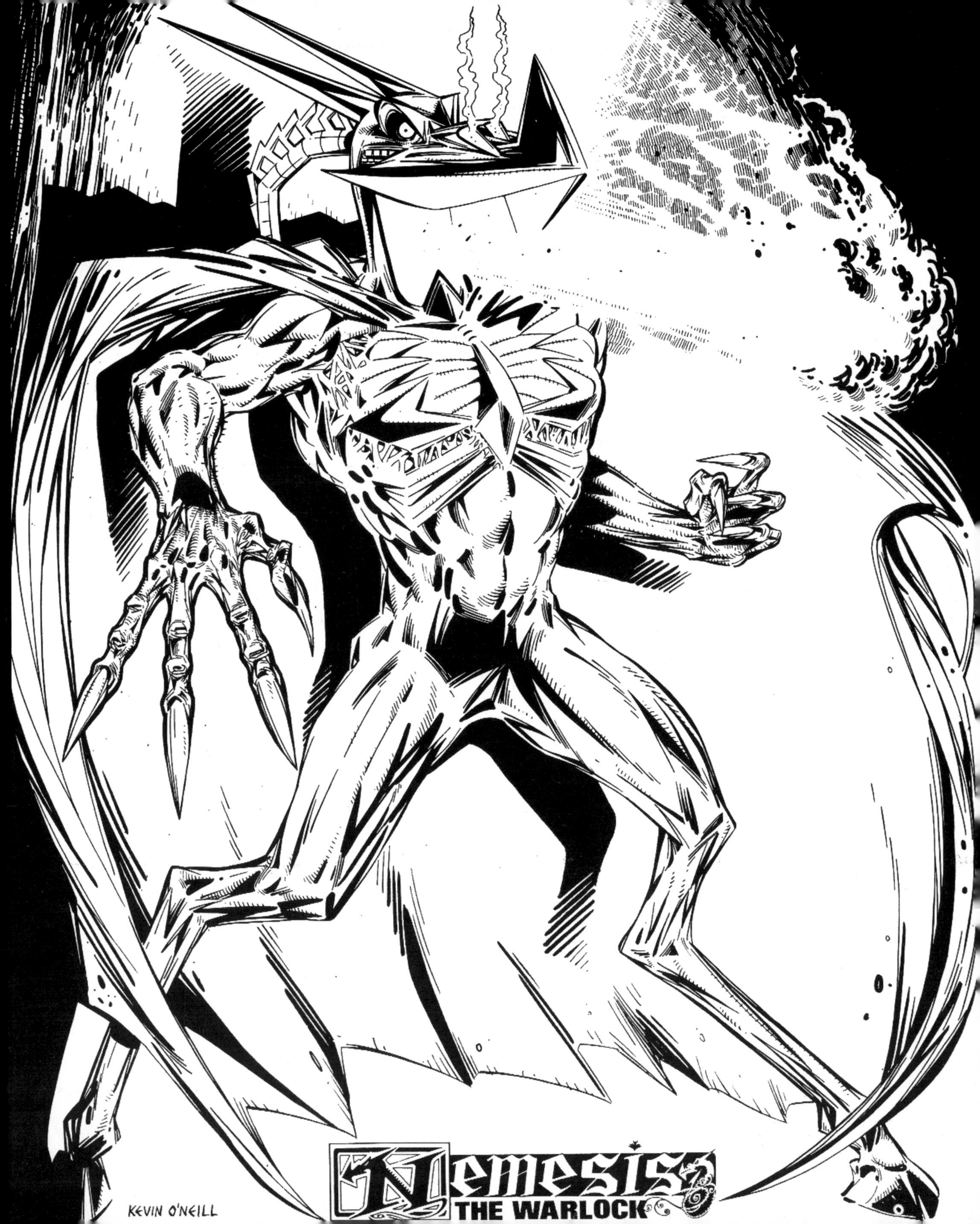
KEVIN O'NEILL
Nemesis
THE WARLOCK

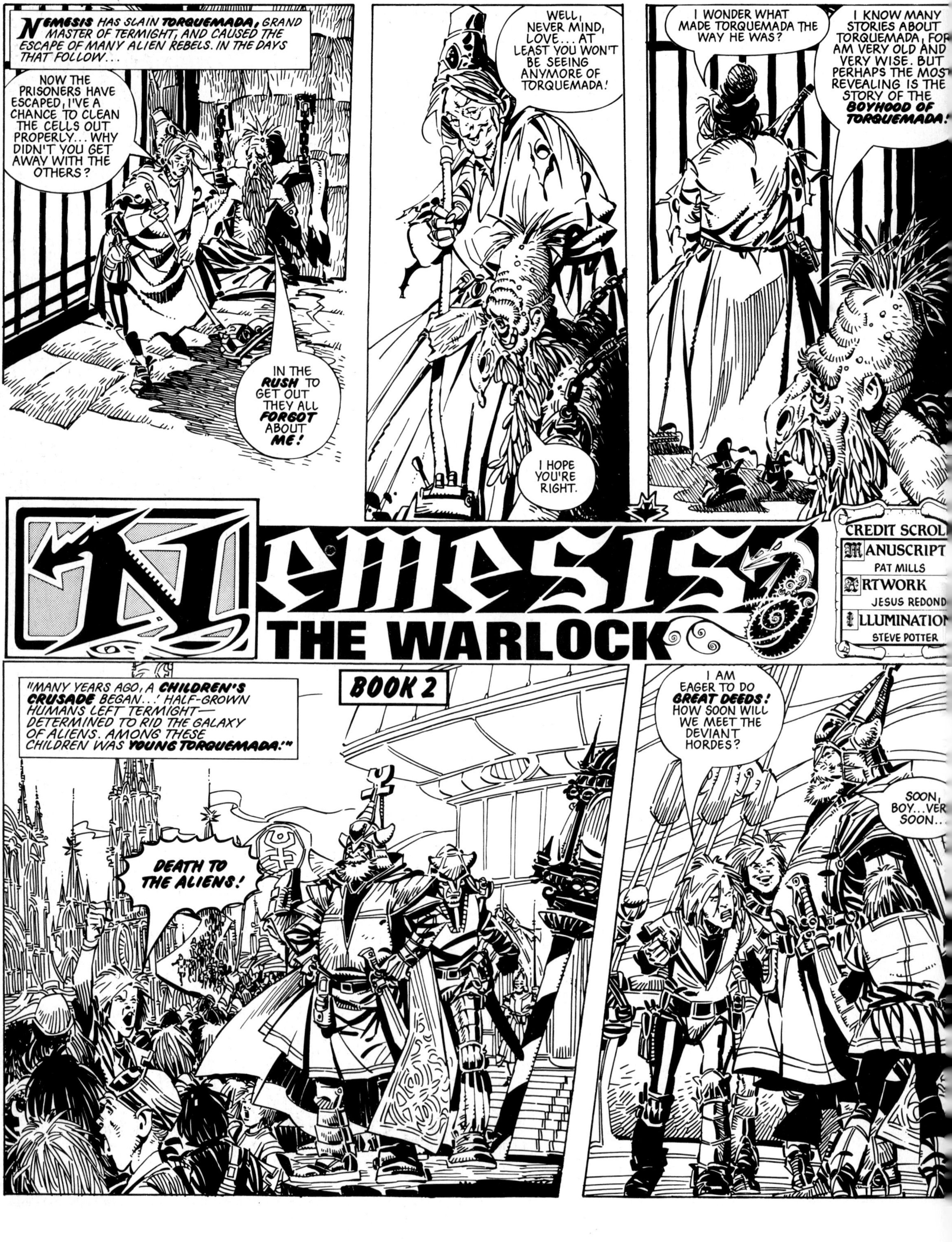
NEMESIS HAS SLAIN TORQUEMADA, GRAND MASTER OF TERMIGHT, AND CAUSED THE ESCAPE OF MANY ALIEN REBELS. IN THE DAYS THAT FOLLOW...
NOW THE PRISONERS HAVE ESCAPED, I'VE A CHANCE TO CLEAN THE CELLS OUT PROPERLY... WHY DIDN'T YOU GET AWAY WITH THE OTHERS?
IN THE RUSH TO GET OUT THEY ALL FORGOT ABOUT ME!
WELL, NEVER MIND, LOVE... AT LEAST YOU WON'T BE SEEING ANYMORE OF TORQUEMADA!
I HOPE YOU'RE RIGHT.
I WONDER WHAT MADE TORQUEMADA THE WAY HE WAS?
I KNOW MANY STORIES ABOUT TORQUEMADA, FOR AM VERY OLD AND VERY WISE. BUT PERHAPS THE MOST REVEALING IS THE STORY OF THE BOYHOOD OF TORQUEMADA!
NEMESIS THE WARLOCK
CREDIT SCROL
MANUSCRIPT PAT MILLS
ARTWORK JESUS REDOND
ILLUMINATION STEVE POTTER
BOOK 2
"MANY YEARS AGO, A CHILDREN'S CRUSADE BEGAN...' HALF-GROWN HUMANS LEFT TERMIGHT— DETERMINED TO RID THE GALAXY OF ALIENS. AMONG THESE CHILDREN WAS YOUNG TORQUEMADA!"
DEATH TO THE ALIENS!
I AM EAGER TO DO GREAT DEEDS! HOW SOON WILL WE MEET THE DEVIANT HORDES?
SOON, BOY... VER SOON...

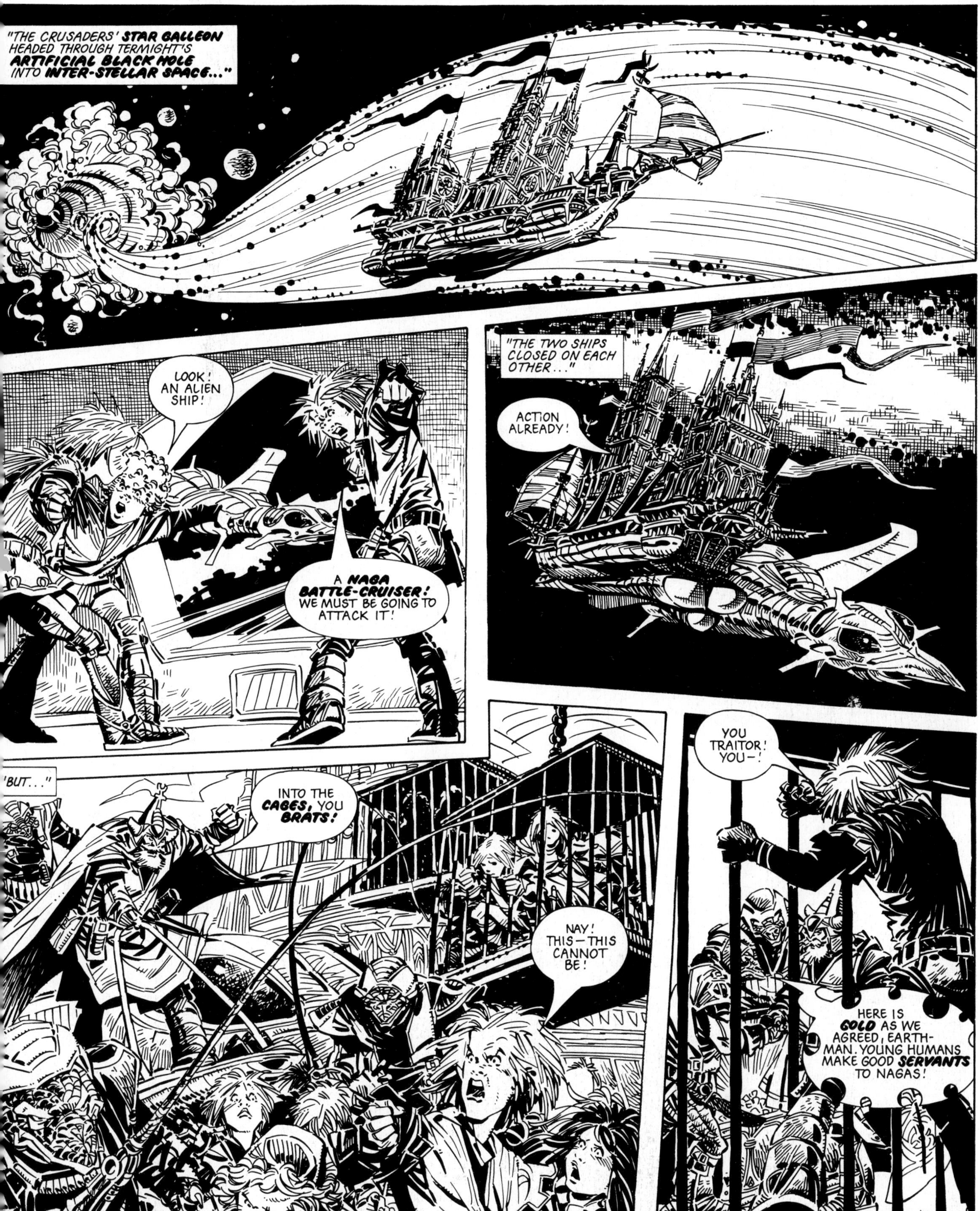
"THE CRUSADERS' STAR GALLEON HEADED THROUGH TERMIGHT'S ARTIFICIAL BLACK HOLE INTO INTER-STELLAR SPACE..."
LOOK! AN ALIEN SHIP!
A NAGA BATTLE-CRUISER! WE MUST BE GOING TO ATTACK IT!
"THE TWO SHIPS CLOSED ON EACH OTHER..."
ACTION ALREADY!
"BUT..."
INTO THE CAGES, YOU BRATS!
NAY! THIS—THIS CANNOT BE!
YOU TRAITOR! YOU—!
HERE IS GOLD AS WE AGREED, EARTH-MAN. YOUNG HUMANS MAKE GOOD SERVANTS TO NAGAS!

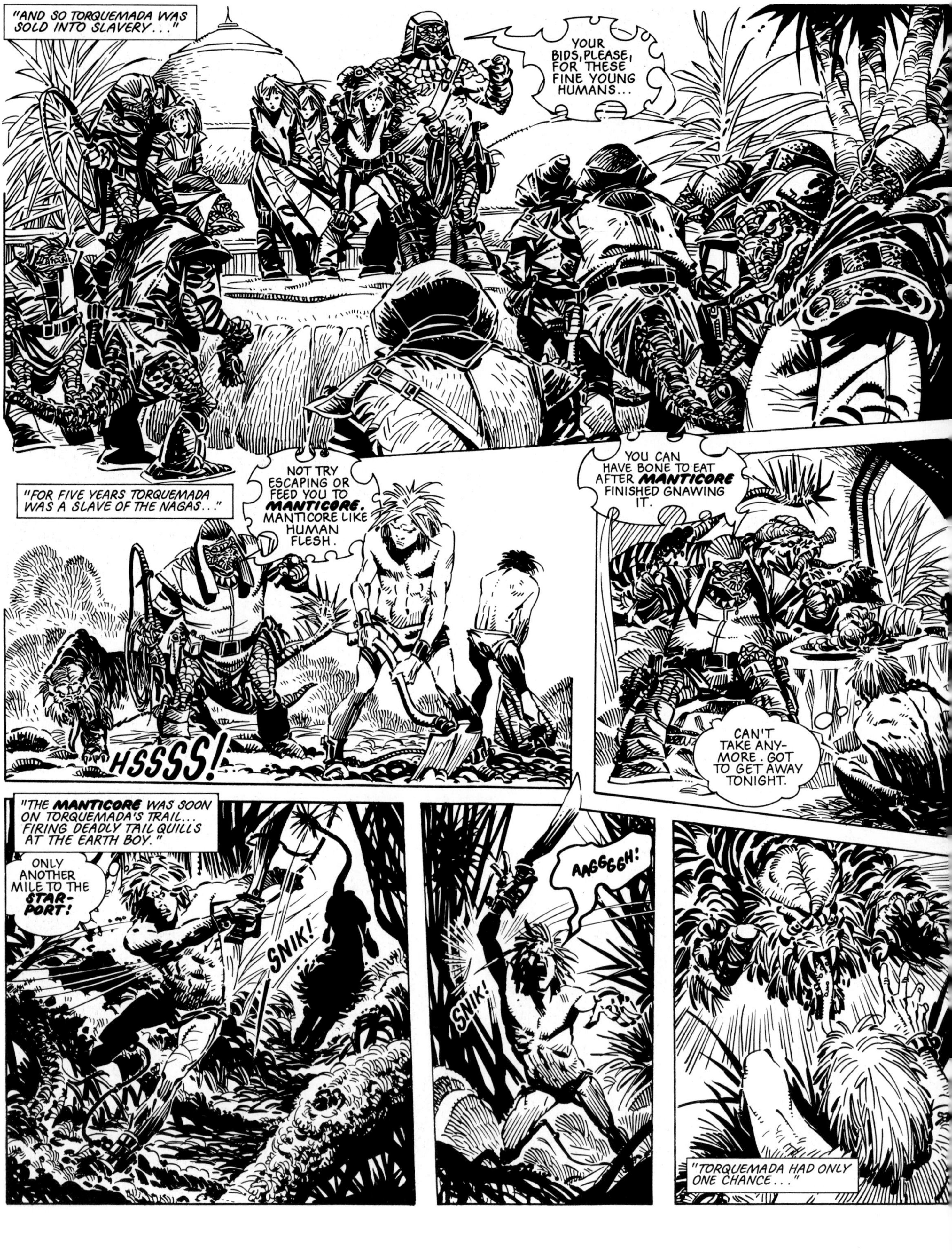
"AND SO TORQUEMADA WAS SOLD INTO SLAVERY..."
YOUR BIDS, PLEASE, FOR THESE FINE YOUNG HUMANS...
"FOR FIVE YEARS TORQUEMADA WAS A SLAVE OF THE NAGAS..."
NOT TRY ESCAPING OR FEED YOU TO MANTICORE. MANTICORE LIKE HUMAN FLESH.
HSSSS!
YOU CAN HAVE BONE TO EAT AFTER MANTICORE FINISHED GNAWING IT.
CAN'T TAKE ANY-MORE. GOT TO GET AWAY TONIGHT.
"THE MANTICORE WAS SOON ON TORQUEMADA'S TRAIL... FIRING DEADLY TAIL QUILLS AT THE EARTH BOY."
ONLY ANOTHER MILE TO THE STAR-PORT!
SNIK!
AAGGGGH!
SNIK!
"TORQUEMADA HAD ONLY ONE CHANCE..."

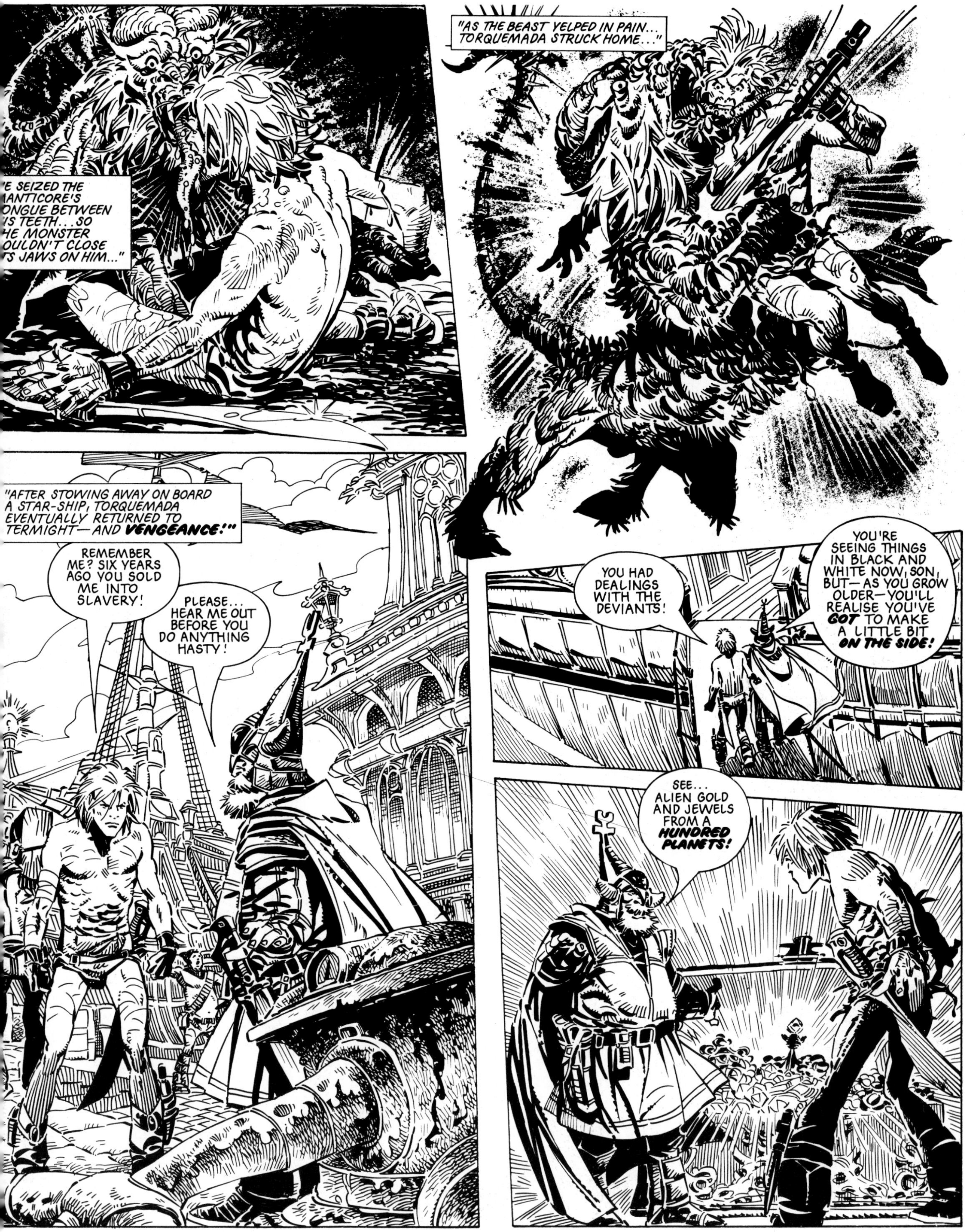

"...E SEIZED THE MANTICORE'S ...ONGUE BETWEEN ...IS TEETH...SO ...HE MONSTER ...OULDN'T CLOSE ...TS JAWS ON HIM..."
"AS THE BEAST YELPED IN PAIN... TORQUEMADA STRUCK HOME..."
"AFTER STOWING AWAY ON BOARD A STAR-SHIP, TORQUEMADA EVENTUALLY RETURNED TO TERMIGHT—AND VENGEANCE!"
REMEMBER ME? SIX YEARS AGO YOU SOLD ME INTO SLAVERY!
PLEASE... HEAR ME OUT BEFORE YOU DO ANYTHING HASTY!
YOU HAD DEALINGS WITH THE DEVIANTS!
YOU'RE SEEING THINGS IN BLACK AND WHITE NOW, SON, BUT—AS YOU GROW OLDER—YOU'LL REALISE YOU'VE GOT TO MAKE A LITTLE BIT ON THE SIDE!
SEE... ALIEN GOLD AND JEWELS FROM A HUNDRED PLANETS!

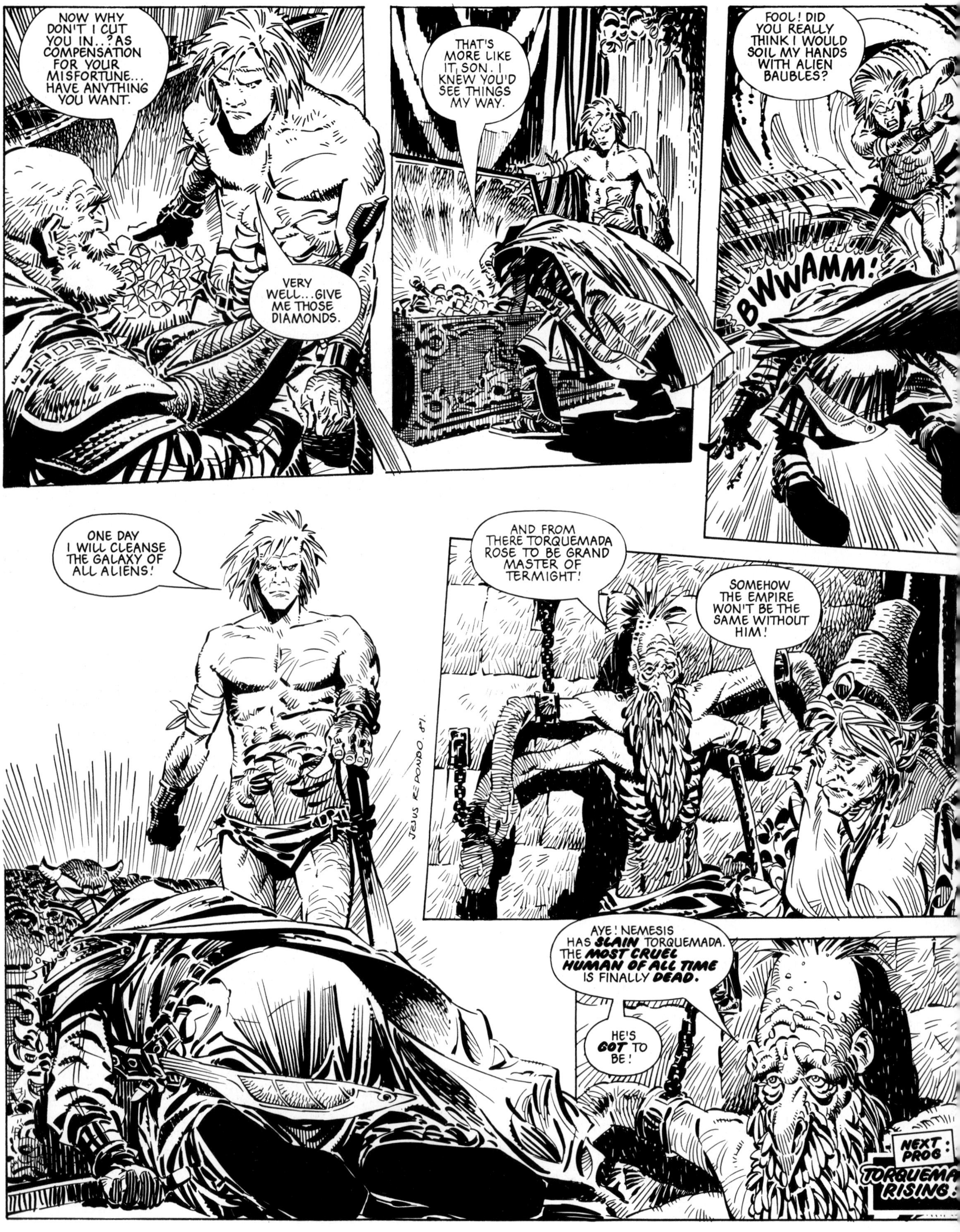
NOW WHY DON'T I CUT YOU IN..? AS COMPENSATION FOR YOUR MISFORTUNE... HAVE ANYTHING YOU WANT.
VERY WELL...GIVE ME THOSE DIAMONDS.
THAT'S MORE LIKE IT, SON. I KNEW YOU'D SEE THINGS MY WAY.
FOOL! DID YOU REALLY THINK I WOULD SOIL MY HANDS WITH ALIEN BAUBLES?
BWWAMM!
ONE DAY I WILL CLEANSE THE GALAXY OF ALL ALIENS!
JESUS REDONDO. 81.
AND FROM THERE TORQUEMADA ROSE TO BE GRAND MASTER OF TERMIGHT!
SOMEHOW THE EMPIRE WON'T BE THE SAME WITHOUT HIM!
AYE! NEMESIS HAS SLAIN TORQUEMADA. THE MOST CRUEL HUMAN OF ALL TIME IS FINALLY DEAD.
HE'S GOT TO BE!
NEXT PROG: TORQUEMADA RISING!

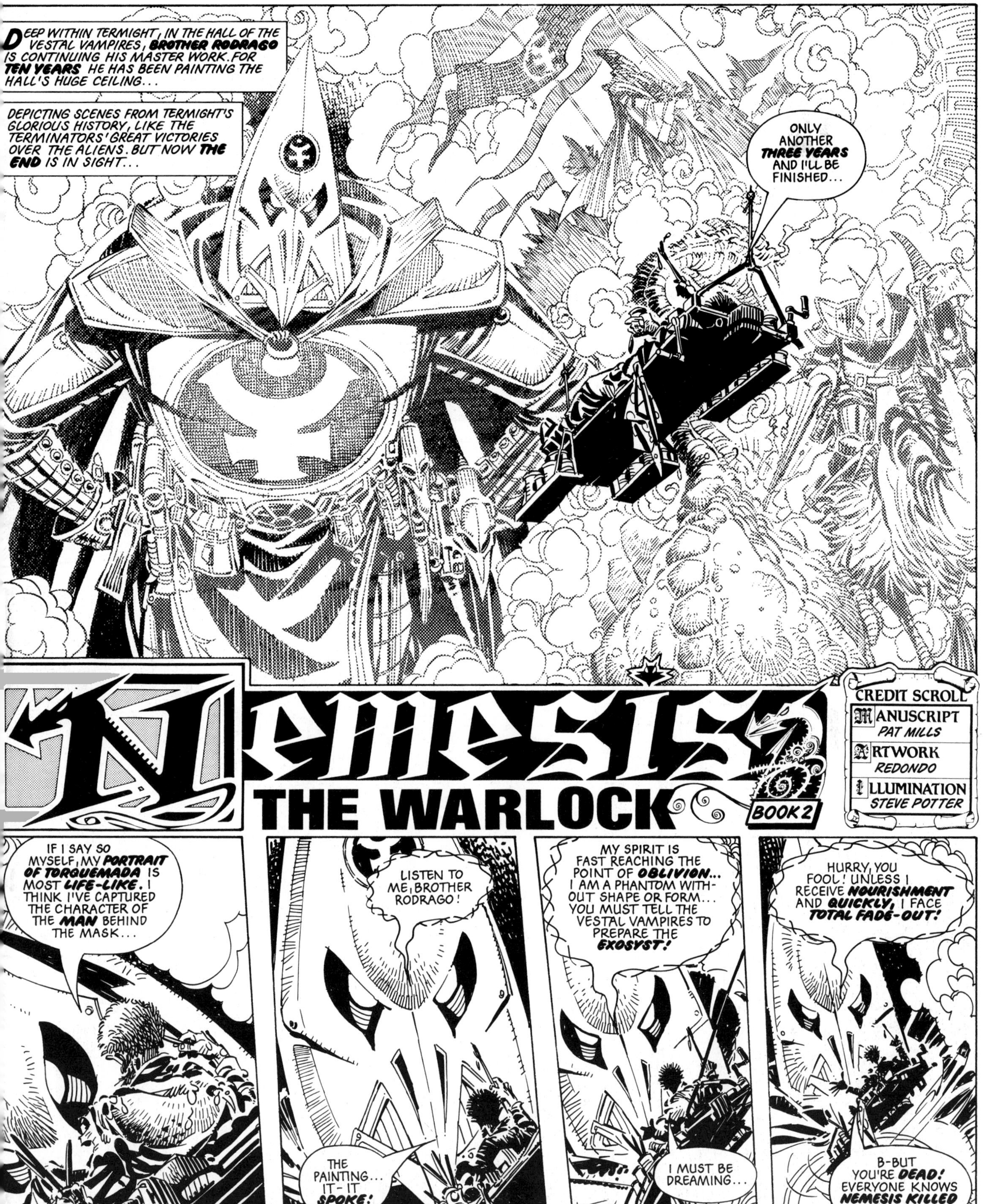

DEEP WITHIN TERMIGHT, IN THE HALL OF THE VESTAL VAMPIRES, BROTHER RODRAGO IS CONTINUING HIS MASTER WORK. FOR TEN YEARS HE HAS BEEN PAINTING THE HALL'S HUGE CEILING...
DEPICTING SCENES FROM TERMIGHT'S GLORIOUS HISTORY, LIKE THE TERMINATORS' GREAT VICTORIES OVER THE ALIENS. BUT NOW THE END IS IN SIGHT...
ONLY ANOTHER THREE YEARS AND I'LL BE FINISHED...
NEMESIS THE WARLOCK
BOOK 2
CREDIT SCROLL
MANUSCRIPT PAT MILLS
ARTWORK REDONDO
ILLUMINATION STEVE POTTER
IF I SAY SO MYSELF, MY PORTRAIT OF TORQUEMADA IS MOST LIFE-LIKE. I THINK I'VE CAPTURED THE CHARACTER OF THE MAN BEHIND THE MASK...
LISTEN TO ME, BROTHER RODRAGO!
THE PAINTING... IT-IT SPOKE!
MY SPIRIT IS FAST REACHING THE POINT OF OBLIVION... I AM A PHANTOM WITH-OUT SHAPE OR FORM... YOU MUST TELL THE VESTAL VAMPIRES TO PREPARE THE EXOSYST!
I MUST BE DREAMING...
HURRY, YOU FOOL! UNLESS I RECEIVE NOURISHMENT AND QUICKLY, I FACE TOTAL FADE-OUT!
B-BUT YOU'RE DEAD! EVERYONE KNOWS NEMESIS KILLED YOU!

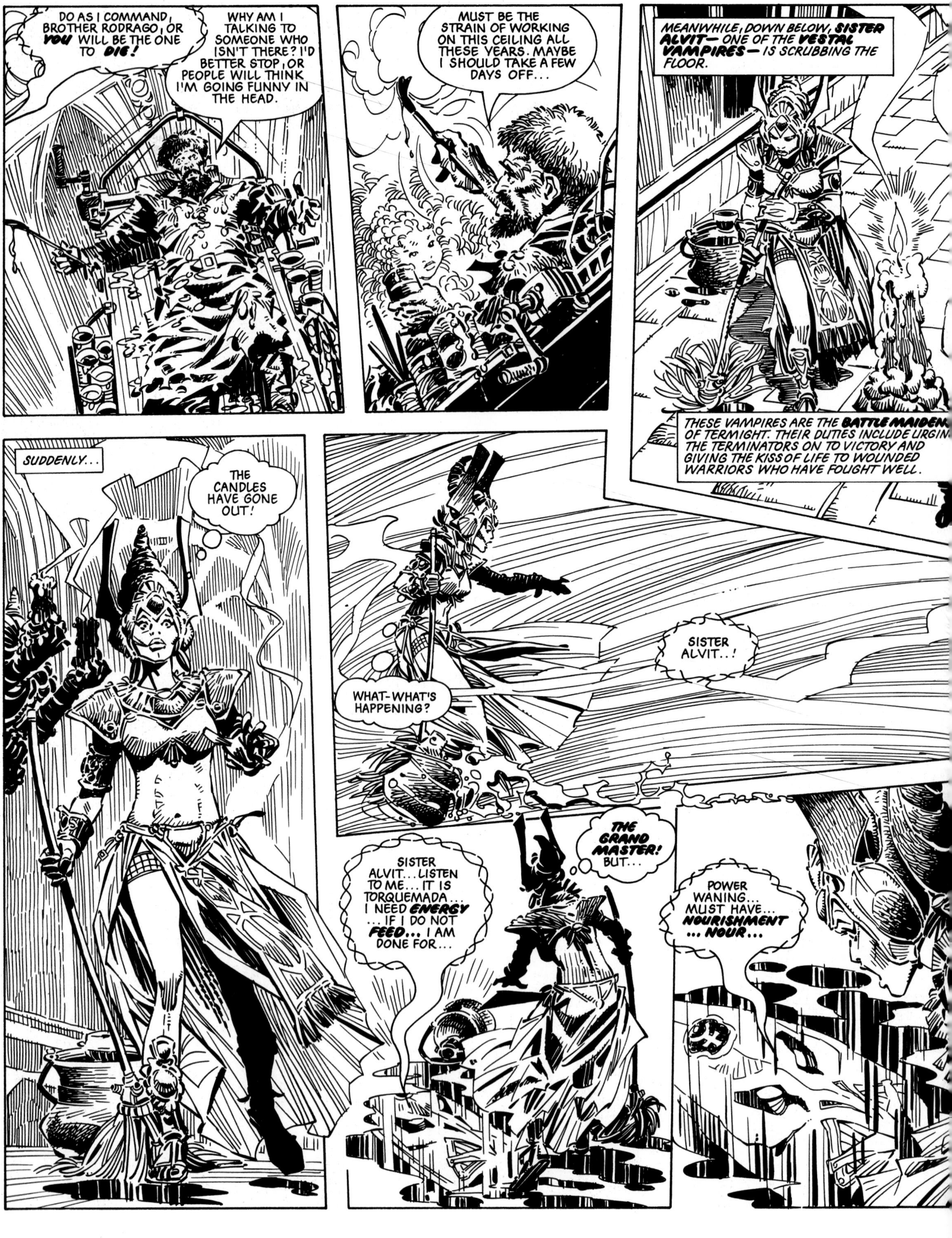
DO AS I COMMAND, BROTHER RODRAGO, OR YOU WILL BE THE ONE TO DIE!
WHY AM I TALKING TO SOMEONE WHO ISN'T THERE? I'D BETTER STOP, OR PEOPLE WILL THINK I'M GOING FUNNY IN THE HEAD.
MUST BE THE STRAIN OF WORKING ON THIS CEILING ALL THESE YEARS. MAYBE I SHOULD TAKE A FEW DAYS OFF...
MEANWHILE, DOWN BELOW, SISTER ALVIT— ONE OF THE VESTAL VAMPIRES— IS SCRUBBING THE FLOOR.
THESE VAMPIRES ARE THE BATTLE MAIDENS OF TERMIGHT. THEIR DUTIES INCLUDE URGING THE TERMINATORS ON TO VICTORY AND GIVING THE KISS OF LIFE TO WOUNDED WARRIORS WHO HAVE FOUGHT WELL.
SUDDENLY...
THE CANDLES HAVE GONE OUT!
SISTER ALVIT..!
WHAT-WHAT'S HAPPENING?
SISTER ALVIT... LISTEN TO ME... IT IS TORQUEMADA... I NEED ENERGY ... IF I DO NOT FEED... I AM DONE FOR...
THE GRAND MASTER! BUT...
POWER WANING... MUST HAVE... NOURISHMENT ... NOUR...

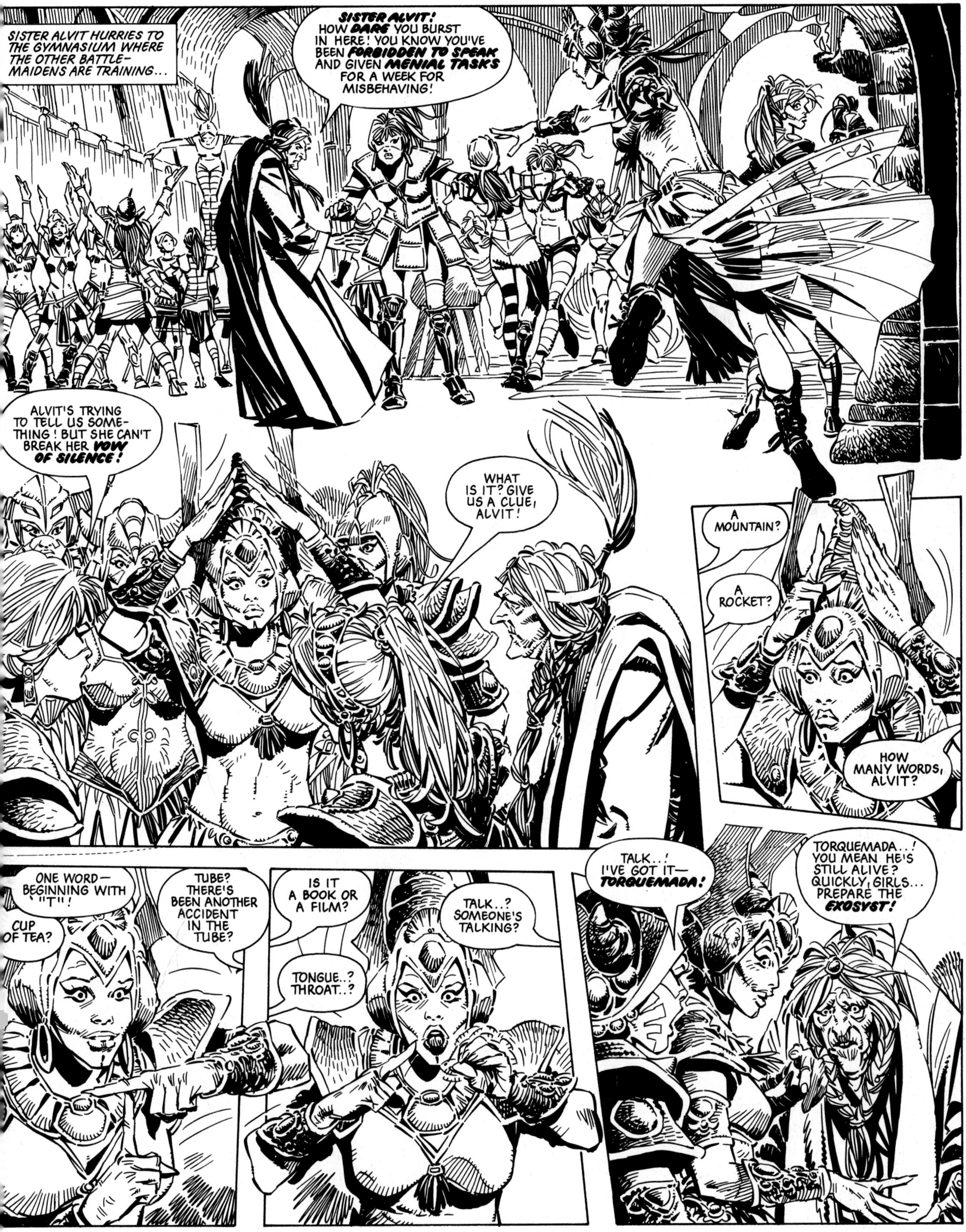
SISTER ALVIT HURRIES TO THE GYMNASIUM WHERE THE OTHER BATTLE-MAIDENS ARE TRAINING...
SISTER ALVIT! HOW DARE YOU BURST IN HERE! YOU KNOW YOU'VE BEEN FORBIDDEN TO SPEAK AND GIVEN MENIAL TASKS FOR A WEEK FOR MISBEHAVING!
ALVIT'S TRYING TO TELL US SOMETHING! BUT SHE CAN'T BREAK HER VOW OF SILENCE!
WHAT IS IT? GIVE US A CLUE, ALVIT!
A MOUNTAIN?
A ROCKET?
HOW MANY WORDS, ALVIT?
ONE WORD— BEGINNING WITH "T"!
CUP OF TEA?
TUBE? THERE'S BEEN ANOTHER ACCIDENT IN THE TUBE?
IS IT A BOOK OR A FILM?
TALK..? SOMEONE'S TALKING?
TONGUE..? THROAT..?
TALK..! I'VE GOT IT— TORQUEMADA!
TORQUEMADA..! YOU MEAN HE'S STILL ALIVE? QUICKLY, GIRLS... PREPARE THE EXOSYST!

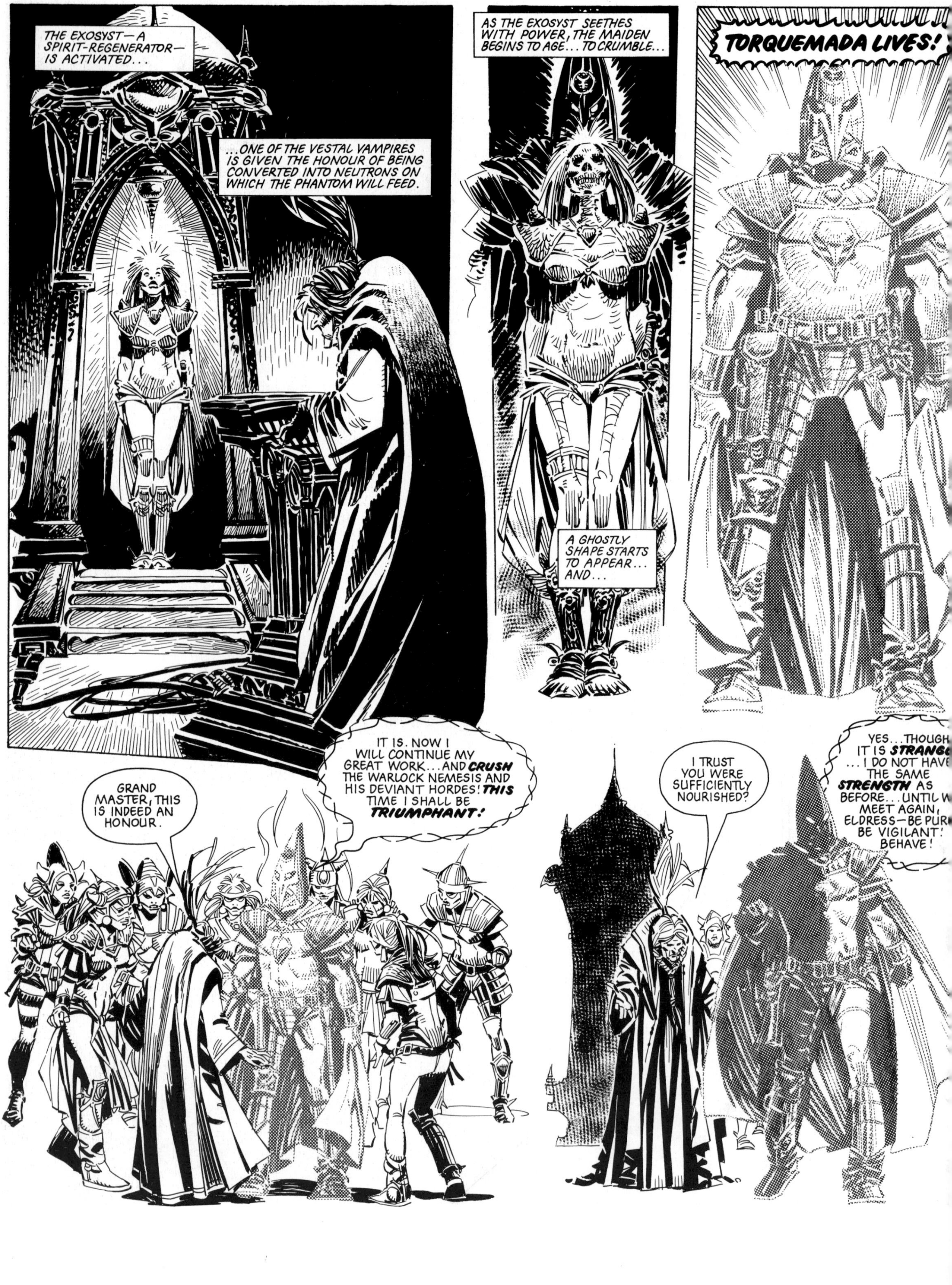
THE EXOSYST—A SPIRIT-REGENERATOR—IS ACTIVATED...
...ONE OF THE VESTAL VAMPIRES IS GIVEN THE HONOUR OF BEING CONVERTED INTO NEUTRONS ON WHICH THE PHANTOM WILL FEED.
AS THE EXOSYST SEETHES WITH POWER, THE MAIDEN BEGINS TO AGE... TO CRUMBLE...
A GHOSTLY SHAPE STARTS TO APPEAR... AND...
TORQUEMADA LIVES!
GRAND MASTER, THIS IS INDEED AN HONOUR.
IT IS. NOW I WILL CONTINUE MY GREAT WORK... AND CRUSH THE WARLOCK NEMESIS AND HIS DEVIANT HORDES! THIS TIME I SHALL BE TRIUMPHANT!
I TRUST YOU WERE SUFFICIENTLY NOURISHED?
YES... THOUGH IT IS STRANG ... I DO NOT HAVE THE SAME STRENGTH AS BEFORE... UNTIL W MEET AGAIN, ELDRESS—BE PUR BE VIGILANT! BEHAVE!

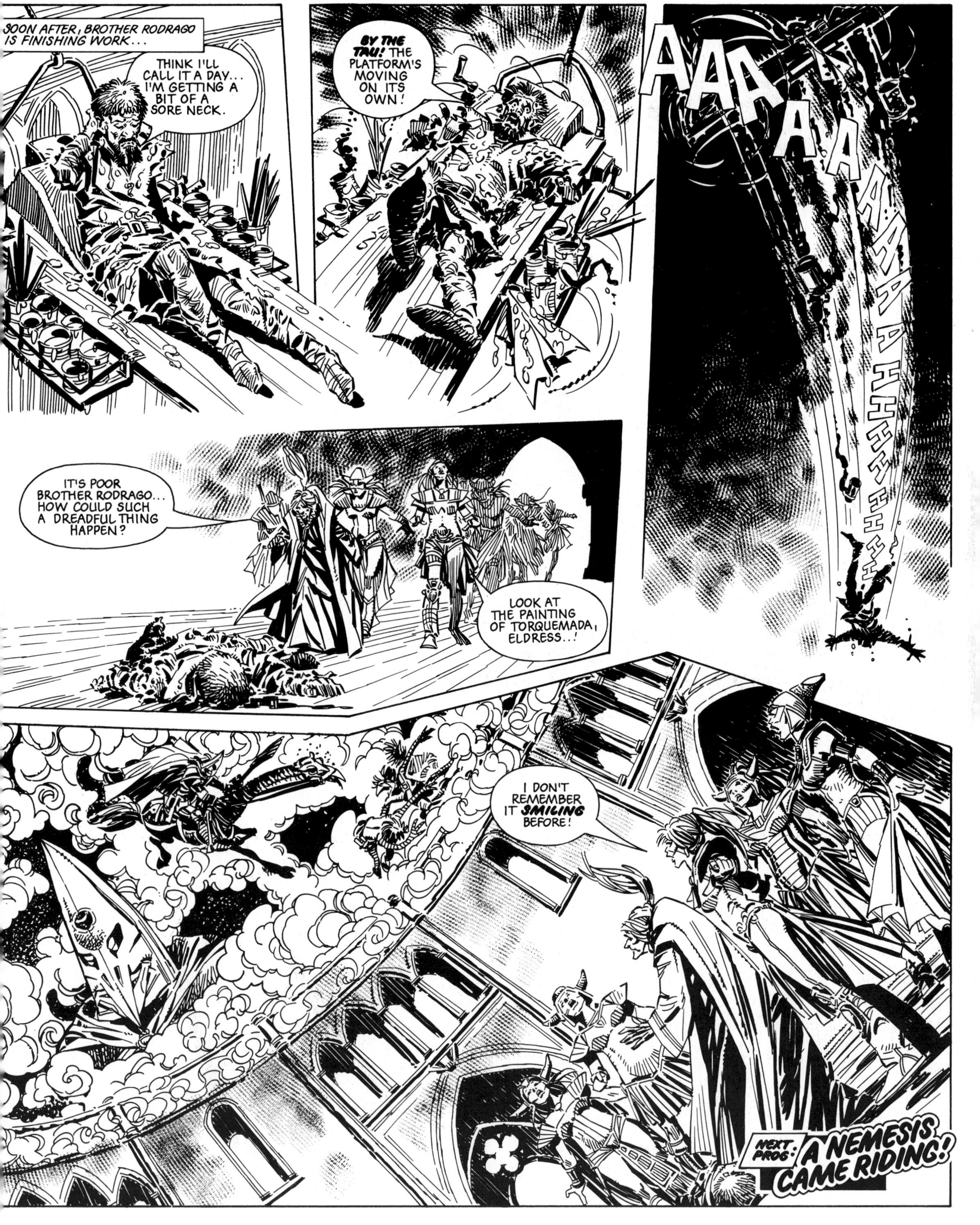

SOON AFTER, BROTHER RODRAGO IS FINISHING WORK...
THINK I'LL CALL IT A DAY... I'M GETTING A BIT OF A SORE NECK.
BY THE TAU! THE PLATFORM'S MOVING ON ITS OWN!
AAAAAAAAHHHHHHHHH
IT'S POOR BROTHER RODRAGO... HOW COULD SUCH A DREADFUL THING HAPPEN?
LOOK AT THE PAINTING OF TORQUEMADA, ELDRESS..!
I DON'T REMEMBER IT SMILING BEFORE!
NEXT PROG: A NEMESIS CAME RIDING!

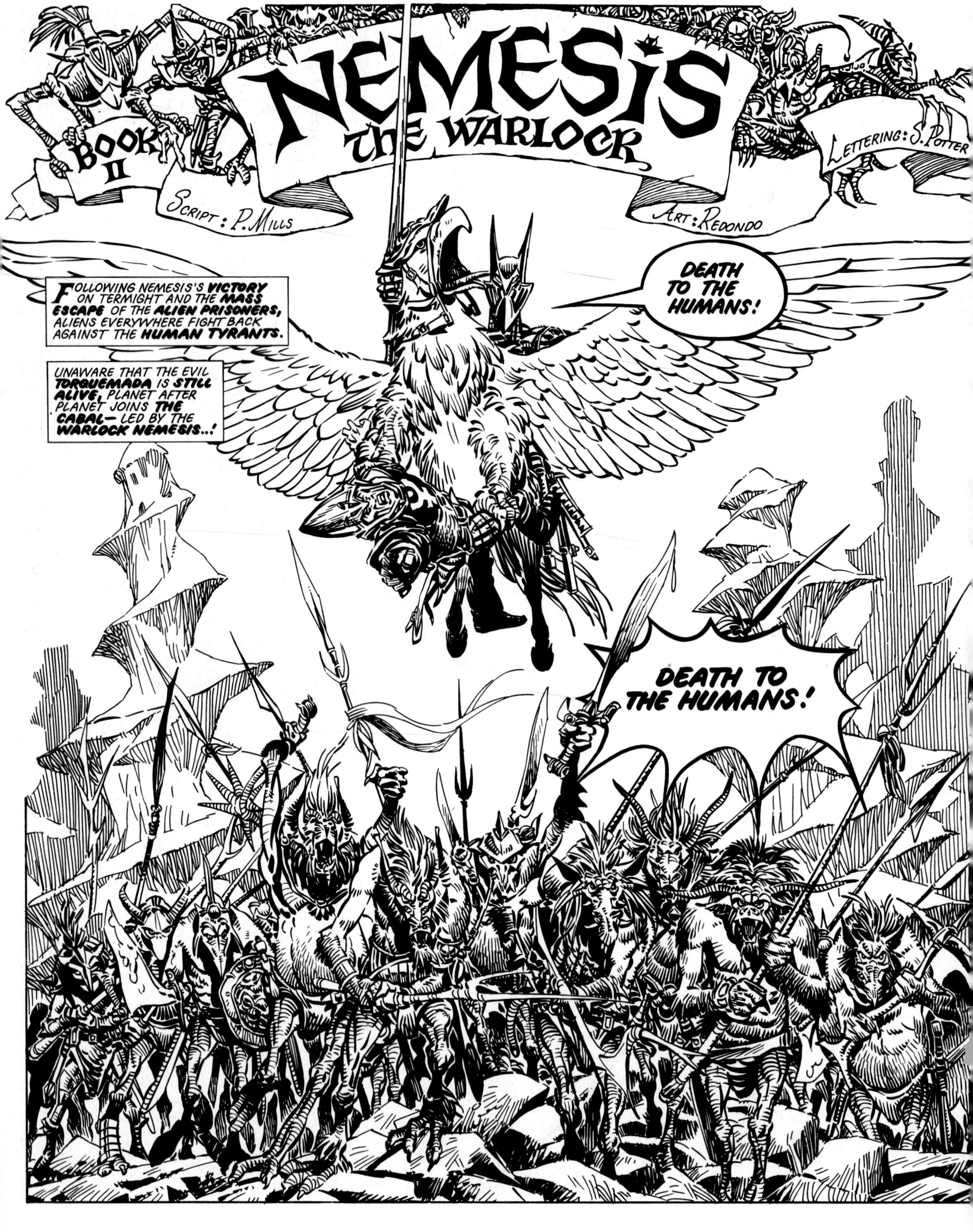

NEMESIS THE WARLOCK
BOOK II
SCRIPT: P. MILLS
ART: REDONDO
LETTERING: S. POTTER
FOLLOWING NEMESIS'S VICTORY ON TERMIGHT AND THE MASS ESCAPE OF THE ALIEN PRISONERS, ALIENS EVERYWHERE FIGHT BACK AGAINST THE HUMAN TYRANTS.
UNAWARE THAT THE EVIL TORQUEMADA IS STILL ALIVE, PLANET AFTER PLANET JOINS THE CABAL— LED BY THE WARLOCK NEMESIS..!
DEATH TO THE HUMANS!
DEATH TO THE HUMANS!

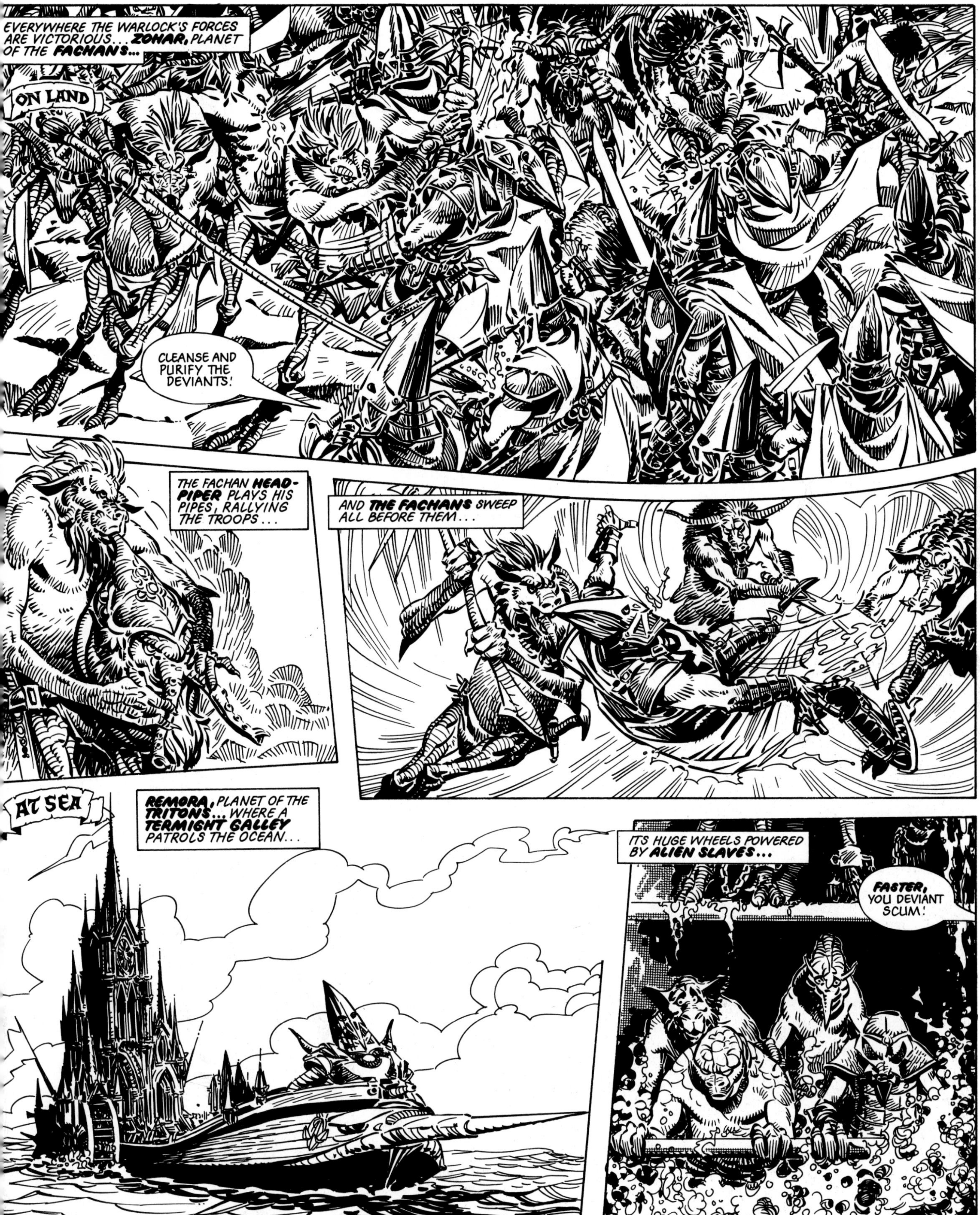
EVERYWHERE THE WARLOCK'S FORCES ARE VICTORIOUS... ZONAR, PLANET OF THE FACHANS...
ON LAND
CLEANSE AND PURIFY THE DEVIANTS!
THE FACHAN HEAD-PIPER PLAYS HIS PIPES, RALLYING THE TROOPS...
AND THE FACHANS SWEEP ALL BEFORE THEM...
AT SEA
REMORA, PLANET OF THE TRITONS... WHERE A TERMIGHT GALLEY PATROLS THE OCEAN...
ITS HUGE WHEELS POWERED BY ALIEN SLAVES...
FASTER, YOU DEVIANT SCUM!

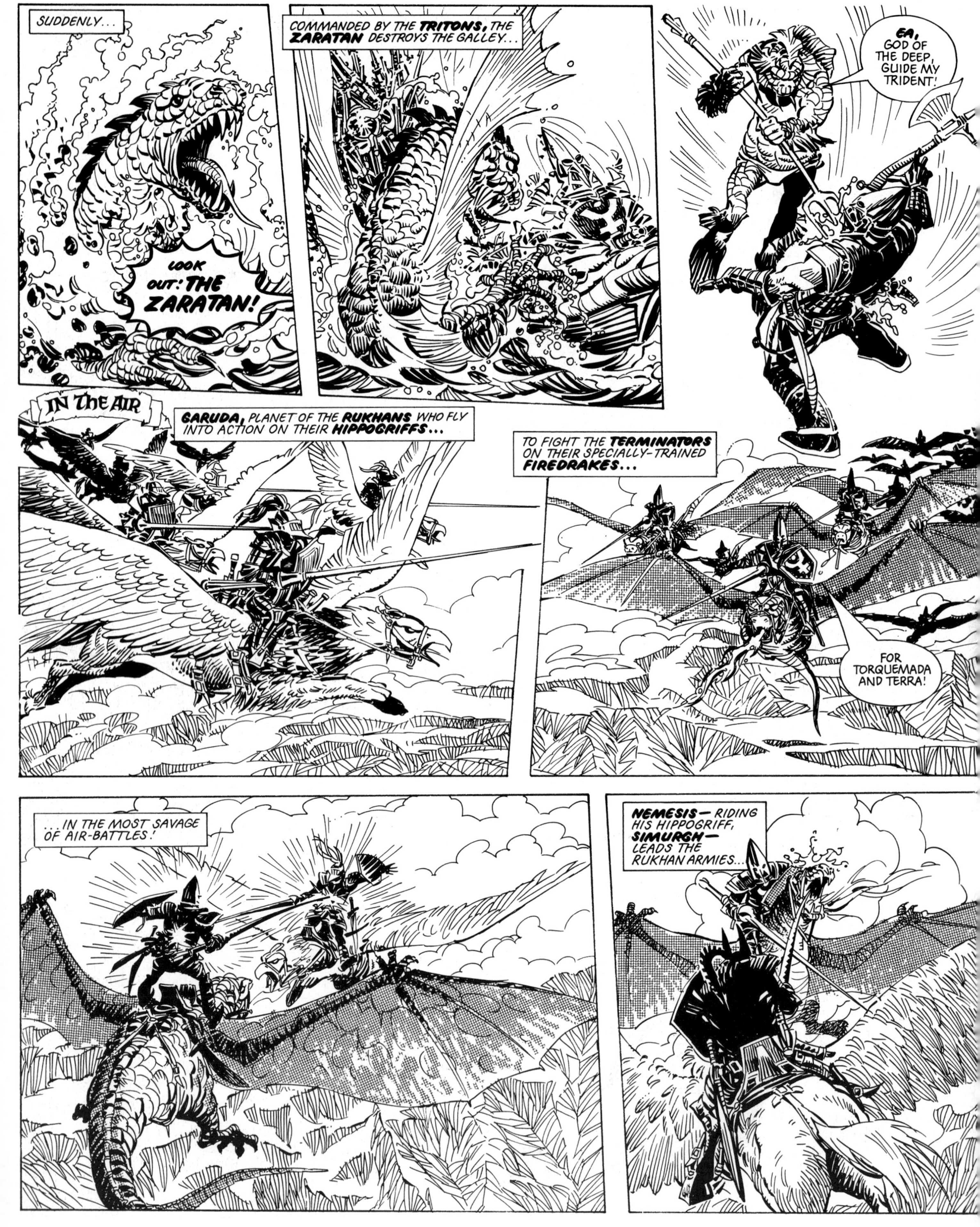
SUDDENLY...
LOOK OUT: THE ZARATAN!
COMMANDED BY THE TRITONS, THE ZARATAN DESTROYS THE GALLEY...
EA, GOD OF THE DEEP, GUIDE MY TRIDENT!
IN THE AIR
GARUDA, PLANET OF THE RUKHANS WHO FLY INTO ACTION ON THEIR HIPPOGRIFFS...
TO FIGHT THE TERMINATORS ON THEIR SPECIALLY-TRAINED FIREDRAKES...
FOR TORQUEMADA AND TERRA!
...IN THE MOST SAVAGE OF AIR-BATTLES!
NEMESIS— RIDING HIS HIPPOGRIFF, SIMURGH— LEADS THE RUKHAN ARMIES...

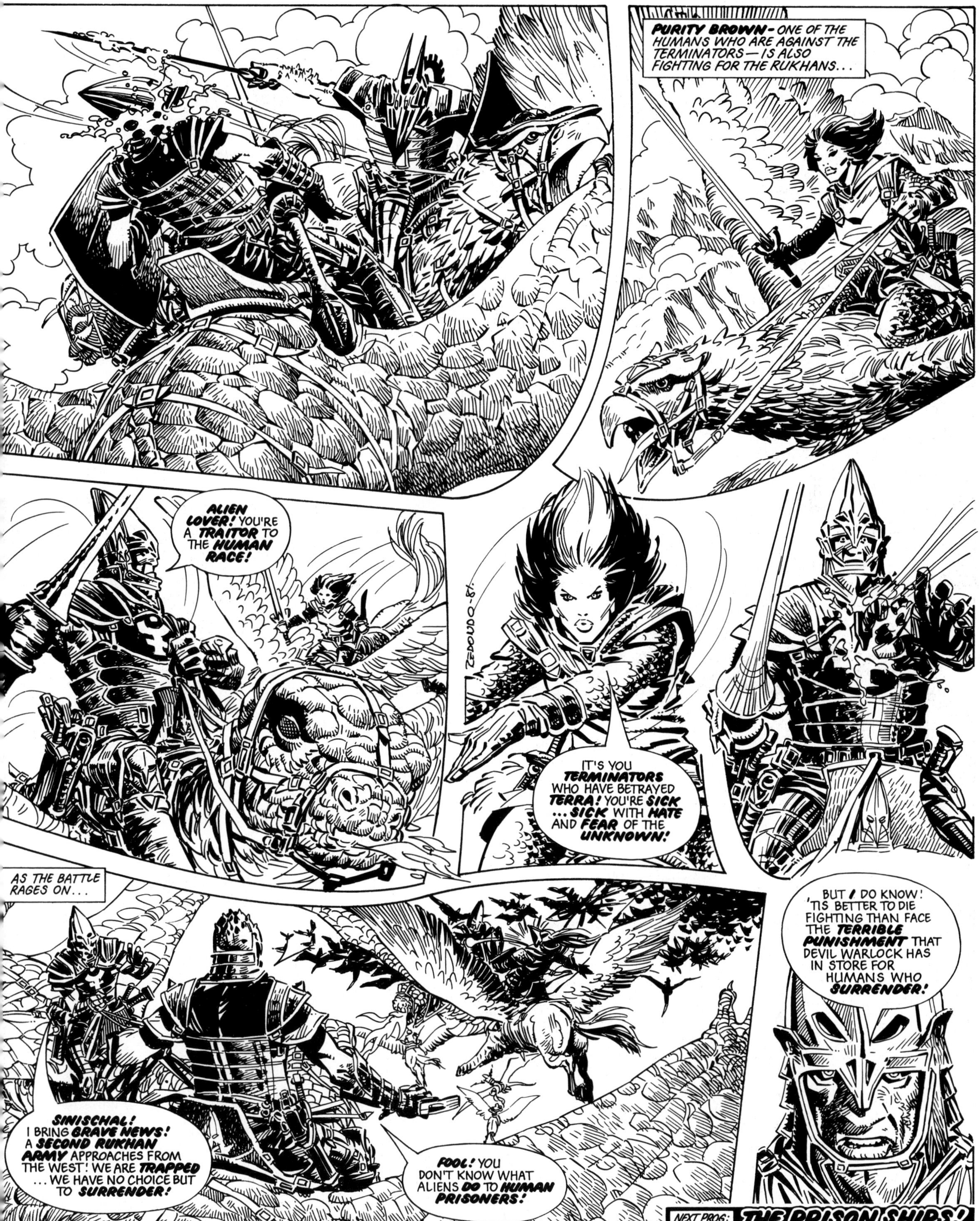
PURITY BROWN - ONE OF THE HUMANS WHO ARE AGAINST THE TERMINATORS — IS ALSO FIGHTING FOR THE RUKHANS...
ALIEN LOVER! YOU'RE A TRAITOR TO THE HUMAN RACE!
IT'S YOU TERMINATORS WHO HAVE BETRAYED TERRA! YOU'RE SICK ...SICK WITH HATE AND FEAR OF THE UNKNOWN!
AS THE BATTLE RAGES ON...
SINISCHAL! I BRING GRAVE NEWS! A SECOND RUKHAN ARMY APPROACHES FROM THE WEST! WE ARE TRAPPED ... WE HAVE NO CHOICE BUT TO SURRENDER!
FOOL! YOU DON'T KNOW WHAT ALIENS DO TO HUMAN PRISONERS!
BUT I DO KNOW! 'TIS BETTER TO DIE FIGHTING THAN FACE THE TERRIBLE PUNISHMENT THAT DEVIL WARLOCK HAS IN STORE FOR HUMANS WHO SURRENDER!
NEXT PROG: THE PRISON SHIPS!

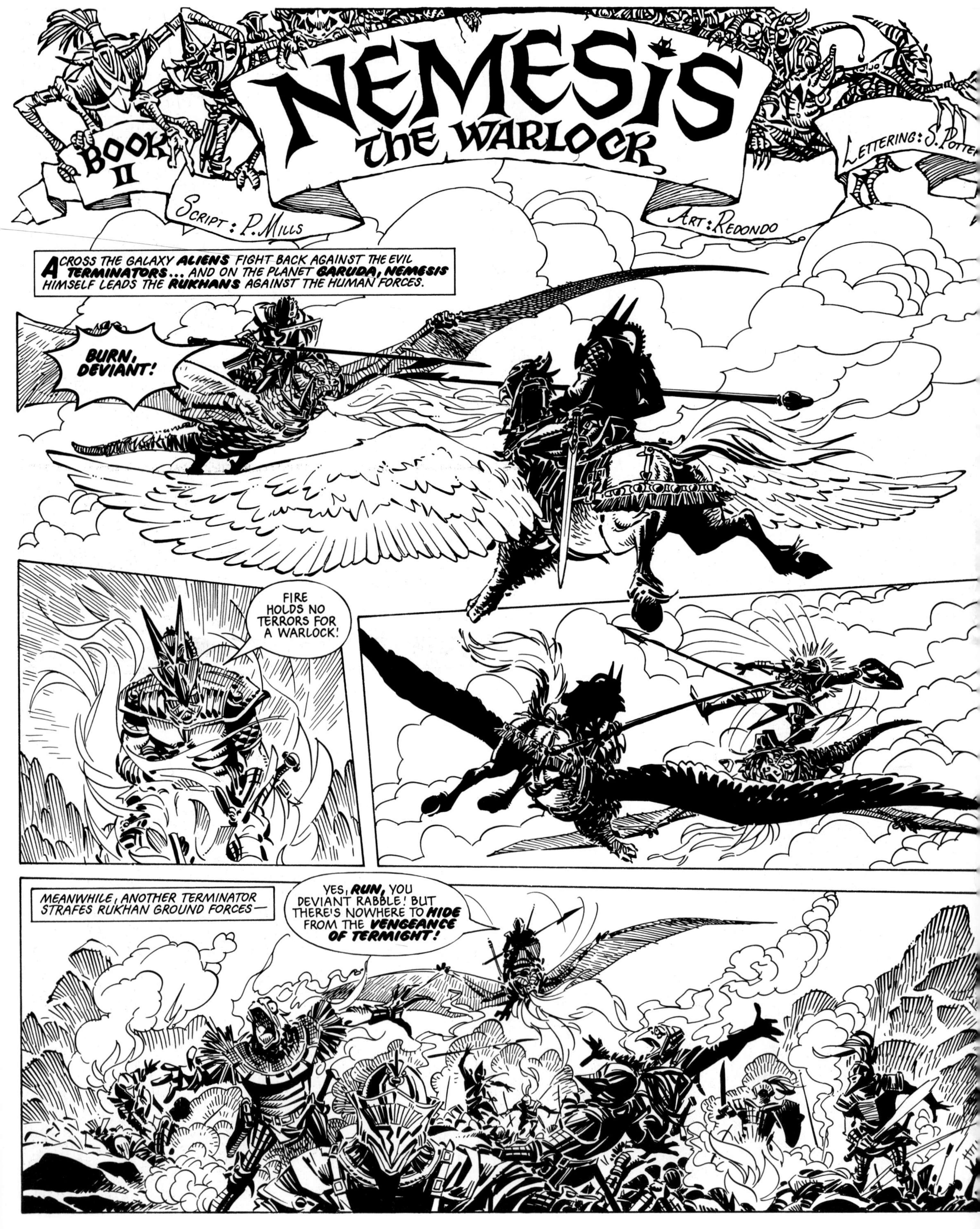
NEMESIS THE WARLOCK
BOOK II
SCRIPT: P. MILLS
ART: REDONDO
LETTERING: S. POTTER
ACROSS THE GALAXY ALIENS FIGHT BACK AGAINST THE EVIL TERMINATORS... AND ON THE PLANET GARUDA, NEMESIS HIMSELF LEADS THE RUKHANS AGAINST THE HUMAN FORCES.
BURN, DEVIANT!
FIRE HOLDS NO TERRORS FOR A WARLOCK!
MEANWHILE, ANOTHER TERMINATOR STRAFES RUKHAN GROUND FORCES—
YES, RUN, YOU DEVIANT RABBLE! BUT THERE'S NOWHERE TO HIDE FROM THE VENGEANCE OF TERMIGHT!

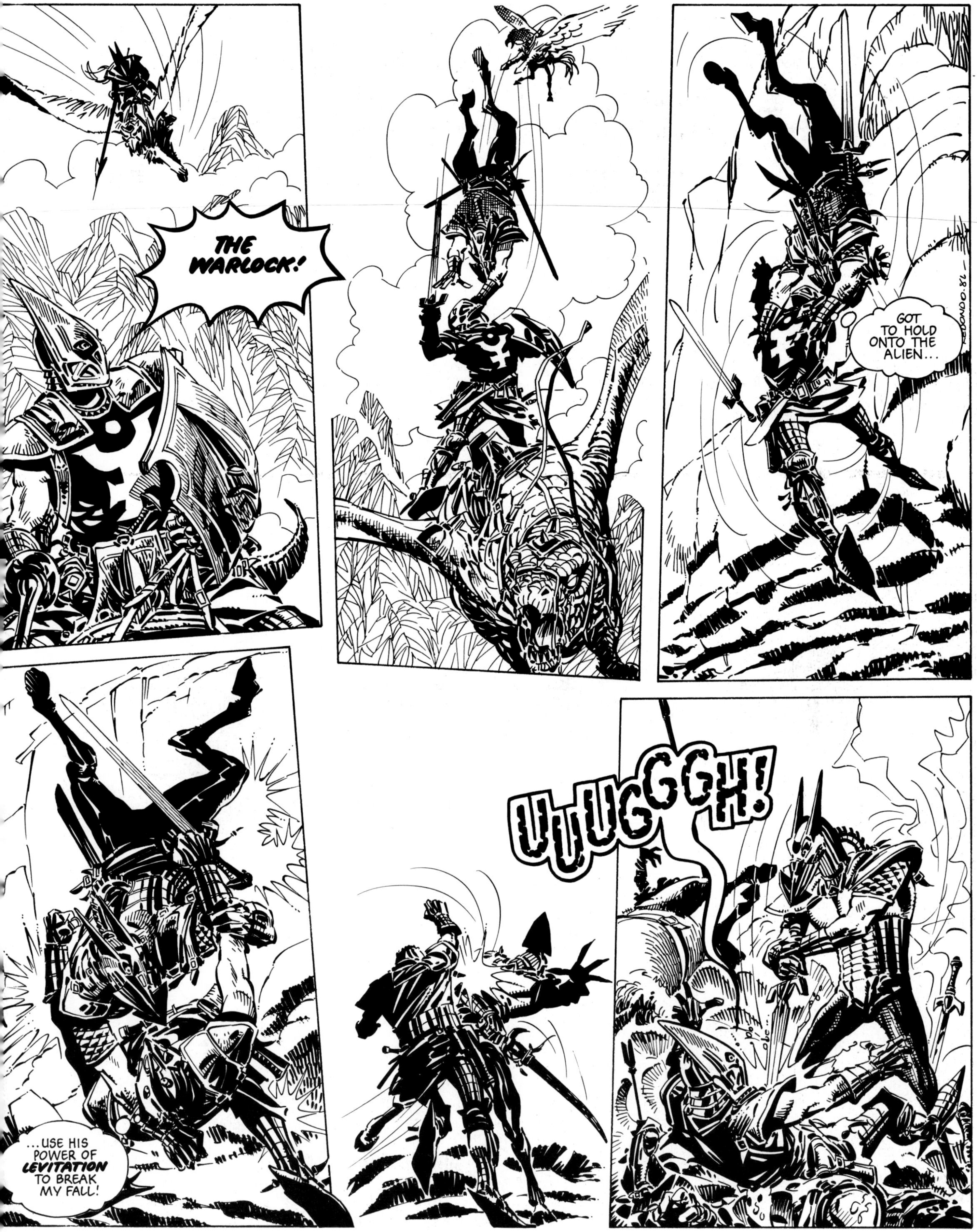
THE WARLOCK!
GOT TO HOLD ONTO THE ALIEN...
...USE HIS POWER OF LEVITATION TO BREAK MY FALL!
UUUGGGH!

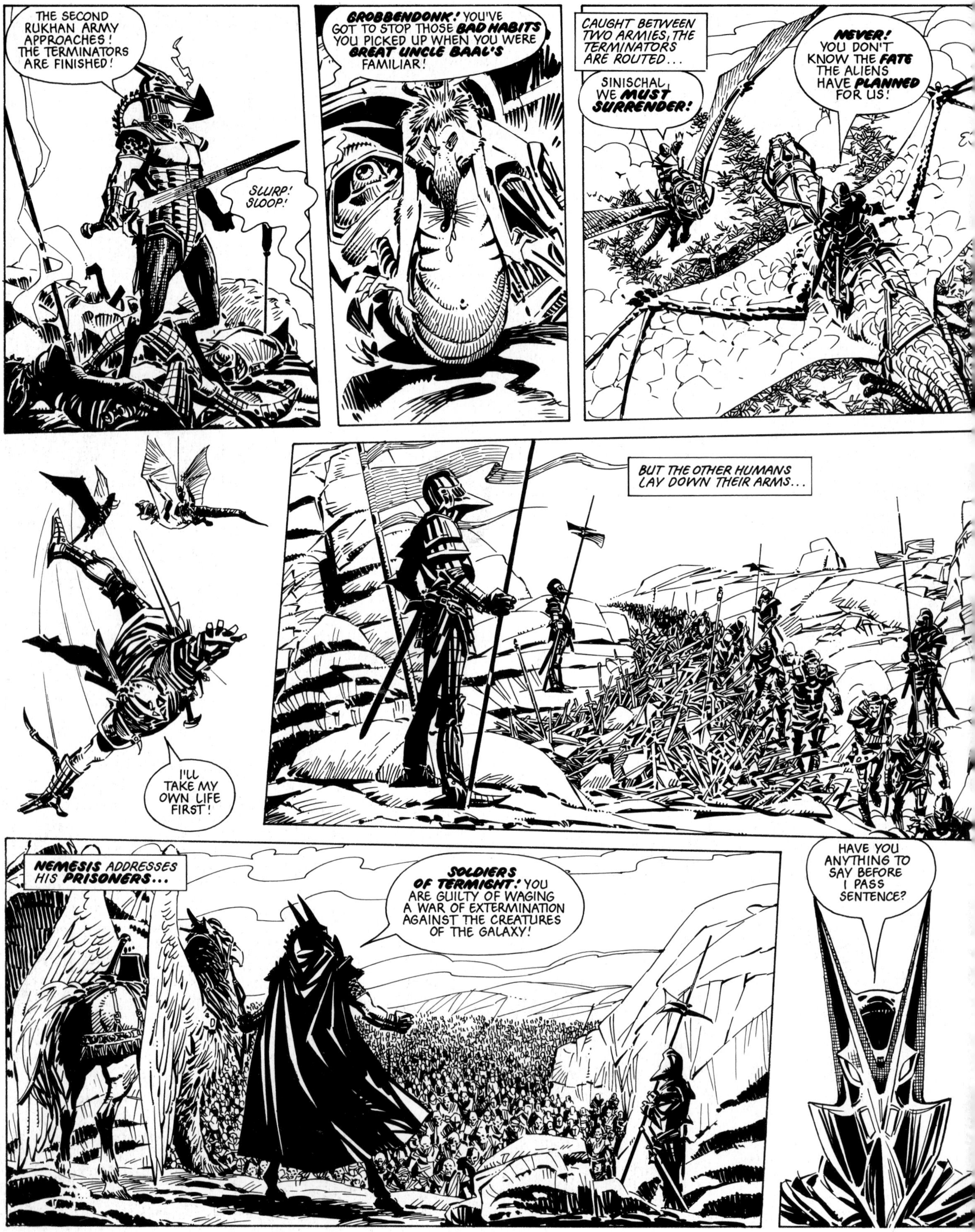
THE SECOND RUKHAN ARMY APPROACHES! THE TERMINATORS ARE FINISHED!
SLURP! SLOOP!
GROBBENDONK! YOU'VE GOT TO STOP THOSE BAD HABITS YOU PICKED UP WHEN YOU WERE GREAT UNCLE BAAL'S FAMILIAR!
CAUGHT BETWEEN TWO ARMIES, THE TERMINATORS ARE ROUTED...
SINISCHAL, WE MUST SURRENDER!
NEVER! YOU DON'T KNOW THE FATE THE ALIENS HAVE PLANNED FOR US!
I'LL TAKE MY OWN LIFE FIRST!
BUT THE OTHER HUMANS LAY DOWN THEIR ARMS...
NEMESIS ADDRESSES HIS PRISONERS...
SOLDIERS OF TERMIGHT: YOU ARE GUILTY OF WAGING A WAR OF EXTERMINATION AGAINST THE CREATURES OF THE GALAXY!
HAVE YOU ANYTHING TO SAY BEFORE I PASS SENTENCE?

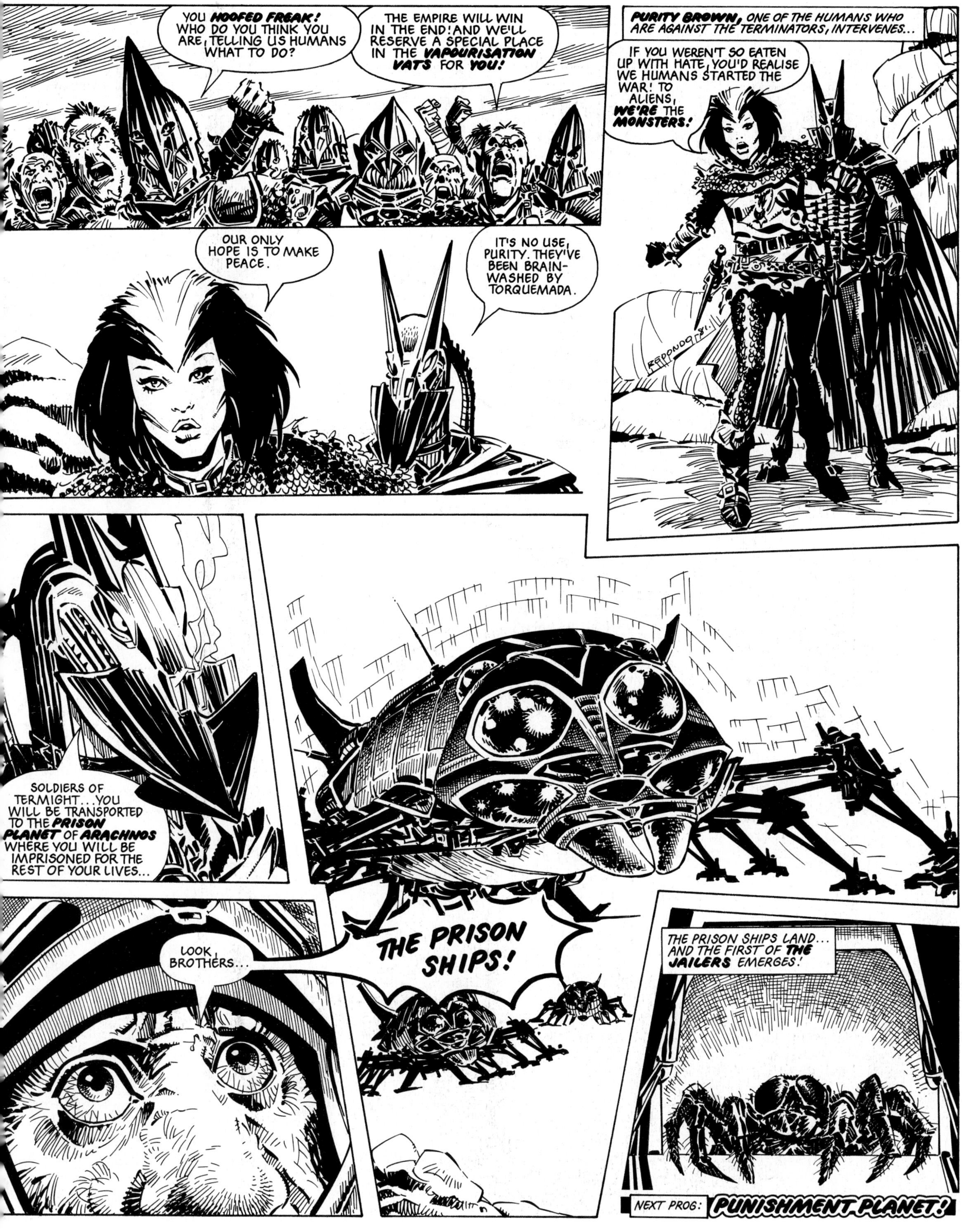
YOU HOOFED FREAK! WHO DO YOU THINK YOU ARE, TELLING US HUMANS WHAT TO DO?
THE EMPIRE WILL WIN IN THE END! AND WE'LL RESERVE A SPECIAL PLACE IN THE VAPOURISATION VATS FOR YOU!
PURITY BROWN, ONE OF THE HUMANS WHO ARE AGAINST THE TERMINATORS, INTERVENES...
IF YOU WEREN'T SO EATEN UP WITH HATE, YOU'D REALISE WE HUMANS STARTED THE WAR! TO ALIENS, WE'RE THE MONSTERS!
OUR ONLY HOPE IS TO MAKE PEACE.
IT'S NO USE, PURITY. THEY'VE BEEN BRAIN-WASHED BY TORQUEMADA.
SOLDIERS OF TERMIGHT... YOU WILL BE TRANSPORTED TO THE PRISON PLANET OF ARACHNOS WHERE YOU WILL BE IMPRISONED FOR THE REST OF YOUR LIVES...
LOOK, BROTHERS...
THE PRISON SHIPS!
THE PRISON SHIPS LAND... AND THE FIRST OF THE JAILERS EMERGES!
NEXT PROG: PUNISHMENT PLANET!

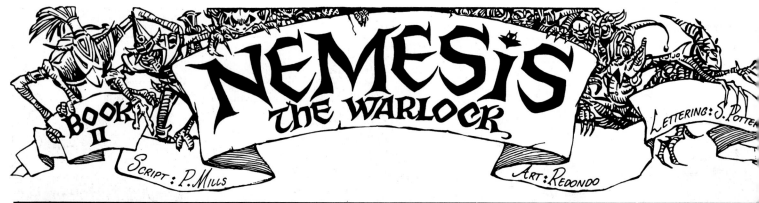

NEMESIS THE WARLOCK

BOOK II

Script: P. Mills   Art: Redondo   Lettering: S. Potter

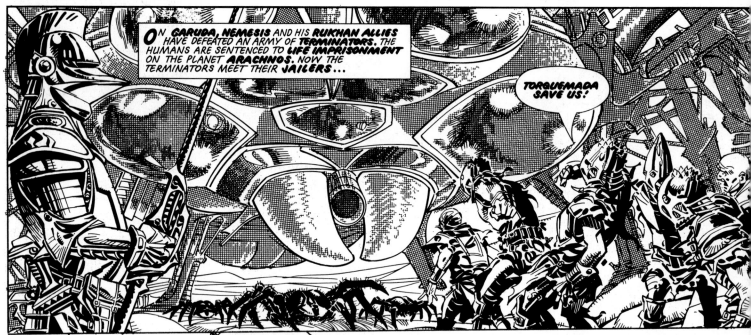

ON **GARUDA**, **NEMESIS** AND HIS **RUKHAN** ALLIES HAVE DEFEATED AN ARMY OF **TERMINATORS**. THE HUMANS ARE SENTENCED TO **LIFE IMPRISONMENT** ON THE PLANET **ARACHNOS**. NOW THE TERMINATORS MEET THEIR **JAILERS**...

TORQUEMADA SAVE US!

ALL HUMANS TO ENTER PRISON SHIP. RESISTANCE IS USELESS!

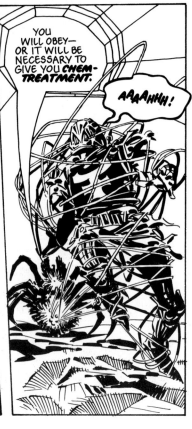

YOU WILL OBEY— OR IT WILL BE NECESSARY TO GIVE YOU **CHEM-TREATMENT**.

AAAAHHH!

IT IS A JUDGEMENT ON US FOR NOT HEEDING THE WORDS OF TORQUEMADA!

STAY WHERE YOU ARE, HUMAN!

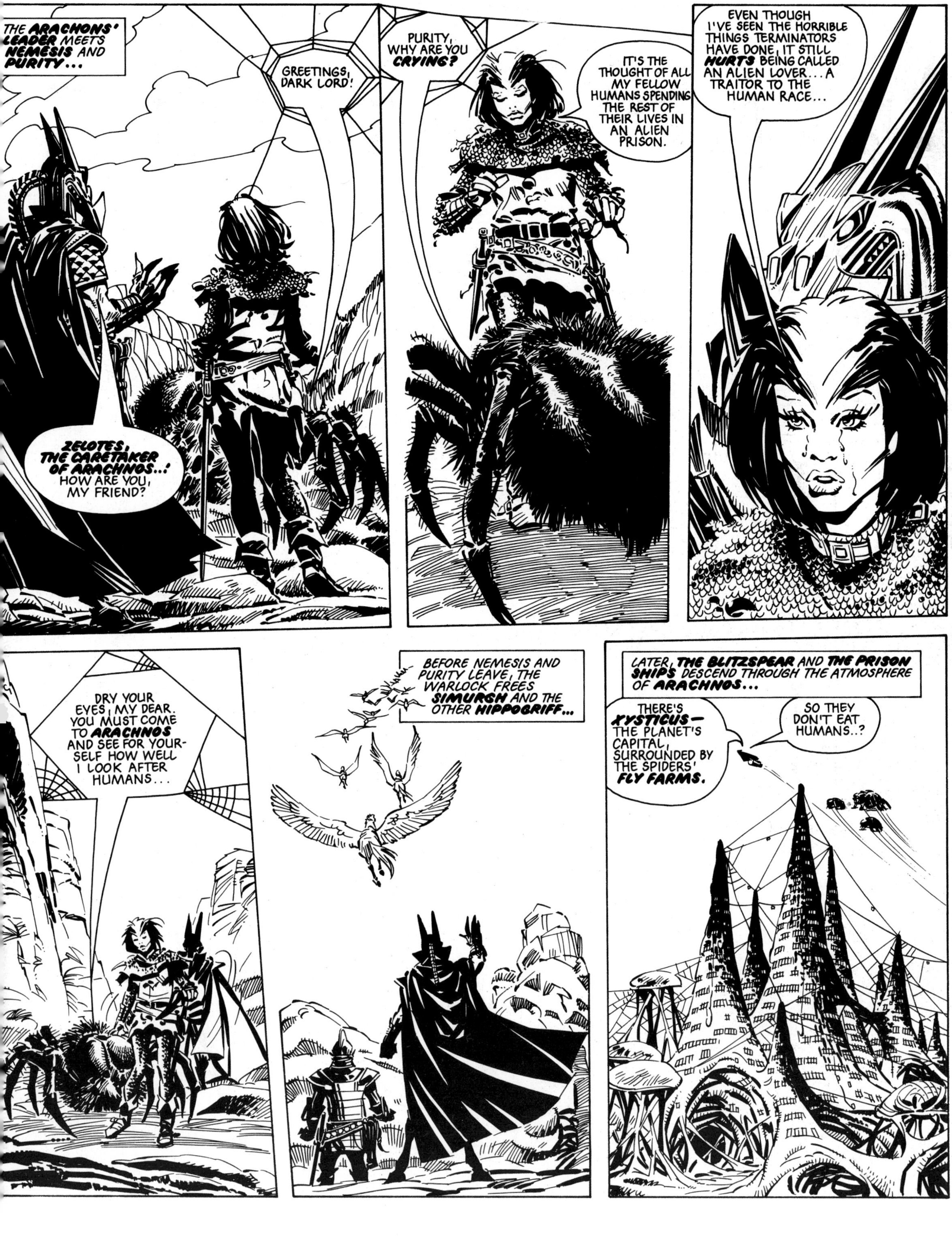
THE ARACHONS' LEADER MEETS NEMESIS AND PURITY...
GREETINGS, DARK LORD!
ZELOTES, THE CARETAKER OF ARACHNOS...! HOW ARE YOU, MY FRIEND?
PURITY, WHY ARE YOU CRYING?
IT'S THE THOUGHT OF ALL MY FELLOW HUMANS SPENDING THE REST OF THEIR LIVES IN AN ALIEN PRISON.
EVEN THOUGH I'VE SEEN THE HORRIBLE THINGS TERMINATORS HAVE DONE, IT STILL HURTS BEING CALLED AN ALIEN LOVER... A TRAITOR TO THE HUMAN RACE...
DRY YOUR EYES, MY DEAR. YOU MUST COME TO ARACHNOS AND SEE FOR YOURSELF HOW WELL I LOOK AFTER HUMANS...
BEFORE NEMESIS AND PURITY LEAVE, THE WARLOCK FREES SIMURGH AND THE OTHER HIPPOGRIFF...
LATER, THE BLITZSPEAR AND THE PRISON SHIPS DESCEND THROUGH THE ATMOSPHERE OF ARACHNOS...
THERE'S XYSTICUS— THE PLANET'S CAPITAL, SURROUNDED BY THE SPIDERS' FLY FARMS.
SO THEY DON'T EAT HUMANS..?

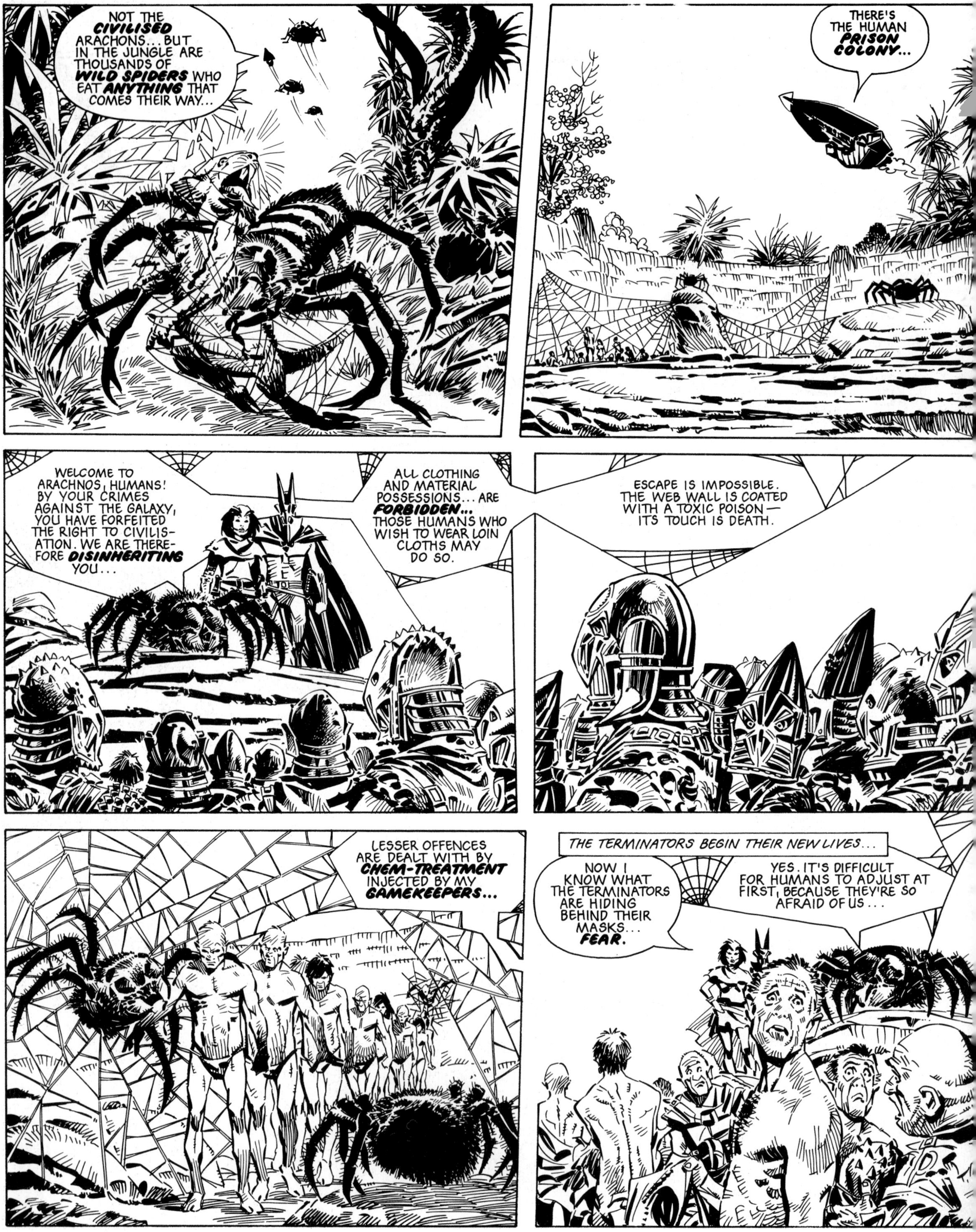
NOT THE CIVILISED ARACHONS... BUT IN THE JUNGLE ARE THOUSANDS OF WILD SPIDERS WHO EAT ANYTHING THAT COMES THEIR WAY...
THERE'S THE HUMAN PRISON COLONY...
WELCOME TO ARACHNOS, HUMANS! BY YOUR CRIMES AGAINST THE GALAXY, YOU HAVE FORFEITED THE RIGHT TO CIVILIS-ATION. WE ARE THERE-FORE DISINHERITING YOU...
ALL CLOTHING AND MATERIAL POSSESSIONS... ARE FORBIDDEN... THOSE HUMANS WHO WISH TO WEAR LOIN CLOTHS MAY DO SO.
ESCAPE IS IMPOSSIBLE. THE WEB WALL IS COATED WITH A TOXIC POISON — ITS TOUCH IS DEATH.
LESSER OFFENCES ARE DEALT WITH BY CHEM-TREATMENT INJECTED BY MY GAMEKEEPERS...
THE TERMINATORS BEGIN THEIR NEW LIVES...
NOW I KNOW WHAT THE TERMINATORS ARE HIDING BEHIND THEIR MASKS... FEAR.
YES. IT'S DIFFICULT FOR HUMANS TO ADJUST AT FIRST, BECAUSE THEY'RE SO AFRAID OF US...

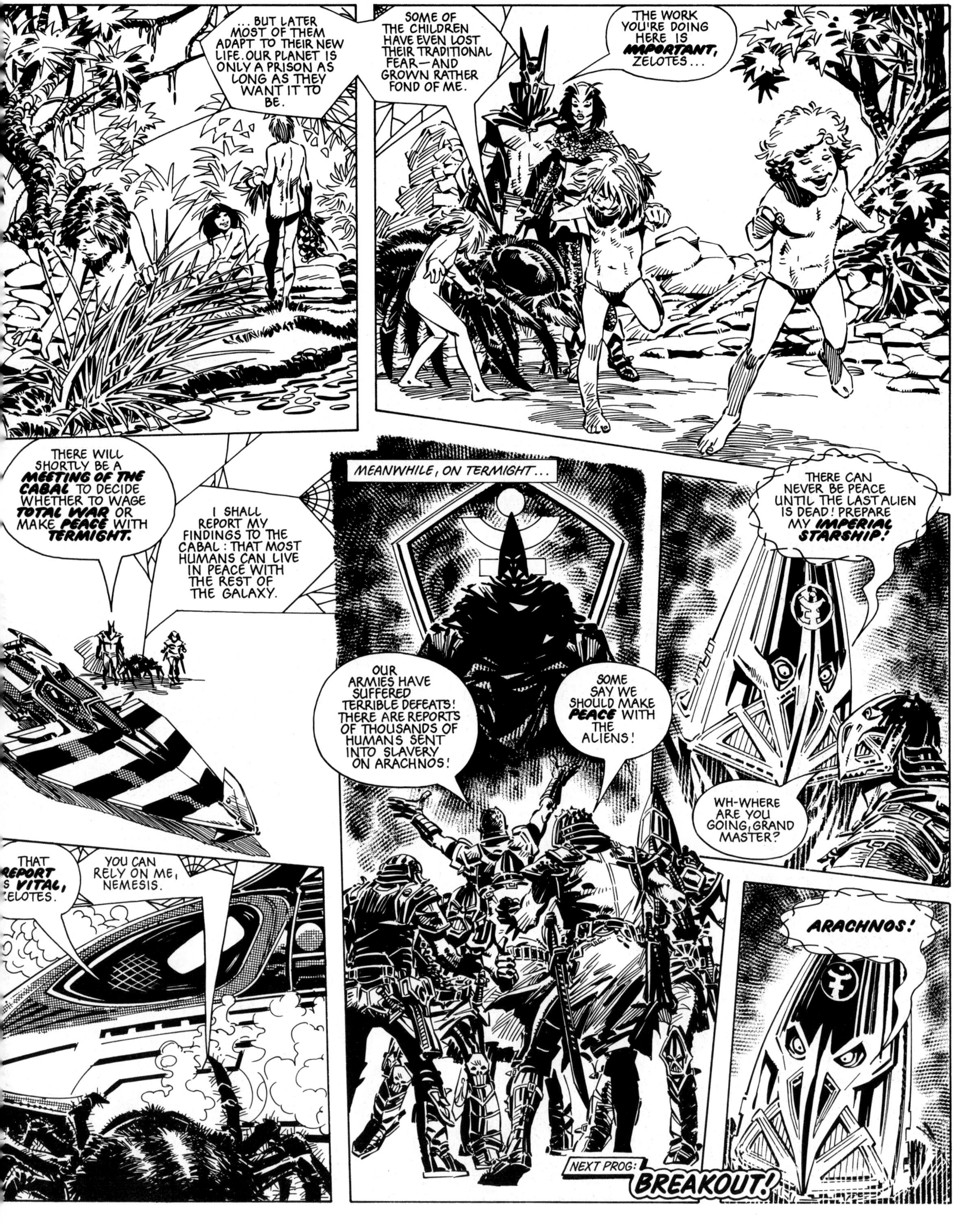

... BUT LATER MOST OF THEM ADAPT TO THEIR NEW LIFE. OUR PLANET IS ONLY A PRISON AS LONG AS THEY WANT IT TO BE.
SOME OF THE CHILDREN HAVE EVEN LOST THEIR TRADITIONAL FEAR—AND GROWN RATHER FOND OF ME.
THE WORK YOU'RE DOING HERE IS IMPORTANT, ZELOTES...
THERE WILL SHORTLY BE A MEETING OF THE CABAL TO DECIDE WHETHER TO WAGE TOTAL WAR OR MAKE PEACE WITH TERMIGHT.
I SHALL REPORT MY FINDINGS TO THE CABAL : THAT MOST HUMANS CAN LIVE IN PEACE WITH THE REST OF THE GALAXY.
THAT REPORT IS VITAL, ZELOTES.
YOU CAN RELY ON ME, NEMESIS.
MEANWHILE, ON TERMIGHT...
OUR ARMIES HAVE SUFFERED TERRIBLE DEFEATS! THERE ARE REPORTS OF THOUSANDS OF HUMANS SENT INTO SLAVERY ON ARACHNOS!
SOME SAY WE SHOULD MAKE PEACE WITH THE ALIENS!
THERE CAN NEVER BE PEACE UNTIL THE LAST ALIEN IS DEAD! PREPARE MY IMPERIAL STARSHIP!
WH-WHERE ARE YOU GOING, GRAND MASTER?
ARACHNOS!
NEXT PROG: BREAKOUT!

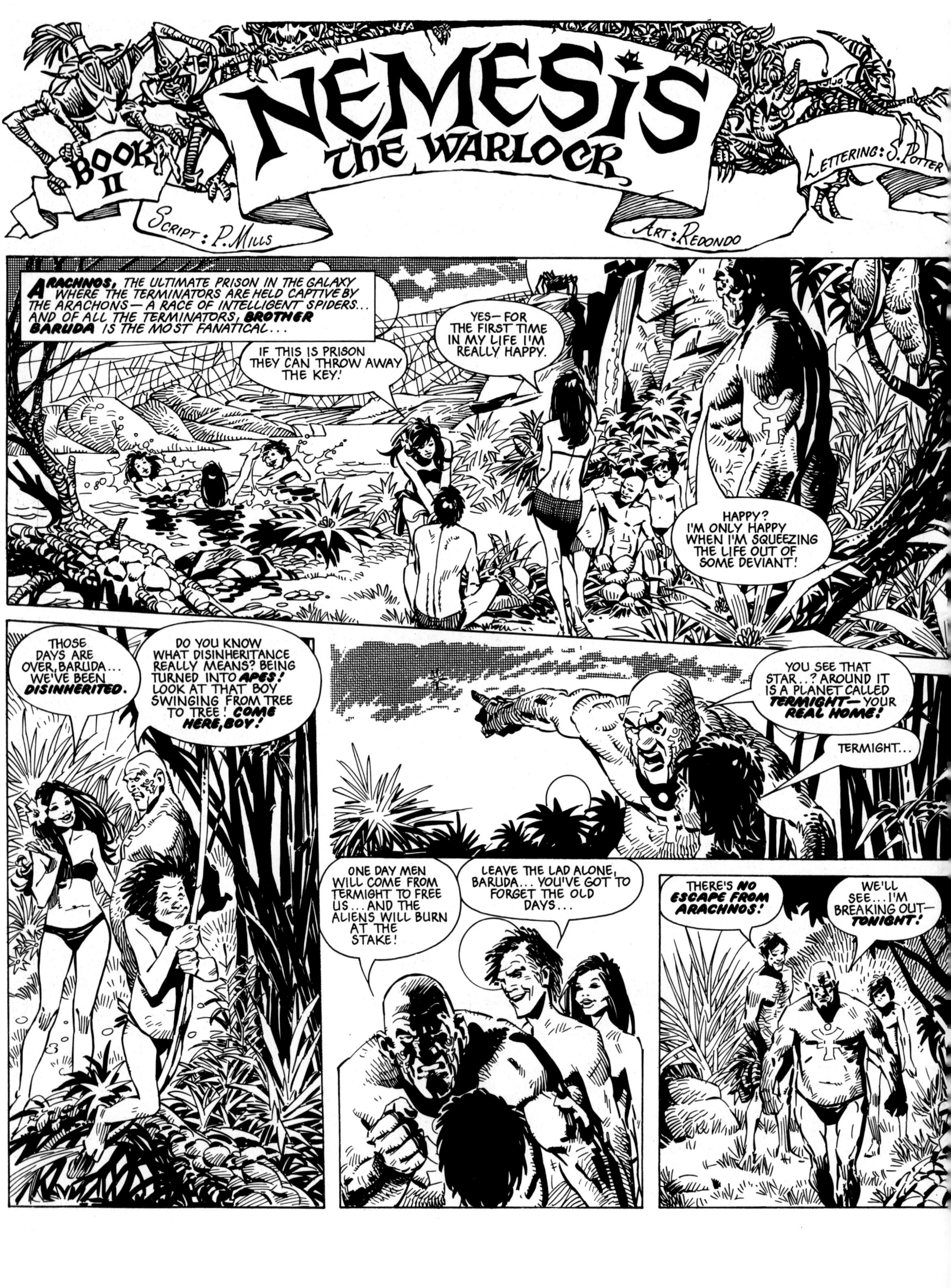
BOOK II
NEMESIS THE WARLOCK
SCRIPT: P. MILLS
ART: REDONDO
LETTERING: S. POTTER
ARACHNOS, THE ULTIMATE PRISON IN THE GALAXY WHERE THE TERMINATORS ARE HELD CAPTIVE BY THE ARACHONS— A RACE OF INTELLIGENT SPIDERS... AND OF ALL THE TERMINATORS, BROTHER BARUDA IS THE MOST FANATICAL...
IF THIS IS PRISON THEY CAN THROW AWAY THE KEY!
YES— FOR THE FIRST TIME IN MY LIFE I'M REALLY HAPPY.
HAPPY? I'M ONLY HAPPY WHEN I'M SQUEEZING THE LIFE OUT OF SOME DEVIANT!
THOSE DAYS ARE OVER, BARUDA... WE'VE BEEN DISINHERITED.
DO YOU KNOW WHAT DISINHERITANCE REALLY MEANS? BEING TURNED INTO APES! LOOK AT THAT BOY SWINGING FROM TREE TO TREE! COME HERE, BOY!
YOU SEE THAT STAR..? AROUND IT IS A PLANET CALLED TERMIGHT— YOUR REAL HOME!
TERMIGHT...
ONE DAY MEN WILL COME FROM TERMIGHT TO FREE US... AND THE ALIENS WILL BURN AT THE STAKE!
LEAVE THE LAD ALONE, BARUDA... YOU'VE GOT TO FORGET THE OLD DAYS...
THERE'S NO ESCAPE FROM ARACHNOS!
WE'LL SEE... I'M BREAKING OUT— TONIGHT!

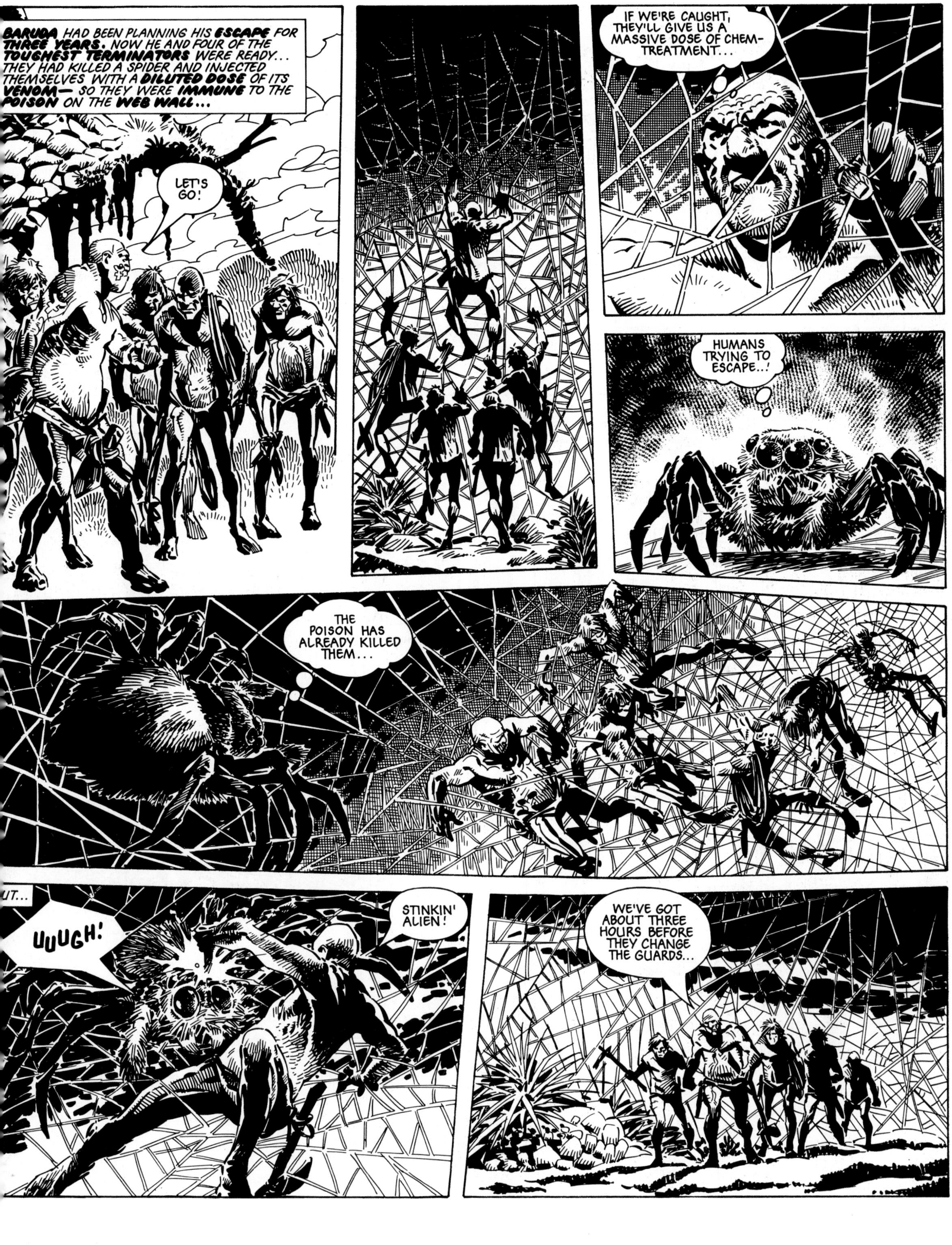
BARUDA HAD BEEN PLANNING HIS ESCAPE FOR THREE YEARS. NOW HE AND FOUR OF THE TOUGHEST TERMINATORS WERE READY... THEY HAD KILLED A SPIDER AND INJECTED THEMSELVES WITH A DILUTED DOSE OF ITS VENOM— SO THEY WERE IMMUNE TO THE POISON ON THE WEB WALL...
LET'S GO!
IF WE'RE CAUGHT, THEY'LL GIVE US A MASSIVE DOSE OF CHEM-TREATMENT...
HUMANS TRYING TO ESCAPE...!
THE POISON HAS ALREADY KILLED THEM...
UT...
UUUGH!
STINKIN' ALIEN!
WE'VE GOT ABOUT THREE HOURS BEFORE THEY CHANGE THE GUARDS...

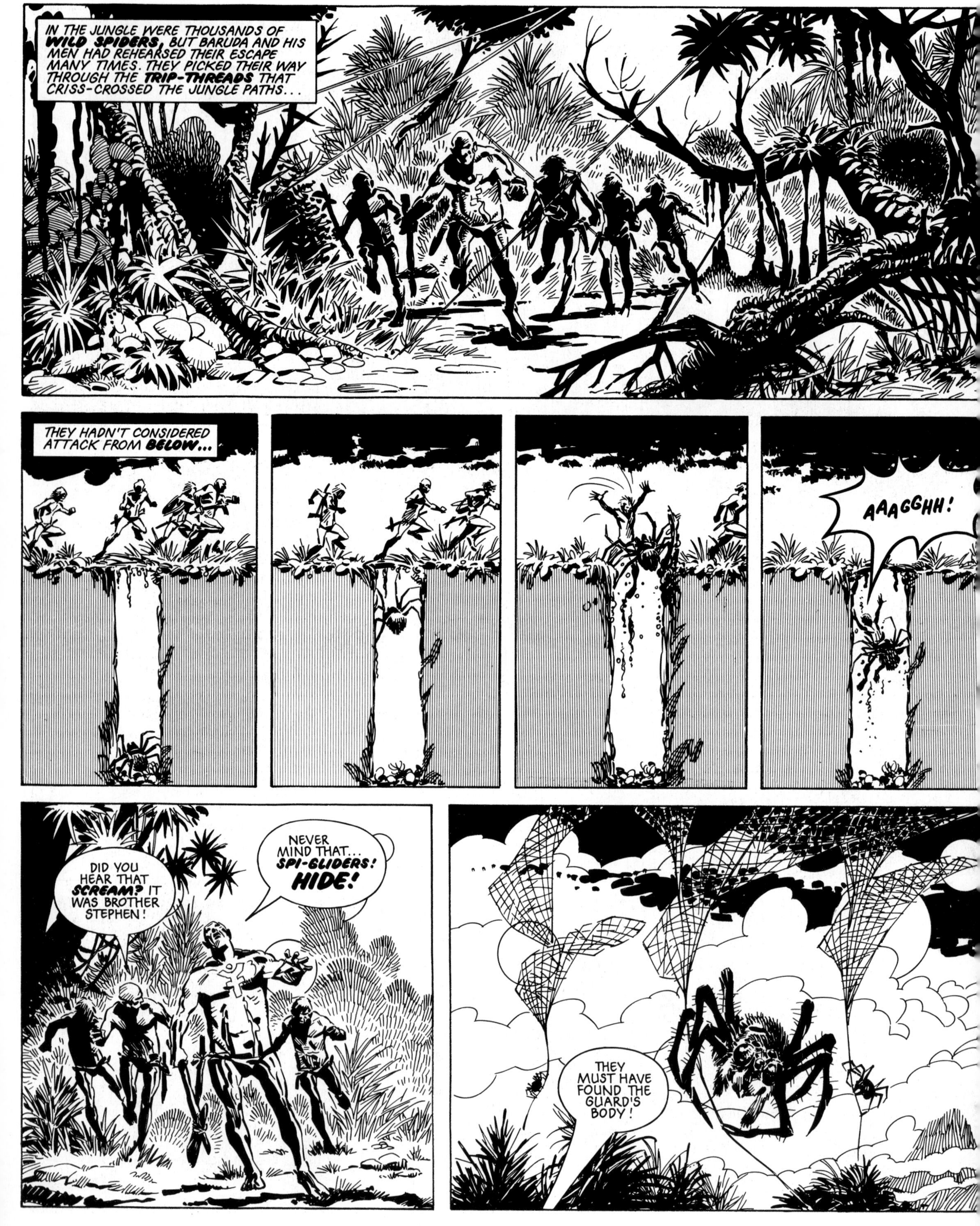

IN THE JUNGLE WERE THOUSANDS OF WILD SPIDERS, BUT BARUDA AND HIS MEN HAD REHEARSED THEIR ESCAPE MANY TIMES. THEY PICKED THEIR WAY THROUGH THE TRIP-THREADS THAT CRISS-CROSSED THE JUNGLE PATHS...
THEY HADN'T CONSIDERED ATTACK FROM BELOW...
AAAGGHH!
DID YOU HEAR THAT SCREAM? IT WAS BROTHER STEPHEN!
NEVER MIND THAT... SPI-GLIDERS! HIDE!
THEY MUST HAVE FOUND THE GUARD'S BODY!

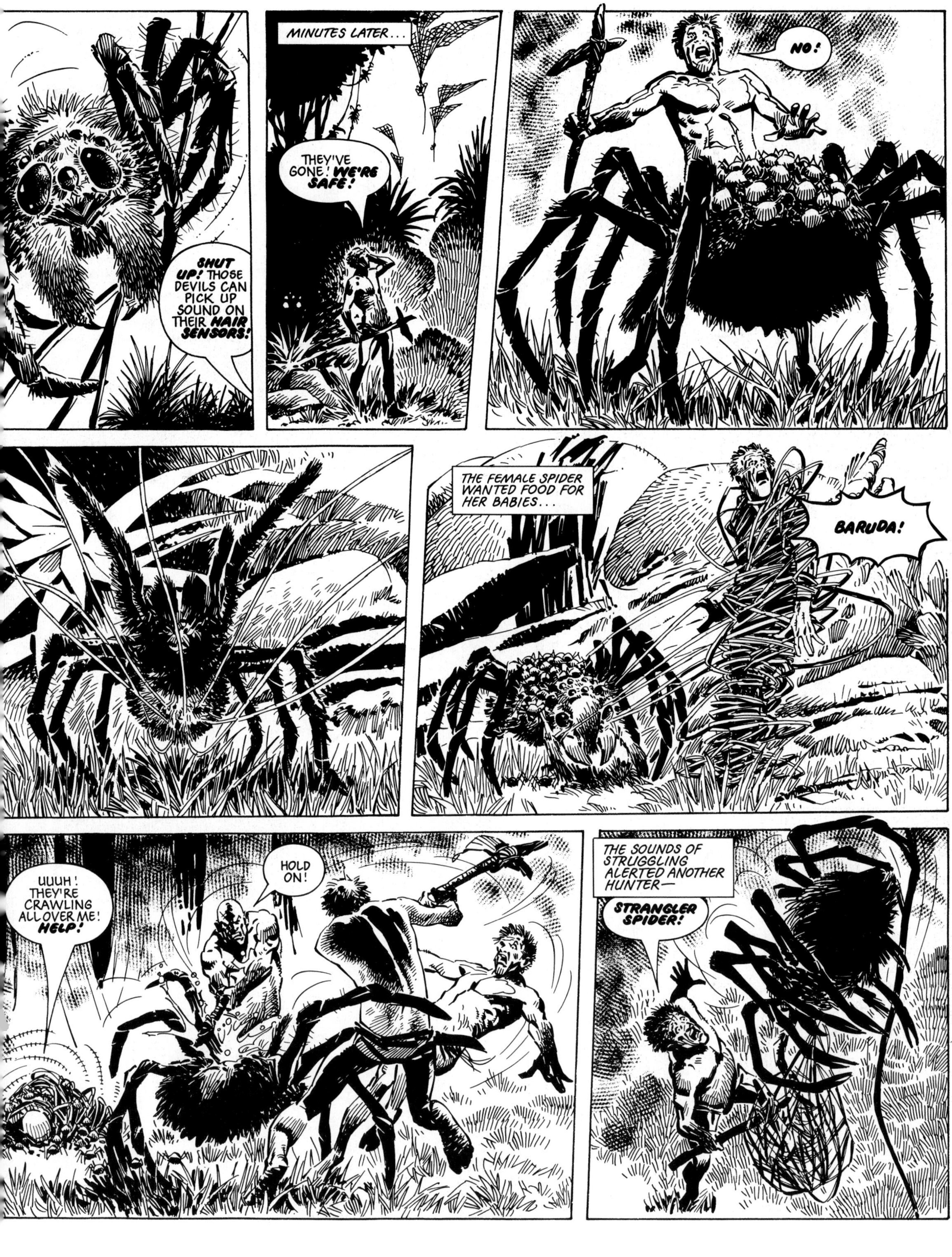
SHUT UP! THOSE DEVILS CAN PICK UP SOUND ON THEIR HAIR SENSORS!
MINUTES LATER...
THEY'VE GONE! WE'RE SAFE!
NO!
THE FEMALE SPIDER WANTED FOOD FOR HER BABIES...
BARUDA!
UUUH! THEY'RE CRAWLING ALL OVER ME! HELP!
HOLD ON!
THE SOUNDS OF STRUGGLING ALERTED ANOTHER HUNTER—
STRANGLER SPIDER!

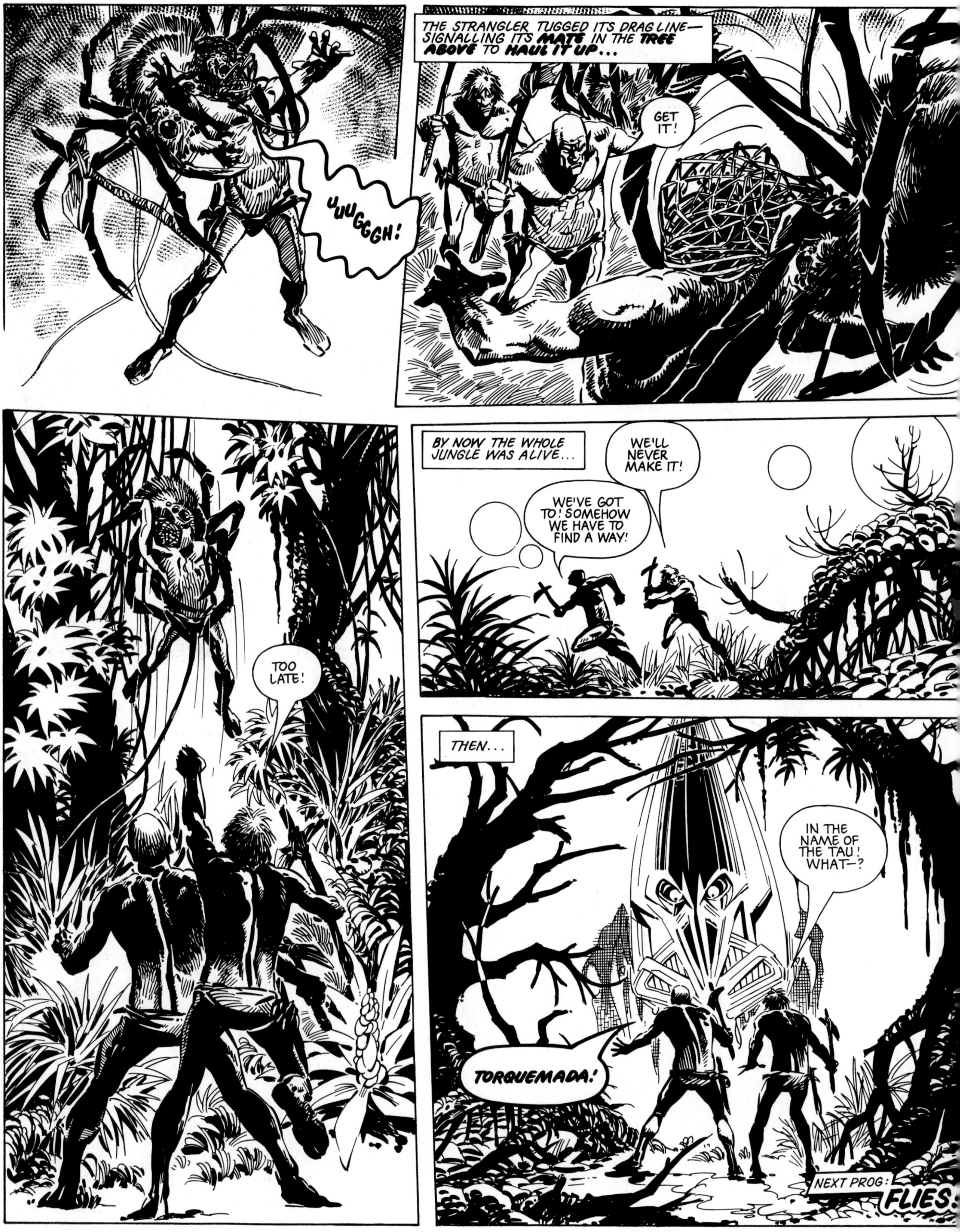

UUUGGGH!
THE STRANGLER TUGGED ITS DRAG LINE— SIGNALLING ITS MATE IN THE TREE ABOVE TO HAUL IT UP...
GET IT!
TOO LATE!
BY NOW THE WHOLE JUNGLE WAS ALIVE...
WE'LL NEVER MAKE IT!
WE'VE GOT TO! SOMEHOW WE HAVE TO FIND A WAY!
THEN...
IN THE NAME OF THE TAU! WHAT—?
TORQUEMADA!
NEXT PROG: FLIES!

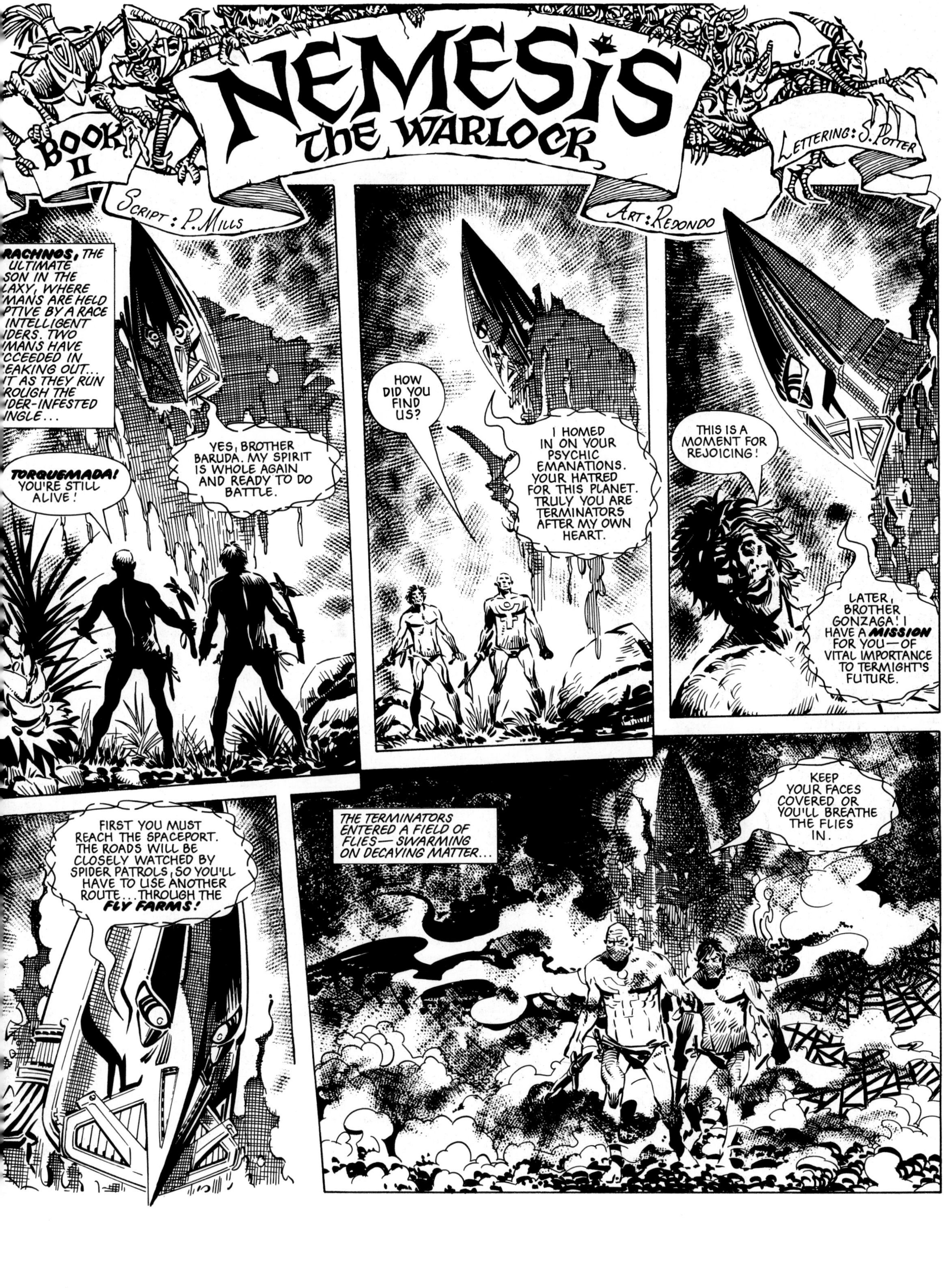
NEMESIS THE WARLOCK
BOOK II
SCRIPT: P. MILLS
ART: REDONDO
LETTERING: S. POTTER
RACHNOS, THE ULTIMATE SON IN THE LAXY, WHERE MANS ARE HELD PTIVE BY A RACE INTELLIGENT IDERS. TWO MANS HAVE CCEEDED IN EAKING OUT... T AS THEY RUN ROUGH THE IDER-INFESTED NGLE...
TORQUEMADA! YOU'RE STILL ALIVE!
YES, BROTHER BARUDA. MY SPIRIT IS WHOLE AGAIN AND READY TO DO BATTLE.
HOW DID YOU FIND US?
I HOMED IN ON YOUR PSYCHIC EMANATIONS. YOUR HATRED FOR THIS PLANET. TRULY YOU ARE TERMINATORS AFTER MY OWN HEART.
THIS IS A MOMENT FOR REJOICING!
LATER, BROTHER GONZAGA! I HAVE A MISSION FOR YOU—OF VITAL IMPORTANCE TO TERMIGHT'S FUTURE.
FIRST YOU MUST REACH THE SPACEPORT. THE ROADS WILL BE CLOSELY WATCHED BY SPIDER PATROLS, SO YOU'LL HAVE TO USE ANOTHER ROUTE... THROUGH THE FLY FARMS!
THE TERMINATORS ENTERED A FIELD OF FLIES— SWARMING ON DECAYING MATTER...
KEEP YOUR FACES COVERED OR YOU'LL BREATHE THE FLIES IN.

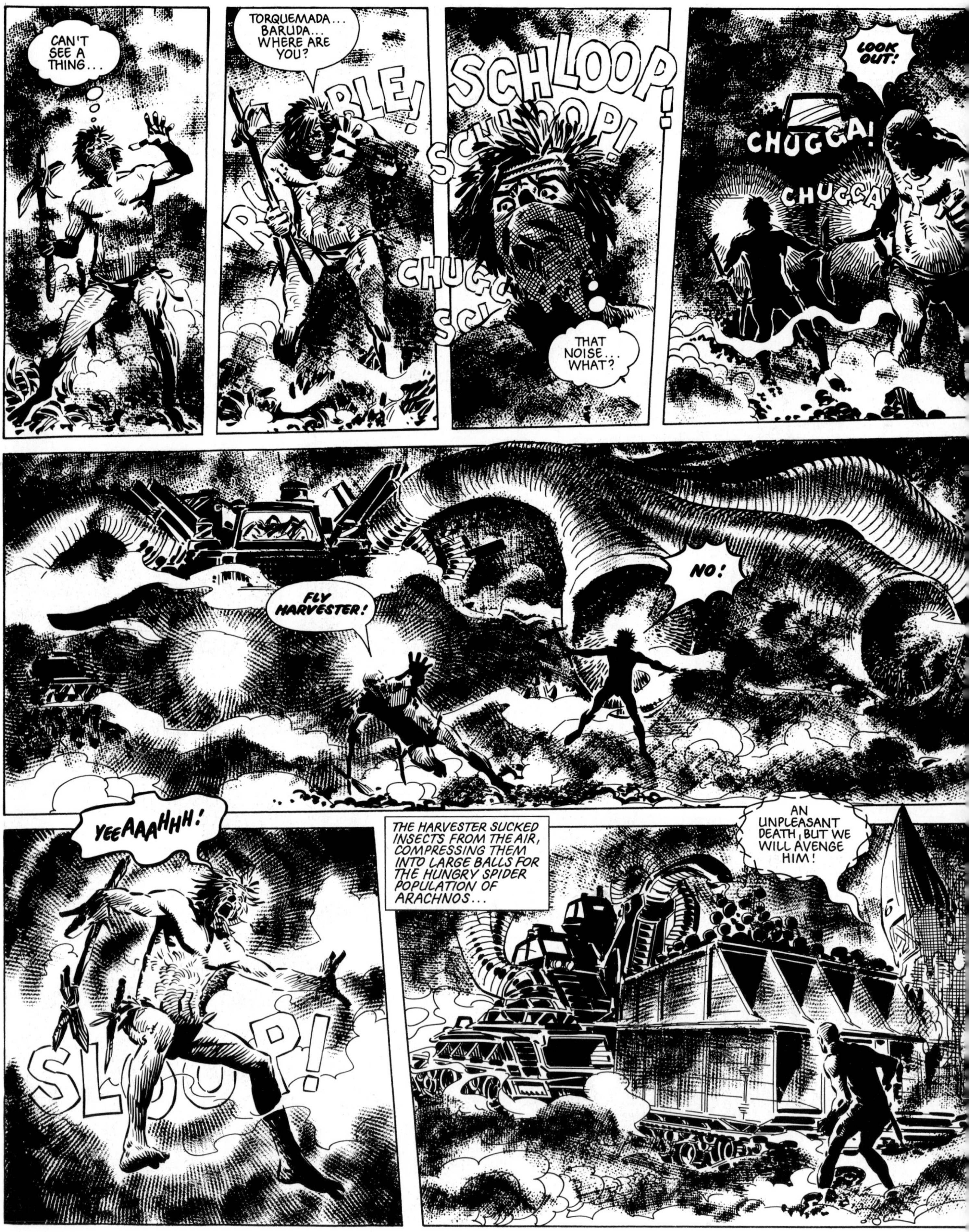
CAN'T SEE A THING...
TORQUEMADA... BARUDA... WHERE ARE YOU?
SCHLOOP!
THAT NOISE... WHAT?
LOOK OUT!
CHUGGA!
FLY HARVESTER!
NO!
YEEAAAHHH!
THE HARVESTER SUCKED INSECTS FROM THE AIR, COMPRESSING THEM INTO LARGE BALLS FOR THE HUNGRY SPIDER POPULATION OF ARACHNOS...
AN UNPLEASANT DEATH, BUT WE WILL AVENGE HIM!

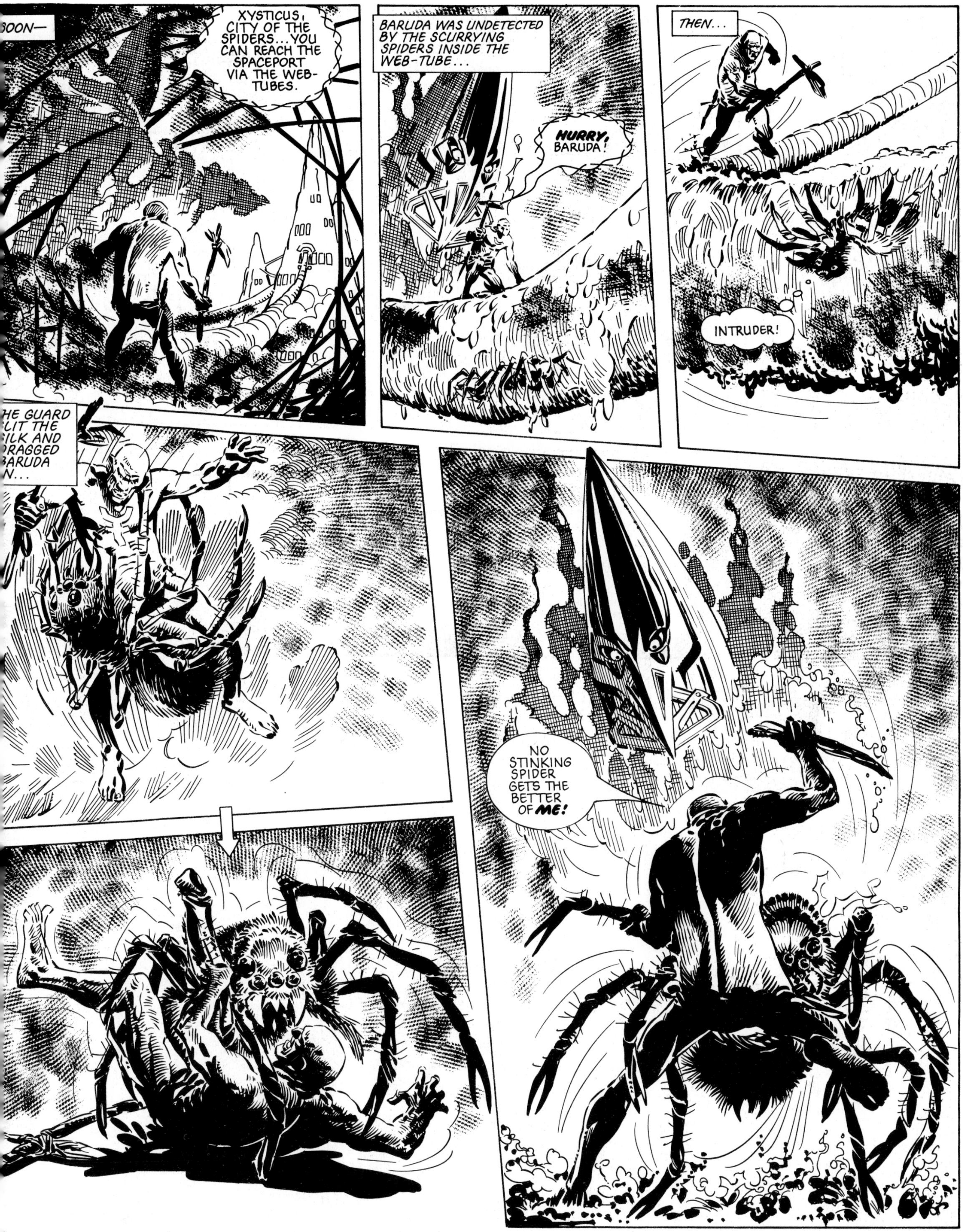

SOON—
XYSTICUS, CITY OF THE SPIDERS... YOU CAN REACH THE SPACEPORT VIA THE WEB-TUBES.
BARUDA WAS UNDETECTED BY THE SCURRYING SPIDERS INSIDE THE WEB-TUBE...
HURRY, BARUDA!
THEN...
INTRUDER!
HE GUARD LIT THE SILK AND DRAGGED BARUDA N...
NO STINKING SPIDER GETS THE BETTER OF ME!

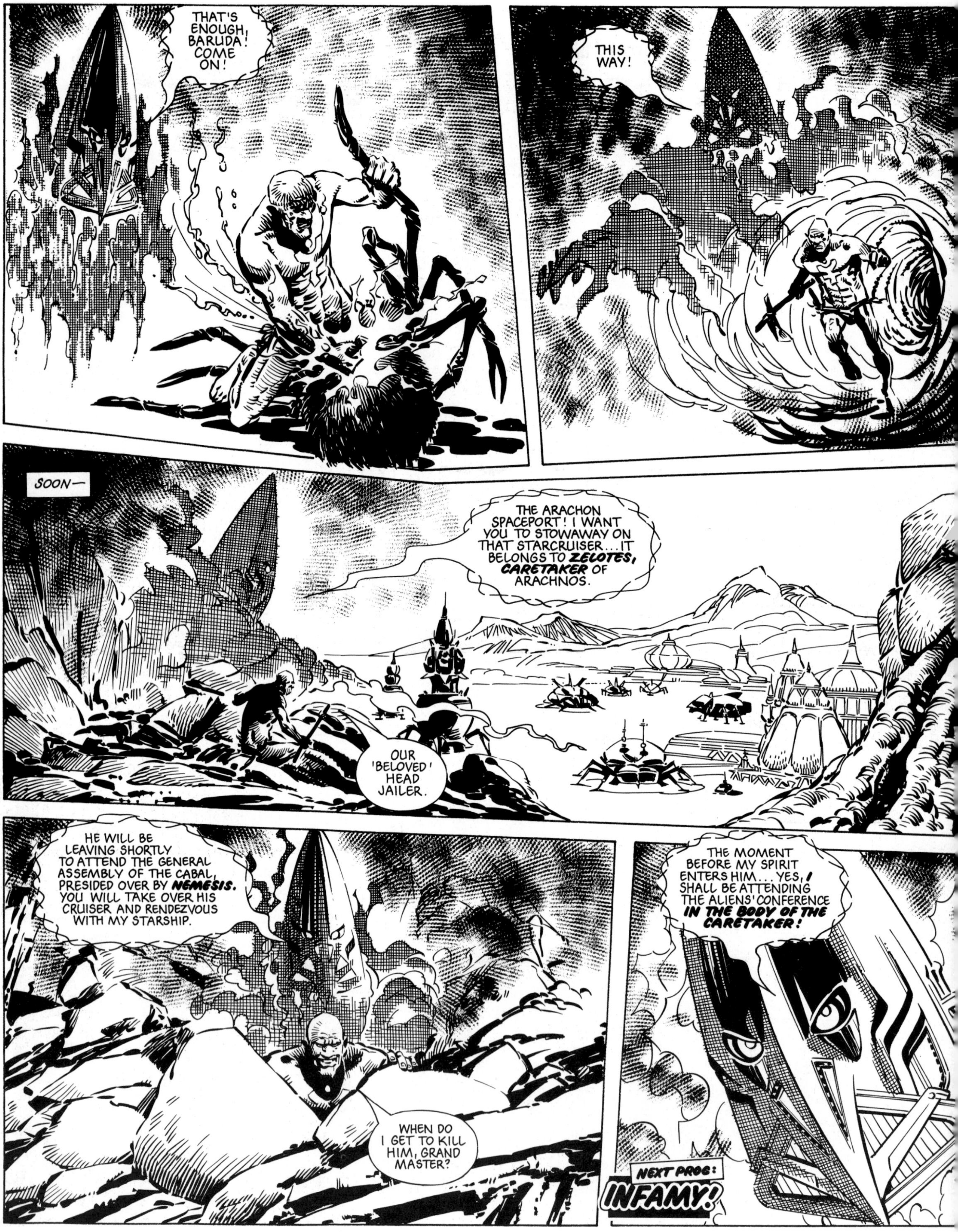

THAT'S ENOUGH, BARUDA! COME ON!
THIS WAY!
SOON—
THE ARACHON SPACEPORT! I WANT YOU TO STOWAWAY ON THAT STARCRUISER... IT BELONGS TO ZELOTES, CARETAKER OF ARACHNOS.
OUR 'BELOVED' HEAD JAILER.
HE WILL BE LEAVING SHORTLY TO ATTEND THE GENERAL ASSEMBLY OF THE CABAL, PRESIDED OVER BY NEMESIS. YOU WILL TAKE OVER HIS CRUISER AND RENDEZVOUS WITH MY STARSHIP.
WHEN DO I GET TO KILL HIM, GRAND MASTER?
THE MOMENT BEFORE MY SPIRIT ENTERS HIM... YES, I SHALL BE ATTENDING THE ALIENS' CONFERENCE IN THE BODY OF THE CARETAKER!
NEXT PROG: INFAMY!

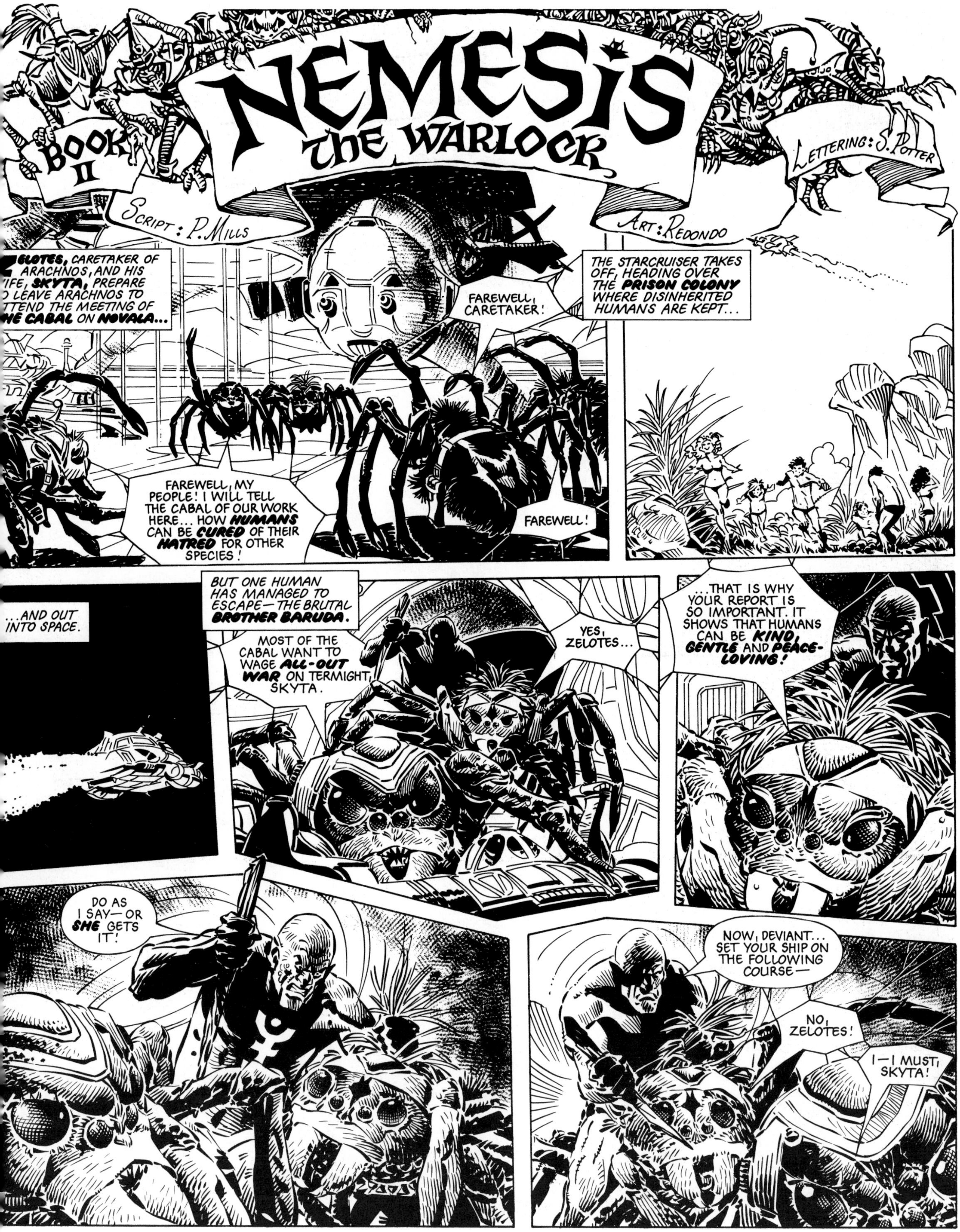
BOOK II
NEMESIS THE WARLOCK
LETTERING: S. POTTER
SCRIPT: P. MILLS
ART: REDONDO
ELOTES, CARETAKER OF ARACHNOS, AND HIS IFE, SKYTA, PREPARE O LEAVE ARACHNOS TO TTEND THE MEETING OF HE CABAL ON NOVALA...
FAREWELL, CARETAKER!
FAREWELL, MY PEOPLE! I WILL TELL THE CABAL OF OUR WORK HERE... HOW HUMANS CAN BE CURED OF THEIR HATRED FOR OTHER SPECIES!
FAREWELL!
THE STARCRUISER TAKES OFF, HEADING OVER THE PRISON COLONY WHERE DISINHERITED HUMANS ARE KEPT...
...AND OUT INTO SPACE.
BUT ONE HUMAN HAS MANAGED TO ESCAPE—THE BRUTAL BROTHER BARUDA.
MOST OF THE CABAL WANT TO WAGE ALL-OUT WAR ON TERMIGHT, SKYTA.
YES, ZELOTES...
...THAT IS WHY YOUR REPORT IS SO IMPORTANT. IT SHOWS THAT HUMANS CAN BE KIND, GENTLE AND PEACE-LOVING!
DO AS I SAY—OR SHE GETS IT!
NOW, DEVIANT... SET YOUR SHIP ON THE FOLLOWING COURSE—
NO, ZELOTES!
I—I MUST, SKYTA!

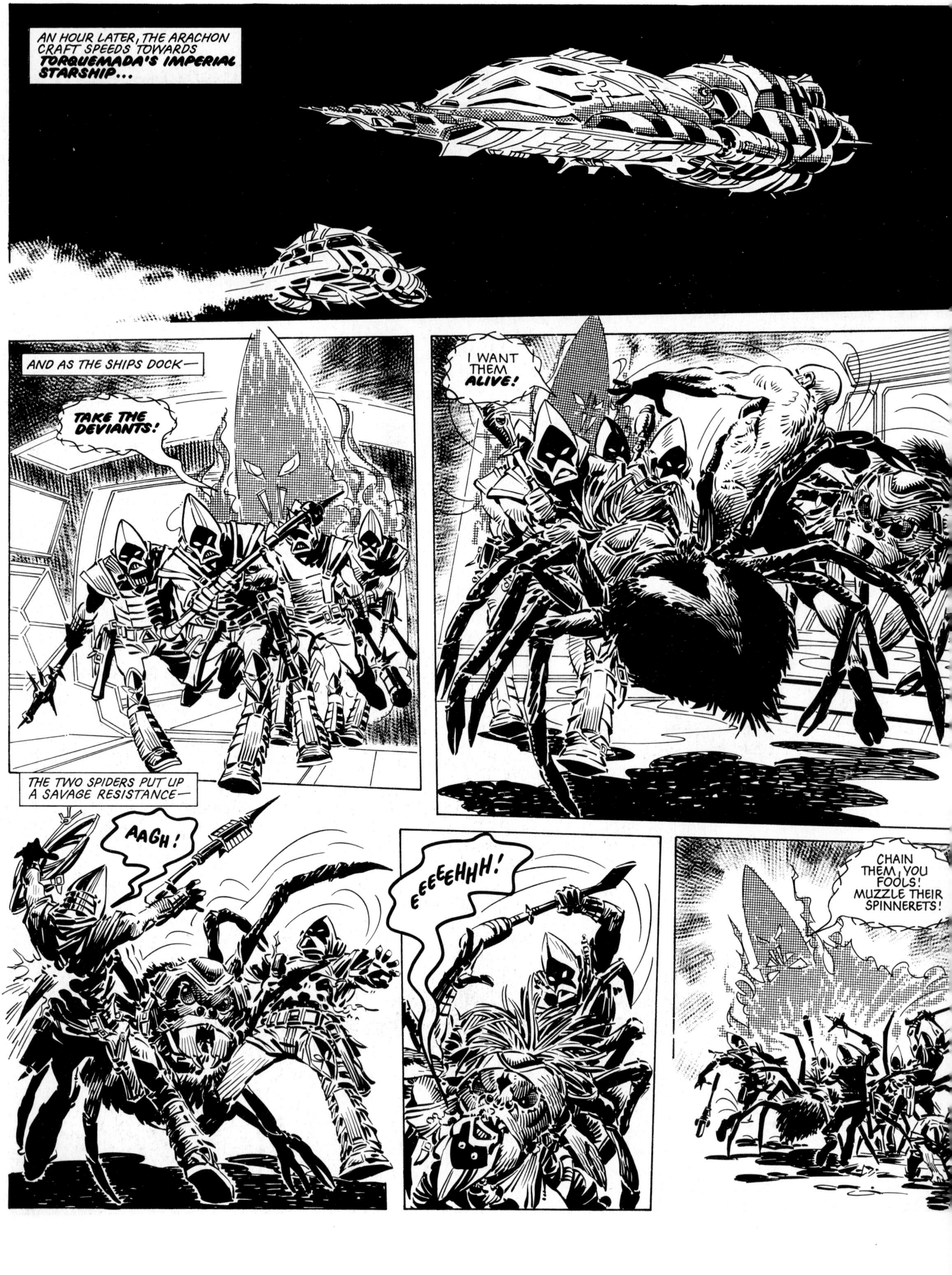

AN HOUR LATER, THE ARACHON CRAFT SPEEDS TOWARDS TORQUEMADA'S IMPERIAL STARSHIP...
AND AS THE SHIPS DOCK—
TAKE THE DEVIANTS!
I WANT THEM ALIVE!
THE TWO SPIDERS PUT UP A SAVAGE RESISTANCE—
AAGH!
EEEEEHHH!
CHAIN THEM, YOU FOOLS! MUZZLE THEIR SPINNERETS!

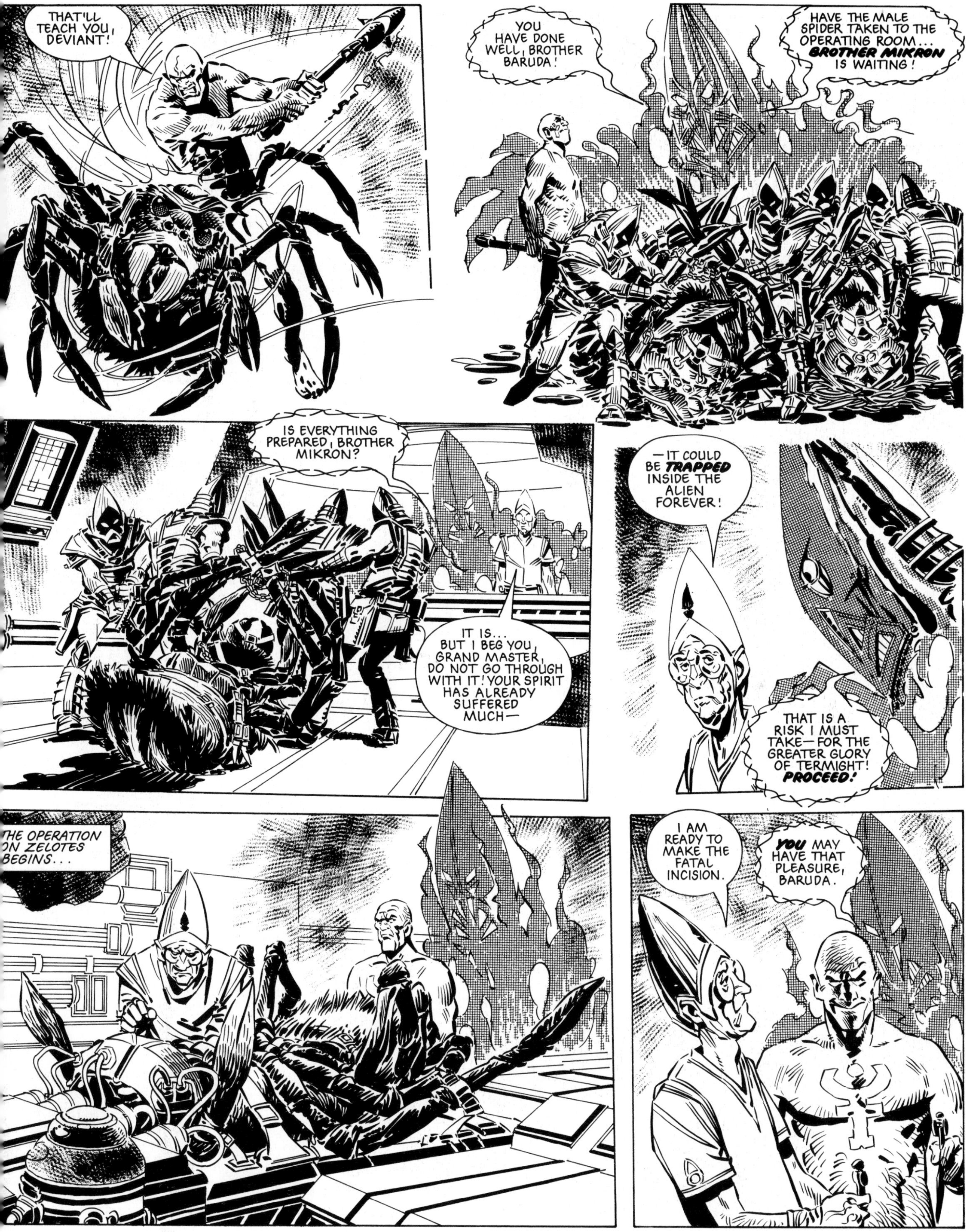

THAT'LL TEACH YOU, DEVIANT!
YOU HAVE DONE WELL, BROTHER BARUDA!
HAVE THE MALE SPIDER TAKEN TO THE OPERATING ROOM... BROTHER MIKRON IS WAITING!
IS EVERYTHING PREPARED, BROTHER MIKRON?
IT IS... BUT I BEG YOU, GRAND MASTER, DO NOT GO THROUGH WITH IT! YOUR SPIRIT HAS ALREADY SUFFERED MUCH—
—IT COULD BE TRAPPED INSIDE THE ALIEN FOREVER!
THAT IS A RISK I MUST TAKE— FOR THE GREATER GLORY OF TERMIGHT! PROCEED!
THE OPERATION ON ZELOTES BEGINS...
I AM READY TO MAKE THE FATAL INCISION.
YOU MAY HAVE THAT PLEASURE, BARUDA.

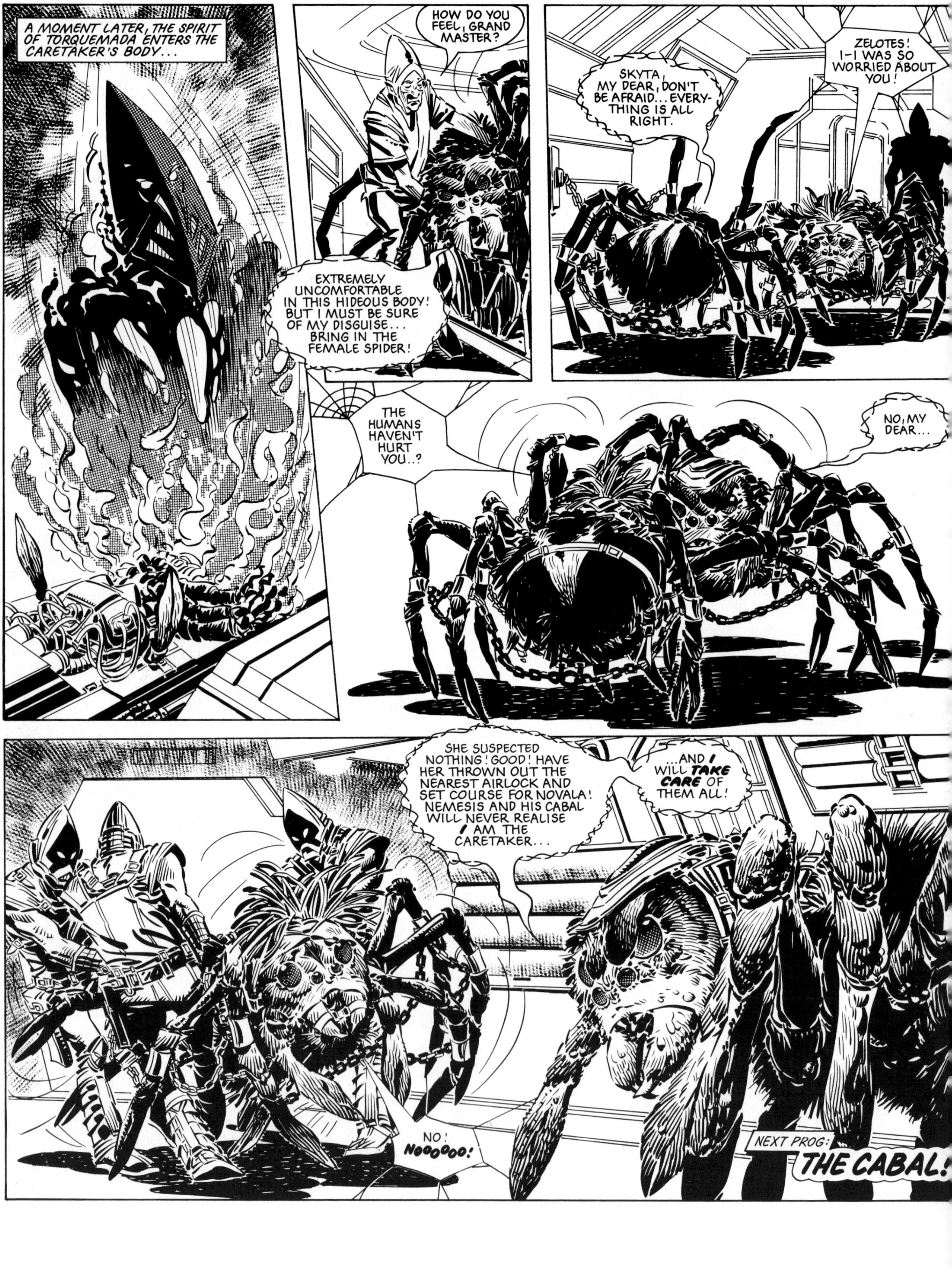

A MOMENT LATER, THE SPIRIT OF TORQUEMADA ENTERS THE CARETAKER'S BODY...
HOW DO YOU FEEL, GRAND MASTER?
EXTREMELY UNCOMFORTABLE IN THIS HIDEOUS BODY! BUT I MUST BE SURE OF MY DISGUISE... BRING IN THE FEMALE SPIDER!
ZELOTES! I-I WAS SO WORRIED ABOUT YOU!
SKYTA, MY DEAR, DON'T BE AFRAID... EVERYTHING IS ALL RIGHT.
THE HUMANS HAVEN'T HURT YOU..?
NO, MY DEAR...
SHE SUSPECTED NOTHING! GOOD! HAVE HER THROWN OUT THE NEAREST AIRLOCK AND SET COURSE FOR NOVALA! NEMESIS AND HIS CABAL WILL NEVER REALISE I AM THE CARETAKER...
...AND I WILL TAKE CARE OF THEM ALL!
NO! NOOOOOO!
NEXT PROG: THE CABAL!

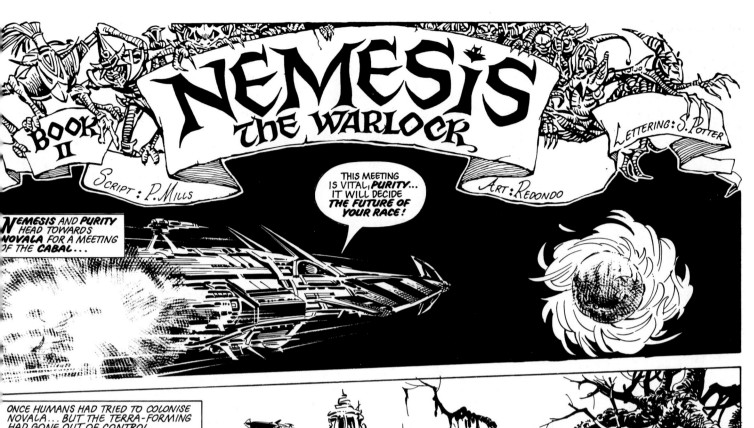

NEMESIS THE WARLOCK

Book II

Script: P. Mills

Lettering: S. Potter

Art: Redondo

THIS MEETING IS VITAL, **PURITY**... IT WILL DECIDE **THE FUTURE OF YOUR RACE!**

NEMESIS AND **PURITY** HEAD TOWARDS **NOVALA** FOR A MEETING OF THE **CABAL**...

ONCE HUMANS HAD TRIED TO COLONISE NOVALA... BUT THE TERRA-FORMING HAD GONE OUT OF CONTROL...

...NOW ITS GREAT CITIES ARE OVERRUN BY DENSE JUNGLE.

A PERFECT HIDE-OUT FOR THE ALIEN REBELS...

NEMESIS! PURITY! WELCOME!

INSIDE, NEMESIS ADDRESSES THE DELEGATES.

MEMBERS OF THE CABAL! WE HAVE WON **GREAT VICTORIES!**

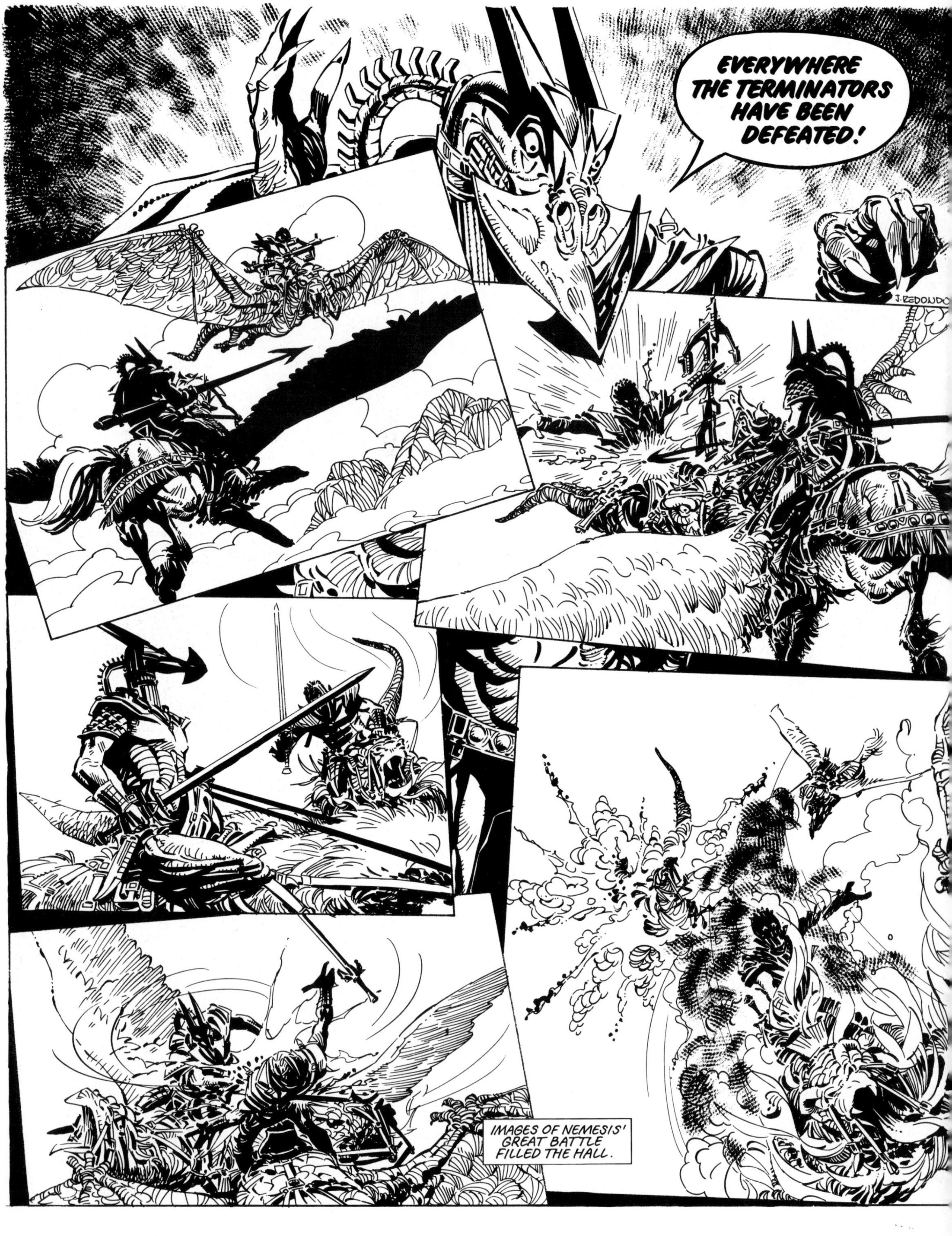
EVERYWHERE THE TERMINATORS HAVE BEEN DEFEATED!
J. REDONDO
IMAGES OF NEMESIS' GREAT BATTLE FILLED THE HALL.

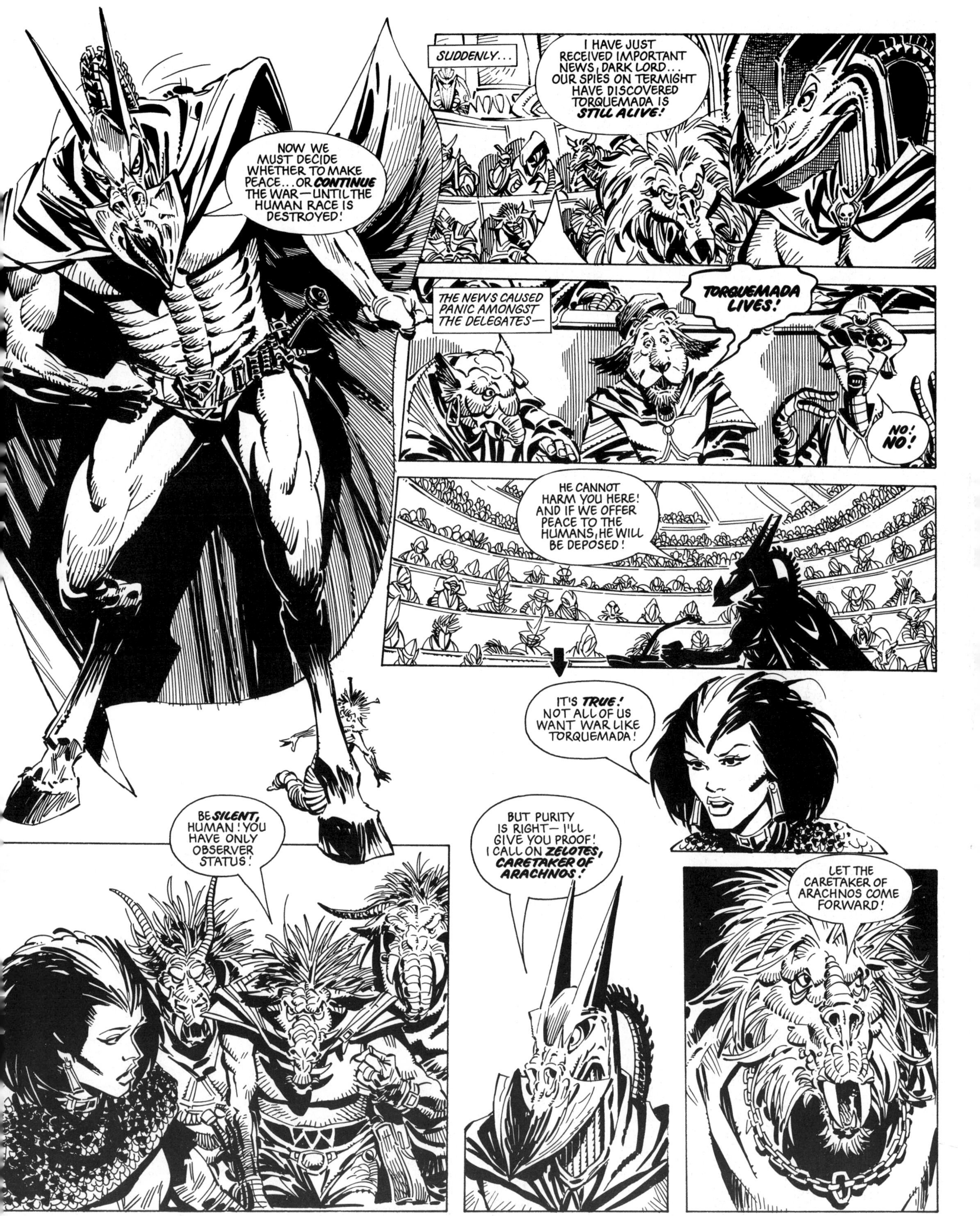
NOW WE MUST DECIDE WHETHER TO MAKE PEACE... OR CONTINUE THE WAR—UNTIL THE HUMAN RACE IS DESTROYED!
SUDDENLY...
I HAVE JUST RECEIVED IMPORTANT NEWS, DARK LORD... OUR SPIES ON TERMIGHT HAVE DISCOVERED TORQUEMADA IS STILL ALIVE!
THE NEWS CAUSED PANIC AMONGST THE DELEGATES—
TORQUEMADA LIVES!
NO! NO!
HE CANNOT HARM YOU HERE! AND IF WE OFFER PEACE TO THE HUMANS, HE WILL BE DEPOSED!
IT'S TRUE! NOT ALL OF US WANT WAR LIKE TORQUEMADA!
BE SILENT, HUMAN! YOU HAVE ONLY OBSERVER STATUS!
BUT PURITY IS RIGHT— I'LL GIVE YOU PROOF! I CALL ON ZELOTES, CARETAKER OF ARACHNOS!
LET THE CARETAKER OF ARACHNOS COME FORWARD!

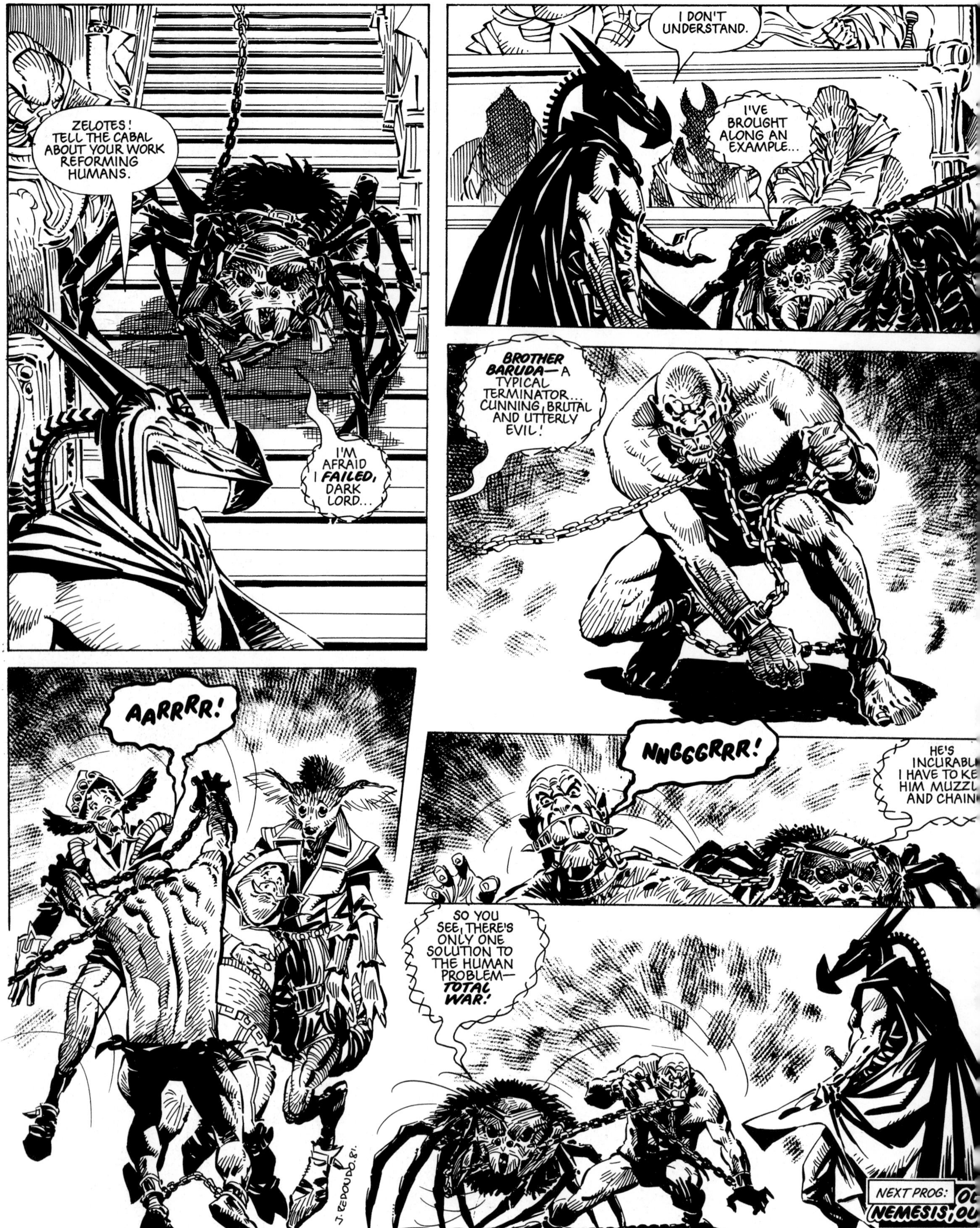
ZELOTES! TELL THE CABAL ABOUT YOUR WORK REFORMING HUMANS.
I'M AFRAID I **FAILED,** DARK LORD...
I DON'T UNDERSTAND.
I'VE BROUGHT ALONG AN EXAMPLE...
BROTHER BARUDA—A TYPICAL TERMINATOR... CUNNING, BRUTAL AND UTTERLY EVIL!
AARRRR!
NNGGGRRR!
HE'S
SO YOU SEE, THERE'S ONLY ONE SOLUTION TO THE HUMAN PROBLEM— **TOTAL WAR!**
J. REDONDO. 81.
NEXT PROG:

NEMESIS THE WARLOCK

BOOK II

Script: P. Mills

Lettering: J. Potter

Art: Redondo

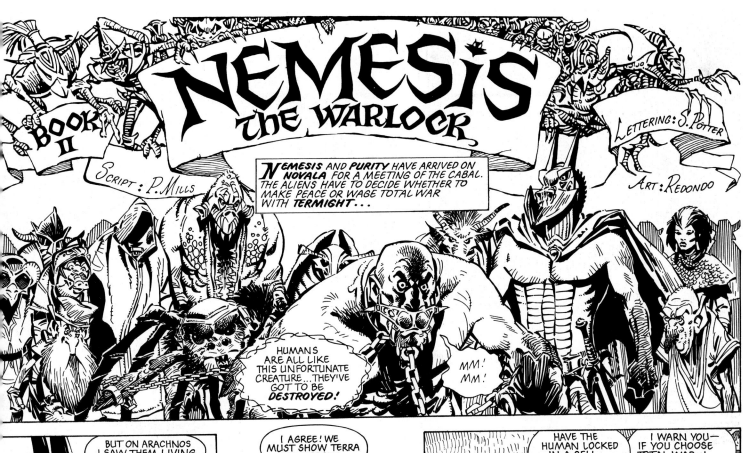

NEMESIS and PURITY HAVE ARRIVED ON NOVALA FOR A MEETING OF THE CABAL. THE ALIENS HAVE TO DECIDE WHETHER TO MAKE PEACE OR WAGE TOTAL WAR WITH TERMIGHT...

HUMANS ARE ALL LIKE THIS UNFORTUNATE CREATURE...THEY'VE GOT TO BE DESTROYED!

MM! MM!

BUT ON ARACHNOS I SAW THEM LIVING IN PEACE.

A PRETENCE, SO THEY COULD TRY AND ESCAPE. HUMANS ARE MORE CUNNING THAN YOU THINK, NEMESIS.

I AGREE! WE MUST SHOW TERRA NO MERCY!

BUT THAT'S WHAT TORQUEMADA WANTS...HE CAN ONLY RULE THROUGH FEAR.

HAVE THE HUMAN LOCKED IN A CELL. THEN WE WILL DECIDE...

I WARN YOU— IF YOU CHOOSE TOTAL WAR, I RESIGN AS LEADER OF THE CABAL.

THE ALIENS VOTED—

WAR!

WAR!

WAR!

COME BACK, NEMESIS! YOU'VE GOT TO MAKE THEM CHANGE THEIR MINDS! YOU CAN'T RESIGN!

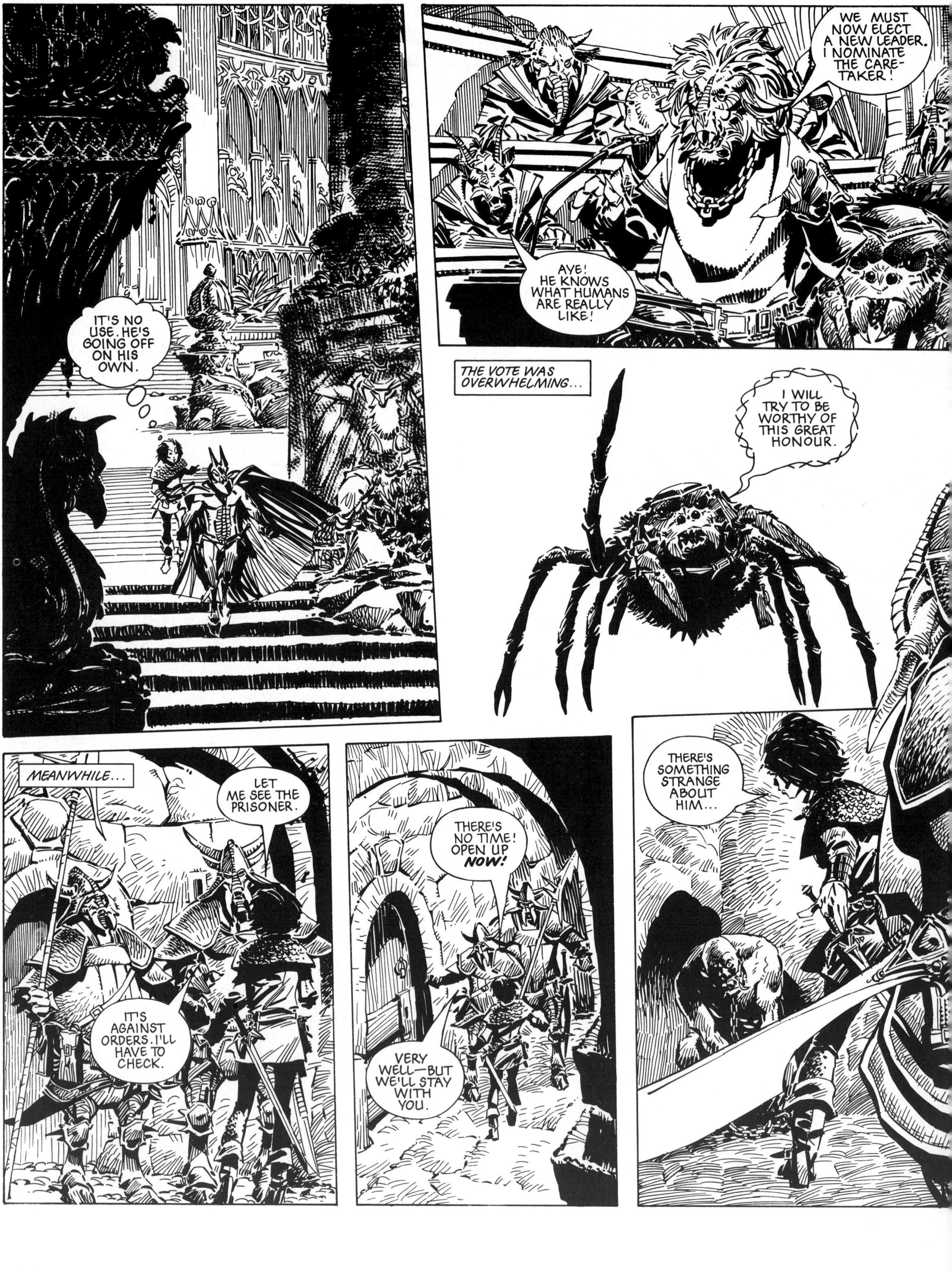
IT'S NO USE. HE'S GOING OFF ON HIS OWN.
WE MUST NOW ELECT A NEW LEADER. I NOMINATE THE CARE-TAKER!
AYE! HE KNOWS WHAT HUMANS ARE REALLY LIKE!
THE VOTE WAS OVERWHELMING...
I WILL TRY TO BE WORTHY OF THIS GREAT HONOUR.
MEANWHILE...
LET ME SEE THE PRISONER.
IT'S AGAINST ORDERS. I'LL HAVE TO CHECK.
THERE'S NO TIME! OPEN UP NOW!
VERY WELL—BUT WE'LL STAY WITH YOU.
THERE'S SOMETHING STRANGE ABOUT HIM...

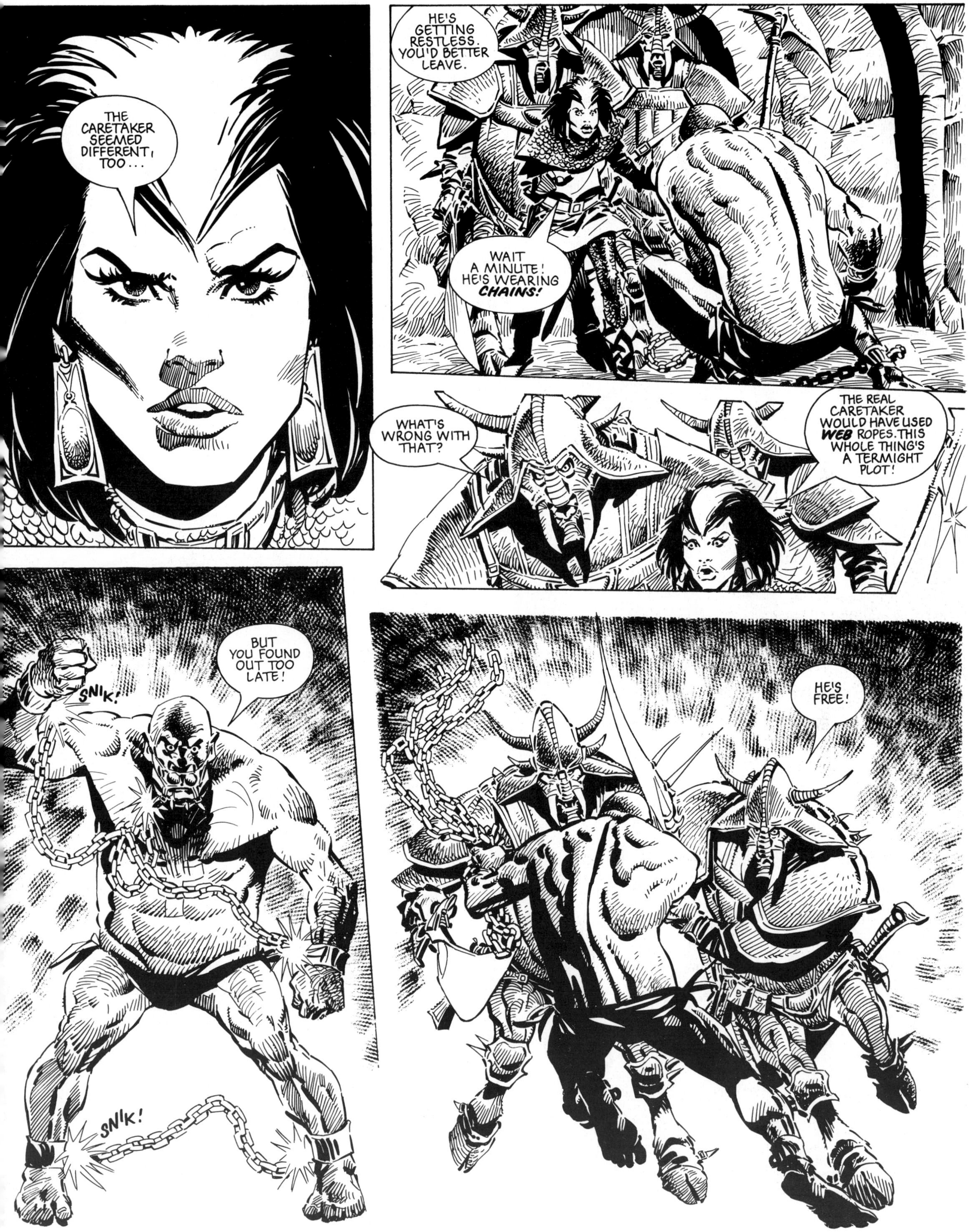
THE CARETAKER SEEMED DIFFERENT, TOO...
HE'S GETTING RESTLESS. YOU'D BETTER LEAVE.
WAIT A MINUTE! HE'S WEARING CHAINS!
WHAT'S WRONG WITH THAT?
THE REAL CARETAKER WOULD HAVE USED WEB ROPES. THIS WHOLE THING'S A TERMIGHT PLOT!
BUT YOU FOUND OUT TOO LATE!
SNIK!
SNIK!
HE'S FREE!

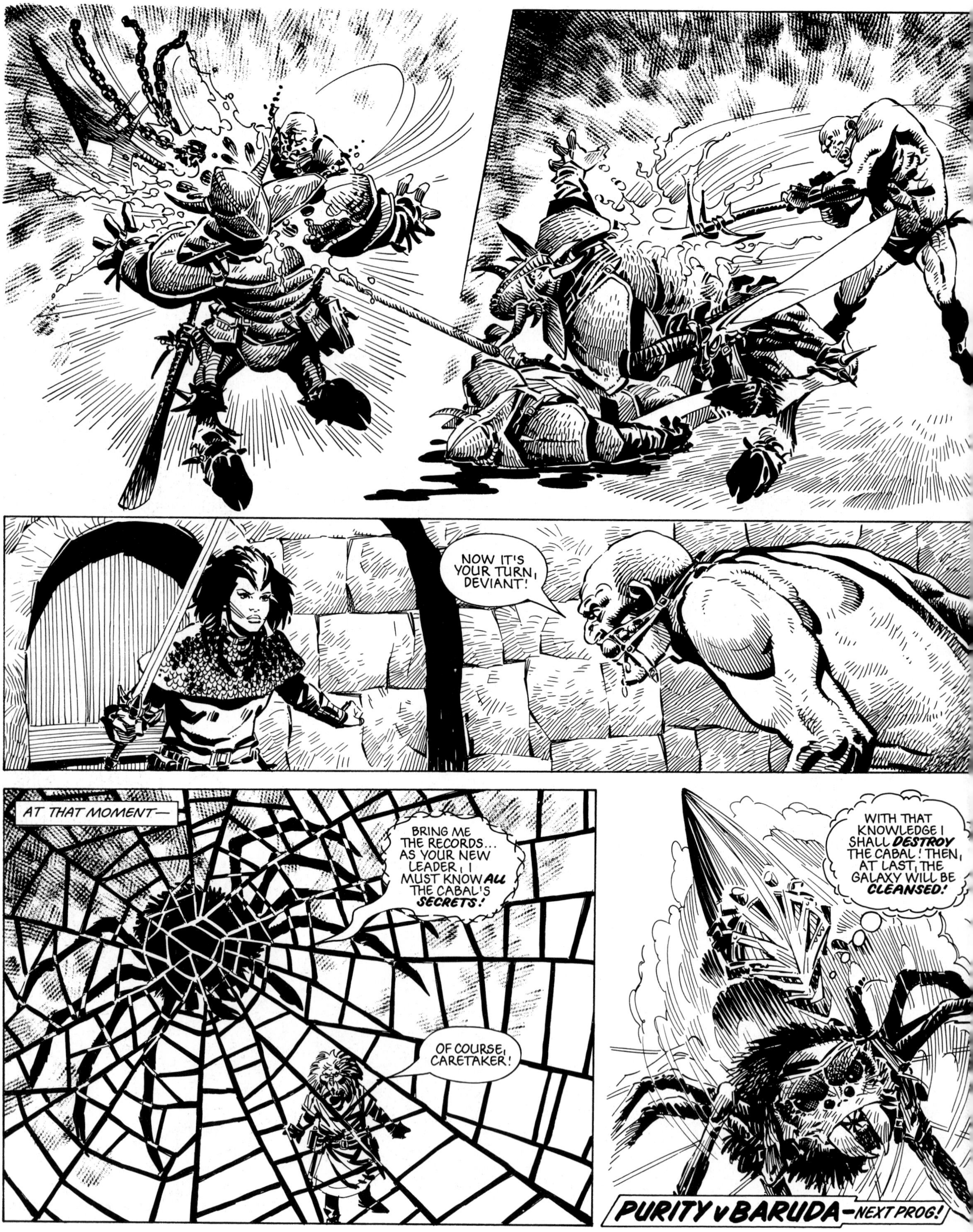
NOW IT'S YOUR TURN, DEVIANT!
AT THAT MOMENT—
BRING ME THE RECORDS... AS YOUR NEW LEADER, I MUST KNOW ALL THE CABAL'S SECRETS!
OF COURSE, CARETAKER!
WITH THAT KNOWLEDGE I SHALL DESTROY THE CABAL! THEN, AT LAST, THE GALAXY WILL BE CLEANSED!
PURITY v BARUDA—NEXT PROG!

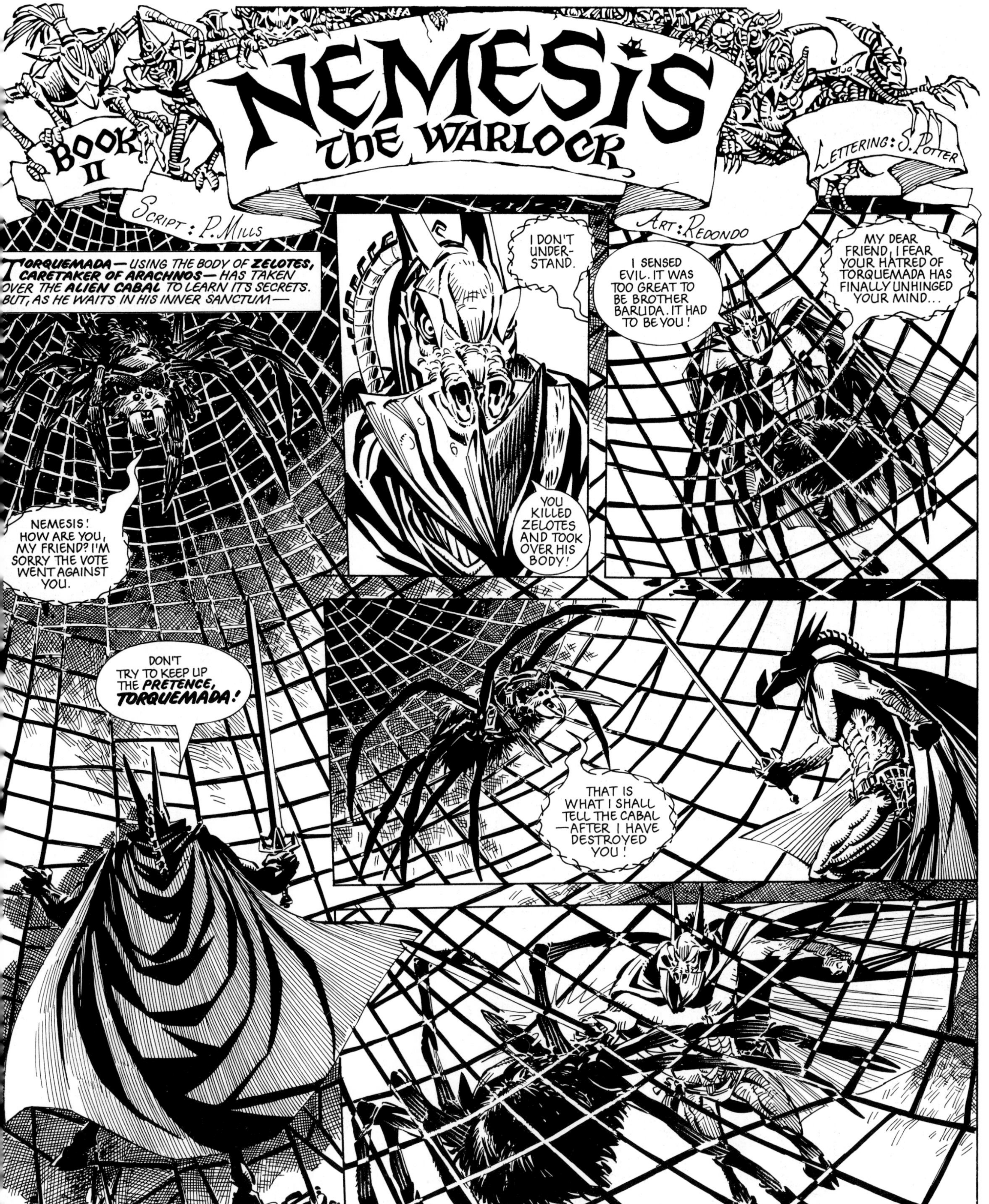

NEMESIS THE WARLOCK
BOOK II
SCRIPT: P. MILLS
ART: REDONDO
LETTERING: S. POTTER
TORQUEMADA — USING THE BODY OF ZELOTES, CARETAKER OF ARACHNOS — HAS TAKEN OVER THE ALIEN CABAL TO LEARN ITS SECRETS. BUT, AS HE WAITS IN HIS INNER SANCTUM —
NEMESIS! HOW ARE YOU, MY FRIEND? I'M SORRY THE VOTE WENT AGAINST YOU.
I DON'T UNDER-STAND.
YOU KILLED ZELOTES AND TOOK OVER HIS BODY!
I SENSED EVIL. IT WAS TOO GREAT TO BE BROTHER BARUDA. IT HAD TO BE YOU!
MY DEAR FRIEND, I FEAR YOUR HATRED OF TORQUEMADA HAS FINALLY UNHINGED YOUR MIND...
DON'T TRY TO KEEP UP THE PRETENCE, TORQUEMADA!
THAT IS WHAT I SHALL TELL THE CABAL — AFTER I HAVE DESTROYED YOU!

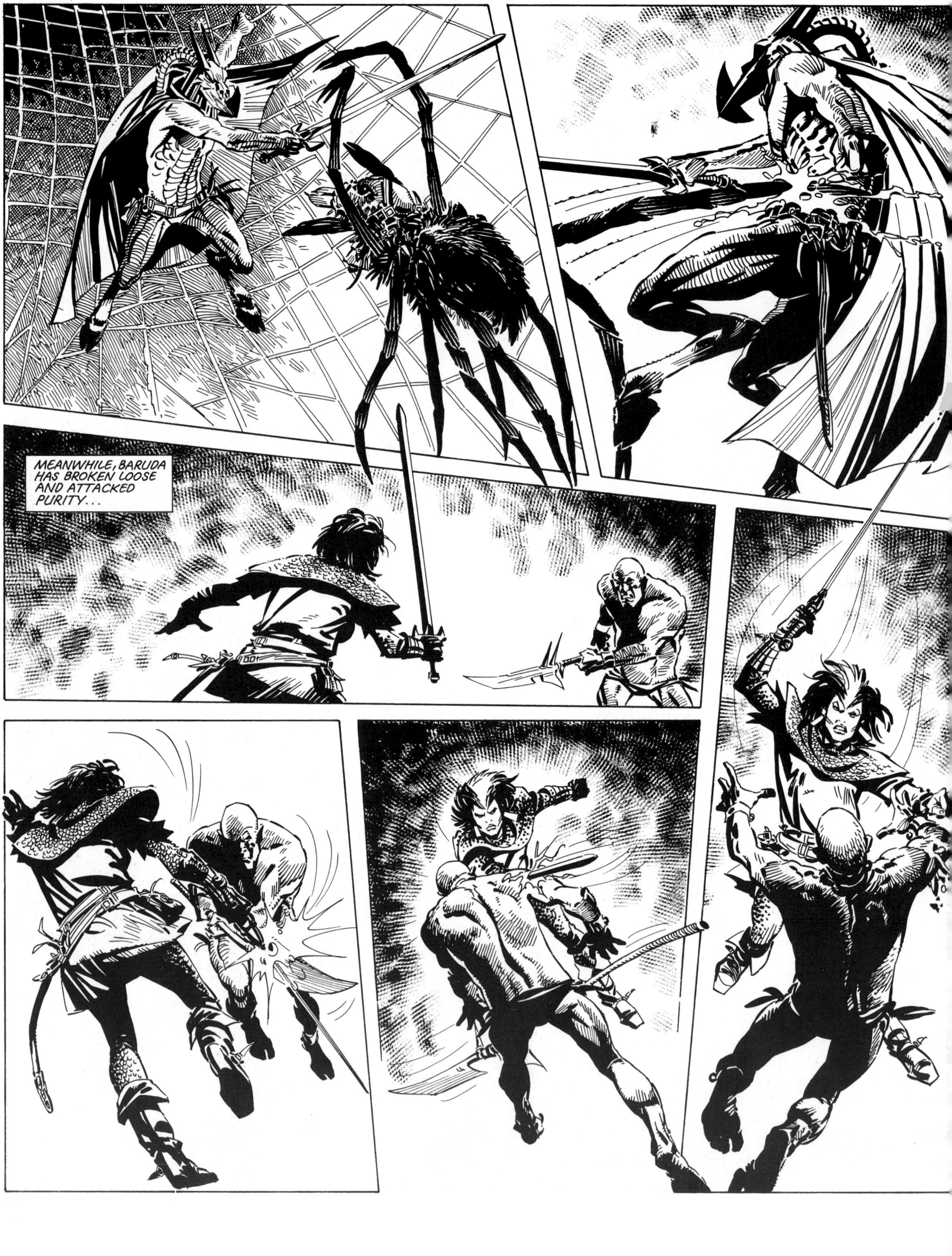
MEANWHILE, BARUDA HAS BROKEN LOOSE AND ATTACKED PURITY...

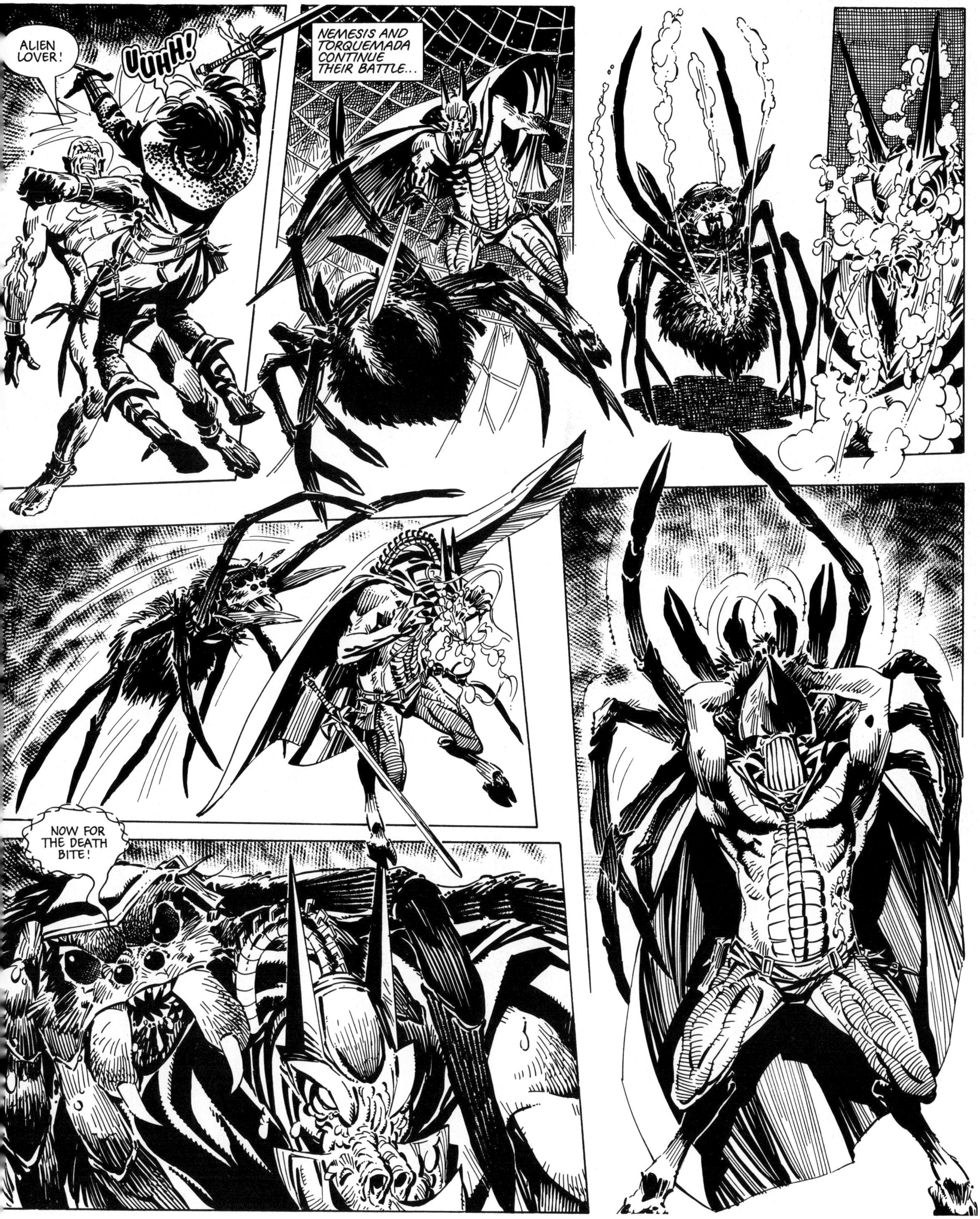
ALIEN LOVER!
UUHH!
NEMESIS AND TORQUEMADA CONTINUE THEIR BATTLE...
NOW FOR THE DEATH BITE!

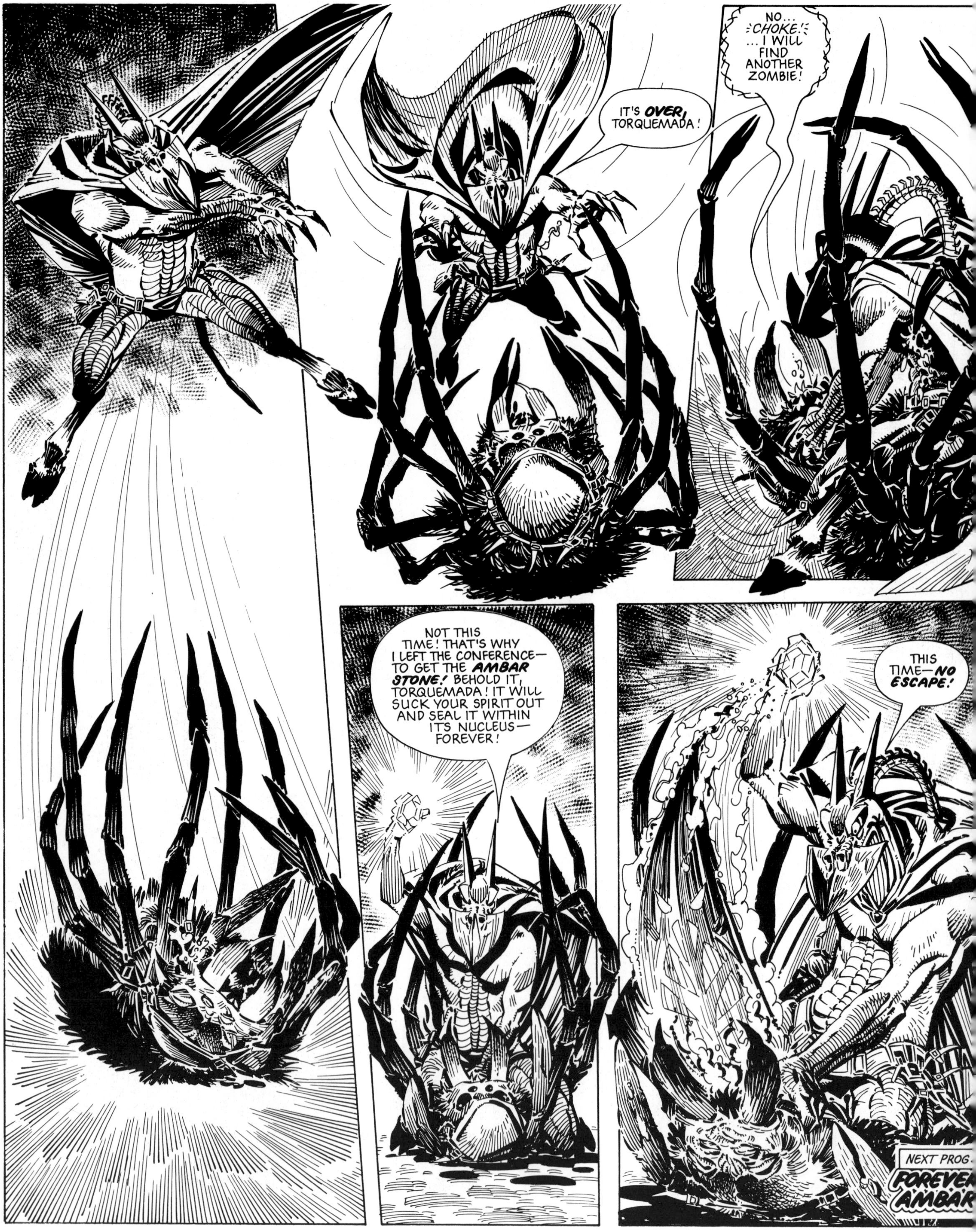
IT'S OVER, TORQUEMADA!
NO... CHOKE! ...I WILL FIND ANOTHER ZOMBIE!
NOT THIS TIME! THAT'S WHY I LEFT THE CONFERENCE— TO GET THE AMBAR STONE! BEHOLD IT, TORQUEMADA! IT WILL SUCK YOUR SPIRIT OUT AND SEAL IT WITHIN ITS NUCLEUS— FOREVER!
THIS TIME—NO ESCAPE!
NEXT PROG

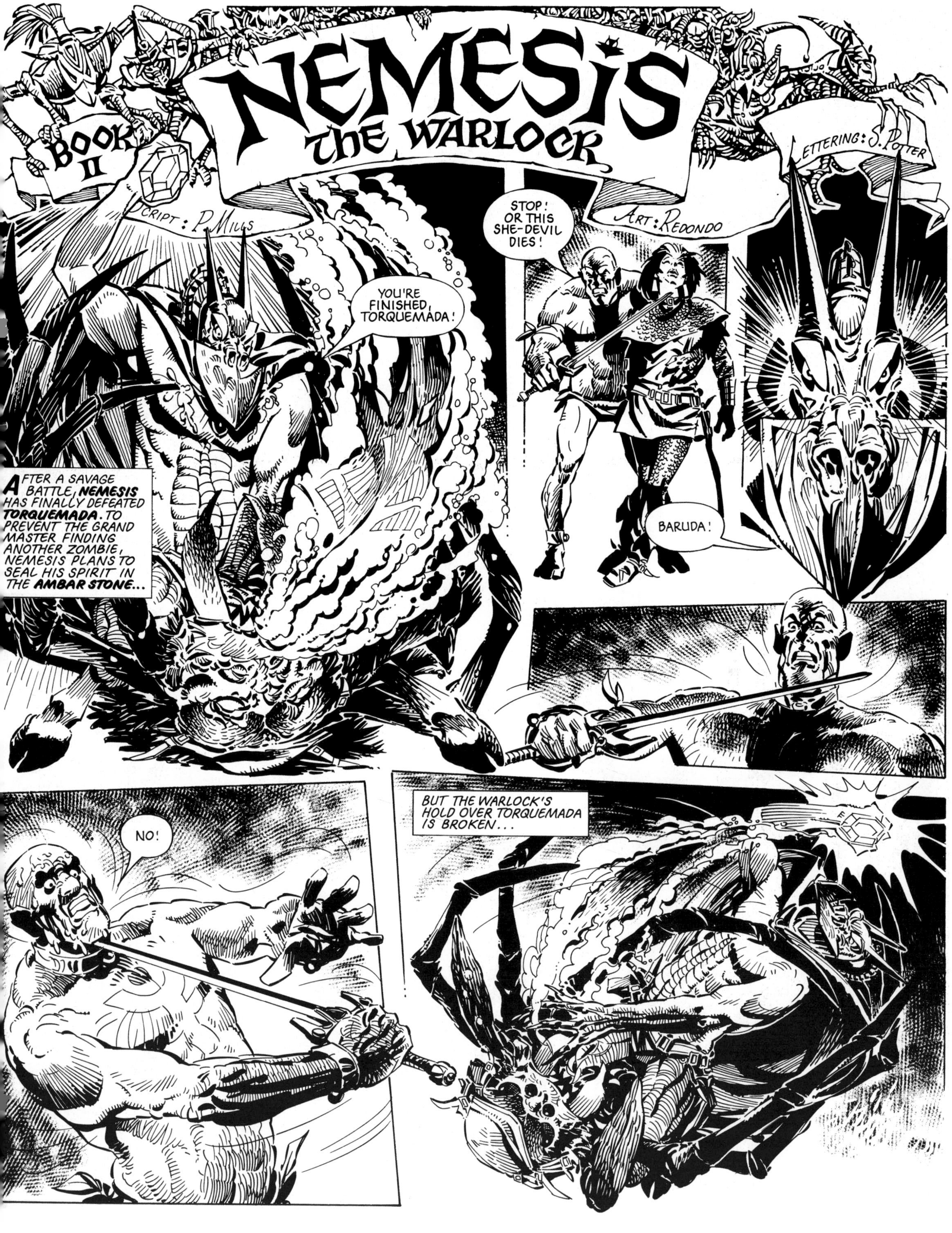
NEMESIS THE WARLOCK
BOOK II
SCRIPT: P. MILLS
ART: REDONDO
LETTERING: S. POTTER
AFTER A SAVAGE BATTLE, NEMESIS HAS FINALLY DEFEATED TORQUEMADA. TO PREVENT THE GRAND MASTER FINDING ANOTHER ZOMBIE, NEMESIS PLANS TO SEAL HIS SPIRIT IN THE AMBAR STONE...
YOU'RE FINISHED, TORQUEMADA!
STOP! OR THIS SHE-DEVIL DIES!
BARUDA!
NO!
BUT THE WARLOCK'S HOLD OVER TORQUEMADA IS BROKEN...

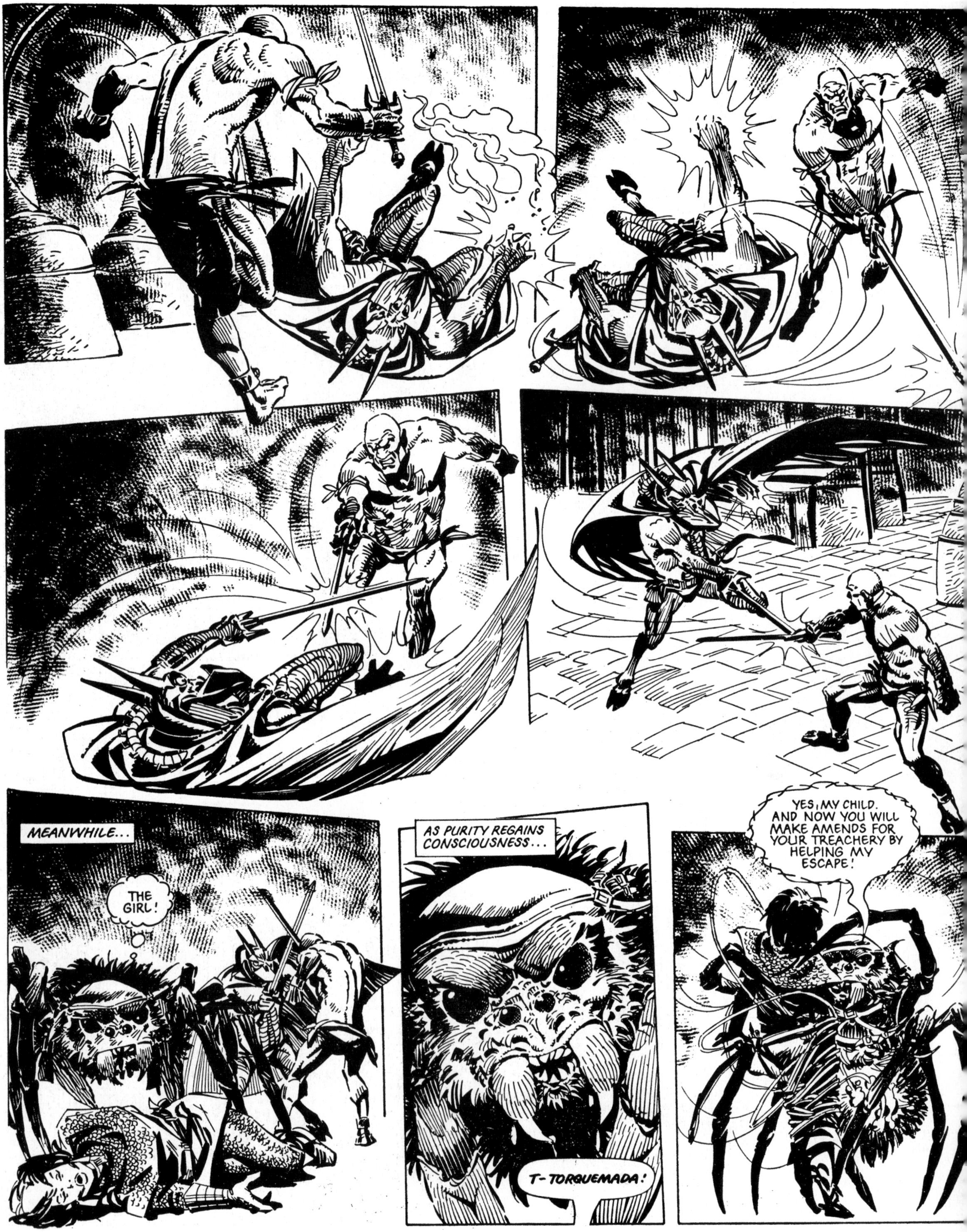
MEANWHILE...
THE GIRL!
AS PURITY REGAINS CONSCIOUSNESS...
T-TORQUEMADA!
YES, MY CHILD. AND NOW YOU WILL MAKE AMENDS FOR YOUR TREACHERY BY HELPING MY ESCAPE!

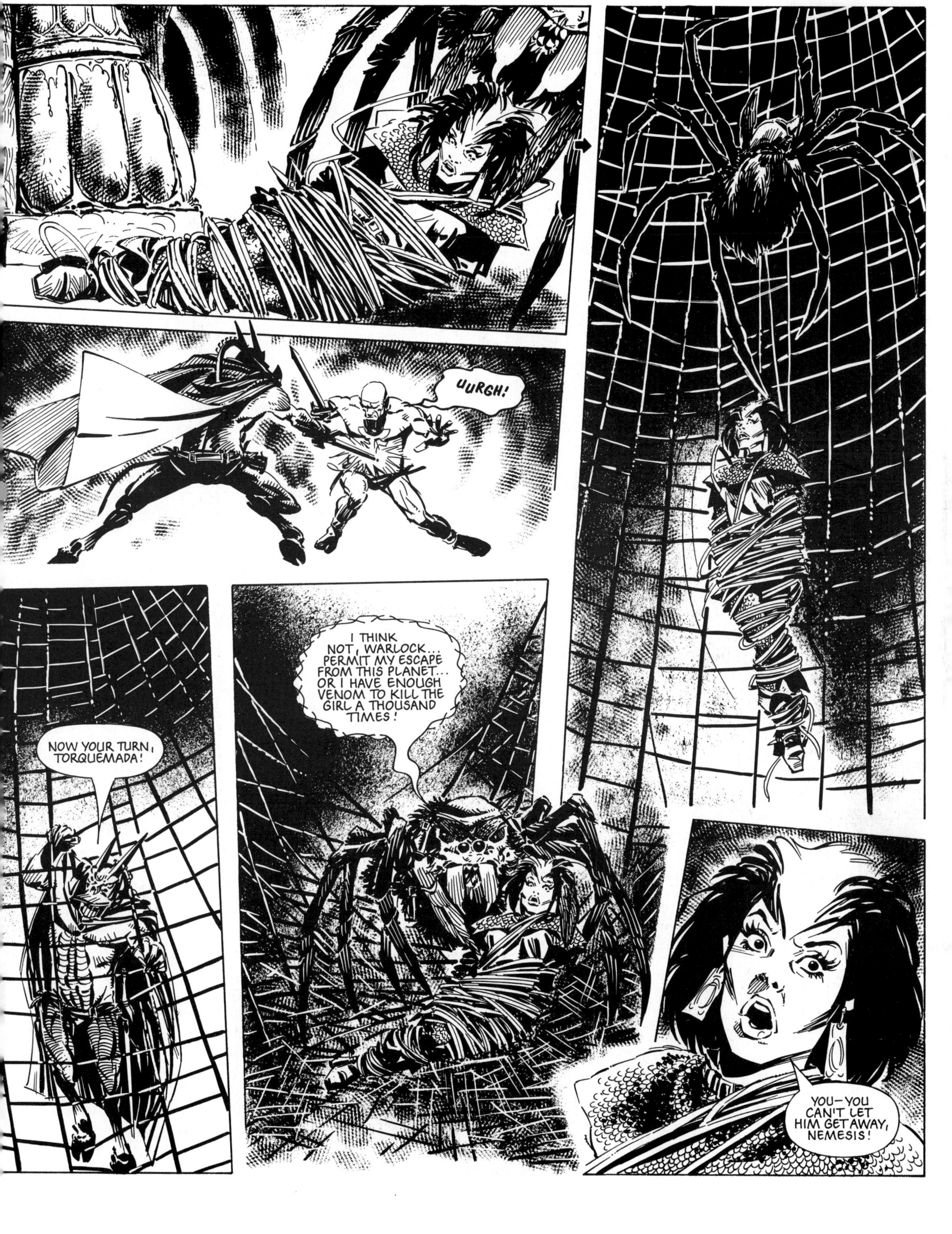
UURGH!
NOW YOUR TURN, TORQUEMADA!
I THINK NOT, WARLOCK... PERMIT MY ESCAPE FROM THIS PLANET... OR I HAVE ENOUGH VENOM TO KILL THE GIRL A THOUSAND TIMES!
YOU—YOU CAN'T LET HIM GET AWAY, NEMESIS!

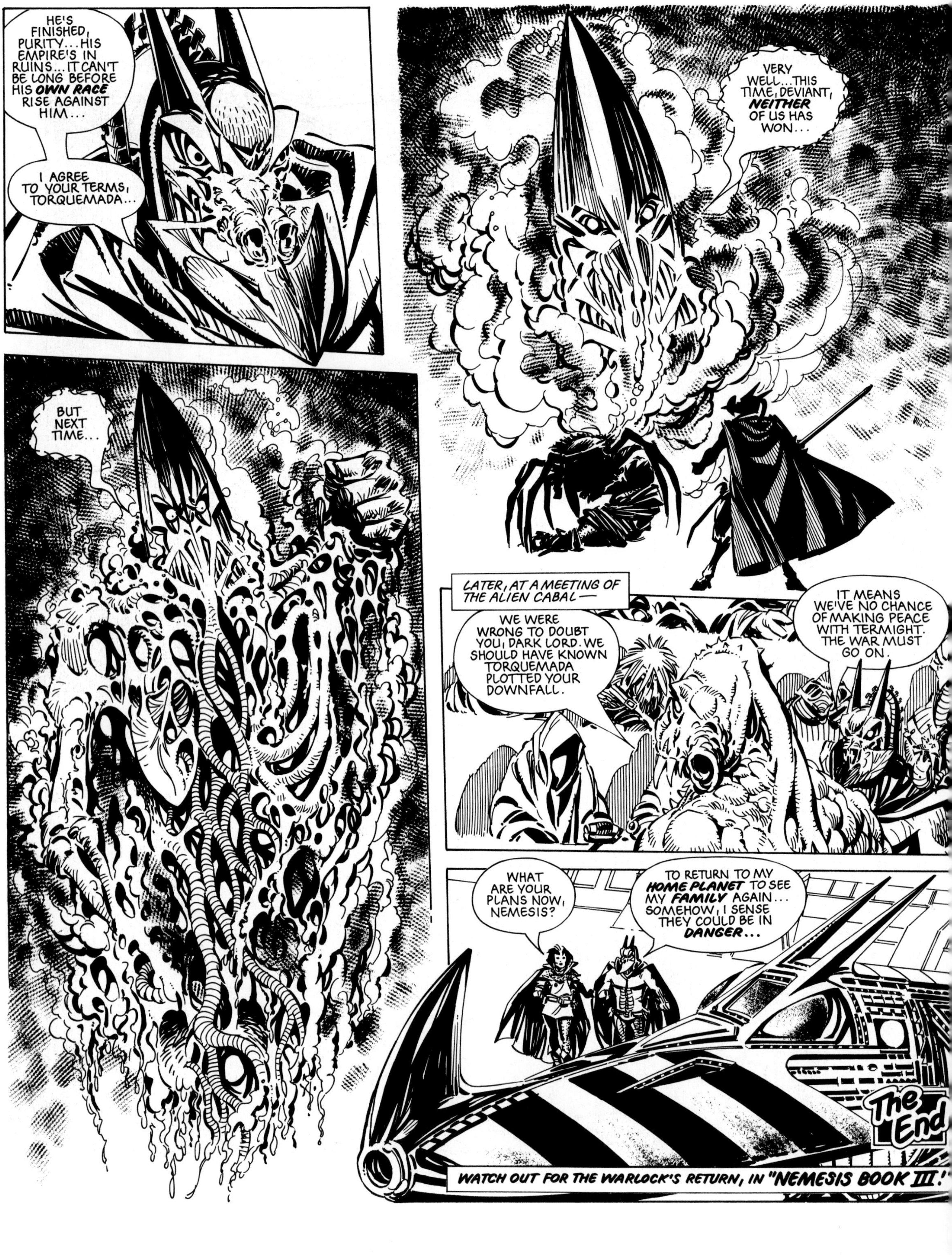
HE'S FINISHED, PURITY... HIS EMPIRE'S IN RUINS... IT CAN'T BE LONG BEFORE HIS OWN RACE RISE AGAINST HIM...
I AGREE TO YOUR TERMS, TORQUEMADA...
VERY WELL... THIS TIME, DEVIANT, NEITHER OF US HAS WON...
BUT NEXT TIME...
LATER, AT A MEETING OF THE ALIEN CABAL—
WE WERE WRONG TO DOUBT YOU, DARK LORD. WE SHOULD HAVE KNOWN TORQUEMADA PLOTTED YOUR DOWNFALL.
IT MEANS WE'VE NO CHANCE OF MAKING PEACE WITH TERMIGHT. THE WAR MUST GO ON.
WHAT ARE YOUR PLANS NOW, NEMESIS?
TO RETURN TO MY HOME PLANET TO SEE MY FAMILY AGAIN... SOMEHOW, I SENSE THEY COULD BE IN DANGER...
The End
WATCH OUT FOR THE WARLOCK'S RETURN, IN "NEMESIS BOOK III."

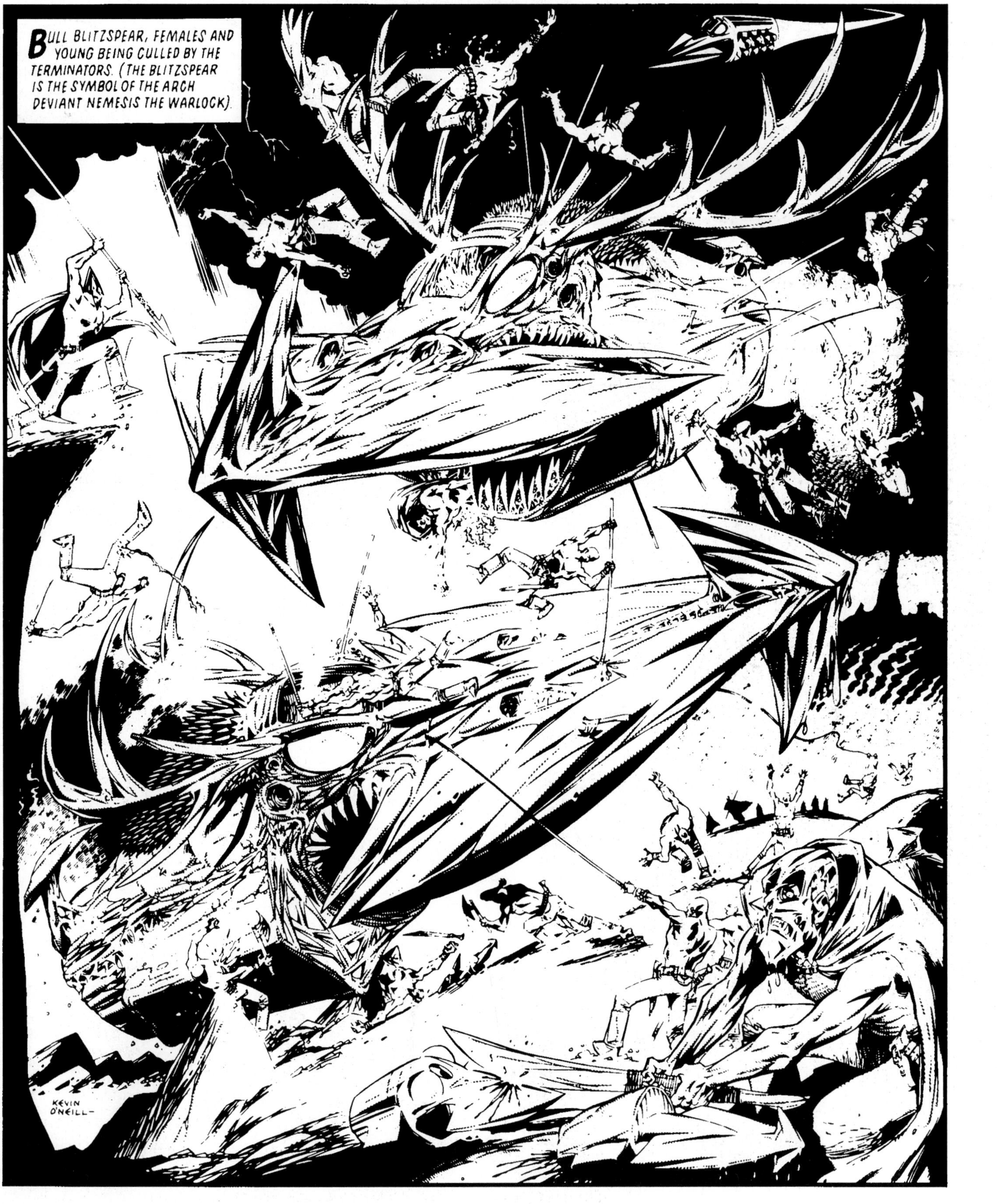
BULL BLITZSPEAR, FEMALES AND YOUNG BEING CULLED BY THE TERMINATORS. (THE BLITZSPEAR IS THE SYMBOL OF THE ARCH DEVIANT NEMESIS THE WARLOCK).
KEVIN O'NEILL

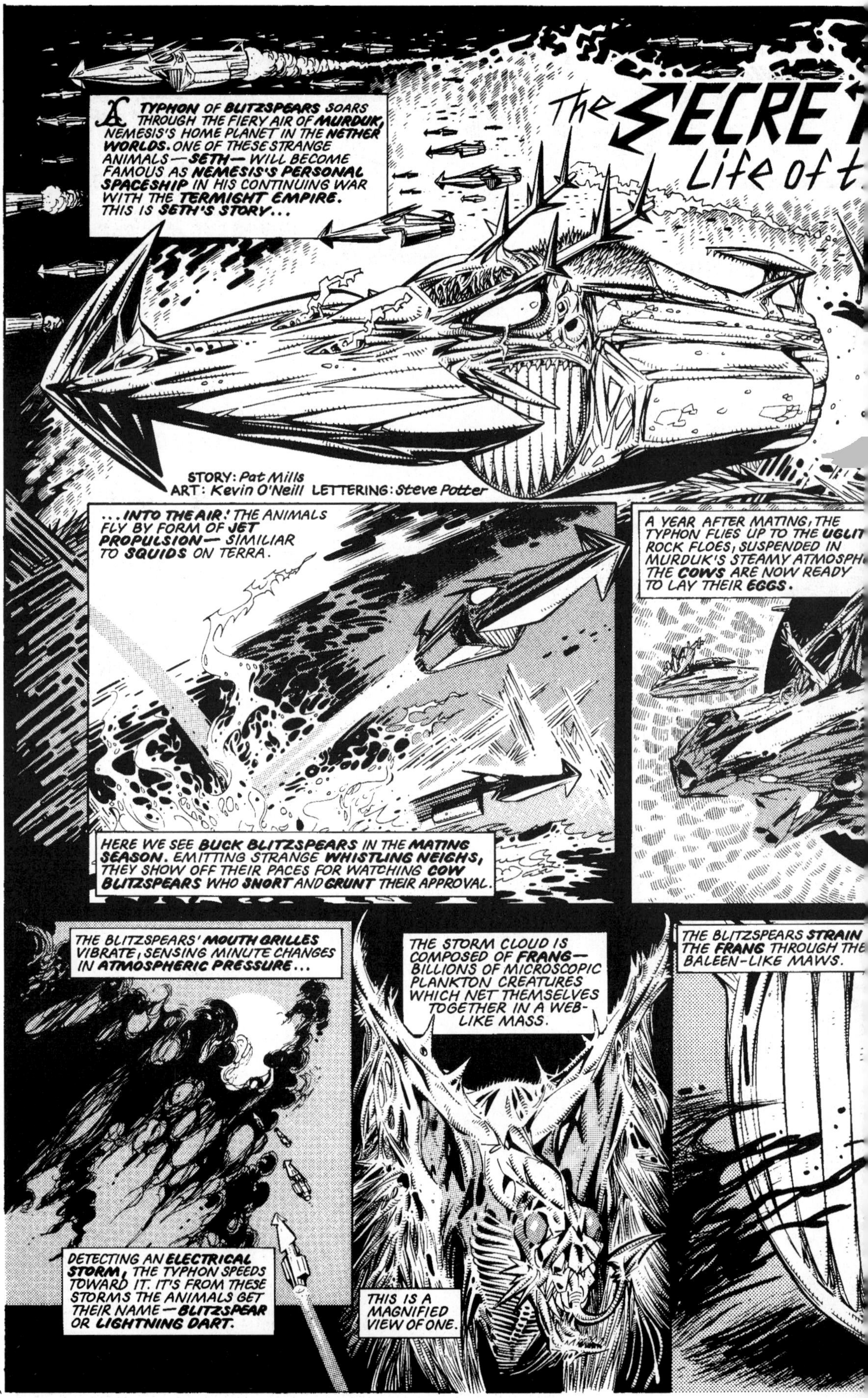

A TYPHON OF BLITZSPEARS SOARS THROUGH THE FIERY AIR OF MURDUK, NEMESIS'S HOME PLANET IN THE NETHER WORLDS. ONE OF THESE STRANGE ANIMALS — SETH — WILL BECOME FAMOUS AS NEMESIS'S PERSONAL SPACESHIP IN HIS CONTINUING WAR WITH THE TERMIGHT EMPIRE. THIS IS SETH'S STORY...
The SECRE
Life of t
STORY: Pat Mills
ART: Kevin O'Neill LETTERING: Steve Potter
...INTO THE AIR! THE ANIMALS FLY BY FORM OF JET PROPULSION — SIMILIAR TO SQUIDS ON TERRA.
HERE WE SEE BUCK BLITZSPEARS IN THE MATING SEASON. EMITTING STRANGE WHISTLING NEIGHS, THEY SHOW OFF THEIR PACES FOR WATCHING COW BLITZSPEARS WHO SNORT AND GRUNT THEIR APPROVAL.
A YEAR AFTER MATING, THE TYPHON FLIES UP TO THE UGLIT ROCK FLOES, SUSPENDED IN MURDUK'S STEAMY ATMOSPH THE COWS ARE NOW READY TO LAY THEIR EGGS.
THE BLITZSPEARS' MOUTH GRILLES VIBRATE, SENSING MINUTE CHANGES IN ATMOSPHERIC PRESSURE...
DETECTING AN ELECTRICAL STORM, THE TYPHON SPEEDS TOWARD IT. IT'S FROM THESE STORMS THE ANIMALS GET THEIR NAME — BLITZSPEAR OR LIGHTNING DART.
THE STORM CLOUD IS COMPOSED OF FRANG — BILLIONS OF MICROSCOPIC PLANKTON CREATURES WHICH NET THEMSELVES TOGETHER IN A WEB-LIKE MASS.
THIS IS A MAGNIFIED VIEW OF ONE.
THE BLITZSPEARS STRAIN THE FRANG THROUGH THE BALEEN-LIKE MAWS.

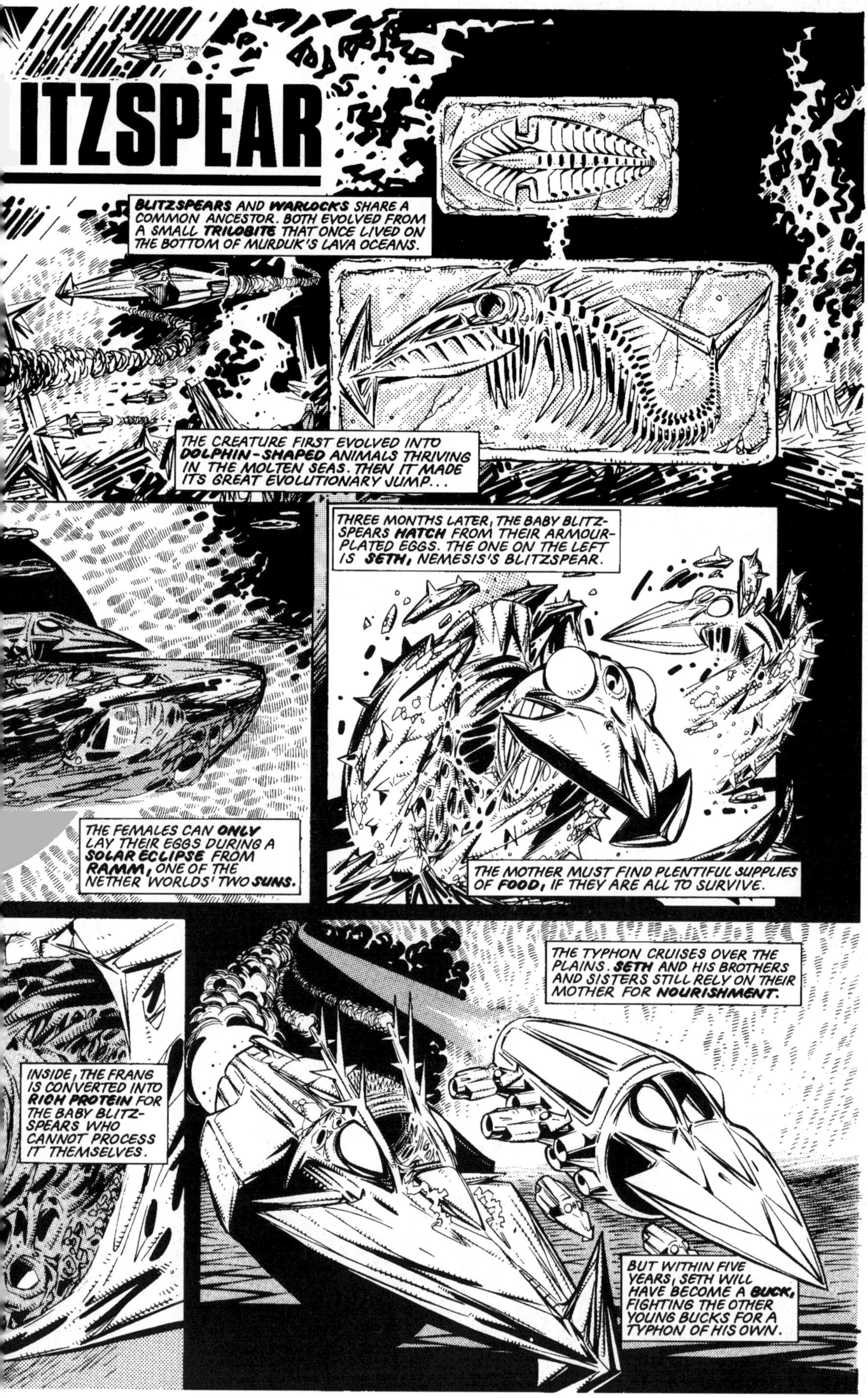

ITZSPEAR
BLITZSPEARS AND WARLOCKS SHARE A COMMON ANCESTOR. BOTH EVOLVED FROM A SMALL TRILOBITE THAT ONCE LIVED ON THE BOTTOM OF MURDUK'S LAVA OCEANS.
THE CREATURE FIRST EVOLVED INTO DOLPHIN-SHAPED ANIMALS THRIVING IN THE MOLTEN SEAS. THEN IT MADE ITS GREAT EVOLUTIONARY JUMP...
THE FEMALES CAN ONLY LAY THEIR EGGS DURING A SOLAR ECLIPSE FROM RAMM, ONE OF THE NETHER WORLDS' TWO SUNS.
THREE MONTHS LATER, THE BABY BLITZ-SPEARS HATCH FROM THEIR ARMOUR-PLATED EGGS. THE ONE ON THE LEFT IS SETH, NEMESIS'S BLITZSPEAR.
THE MOTHER MUST FIND PLENTIFUL SUPPLIES OF FOOD, IF THEY ARE ALL TO SURVIVE.
INSIDE, THE FRANG IS CONVERTED INTO RICH PROTEIN FOR THE BABY BLITZ-SPEARS WHO CANNOT PROCESS IT THEMSELVES.
THE TYPHON CRUISES OVER THE PLAINS. SETH AND HIS BROTHERS AND SISTERS STILL RELY ON THEIR MOTHER FOR NOURISHMENT.
BUT WITHIN FIVE YEARS, SETH WILL HAVE BECOME A BUCK, FIGHTING THE OTHER YOUNG BUCKS FOR A TYPHON OF HIS OWN.

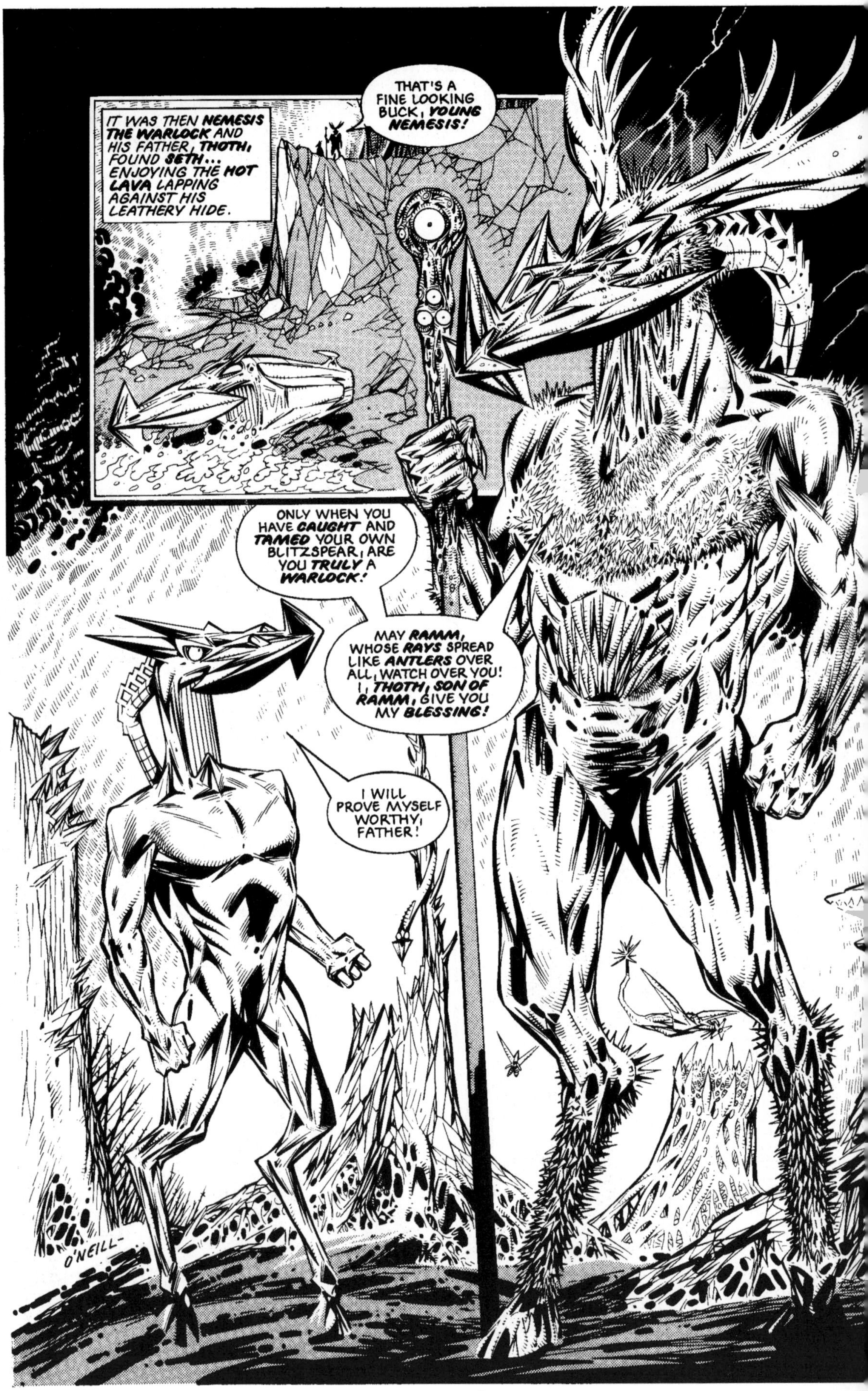
IT WAS THEN NEMESIS THE WARLOCK AND HIS FATHER, THOTH, FOUND SETH... ENJOYING THE HOT LAVA LAPPING AGAINST HIS LEATHERY HIDE.
THAT'S A FINE LOOKING BUCK, YOUNG NEMESIS!
ONLY WHEN YOU HAVE CAUGHT AND TAMED YOUR OWN BLITZSPEAR, ARE YOU TRULY A WARLOCK!
MAY RAMM, WHOSE RAYS SPREAD LIKE ANTLERS OVER ALL, WATCH OVER YOU! I, THOTH, SON OF RAMM, GIVE YOU MY BLESSING!
I WILL PROVE MYSELF WORTHY, FATHER!
O'NEILL

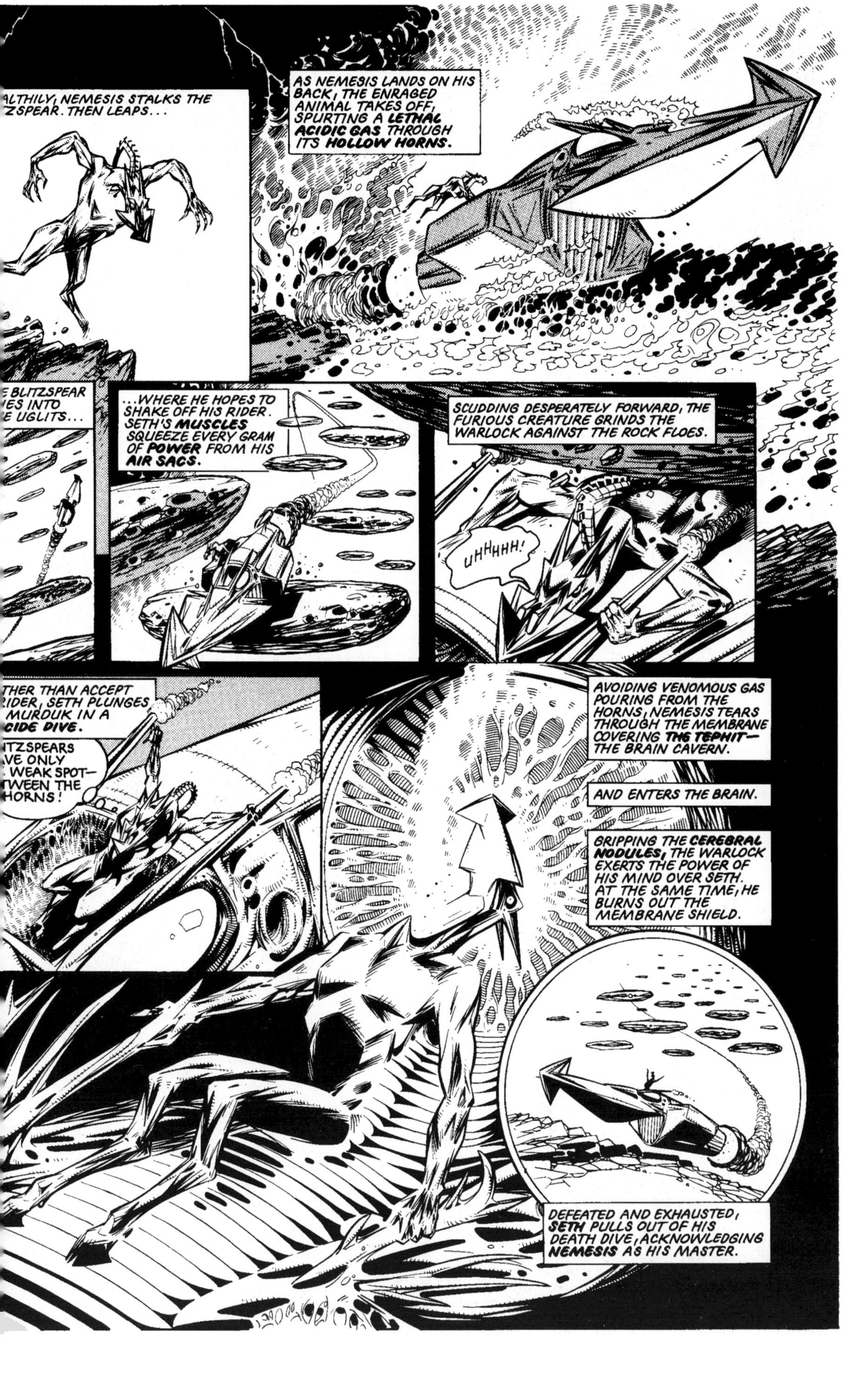
ALTHILY, NEMESIS STALKS THE
TZSPEAR. THEN LEAPS...
AS NEMESIS LANDS ON HIS BACK, THE ENRAGED ANIMAL TAKES OFF, SPURTING A **LETHAL ACIDIC GAS** THROUGH ITS **HOLLOW HORNS**.
E BLITZSPEAR IES INTO E UGLITS...
...WHERE HE HOPES TO SHAKE OFF HIS RIDER. SETH'S **MUSCLES** SQUEEZE EVERY GRAM OF **POWER** FROM HIS **AIR SACS**.
SCUDDING DESPERATELY FORWARD, THE FURIOUS CREATURE GRINDS THE WARLOCK AGAINST THE ROCK FLOES.
UHHHHHH!
THER THAN ACCEPT RIDER, SETH PLUNGES MURDUK IN A **CIDE DIVE**.
ITZSPEARS VE ONLY WEAK SPOT— TWEEN THE HORNS!
AVOIDING VENOMOUS GAS POURING FROM THE HORNS, NEMESIS TEARS THROUGH THE MEMBRANE COVERING **THE TEPHIT**— THE BRAIN CAVERN.
AND ENTERS THE BRAIN.
GRIPPING THE **CEREBRAL NODULES**, THE WARLOCK EXERTS THE POWER OF HIS MIND OVER SETH. AT THE SAME TIME, HE BURNS OUT THE MEMBRANE SHIELD.
DEFEATED AND EXHAUSTED, **SETH** PULLS OUT OF HIS DEATH DIVE, ACKNOWLEDGING **NEMESIS** AS HIS MASTER.

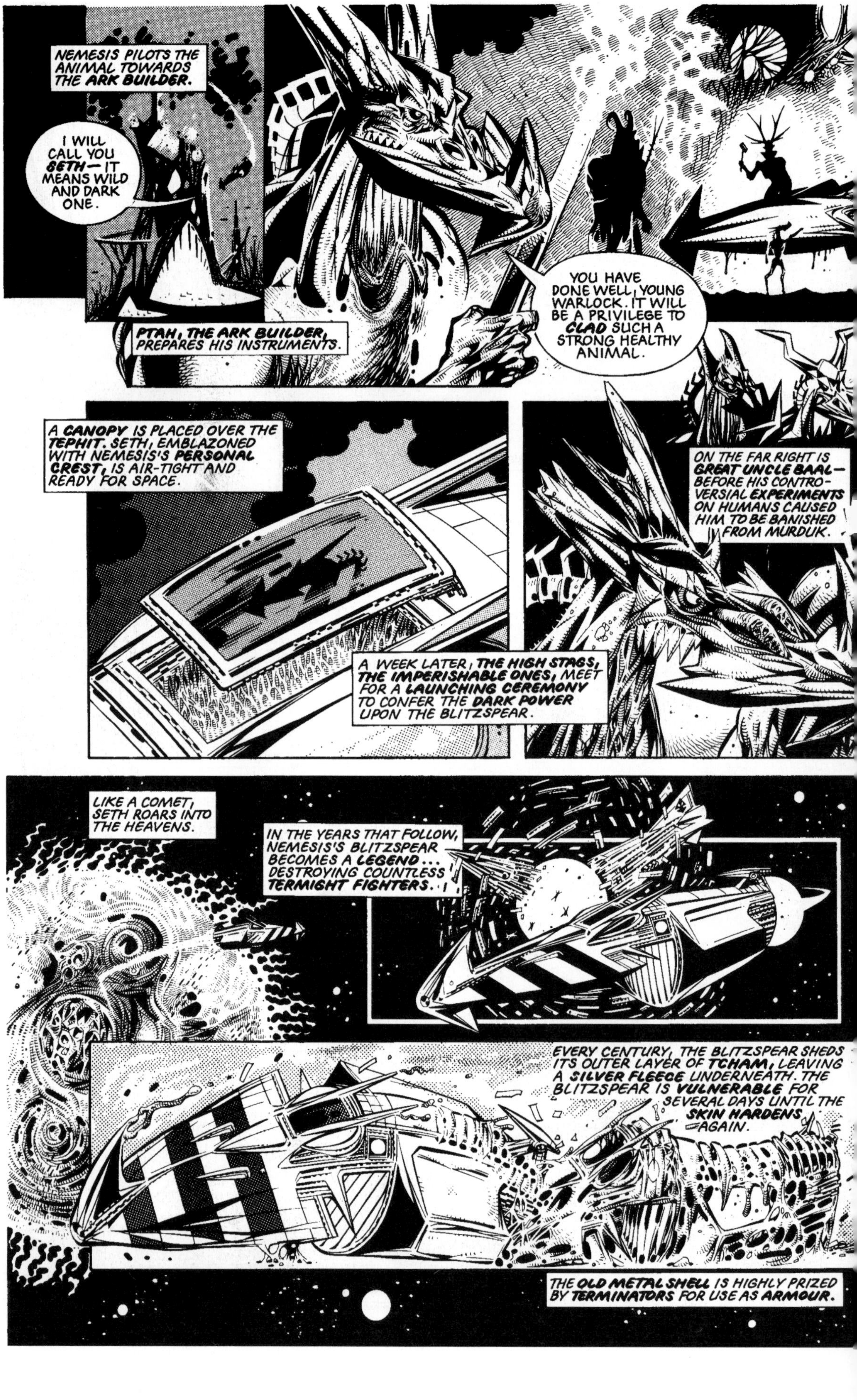
NEMESIS PILOTS THE ANIMAL TOWARDS THE ARK BUILDER.
I WILL CALL YOU SETH— IT MEANS WILD AND DARK ONE.
PTAH, THE ARK BUILDER, PREPARES HIS INSTRUMENTS.
YOU HAVE DONE WELL, YOUNG WARLOCK. IT WILL BE A PRIVILEGE TO CLAD SUCH A STRONG HEALTHY ANIMAL.
A CANOPY IS PLACED OVER THE TEPHIT. SETH, EMBLAZONED WITH NEMESIS'S PERSONAL CREST, IS AIR-TIGHT AND READY FOR SPACE.
ON THE FAR RIGHT IS GREAT UNCLE BAAL— BEFORE HIS CONTROVERSIAL EXPERIMENTS ON HUMANS CAUSED HIM TO BE BANISHED FROM MURDUK.
A WEEK LATER, THE HIGH STAGS, THE IMPERISHABLE ONES, MEET FOR A LAUNCHING CEREMONY TO CONFER THE DARK POWER UPON THE BLITZSPEAR.
LIKE A COMET, SETH ROARS INTO THE HEAVENS.
IN THE YEARS THAT FOLLOW, NEMESIS'S BLITZSPEAR BECOMES A LEGEND... DESTROYING COUNTLESS TERMIGHT FIGHTERS.
EVERY CENTURY, THE BLITZSPEAR SHEDS ITS OUTER LAYER OF TCHAM, LEAVING A SILVER FLEECE UNDERNEATH. THE BLITZSPEAR IS VULNERABLE FOR SEVERAL DAYS UNTIL THE SKIN HARDENS AGAIN.
THE OLD METAL SHELL IS HIGHLY PRIZED BY TERMINATORS FOR USE AS ARMOUR.

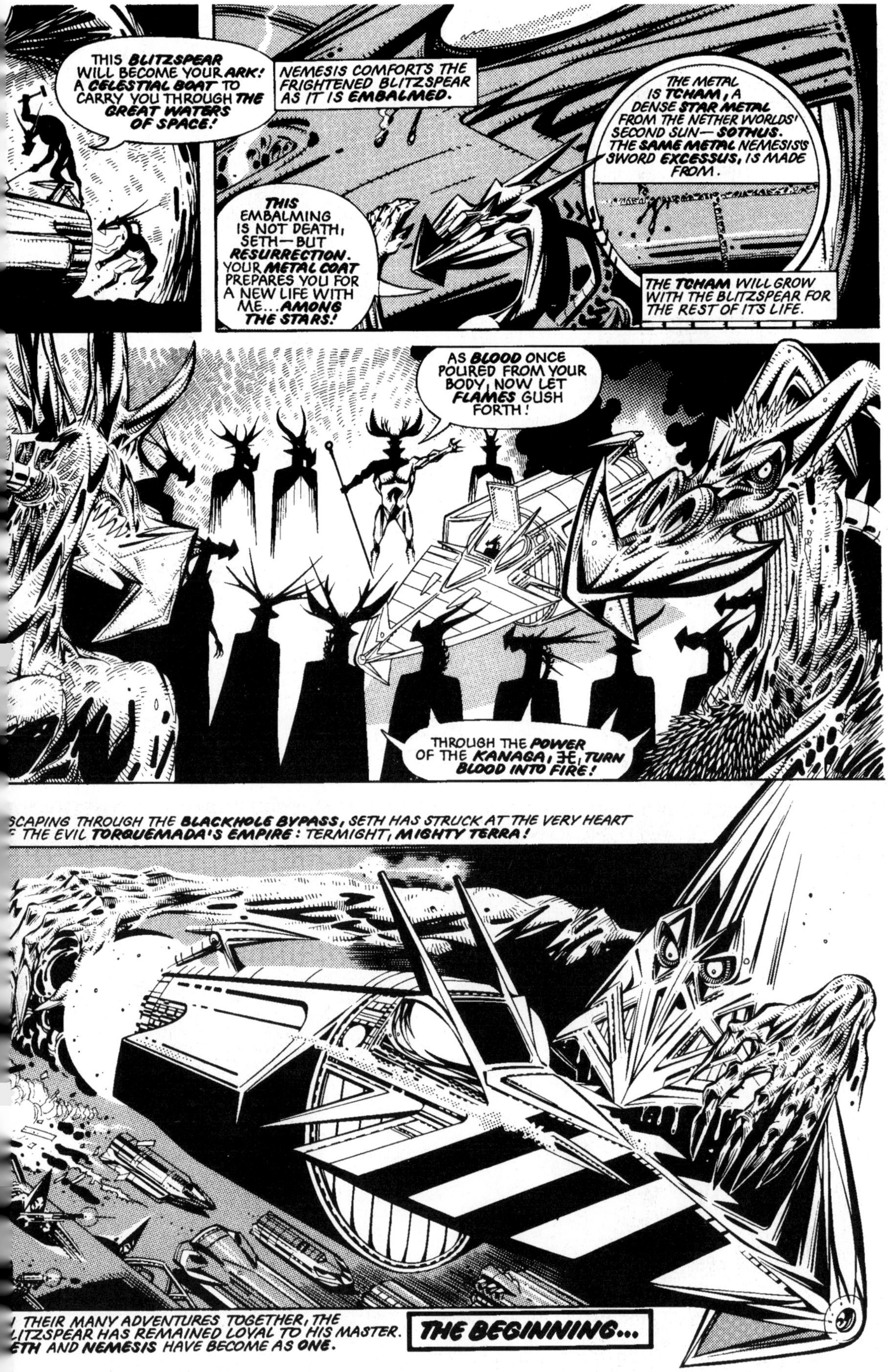
THIS BLITZSPEAR WILL BECOME YOUR ARK! A CELESTIAL BOAT TO CARRY YOU THROUGH THE GREAT WATERS OF SPACE!
NEMESIS COMFORTS THE FRIGHTENED BLITZSPEAR AS IT IS EMBALMED.
THE METAL IS TCHAM, A DENSE STAR METAL FROM THE NETHER WORLDS' SECOND SUN— SOTHUS. THE SAME METAL NEMESIS'S SWORD EXCESSUS, IS MADE FROM.
THIS EMBALMING IS NOT DEATH, SETH— BUT RESURRECTION. YOUR METAL COAT PREPARES YOU FOR A NEW LIFE WITH ME... AMONG THE STARS!
THE TCHAM WILL GROW WITH THE BLITZSPEAR FOR THE REST OF ITS LIFE.
AS BLOOD ONCE POURED FROM YOUR BODY, NOW LET FLAMES GUSH FORTH!
THROUGH THE POWER OF THE KANAGA, ƎE, TURN BLOOD INTO FIRE!
SCAPING THROUGH THE BLACKHOLE BYPASS, SETH HAS STRUCK AT THE VERY HEART F THE EVIL TORQUEMADA'S EMPIRE: TERMIGHT, MIGHTY TERRA!
I THEIR MANY ADVENTURES TOGETHER, THE LITZSPEAR HAS REMAINED LOYAL TO HIS MASTER. ETH AND NEMESIS HAVE BECOME AS ONE.
THE BEGINNING...

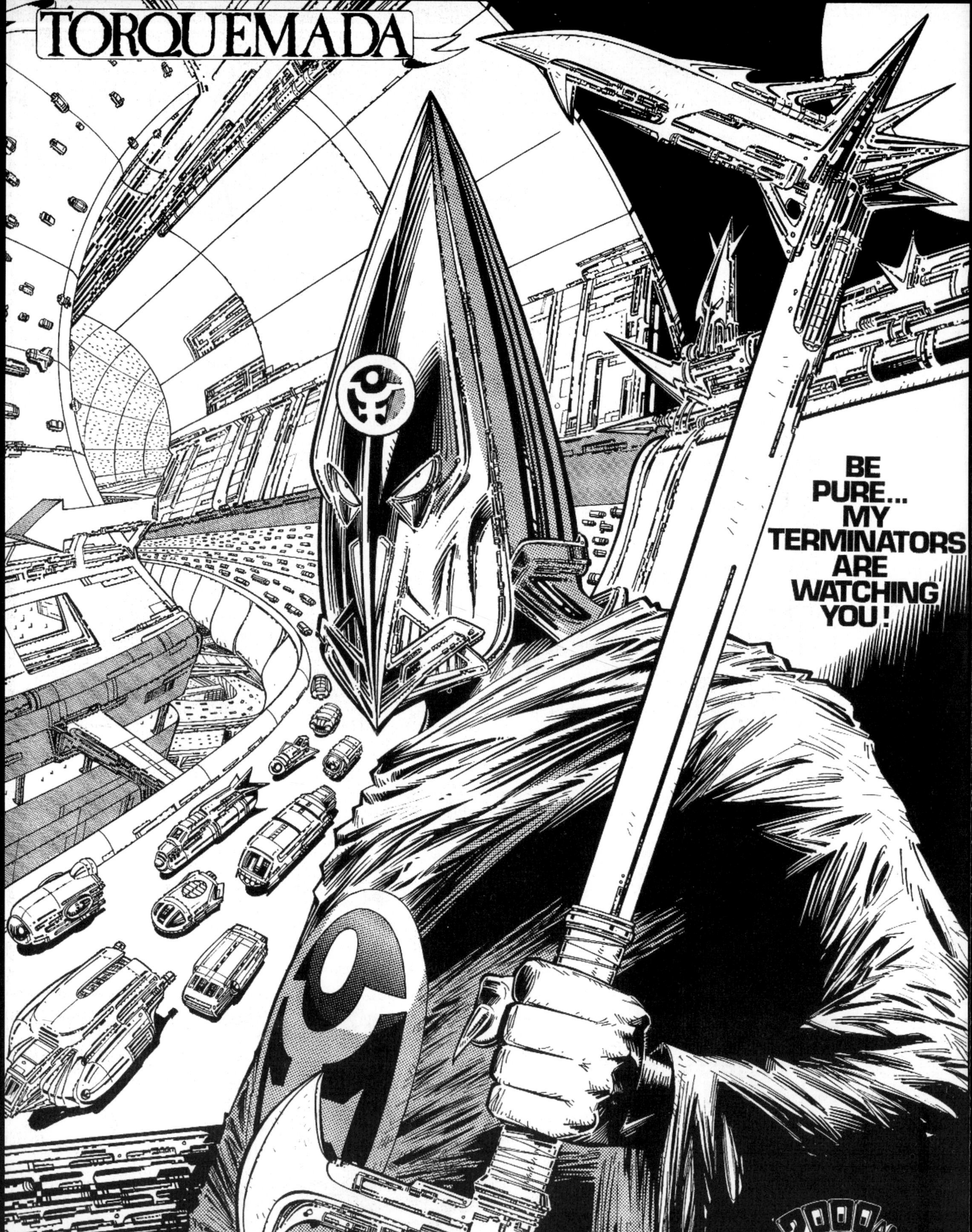
TORQUEMADA
BE PURE... MY TERMINATORS ARE WATCHING YOU!
2000 AD
JUDGE DREDD
STAR PIN-UP

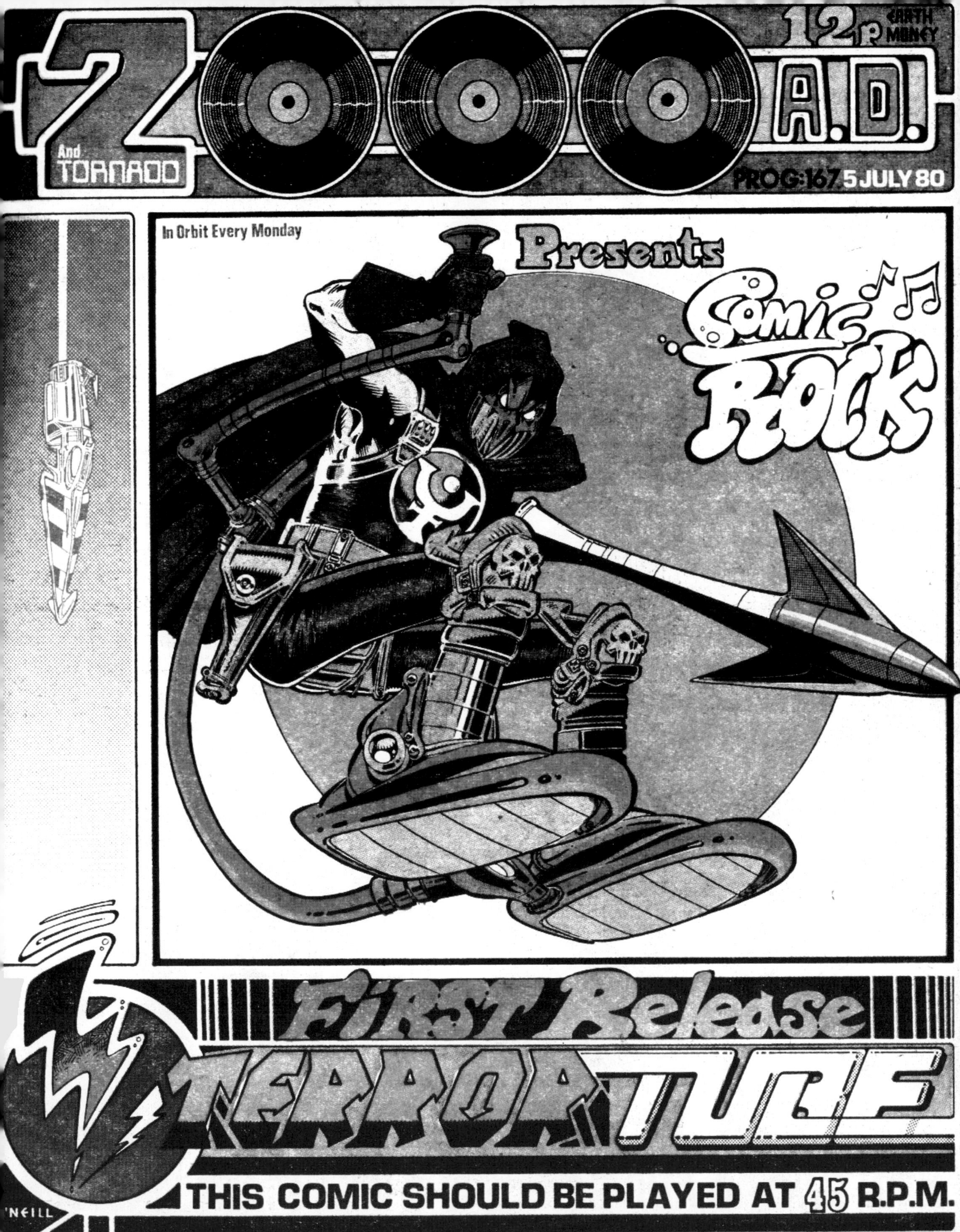

2000 A.D.
And TORNADO
12p EARTH MONEY
PROG:167 5 JULY 80
In Orbit Every Monday
Presents
Comic ROCK
FIRST Release
TERROR TUBE
THIS COMIC SHOULD BE PLAYED AT 45 R.P.M.
'NEILL

Malaysia $1.00; New Zealand 40c; Australia 40c

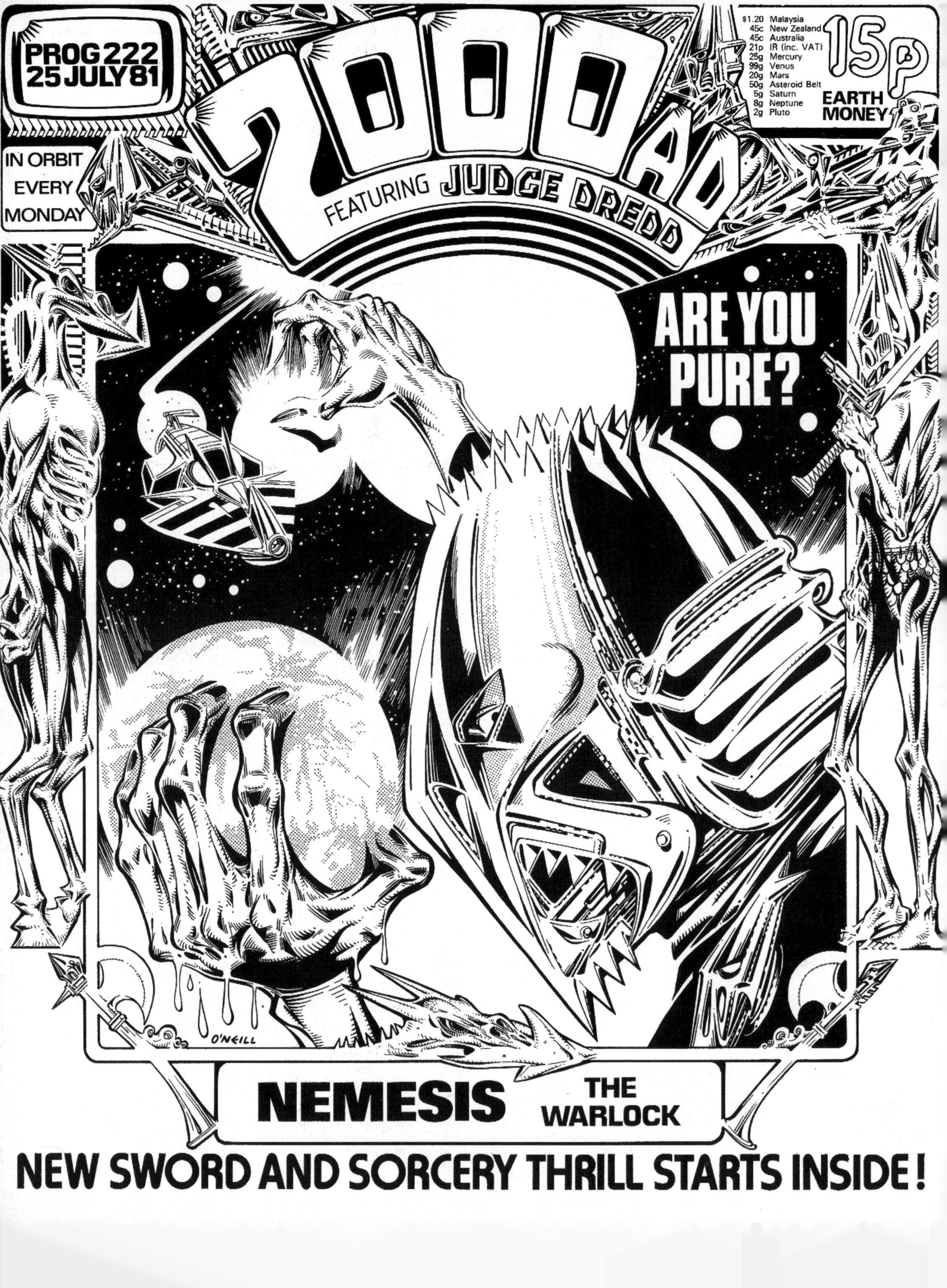
PROG 222
25 JULY 81
2000 AD
FEATURING JUDGE DREDD
$1.20 Malaysia
45c New Zealand
45c Australia
21p IR (inc. VAT)
25g Mercury
99g Venus
20g Mars
50g Asteroid Belt
5g Saturn
8g Neptune
2g Pluto
15p
EARTH MONEY
IN ORBIT EVERY MONDAY
ARE YOU PURE?
O'NEILL
NEMESIS THE WARLOCK
NEW SWORD AND SORCERY THRILL STARTS INSIDE!

SIMPLY LIGHT YEARS AHEAD!

PROG 252
20 FEB 82

2000 AD FEATURING JUDGE DREDD

$1.25	Malaysia
45c	New Zealand
46c	Australia
23p	IR (inc. VAT)
25g	Mercury
99g	Venus
20g	Mars
50g	Asteroid Belt
5g	Saturn
8g	Neptune
2g	Pluto

16p EARTH MONEY

IN ORBIT
EVERY
MONDAY

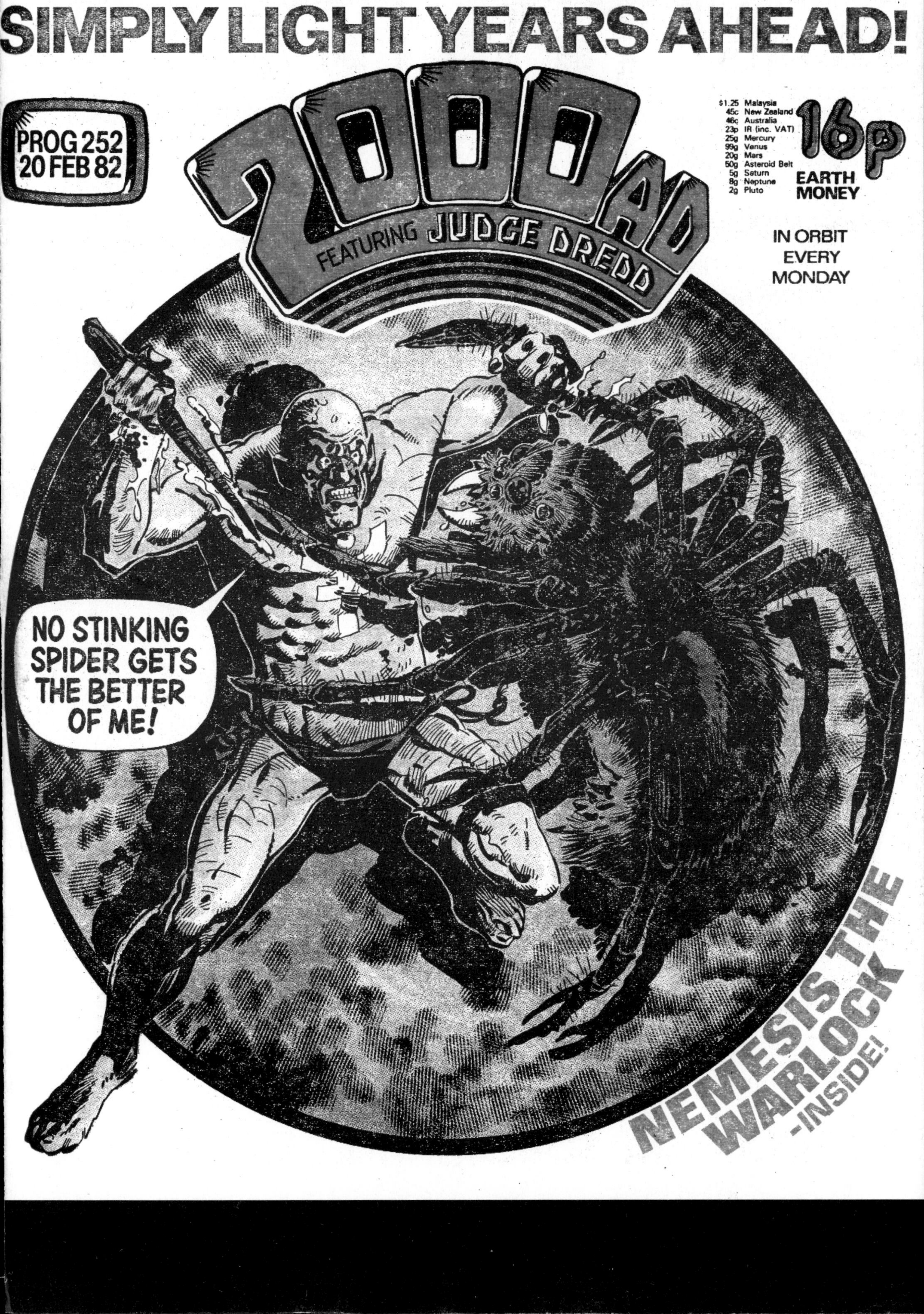
NO STINKING SPIDER GETS THE BETTER OF ME!

NEMESIS THE WARLOCK
-INSIDE!